C000183012

ROBERT ALAN JAMIESON was bor
and grew up in the crofting com
University of Edinburgh as a mat
William Soutar Fellowship in Per
Review, 1993–98, and writer in re
and Strathclyde, 1998–2001. Since then he has tutored creative writing
at the University of Edinburgh. He is the author of three novels, three
collections of poetry and two plays, and has edited a number of anthol-
ogies. Through his occasional work with the organisation Literature
Across Frontiers, his poetry in Shetlandic Scots has been translated into
more than a dozen languages, and he has translated over 20 contemporary European poets into Shetlandic Scots.

Praise for *macCLOUD FALLS:*
An important book both for Scottish and Canadian readers, calling
attention to the often-erased role that First Nations people played
in the so-called settlement of North America, and to the need for
ongoing reconciliation. LEITH DAVIS, THE BOTTLE IMP

How effective can fiction ever be in showing the landscape as a
palimpsest going all the way back to that time before the colonists
came? That's one of the challenges Jamieson has set himself, but he
is well able for it. DAVID ROBINSON, BOOKS FROM SCOTLAND

Postmodernism teaches that history is malleable, sources are muddy,
'truth' doesn't exist. Jamieson's excellent novel doesn't necessarily
eschew that theory; rather, it gives it a twist, saying, 'we can trace
history more easily than that. It just might not turn out to be what
you expect'. LESLEY MCDOWELL, THE NATIONAL

Praise for *Da Happie Laand:*
Robert Alan Jamieson's strange masterpiece *Da Happie Laand* haunts
dreams and waking hours, as it takes my adopted home of Shetland,
twisting it and the archipelago's history into the most disturbing,
amazing, slyly funny shapes. SUNDAY HERALD

A work of complexity, a novel to be savoured and one that will only
get better with age. NEW SHETLANDER

Jamieson achieves something quite extraordinary... [he] combines a compelling modern mystery with 500 years of history in a typically experimental style that leaves many of his contemporaries lagging. THE LIST

Robert Alan Jamieson is one of this country's finest, most distinctive writers, and Da Happie Laand is his best work yet. Vast in scope but understated in tone, big in ambition and beautifully rendered from beginning to end, if there's any justice this potent tale of a very unreal world and another very real one should find a wide audience of readers who will come away feeling inspired and uplifted. RODGE GLASS

By the same author:
Soor Hearts, Paul Harris Publishing, 1984
Thin Wealth: A Novel from an Oil Decade, Polygon, 1986
Shoormal, Polygon, 1986
A Day at the Office, Polygon, 1991
Ansin T'Sjaetlin: Some Responses to the Language Question, Samisdat, 2005
Nort Atlantik Drift: Poyims Ati' Shaetlin, Luath Press, 2007
Da Happie Laand, Luath Press, 2010

macCLOUD FALLS

A NOVEL

ROBERT ALAN JAMIESON

Luath Press Limited

EDINBURGH

www.luath.co.uk

First published 2017
This edition 2020

ISBN: 978-1-912147-44-1

The author's right to be identified as author of this book
under the Copyright, Designs and Patents Act 1988 has been asserted.

The paper used in this book is recyclable. It is made from low
chlorine pulps produced in a low energy, low emission manner from
renewable forests.

Printed and bound by iPrint Global, Ely

Typeset in 10 point Sabon by Lapiz

The historical core of this novel is based on the life of
James Alexander Teit (1864-1922). The remainder is fiction.

This book is dedicated to the memory of three dear friends who
passed away during its writing: Gavin Wallace, my old co-editor on
the *Edinburgh Review*, whose encouragement and enthusiasm for the
idea was invaluable at the outset; Richard McNeil Browne of Main
Point Books, a friend of almost thirty years, whose kindness, wit and
wisdom I greatly miss; and finally, Isaac, the King of Shelties, finest of
canine companions, the true 'Hero' of this tale.

Acknowledgements

Thanks are due to Creative Scotland for a major bursary that allowed me to make nine visits to British Columbia during the writing of this book; to the University of Edinburgh for its continued indulgence and support; to my friends at Luath Press, Jennie Renton and Gavin Mac-Dougall, for continuing to make publishing both pleasurable and easy; to staff at the BC Archives, Simon Fraser University, University of British Columbia, Vancouver Public Library, Nicola Valley Museum and Archives, and Kamloops Museum and Archives for their assistance; to Karen Dawson for making it possible to spend two memorable months writing in Italy, and Patrick Jamieson for his companionship then; to my neighbour Barry Smith for the Ryga book; to the many friends in Canada who contributed good times, knowledge and sometimes accommodation, especially Adam Pearson, Byron and Sheila Anderson, Michael Elcock and Marilyn Bowering.

Most of all, thanks are due to the Vancouver poet, Miranda Pearson, who appeared as if by magic in the skies over Scotland in 2010 and helped to seed the idea, who has remained magical ever since.

DANCE PROGRAMME

First Dance
Oldest Inn in 'New Caledonia'
(Boston Two-step)

SHE THREADED HER fingers through the worn metal handle, put her thumb on the old-fashioned latch and a little bell rang above her head as the door rattled open. 'Come on lad,' she said to her dog. After the dazzling sunshine she'd left outside, her eyes took a moment to adjust. It was certainly quaint inside, like something out of a movie, maybe some old spaghetti western. Gil had said it was built in the Mexican style. The arch that welcomed them into the foyer had a low adobe curve, and the whole place seemed made of terracotta.

'Are you the innkeeper?' she asked of the only person visible, a figure crouched at the desk across the hall who sat up as if he'd been dozing. The question hung in the hazy violet light that framed the speaker, the tall brunette woman in a deep purple dress who had entered with a dog at her heel. It was one of the Lassie breed.

'Can't say I've ever been called that before,' he answered in a voice from the east. In a second, it seemed she crossed the foyer in long strides and stood above him. He looked up, was caught by her intense brown-eyed gaze, still half-asleep.

'But this is the inn, isn't it?' Her tone was impatient, dismissive, her accent foreign somehow.

'Sure. The oldest inn in the province, though I guess it's more of a motel these days. Back then, they had no mo, y'know.' He smiled, as if the line was well-rehearsed, awaiting a response.

She stared down at where he sat, gently oozing sweat despite his being dressed in thin grey t-shirt and khaki shorts, and the fan spinning with a periodic squeak above his head. 'I don't understand?'

'No motors. No autos. Back when they named it the inn.' If it was intended as a joke, she wasn't amused. The dog circled her heels and sat down, facing up at him, its expression as blankly insistent as the woman's.

'You have a Scotsman staying with you?' she asked.

He stood up from his stool behind the desk, a small slight fella, hardly as tall as her shoulder. He hesitated as if weighing her enquiry, then nodded. 'Sure. Mr. Johnson.'

Her tone remained urgent. 'Can I see him?'

The innkeeper shook head. 'He's out right now.'

'Is he okay?'

'I think so, yes. Why?'

At that, she gave out a deep sigh. 'Thank God,' she said softly, and bent to pet the eager dog. 'We've been so worried about him, haven't we, lad?'

'Why?' the voice asked again.

She stood up and gave him the once-over, before adding. 'I think he may be planning to kill himself.' She spoke quite matter-of-factly and the innkeeper didn't appear too shocked at first, but as the meaning of her words struck him, he gave a little gasp.

'And what makes you say that?' he asked slowly, as if trying to gauge her sanity.

The tall dark woman gazed around her, seeking for some inspiration as to how to turn her feelings into words. 'Well, it's hard to explain. He sent me a postcard the day he got here, a picture of the river. It said 'Sometimes I take a great notion.' And he was reading a book about a Scotsman who travelled into the north of Canada to die.'

The innkeeper scratched his head behind his ear. 'I don't really get what you're saying.'

She stared down at him. 'In Vancouver. Or rather, when I met him on the plane. About ten days ago.'

The innkeeper smiled again, shook his head. 'Nah, you're gonna have to explain. Sometimes I take a great notion to what?'

'We were walking down at Jericho Beach, you know in Vancouver. We passed a bench, and you know how they have these little plaques? Well this one said 'I'll see you in my dreams' and Gil, your Mr Johnson, sang 'Goodnight Irene.' I asked what it was and he said it was a song his mother loved. And he sang that line to me. Sometimes I take a great notion, to jump in the river and die.'

'Goodnight Irene,' the innkeeper said. 'Sure. I know it. But it's just a song. Doesn't really mean he wants to jump in the river, does it?'

Not dissuaded, she carried on. 'But the book he was reading, Sick Heart River – he told me, that's exactly what the Scotsman in that book wants – to die. It's why he comes to Canada.'

'Sick Heart River?'

'That's what the book's called.' For a second the two stared at each other, as the dog looked from one to the other, unsure what was passing between them.

'Okay,' the innkeeper said. 'Maybe could you go back to the beginning, please? I'm kinda confused.'

'The beginning? Well, I met him on a plane from Calgary... last week. I mean, I got on at Calgary, but he was travelling from Scotland. We got talking and when he was in Vancouver – before he came up here – we hung out a bit.'

He stood a while, gauging her, as if unsure what to say next. 'So you've come all the way up here from Vancouver because of this.'

'I couldn't get in touch with him, I sent messages, texts, but...'

He laughed at that, and came out from behind the desk, his arms splayed and his palms upraised. 'We're off-radar, is all. None of that works here in the canyon. So he won't have got your messages, is all.'

'But I tried to phone here and it just rang and rang and nobody answered.'

'Ah,' the innkeeper said. 'Well, you know, I'm on my own here right now. Since my wife left. And sometimes I have to go out.'

She stared at him for a few seconds, as his words took meaningful shape in her mind. When she spoke, it was only to say with some incredulity, 'We drove up. Six hours.'

'We?'

She indicated the dog.

'Must be good to have a dog to split the driving with,' he said, but again she wouldn't laugh. 'Listen, you look like you could use a strong drink, and maybe your dog would like some cold water? It's pretty hot up here right now. Come out onto the terrace and into the shade, and tell me why you've driven six hours to get here, why you think our Mr Johnson may be planning on killing himself. Cause the reasons you've given me so far don't seem like good ones.'

She studied his face for a moment. 'Well maybe a cup of mint tea would be welcome.'

'How about ordinary tea?'

'Okay.'

He led her through the empty dining room, out onto a terrace over-looking the river. She sat in the shade at an ironwork table, with the lassie dog at her feet, while he boiled a kettle behind the little bar. 'And that is quite a river, like Gil said,' she breathed, patting the dog while gazing over the bank that led down to the vast urgent flow of flinty grey water racing down through the canyon. The high rocky face opposite was mostly in shadow, but the very top of the crags caught the last of the setting sun.

'Sick Heart River,' he said, when he returned. 'You know, I think my wife may have read that. Title seems familiar.'

'I don't know much about it,' she answered. 'Just what Gil... Mr Johnson told me. It's by some Scotsman who was an early Gover-nor General.'

He put a tray with a small blue teapot and cup on the table, then sat down opposite her. 'So tell me, why do you think he would he want to kill himself? I thought he was a writer, here to research a story.'

'He's not a writer,' she said. 'He's an antiquarian bookseller. He told me he'd always wanted to write, but never had.'

Again, the innkeeper looked non-plussed. 'So he sent you a post-card, so he's a reading a book about someone dying, you couldn't get a reply to your messages, you panicked a bit. I can understand all that. But that's no reason to drive up here, surely?'

She sipped her tea. 'No, there's more. His mother just died. And there's the cancer.'

'What cancer?'

'Didn't I say?'

'No.'

'He's got cancer. He told me on the plane, how he wants to make one big journey before he dies.'

The innkeeper's expression had changed at the dread word. 'Here?'

She nodded. 'I guess so.'

'Hmmm.' He took a sip of his tea and stared out across the river towards the little town on the other side. 'So, you met a guy on a plane a couple of weeks ago who told you he had cancer, who was talking about death, suicide. Then he sends you postcard with a cryptic note on it about jumping in the river and dying. You can't get a reply to the messages you send?'

'It's more than that. I had this really strong feeling. Like a premo-nition or something, you know?'

The innkeeper sat silently studying her for a while. Then he said quietly, 'Sounds a little crazy,' as much to himself as to her.

The word made her flinch. 'You think so?' she asked, an edge of annoyance in her voice. 'It happens, you know.'

He shrugged. 'Well, no, I don't know. But I'm a little worried too now.'

'It's such a strong sense that something's wrong.' She looked at her watch. 'It's getting late. Where could he be, do you think? Isn't there someone you could call?'

'Just hang on. Let me think a moment.' They sat in silence for a while, the dog panting at her feet. The innkeeper, as she'd called him, stared out across the river. His gaze was focused, as if checking all the houses and buildings he could see, eliminating one by one the places where the Scotsman couldn't be. Then he went inside to phone while she stayed on the shady terrace, sheltered from the baking sun. She could hear his voice in the distance asking questions of whoever was on the other end of the line.

She stood up and leant against the wall of the veranda, so she could see the little town in the canyon properly. It was desert alright, like Gil had said it was - the end of that arid belt that stretches north from Mexico through the US into western Canada. She ran her eyes over the town across the great river and counted maybe fifty houses at most. Surely he couldn't be too lost in such a small place? But no, she had a bad feeling she couldn't explain away.

'Sorry,' the innkeeper said as he reappeared in the doorway, his flip-flops slapping the tiles. 'I called around the likely places. Nobody's seen him today.'

Call it intuition, whatever, she wasn't surprised. 'Something's happened. I know it has. We should call the police.'

'Mounties to the rescue?' he smiled. 'No, there could be any number of explanations. Besides, why would he want to harm himself when he's so busy with this research? He's been meeting a lot of people since he got here, he could easily be in someone's house. You know, interviewing somebody.'

She sighed deeply and the dog looked up, as if recognising the sound and what it indicated. The innkeeper watched as she sat upright, brown hair falling around her face. She was very striking, and somehow familiar, so much so he seemed to know her face from somewhere. Was she an actress or something?

'I don't know. Can I see his room?' she said suddenly, quite firmly. 'He may have left a note.'

The innkeeper was so captivated by her resemblance to someone he couldn't quite recall, he was about to consent, but then he hesitated. 'Now, I don't think I can do that. It wouldn't be right. I can see you're worried, but really…'

She interrupted. 'You have a pass key?'

'Sure, but…'

'You enter his room each day to fix it?'

'Sure, at least the maid does.'

'I only want to look around.'

'Well, I don't know, I mean you just turn up here, you could be anybody. I don't know you, though I feel as if I should.' He hesitated again. 'Are you someone famous, on TV or something?'

'I'm here because I care. That's all you need to know.'

So, perhaps just to pacify her, he relented and led her up the narrow winding staircase to a door marked with a 14. The dog was at her heel all the way, panting with the heat but always no more than a step behind her.

'This is it,' he said, and opened the door with his pass key. Inside, a video camera on a tripod pointed out the window across the river towards the houses on the far bank, and a long desk under the window was stacked with books, some open at a particular spot. It looked like a scholar's den, even though he'd only been there a few days.

'I don't understand. Where did he get all these?' she asked.

'Ah. Now that I can explain. He went through my wife's library the other day. She hasn't taken her things away yet so I told him he was welcome to borrow whatever was useful.'

She and the dog moved forward as one, and she began to read the titles on the spines. *Indian Myths and Legends from the North Pacific Coast of America*, *The Thompson Indians of British Columbia*, *Our Tellings*, *Skookum Wawa*, and another twenty or so piled high.

'Mostly he's interested in the history of the province,' the innkeeper observed. 'I guess it all relates to this guy he's…'

'Lyle?'

'Yes. James Lyle.'

Hidden behind the stack of books, they saw his laptop, lid down and switched off. It would be passworded, no doubt.

'Well, no suicide note that I can see,' the innkeeper said with a smile. She didn't answer, but moved elegantly forward with slow steps, her brown eyes searching the room. The bed was neatly made, his clothes all hung up, with the exception of a couple of shirts and a pair of shorts lying across an armchair. She went to the bedside cabinet and pulled the drawer open. Nothing but tourist brochures.

'Maybe we shouldn't…' the innkeeper began, but she silenced him with a glance. 'What's that?'

She flicked, eyes seeking content, through a few pages of a note-book on the desk. 'His writing, it seems.' As she stood scanning the pages, the innkeeper moved nervously around her, while the dog stood still, watching him with its dark eyes.

'What if he comes back and finds us here?' he said.

'I'll take responsibility,' she said imperiously, and took a pair of expensive-looking pink-rimmed glasses from her purse. 'It seems to be a diary,' she added.

From outside, the sound of a fire-door opening echoed up the stairs. 'Put it back,' he said anxiously, but then relaxed when he heard voices. 'Ah it's only the tree-planters coming in. I could ask them if they've seen him.'

'The tree-planters?'

'They're working up north, stayin here. Mr Johnson is quite friendly with them.'

She didn't answer, but turned another page in the large notebook. The innkeeper's reservations seemed to have evaporated. 'Look at the end,' he suggested. 'The last thing he wrote.'

She thought for moment and then, as if deciding that was good advice, she flicked forward through the handwritten pages, until she came to an unfinished one.

'It says "Today, the sacred valley",' she said. 'Where's the sacred valley?'

'I don't know.'

'Isn't it somewhere round here?'

'If it is, I never heard of it. But we only moved here three years ago. My wife might know, though. She's very interested in all that local history stuff.'

'Could you call her?'

'I guess. Though we don't talk much anymore.' He pointed to the journal in her hands. 'Maybe if you read farther back a bit, it'll tell you what he means?'

'I will.' Her eyes were taking a ranging view of Gil's writing. 'You go ask around – see if anybody knows where this sacred valley is.'

Again he hesitated, still unsure of whether he was doing the right thing in helping her root around in his guest's room. Then it struck him. 'Sigourney Weaver! That's who it is,' he exclaimed. She looked up at him over the rim of her spectacles and smiled, then shook her head, as if she'd heard the same idea endlessly repeated.

'Don't… please,' she said.

'But you're not… not really?' he asked, confused.

'Oh, just go already, will you!' she commanded. The dog had been watching her every movement and lay down at her feet, panting with the heat, as if scolded. The innkeeper began to apologise to her, still seemingly uncertain as to the woman's true identity, but she shooed him out the door.

Once he'd left, the woman who was tired of looking like Sigourney turned her attentions to her dog and said, 'Poor boy, it's way too hot for you here.' She sat on the end of the bed. He jumped up beside her and she patted him lovingly with one hand as she flicked back through the pages from the last entry in the missing man's journal. 'Let's see if we can find another mention of this sacred valley,' she said, perhaps to herself, perhaps to the dog, as she scanned the pages in reverse, making her way back towards the beginning. It seemed to be a record of his movements here in Cloud Falls – but it was written in the third person for some reason. No other mention of this valley caught her eye.

Instead, she began to read the first page.

Coincidence is – perhaps – a symptom of fate. Perhaps, because it arises per hap: through chance. Imagine: you have spent a summer sitting in the garden of the place you are living in, watching planes fly low overhead as they approach the nearby airport. You have watched them knowing that you may never fly again, because you are being treated for cancer by radiotherapy. Your throat is a dried-up wrinkling, red-hot on the inside, red-skinned on the outside. You have no energy, no enthusiasm for an active life, except to watch – you watch the swifts and the swallows as they zip and flit above the river, feeding among the floating specks of insects lit up by the setting sun. Your view is to the west, the end of day, the end of life. But by the time that the first leaves are yellowing, you find yourself on an aeroplane, leaving that airport, flying above your riverbank retreat towards a place you have never been. Yet somehow you are returning to source, swimming upstream. Your seat is in the last row, at the rear of the cabin – you do not greet each other. She is intent on reading, and so are you. After half an hour, you are flying somewhere over the mountains, heading west, when the voice from the cockpit announces a problem with one of the engines, and so the plane will make a forced landing at another airport. You glance at your fellow traveller, the invisible wall of separate concentrations suddenly melted away. There is a look of panic in her eyes – her very dark brown eyes. But as the sun catches her face, a flash of gold among the brown surprises you. There is light and terror in her look, a glancing fear that sparks your interest. But you do not speak. Instead, you gaze down at the mountains and valleys below. A lake, a river, a snaking sliver that cuts the landscape.

From up here, life is tiny. Your life is tiny. And you have thought about that, sitting in the garden of the riverbank cottage, watching the planes. How tiny your life is, and how short it has been. Cancer sharpens awareness, even as it clogs the body with unwanted, non-functioning cells. In the past few months, you have come to terms with death, have put your affairs in order, said goodbyes. If this plane crashes, and you die, it could not happen at a more opportune moment. Thanks to the cancer, all is ready. But she looks as if she has life ahead of her, things she must do, and places she must go. People to see, perhaps children to care for, a husband.

The plane circles above the metropolis, banks to make its approach to the runway. You can feel the collective intake of breath amongst the passengers. It is tangible, palpable, visceral, in that little tube of pressurised air. And the outbreath as the wheels bump and find the tarmac. You have not died – yet. The worried face of your fellow traveller relaxes its frown. You are the last to leave, the stricken... A lot of people left the plane at Calgary. It was a relief, after being squashed in the window seat for seven hours, when the Glaswegian couple took their bags and filed out. A few new faces replaced those who'd reached their destination, but not nearly so many. The remaining passengers spread out, filling empty seats. Some stretched out across a middle three. After walking around a while, peering out at the runway, the airport, the faint cityscape on the plain and the line of distant mountains, he went back to his window.

'He's changed person in the middle of the paragraph,' she said. But she carried on, intrigued.

This was the leg of the journey he'd been waiting for – sunset over the Rocky Mountains – so he didn't even notice her at first, until she stopped and checked the seat number, then sat with a smile in the outer of three. 'Hey,' she said, casually, not inviting a response. He glanced at her, then went back to fiddling with the buttons on his Nikon. But he noticed the book she brought from her bag – it was 'Anna Karenina', but in Russian, judging from the Cyrillic script on the cover. He was snapping automatically, trying to get an angle on the incredible white peaks, the blue lakes, the snaking silver rivers, that would exclude the sun's glare just enough for clarity, when the pilot announced turbulence and the seatbelt sign went on. 'Shit,' she said, half to him, half to herself. 'I knew I should've ordered a drink. If I'm going to die, I want to die happy.' He took one of the full miniatures of Johnnie Walker from his bag, and the second unused plastic cup that had encased the one he'd been drinking from, offered them to her. She looked at it, at him. 'If you want it, it's yours,' he said. She hesitated, then smiled. 'Thanks, that's kind. But I don't like whisky. A gin and tonic's what I need.'

'Well,' she said to the dog, 'That never happened. And it's all confused. If that's the kind of writing he does, I'm not surprised he hasn't been published.' But the dog wasn't listening, it had heard someone coming upstairs, footsteps that stopped outside the partly opened door of room 14, and it growled as a couple of faces peered in. When the interlopers heard that, and she looked up, they ducked out of sight. 'Nah, that's not her,' a disappearing voice said as they went back downstairs. 'Sure looks like her though,' said another. She frowned behind her pink-rimmed glasses. 'Silly men,' she said, patting the dog, but her interest was in the journal. He'd written about them, their meeting on the plane – though he'd changed things here and there.

Her eyes flitted quickly over the lines, as she turned page after page back through the outsized notebook, till noises from the terrace below rose up and in the open window. The two spies were down below and their conversation drifted upwards.

'I'm telling you, man, she definitely bought that big house right down on the shore in West Van. We saw it from the water when we was out in the boat, my cousin Dan an me.'

'Na, that was Oprah. Everybody knows bout that.'

'No, it's not that house.'

'So what would she be doing up here in the canyon, anyway?'

'Maybe the Scotch guy's a scriptwriter?'

'He's from Scotland, bro.'

'They make movies there. Braveheart.'

It was far from the first time Sigourney's image had got in her way. She'd given up trying to stop the misapprehension. At times it even opened doors. So she got up from the bed and pulled the window shut on the conversation. Her dog lifted its head expectantly, but the long legs those canine eyes watched walked back to the bed, where she flicked through more pages impatiently, looking for another mention of the valley. 'I know, it's hot, honey. But it'll be cooler soon and we'll take a walk then. Maybe Gil will have turned up,' she told the dog. 'You like Gil, don't you?'

Exasperated with her fruitless search, she stopped her backwards scanning, and turned to the beginning again. She started to read, and her expression changed from one of frustration to amazement. 'Oh my God!' The dog looked at her, as if understanding the phrase and what it signified. 'He's changed our names.' And she began to read intently, her eyes flitting over the words at speed behind her pink-rims.

On the plane, unprompted, she'd said 'You're a little late, aren't you?'

I looked up at her, puzzled. 'Late? Why?'

She pointed at the *Handbook to the Goldfields* on my knee, an 1862 edition from the bookshop in Edinburgh. 'The gold rush ended about 150 years ago.'

'Well,' I answered, laughing. 'I thought there would still be a few nuggets left here and there.'

'So you're a prospector? No, I don't expect so. But you're Scotch. That much I can tell from your accent, and the whisky. There are a lot of you Scotch in Canada.'

'The Scots built Canada, according to some books I've read. And the country I'm going to used to be known as New Caledonia, in the days before it became British Columbia.'

'So where is it exactly you are going to?'

'Well, I'm going to spend a week in Vancouver – I've rented a room on MacDonald Street, which just makes my point about the Scots – and then I'm going to head into the interior, up the canyon to a place called Cloud Falls.'

'MacDonald is near where I live. But I don't know Cloud Falls. Where is that?'

'In the Gold Country, of course.'

'Touché. But you're not really going to look for gold.'

'No. Anyway, most folk probably won't have heard of Cloud Falls. It's only about a hundred people.'

'So if it's not gold you're searching for, what is so special about this little town?'

'I'm doing research on a man who went to live there, about 150 years ago.'

'You're a journalist?'

'No. It's a long story. I think he's a relative of mine. I've been ill. I've wanted to make this trip for a long time and when I got my strength back, I thought this was as good a time as any.'

'I get it. Bucket list. I thought you looked sick. You're so thin. What was wrong with you?'

'Cancer.'

She shook her head, as if disbelieving. 'Wow,' she breathed.

'Anyway, here's to life ongoing,' he said, raising the plastic airline cup.
'And gold.'
'I hope so,' he answered. 'Both.'

It took her a moment to realise that the writer had switched person in mid-passage again. What made someone so unsure of who they are?

'So this is your first time crossing the Rockies,' she said.
'How can you tell?' he asked, camera in hand.
'Oh, just all those pictures you were taking earlier.'
'Well, you're right. And you?'
'Oh, many times. I live in Vancouver now. Though not always.'
'I guessed that. Your accent is...?'
'Czech.'

Hah! He'd made her Czech!

'Not Russian?' He pointed at the Tolstoy, protruding from her bag.
'No! Definitely not Russian. Though like a lot of Czechs of my generation, I can read Russian as a result of classes at school. But I've never read *Anna Karenina* before.'
'It's always good to leave a few classics for later life,' he said and tossed back his dram.

He didn't say any of that. He was nowhere near as eloquent.

'So now you're reborn?'
'I had to re-evaluate everything. And stop smoking, of course. I don't know what lies ahead.'
'Smoking, ah...'
'I feel as if I've lived a very safe life, as if I've never done anything dangerous or foolish and it's almost over.'
'But you smoked, surely that's dangerous and foolish...'
Yes, he had smoked – from the moment he first opened his father's tobacco drawer and smelled the freshly aromatic scent tempting his olfactory nerve, he'd had warm associations with the wicked weed.
And so above the Rockies, you told this stranger the story of your quarry.

He'd switched again! What's the matter now?

You told her the story of Jimmy Lyle and his wanderings, as you had heard it from your great-grandmother, how she remembered his solitary homecoming in 1901. Of a nineteen-year-old travelling five thousand miles in 1884 from the bare island hills, by sea and land, and sea and land, and much more land, into a desert canyon. And back again, seventeen years later, by horse, train and ship. Of that old magazine in your great-grandmother's kitchen in Leith with the story about him entitled, 'Friend to the Indians'. And the photo with his Native wife, and his dog, in front of the log cabin. Of how he'd been 'Aly', then 'Jimmy', then 'Jacques'. All the things you knew about a place you'd never been to. Dead people you'd never met.

You looked at her face and she slept, so you ceased. Unlike anyone, and yet from somewhere among the thousands of faces you'd glimpsed or got to know, some recognition seemed to flow.

'You stopped,' she'd said quietly, without fully opening her eyes.

'I thought you were sleeping,'

'No, not now.'

So you'd shared a taxi from the airport, you were travelling to the same part of the city, only a few blocks apart. And when she gave you the neat printed card with her name and address, her phone and email, and you exchanged that for a slip of paper from your wallet with your phone number, you felt that you'd connected, somehow.

If I'm going to die, I want to die happy, she had said. What you did not tell her was that while you'd lain in your mother's garden and gazed up at the clouds last summer, you'd come to know a younger self that you'd ignored, someone bold and ambitious, eager for challenge and willing to take risks. You didn't tell her that younger self was angry with you, that you felt him on your shoulder urging you on, to try at least to do one big thing while you still had time. You had been the tethered bear, walking that circle, for just too long.

When the innkeeper tapped the open door of room 14, she looked lost in the Scotsman's journal. He cleared his throat and tapped again. His face seemed uncertain as to whether he'd done the right thing in letting her into the room.

'So you found out what this sacred valley is?' she said, without more than a glance in his direction.

'No. Nobody seems to know about it. Did you find anything in his journal? Because I'm kinda worried myself now.'

'Not yet.' She laughed a little, the first time he'd seen her smile and he stared intently, as if trying to compare it with what he remembered Sigourney Weaver's smile to be like. 'But I found myself,' she said. She was about to add something, but a sudden grinding, clashing roar arose from somewhere outside, gradually growing so loud that it felt as if the little inn was shaking, and the dog leapt up, barking and howling.

'CPR,' the innkeeper shouted over the uproar. 'It'll be over soon.' But the noise got louder, and the roaring and barking went on for some long minutes more.

'That can't do much for trade,' she said, when the commotion was finally over. 'How often does that happen?'

'A few times a day,' he answered. 'You kinda get used to it.'

'Do you?' She put her glasses back on, and picked up the journal which was not a journal but a story, and a story about her, or some version of who she was. How this dying Scotsman saw her.

'So...' he hesitated. 'What do you want to do now?'

'Me, I'm going to read this. If Gil – Mr Johnson - turns up, then let me know. And in the meantime, I want you to find out where that valley is. Someone must know. Phone around, speak to people. And I want you to bring me some more tea. And some water for him.' She gestured towards the dog.

Her tone was so naturally commanding, she could well be some big movie star. 'Up here?'

'Sure, why not? It's a pretty nice room. And quiet, except for those trains.'

The innkeeper hesitated again. She had invaded his domain and now was dismissing him like a servant.

'What is it?' she asked.

'It's just...'

'What?'

'Are you really who I think you are...?'

'What do you think... what is your name, anyway?'

'Rick,' he said. 'And I just wondered, what your plans are, if you're going to drive back to Vancouver or carry on elsewhere, because if you want a room here I'll need to get one ready. And if you want food, then...'

She interrupted, 'I'm just going to wait here for now,' but she was already drifting back into the journal.

'Shall I close the door?' he asked.

'On your way out, yes,' she said, and turned her attention back to the Scotsman's handwriting.

What was this, a poem?

> You hear the kaark kaaark kark of consciousness.
> Hugin and Munin flee ilk day,
> owir da spacious eart.
> Though I vex for Hugin
> that he'll no come back,
> it's for Munin I'm maistlie feart.
> Two ravens flew from your shoulders,

Hugin to the hanged
Munin to the slain,
light stealers, shape-shifting
fellow travellers.
Thought and Mind
arguing forever over
the last bean in the can

That was all it said. No context, no notes. She turned the page, found the narrative thread from before.

He woke wondering where the hell he was, remembering a dream about ravens, pulled back the heavy drapes and it seemed to be getting dark. There were a few complimentary groceries in the kitchen of his suite, so he made a cup of tea and ate a biscuit, switched on the TV to discover it was early morning, not evening. His watch still had Greenwich Mean Time. He tried to calculate the time difference, and just how long he'd slept, but the arithmetic was beyond him at that moment.

So this really was British Columbia. He vaguely remembered landing, the airport with its native carvings, the long queue at passport control, coming through, drunk on whisky miniatures, feeling jet-lagged, weakly dragging his suitcase, wondering if the woman he'd met on the plane would be there at the other side of Customs as she'd said she would be. And then her waiting with her small red case, smiling at him, the taxi through the suburbs to the door outside, where she'd left him.

As the morning brightened, he went out to look around. The suite he had rented was a largish room with small kitchen on the ground floor of a wooden heritage house, painted fashionable grey. The neighbourhood was one of similarly smart suburban houses, some like Swiss cottages, others more Arts and Crafts. In one direction, the road dipped out of sight and in the distance he could see white-capped mountains across the bay. After breakfast, he'd walk there.

MacDonald Street was quite busy, a bus route to downtown, and it intersected with the much busier 4th Avenue a couple of blocks away. Commuters were already moving to wherever they were headed. He was waiting to cross at the lights, amused by the novelty of the Canadian signals, when he got a text.

hope u slept. j-lagged? if not, can i show u something? Martina

So she was real. He found a café on the corner of 4th and Bayswater, where he ate a muffin and drank coffee while he texted back: *OK what? Where?*

Jericho - native daughters.

OK

An hour later, she picked him up outside his suite in a green VW. As he opened the passenger door, hesitating briefly to check it was the correct side, she glanced at him curiously, as if she had doubted he'd existed too, and wanted to see him again just to prove that he did.

'Hey,' she said, as he got in. 'You sleep?'

'Yeah. But I woke too early, thanks to a flock of crows – or maybe they were ravens?

'You sure you feel like doing this? Not too jet-lagged?'

'Haha, I wouldn't even know what that feels like,' he said. 'But when I woke, I thought it was night. I put on the tv and it was breakfast news, the anchorman was a Campbell and he was interviewing a MacAllister. There's Scots everywhere. Very strange. So where are we going?'

'I just thought you might like to see the oldest building in Vancouver. Thought it might get you on the road with your historical research.'

'Sounds interesting,' he said. In fact, he felt surprisingly good, good to be with her, good to be alive. The car came to a four way stop where a skateboarder was crossing.

A huge laminate photo image of a couple, embedded in the wall of an elaborate timber house on the corner, caught his eye. They were dressed in what seemed like smart 1950s fashions to him, posed almost nose to nose, though she was standing a step above her sweetheart. He read the picture title out loud: 'John and Dimitra. Together Forever. So who were John and Dimitra?' he asked.

'I don't know,' she replied, pulling away. 'Some dearly departed Greek couple. I think one of their kids keeps the place as a kind of shrine to them now. Check out the gardens. The white picket fence is plastic, by the way.'

'Happy in the ever after,' she added. 'There's a big Greek community here. It's not all Scottish.'

'But a lot of it is,' he suggested. He examined the image again. John stood a step below, looking up into Dimitra's adoring face. She was displaying a large ring on her wedding finger. 'They're the perfect married couple, whoever they are.'

As she pulled away from the stop, she smiled. 'Maybe. One photo doesn't prove anything.'

At the bottom of the hill as she turned left, he caught a glimpse of skyscrapers glinting in the sun in the other direction. Downtown, obviously.

'Beautiful,' he said, not thinking.

'Isn't it?' she answered. Then neither spoke for a while. She drove quickly and confidently along a main road skirting the shore. The view across the bay skipped in and out of sight between large mansion houses on the cliff edge, towards tall peaks across the sea. He could tell it was very beautiful and wanted to go down there, to be able gaze out across that Pacific water at the mountains and the skyscrapers, to think about all the distance he had travelled.

'You know, that would be one of the things on my bucket list,' she said, thoughtfully.

'What is?'

'You'll laugh, I know. It's to get married.'

'Married? Who to?'

'Oh, that doesn't matter so much. I just want to be a bride. If I was dying, it wouldn't matter who it was, any one of my single friends would do.'

He studied her face as she drove, saw the golden glint of mischief he'd sighted the day before. It was hard to tell if she was serious. 'But there wouldn't be any together forever,' he said.

'That's the point, clever. Just a big party where I could be the bride. Never having been one. Yet.' The automatic gear change clicked and the engine eased into top, as they sped away from town.

'I don't really understand,' he said, after a while.

'Maybe it's a girl thing. My girlfriends all understood.'

'No, I mean marriage. The need. The urge. At all. Think I've lived alone too long. To be with someone in that domestic way.'

'That's not what I wanted. And maybe that's why I never got married. No, it's just the life event. I want to experience it. Every little girl thinks about it, or at least they did where I come from. Her wedding day.'

'Where do you come from?'

'It's a little town in Czech Republic. You wouldn't know it.'

'And any groom would do in this bucket list wedding, would they?'

'Well, they'd have to look good in the photos. And play the role well on the day. You know, speeches, that sort of thing. And then leave me alone whenever I said so, once it's all over. And divorce me if I lived.'

She put down the journal on the bed, a puzzled look on her face. Hero stared at her with his mind-reader's eyes and she stroked his head. 'Weird, Hero,' she said under her breath. 'We did say these things, or something like it.' He'd captured something. Her eye fell on the next word and she read on.

'So pretty straight forward then?'

'Sure - interested?'

'I'm afraid I'm not available. Dying men don't make good husbands to be. You don't know if they're going to make it to the altar. Anyway, a beautiful woman like you has no shortage of men to choose from, I'd guess,' he teased.

'Not only men,' she said. 'This is Vancouver, after all,'

She turned off the main road, and down towards the shore, where a marina arced out into the bay. Behind a sandy cove stretched, the tide far out. They approached a small dilapidated wooden building, peeling a strange shade of dusty pink paint.

'Jericho Beach,' she offered.

'So someone blew trumpets?'

'What do you mean?'

'The Bible story. When Jeremiah brought the walls of the city of Jericho down just by blowing trumpets.'

'Now he's making things up, Hero. Taking liberties. He didn't say any of that clever stuff about the Bible.'

'I'm afraid I don't know bible stories. I grew up in Soviet times.'

Hah!

'Of course. It's not important.'

She stopped and faced out across the wide bay, to the mountainous steeps on the far side, where streets of houses stretched up from the city below. 'I think the name is a corruption. I read somewhere that an early settler had a lumber mill here and the beach was known as Jerry's Cove, which got shortened to Jericho. Though there was a Squamish settlement here before that.'

'And I never said that either.'

'I sometimes try to imagine what it must have looked like, before Europeans arrived. There were three Squamish villages along the south coast here alone. And this is Hastings Museum, or the old Hastings Mill Store, as it was called. The home of the Native Daughters. It was the heart of the first lumber mill here, where downtown is now, then they towed it up here.'

'So I suppose when the gold ran out, it was all about timber here, in the early days?'

'In the early days of the white settlement, yes. That and salmon.'

'I guess it was a hunter's paradise, forests everywhere. Wild animals. Bears, wolves, beavers.'

'But you know, they discovered a garbage pit downtown a while back while they were building, and the remains were at least 2,500 years old. You know, shells and bones and stuff. Some expert said it could be as old as 9,000 years.'

'A midden?'

'Yes. That's it. A midden.'

'Good Scots word,' he said as he got out and wandered over to the front door, where an old iron bell swung from a new support. She hung back by the VW, sat on the bonnet and smiled, as he pulled out his Nikon and began snapping the front of the store, its shuttered windows and signs.

'Like it?' she asked.

He turned and looked at her sitting there watching. 'As you say over here, sure.' And he turned the lens towards her, focused. She crossed her legs, lifted her chin, posed, and he pressed the shutter. Gazing into the camera at the recorded image, he said 'You don't look very Czech,' with a grin.

'How should I look?'

'Well, I always thought Czech women were tall and blonde. You know, like the tennis player.'

'But I refuse your stereotyping. You don't have ginger hair and a kilt.'

He clicked the shutter again, checked the picture. Again, he had the feeling she reminded him of someone. 'True. I'm a poor specimen of my race.'

'You are indeed. So very thin and... what's the word?'

'Thrawn?' he offered, but she didn't respond.

Instead she stood up. 'If you say so. Anyway, I'm going in now.'

'Let's...'

She laid the journal down as Hero's ears pricked up, and they both listened as a distant rumble grew. But it passed, just a truck on the highway. Turning back to the story in front of her, she said 'It all seems a bit stagey, buddy. I'm not sure what to make of it. What is this Scotchman of ours up to?' But she carried on.

He pushed the old wooden door of the museum open for her, and she went to squeeze past, into the gloom. For a moment they were nose to nose, eye to eye, and he realised she was exactly as tall as he was. Her scent filled his nostrils like a potent smoking drug, then she had passed him by.

Inside was a porch, with various signs and pennants pinned to a v-lined wall. A second door led to the dark interior, like a large schoolroom, or indeed a store. The air inside felt heavy with dust, laced through with the aroma of slowly aging decay, barely masked by furniture polish. It reminded him firstly of a church and then, with an aftertaste of bibliochor, his bookshop in Edinburgh, and for a moment he was back in familiar territory.

In the gloom, behind a long heavy wooden shop counter acting as a desk, a woman sat crocheting. She glanced up as they entered, as if she wasn't expecting anyone, as if they may be the first and only visitors of the day. She put her crochet down and sat up.

'Well, hi,' she said. 'Come on in. Welcome to the oldest memorial to Vancouver's pioneer past.' He gazed around the room at the mass of assembled artefacts. All seemed faded, sepia-coloured, a multi-paned window on an earlier era. Not a smart modern museum full of interactive gizmos, the past sealed behind plexiglass casing, here the building itself was an exhibit.

'It dates from 1865?' Martina asked.

'That's correct. Though at that time it wasn't out here at Jericho. You have to imagine the whole of the city as virgin forest,' the woman at the desk went on. 'Ancient old growth trees, more than 300 feet tall. Then in 1865 an Englishman by the name of Stamp began to build a lumber mill down by the shore there, at the foot of Dunlevy. They took a flume from Trout Lake to provide steam power, and built this store to service the camp. It sold everything you could think of back then, a true emporium.'

Listening, he wandered through the exhibits, arrayed as if in a country schoolroom or a very plain Protestant chapel, yet the most fabulous of obscure objects to him lay within reach. Old mangles, pots and pans, various tools, many of them carved from wood. As he nosed around, peering at the old photos and artefacts, it occurred to him that Vancouver was almost exactly the same age as Lyle. The idea of the lumber mill would have been gestating in Stamp's mind just as Jimmy was entering the world, five thousand miles away in Shetland, in the spring of 1864.

'Are you from round here?' the woman asked, curiously.

'I live nearby,' Martina said, 'But I've never been in here before, although I have driven past many times. My friend is from Scotland and very interested in the history of the province.

'Well, there's plenty of history in here. And one of the early mill owners was a Scot, you know, after Stamp gave the mill up. He was a Campbell.'

'Did you hear that?' Martina called over to him, then turned back to the figure at the desk. 'He thinks everything here is from Scotland. He points to street names as we drive past and tells me they're all Scottish.'

Gil smiled over at the two women as they talked by the desk. The curator laughed. 'Well, you know, lots of Scots came here at first, my dear. He's right about that. And it's from them we take much of our inspiration, them and others like them.'

'Exactly, just as I told you.' he said. 'Is it all right to take a few photos?'

'For a small donation,' the woman replied, nodding towards a large wooden collection box on a table by the door.

'So when did the store move up here?' Martina asked her.

'1930. They were going to demolish it, and so a group of ladies came together and insisted that it should be preserved. They towed it up here from Burrard Inlet, through the Narrows across English Bay, and lifted it up here on rollers. There's a film of it you can watch if you like, just by the entrance to the Hansom Cab over in that corner there.'

The two visitors peered into the gloom in the direction she indicated.

'It's quite wonderful,' she went on. 'There's footage of the Native Daughters aboard the Harbour Board yacht, serving a special tea. It was quite an event, you see, the mill store had a very special place in people's hearts, because it had survived the great fire of 1866. And it had been the first post office, the first schoolroom, the first drugstore anywhere round here.'

'There was a fire in 1866?' he asked. He was calculating in Lyle time, that Jimmy would have been in Cloud Falls for two years by then.

'Yes,' Martina said. 'Almost the whole of the town was destroyed, wasn't it?'

The curator grimaced. 'Sure, it was terrible. Not that there was so much to destroy back then, but it was all made of timber and went up like a rocket. They were clearing land because Vancouver had been selected as the terminus for the CPR railway, and a squall swept up a brush fire that the workers had started. The sparks fell on the town and it just exploded, and kept on burning till it was just about on top of the store. Then, like it was the hand of Providence at work, the wind changed and the store was spared. The millstore here became an emblem. It still is, to those who know the story.'

Gil was snapping photos as he listened, thinking about the news of the great fire making its way up country to the young Lyle on his uncle's ranch in Cloud Falls. With no railway at that time, the news would have travelled by stagecoach or horseback, probably – no doubt fiercely discussed and debated, the fire and its causes, the miracle of the wind change. The story would have grown with each telling. Jimmy Lyle would have known this building and its story well.

The curator went on with her tale. 'After the fire, the store was at the heart of the recovery operation, doling out food and emergency supplies, even acting as a morgue for the dead.'

He wandered about after that, looking at the exhibits, the thought of death vivid, as if the memory was somehow encoded in the timbers of the store. His eyes picked out a massive wooden plough, old sledges, a wooden washing machine. Cannons from 1867 when the settlement still had need of them, the Hansom cab, the old Hastings Mill safe. Some period dresses. A vast collection of woven baskets like the kind he knew Lyle had collected for the museums back east.

Then they watched the grainy film of the Native Daughters serving tea on the day in 1930 that the millstore was brought to Jericho by barge.

Afterwards Martina asked the curator, 'So just who are the Native Daughters of BC?'

'We are an organisation of women born here in the province. Pioneers.'

'So I couldn't join because I was born in Czechoslovakia?'

'No, dear. Not if you aren't born here.'

'So this has nothing to do with First Nations natives?' he added.

'Not much,' she answered, not elaborating, then to Martina she said, 'You are, my dear, lovely as you are, what back in the old days, they used to call a 'cheechako'. Someone who migrates here, in the Chinook parlance.'

'Yes, I am a cheechako,' Martina said, and looked to him, suddenly, with a vague glare of annoyance. She seemed somehow upset at the idea.

'There's a book of Robert Service's poems, *Ballads of a Cheechako*,' he volunteered, inadvertently making a no-man's land between the curator and the cheechako.

'Ah, Robert Service,' the woman said. 'Now he was a poet. We Canadians are very proud of him.'

'But in Scotland, where he came from, he's hardly mentioned these days.'

For a second the woman looked puzzled. 'Scotland? Are you sure?'

'He grew up in the shire of Robert Burns, and was schooled in Glasgow. He came out here as a banker. He ended up as the biggest-selling poet of the twentieth century, living the life of Riley in Paris.'

'You,' Martina laughed, 'would have everything Scottish. But surely that can't be correct. What about Eliot and his cats? That must have made millions.'

'I'm only repeating what I've read,' he said, holding his palms up to both.

There had been a dusty old settled pride about this native-born lady as she sat behind the old shop counter, but as she shifted into a beam of light that streamed from the window, a glamour of well-to-do assurance came over her. She stretched out across the small desk and the sunlight caught her profile.

'I think you'll find I'm right about Mr Service,' she said firmly. For a second he was tempted to spout a challenge, and probably appear quite pedantic, but he smiled instead.

'Ah well, maybe you are. I'm only a bookseller, after all,' he said. And he put a twenty-dollar bill in the collection box by the door as they exited. No gift shop here.

Afterwards, outside, they stood silently for a while, looking out over the grandeur of the harbour to the mountains beyond.

'That woman annoyed me,' she said.

'Really?' he asked, and smiled in a slightly twisted way that didn't turn out right. 'I'd never have guessed.'

'Are you teasing me?' she said sharply. Did he twist his smile because she seemed annoyed, or because he was nervous?

'Maybe. So what if you're a Czech cheechako?'

She laughed. 'And you're very cheeky.'

'And this is the cheek of a Czech Cheechako,' he added and, for no reason, kissed her on the side of her face, as a joke maybe.

She put down her glasses, checked the time on her cell. Hero raised his head from the cushion of his paws, hopefully. She patted his neck fur, and said, 'This is weird, buddy. I'm in a story.' And she put her spectacles back on.

'So,' he said, 'Tell me what I'm looking at here. What are these places called?' And so, slowly, she began to name the various sights, from Vancouver Island in the distance, to the Sunshine Coast, Bowen Island, West Vancouver and the mountains of Cypress, Grouse and Seymour all opposite, and then Point Grey on the same shore. He tried to memorize all the names, but his mind was still reeling gently from the jetlag.

'Okay. Enough,' he breathed. 'That's all my brain can take in for now.'

'You must be tired,' she said, examining his face. 'You probably want a timeout.'

'No,' he answered. 'I'm enjoying this. I'll tell you when I've had enough.'

'Well, the tide's out. We could walk back along the shore? It's not too far to where you're staying?

'What about your car?

'I can pick it up later. I could do with the walk. And you should see this piece of shoreline. It's the last wild part, the rest has all been landscaped. There's a nice place below MacDonald where one of the Squamish villages used to be. Tsumtsahmuls, they called it. The name's lost now.' So they clambered down onto the beach, and went treading their way through the wet stones and slippery surfaces.

'You must tell me more about why you're here,' she told him, as they walked in the ebb along the shore. Shells crunched underfoot.

'I told you. I want to write a book.'

'I sense there's more to it than just the book.'

'Well, I suppose it's my top bucket-list item,' he said. 'Things to do before you die.' Along the seawall an impressive line of graffiti caught a blaze of sunlight. It lit up shapes and slogans unfamiliar to him, though one smallish piece *Uncle George – get well soon!* made them both laugh. They walked on a little further, around a headland, picking careful steps across rock and sand.

'But why? I think I deserve a little more information. I've brought you to one of my secret places. You owe me more about your secrets.'

A large flock of ducks and ducklings made darting bobbing passage along the shallows. A few went far out, some were left behind.

'Well, you are right. There is more. It's to do with my father. Something I always wondered about. You see, he was much older than my mother, a widower, and he died when I was a boy so I don't – I didn't even have the chance, you know, to find out much about him, other than what my mother told me, and she had her own issues with him. She always seemed to end up talking about those.'

He stopped and peered out across the water. 'Downtown's stunning from here,' he said, 'the way the city seems to try to compete with the mountains in scale...'

'But completely fails,' she finished.

'So far.'

'They'll never tame it,' she said, with absolute certainty. 'The buildings will all be thrown down and overgrown.'

'Prophecy of doom?'

'Certainty, in cosmic terms.'

'You know a bit about the cosmos?'

'It's innate. Stardust, you know, like the song says we are.'

'Ah yes, the great Canadian songstress.'

'You know Joni?'

'I grew up with her.'

'Me too. I learned so much from her songs. About art, emotions. And America. Funny we should share that.'

'Her background was Scottish, I think.'

'Shut up,' she said. 'Enough already.'

Nine freighters were anchored in the depth of the harbour, various combinations of rust-proof red and salty black, a little sallow yellow or white for the superstructure. Flags lay at mast in the stillness. They could be from anywhere, this metal leviathan school, carrying containers across the Pacific, to and fro from China, Japan, Russia, full of everything that can be bought and sold.

'So what's the mystery? Are you going to tell me?' she asked.

'The family secret? It's not so great, and I don't know the answer. I may find out when I go north.'

'North?'

'Yes, next week. To Cloud Falls. I'm following his trail, really, coming here, going there.'

'To where your Lyle fella lived?'

'Oh, he's part of it. My father was there too. After the First World War, he emigrated. At least I think so. He was married, settled, but his wife died, and he went back to Scotland. Or so I think. So far it's not proven, as we say in Scotland.'

'And you are here to prove it,' she said, with that same tone of certainty he was growing used to. He didn't bother to confirm. She had decided, and he understood.

'It's a complicated family,' he added.

'Aren't they all?' She stopped, sat on one of the huge tree-trunks that had washed ashore in some high tide or other. He sat beside her, close enough to feel her warmth, or to imagine that he did.

'This,' she said, 'is what used to be called Tsumtsahmuls by the Squamish. That's all Stanley Park across there, to the right. And over there, where the forest ends, you can just see Siwash Rock.'

'You mean that little rocky pinnacle?'

'Yes. It's a famous landmark. There's a story about it, you know, in native myth.'

'Which is?'

She took a breath before replying. 'I don't remember it all, but from what I recall, Siwash was a virtuous young man. His new wife was pregnant and so he swam every morning to kinda purify himself before becoming a father. Soon after the baby was born, one morning he found himself in the path of a great canoe that was making its way south along the coast and on a course to go through the channel where Siwash was swimming. And he refused to move out of the way. His ritual demanded that he didn't stop. He didn't know it, but the canoe belonged to the four grey men of the north, and they were like wizards.' She stopped, as if trying to find the right words.

'What happened?'

'Well, he explained to them that he couldn't turn aside without breaking his vow. The phrase sticks in my mind - clean fatherhood, it was called. So anyway, they turned him into that rock, saying that it would be a reminder to people of the importance of uprightness forever.'

'That's quite sad. What happened to the young wife and child?'

'Ah well, the men of the north took pity, and turned them to stone too. There are two other smaller rocks hidden in the forest near Siwash, supposed to be his wife and child.'

He whistled in surprise. 'A rather harsh form of pity. But I suppose they're together forever,' and at the same moment, both of them exclaimed, 'John and Dimitra!' Laughing at the coincidence, they looked directly at one another, their eyes locked together for a millisecond. Again he saw that golden light radiate from brown. She did so remind him of someone.

A surprised silence grew as they listened to the gentle rhythm of the waves. The calls of the seabirds played a shrill melody above. In the harbour, the freighters had multiplied to eleven, as new hulls which had been hidden from sight came into view behind the foregrounded few.

'The story with my father relates to Jimmy Lyle,' he said after a while. 'I think Lyle may have been my grandfather.'

She turned to stare at him. 'Really? How come?'

'Well, when Lyle left Scotland to come out here, he left behind a pregnant woman.'

'His kid?'

'I think so. But I can't prove it. Yet.'

'Wow,' she said. 'So were they married?'

'No. She was an older woman. A widow in her thirties. I don't know the truth of it, but it seems from what I can find out that the child was his. And that child, I believe was my father.'

'So he ran out on them?'

He shrugged, gave her a look of uncertainty. 'Could be. He was just a lad, barely eighteen. I expect it was a scandal.'

'And that's why you're so interested in him?'

'Not only that,' he said. 'Otherwise, he lived this heroic sort of life. From what I've been able to find out.'

After a long time, she added, 'I can take you to Siwash, maybe. Maybe on Thursday?'

'That would be great.'

'I'll text you.'

'So, anyway, your story about clean fatherhood. From my family's perspective, your Siwash has a point.'

'He has a rock.'

'A rocky point.'

'Or a pointy rock.' They both began to giggle, he started coughing and he signed that she should slap his back, which she did, repeatedly. When he'd recovered, he said, 'I still find laughing hard on the throat.'

'After the radiation?'

'Yep.' That reminder shifted the mood like a breeze from elsewhere, a colder place, paradoxically filled with the memory of lasers burning. Being strapped down and hit with beams. She seemed to stiffen, breathing in the sea air deeply.

'I wanted to tell you, on the plane, when you told me about your illness...' She paused.

'What?'

'It happened to me to.'

'What?'

'Cancer.'

'You?' They looked at each, eyes wide, as her secret wound its way around them, drawing them closer still.

'I was having radiation more or less at the same time as you were.'

'Good God,' he said.

'So we're radiation twins, in a way.'

'I suppose so. Are you okay? What's the story?'

'Yes, all clear at the moment. Regular checks. Some post-surgery pain, but I'm okay so far.' She touched her left breast with her open palm, and he understood.

'So you're still healing, like me?'

'Yes, still a distance to go. In lots of ways.'

'Well well.' For a while they sat in silence, then without thinking, he said, 'I wonder if it will ever be like it was before?' It was a question neither of them thought worth answering.

The ebb was low. Mist was embracing Mount Seymour. Above those downtown tower blocks, the high forest ridges of the valleys inland slipped mysteriously into a grand enveloping shroud. From here, the city was shining towers, striations where balconies marked out floors, altogether like a single bent-back crouching creature with skyscraper spikes and streets for stripes, like some giant armadillo. It did not move, this beast, but smaller creatures moved within it. Tiny struggling creatures, forever going nowhere.

'Did you ever think about not going through the treatment, just letting go?' he asked, after a while.

'What do you mean? Wouldn't that be a bit like committing suicide?'

'Sort of, I suppose. Just letting it all go. Having the cancer do its thing.'

She frowned at him. 'No. Did you?'

'I did. At the start, when I knew I was ill but before I found out what lay ahead.'

'What happened?'

'I suppose I couldn't imagine how I could do it. Where. But the why seemed obvious.'

She shook her head slowly, leant down and picked up a pebble, then threw it towards the distant waterline where it skipped once and submerged. 'I just try to deal with it, matter-of-factly. As a thing that's happening to me. Something I have to get through. Somehow.'

'And are you? Getting through?'

'I'm still on sick leave. And it was a huge shock, okay, that's for sure.'

Now the mist was slipping behind Stanley Park and the wooded outline was vivid against the white wall. Siwash rock was perfectly framed, clearly separated from the main cliff at this angle. In the foreground, the small boats in the visible marina were all anchored. The natural harbour lay beyond, hidden from the ocean behind the strait. He imagined the coming of the Europeans, how Captain Vancouver's crew must have welcomed the sense of shelter, the safety from the open sea it brought, as they sailed into this great fjord. And here, at Tsumtsahmuls, someone would have watched, perhaps whilst gathering shellfish, astounded by the other worldly vessels approaching.

'Radiation twins. Well well,' he said after a silence.

'You don't still think of it, do you?'

'What?'

'You know, suicide.'

'Ending it all, as they say? Oh I don't know, I suppose it will end soon enough, whatever.'

She gave him a hurried concerned look, then smiled and slapped his back again. 'All more reason to live, to write your book!'

'Ah yes,' he said, with a faraway look, 'The great book. I'm not so sure that's so easy.'

She frowned. 'You're sounding depressed – and it's depressing me. Stop it.'

'Sorry.'

'And don't say sorry. Just live. Breathe. It's not so hard. And none of it is so heavy as you think. Look, see those mountains. Feel how light they are in your mind. Make your troubles as light as those. Distant.' His eyes followed her tanned arm as it waved towards the ridge of peaks in the far distance.

'Easy to say,' he muttered. ''Easy to say.'

As they sat, side by side on a giant sea-worn trunk, the great harbour shimmering in front of them, she put her hand on top of his, on top of the worm-filled log. Their legs dangled like those of children, as they sat and stared and watched a flotilla of paddle boarders pass slowly, the voices echoing from the edge of hearing. At the marina to the west, a fleet of little dinghies sailed.

'I can see I'll have to look out for you, Mr Sick Heart,' she said, then pulled her hand away and stood up. 'I'll walk back to get the car. You just have to go up the steps there, and you'll see MacDonald. Just walk up a couple of blocks and you'll see your place.'

As he watched her walk away, her tall figure receding into the distance as she rounded the great tree trunks washed ashore, stepping delicately over the green seaweedy stones, he felt the weight of insignificance return. The weight that was a lightness, like Kundera suggested. Dying was easy. Living was the hard part. Had he travelled all this way, just to realise that? He could surely have realised that back home. A shoreline is a shoreline, an ebb an ebb, Atlantic or Pacific. The slap and slush of the barely moving, the strange charm of the lolling water's incantation. Yet the shape of this inlet had its own unique shape, and so the movements of tides did too. What gullies filled, what disappeared from view as the waters encroached, how each shapes the other.

For so long he'd been alone, ever since his mother died, with no one for company but doctors and nurses. Now, in just one day, this other person had penetrated his solitude and now he knew that she had suffered as he had done. Alone in Scotland, he had accepted that he was nothing, an infinitesimal detail in the vast cosmic flux. It seemed unbelievable, somehow, that he had travelled 5000 miles to meet a woman who understood, who had faced the same trial, this stranger who'd had a visit from death just like he had, and knew, like he did, that it would be back to stay at some stage.

Did it matter? Any of it? Was the oyster shell important, this one he picked from the shore as the crows attempted their clam-opening trick, of flying high up to drop it on a rock. To the oyster, maybe. In the grand scheme, as one of a species, maybe no and yes. What was one more oyster? Another few hours of mindless life. Yet its shape is perfect, a closure, the mollusc mouth straining, the seal so tight, as he had been sealed, grimly awaiting death. But he was still alive, and now someone was prising him open again. And how long before the shell is simply dust again, a scattered calcium strain in a sand of many colours, drenched in mud?

The growing hum and judder of the small plane flying in over Stanley Park broke his thought, finally sounding huge in the silence of this natural amphitheatre. It reminded him of those months in the garden at his mother's house near the airport, watching the planes, as he endured the radiotherapy.

And then a series of explosions, like heavy gunfire, maybe six or seven shots in a row, sounded in the distance. As they echoed away, birds dominated the soundscape again. Gulls and crows, some geese in the water. A heron's *kaarrik* counterpointed a crow's *kark*. Some of the crows were still apprentice in the art of cawing, this year's hatchlings, awkward in their grown-up feathers. Had they mastered the art of the clam drop, was it innate?

The curved question marks of two goose heads appeared in the distant water, then disappeared underwater, seeking their missing dots. Voices carried, words inaudible, from a little cruiser passing.

On the seawall, someone was building a barricade of giant iron baffles, angles cut to keep the waves away. Like Richard Serra in domestic mood. The metal had immediate age, and already the graffiti artists of the foreshore had marked their claim of right. But in a city built on timber, the boldness of such an intrusion became a symbol of industrialisation. The oldest Vancouver was built on what had grown here, was itself a product of the land, and was reclaimed by it in fire. What remains, the solitary Hastings Mill, is a delicate tinderbox, towed far from the glass and steel of downtown, moored in Jericho.

Jericho. Tsumtsahmuls. MacDonald. The right to name, the language of power, the dominant narrative. That much was the same in old Caledonia and in New Caledonia, as the early settled country was called before Queen Victoria decided that, as the French already had a New Caledonia, British Columbia it should be.

Tsumtsahmuls was left off the map. The old world cartographers brought their own language to add to the first people's, the names of their hometowns from the old country, their great figures, their leaders and chiefs, their clans, at first just a few, then to swamp those first names in a torrent of syllables.

38 maccloud falls

Then he felt a buzz in his pocket, and took out his phone. It was a text from her.

Want 2 watch hockey 2night? Big game.

He called her back.

'Well now,' she said to her canine companion, and laid down her pink-rimmed glasses. Hero looked up at her, expectantly, as if he had been waiting jealously for attention. 'Very strange. It's a story with someone like me doing things very like some things I've done. But it isn't me and it isn't what happened. At least, not as I remember it.' She bent down and petted the dog. 'Our friend Gil has put us in a story. He is a strange guy.' She stood up and walked over to the window, where the video camera stood on a tripod, pointing out across the river towards the little town. 'I wonder what he's been recording on this,' she said. The dog got up and walked obediently to her side. 'Shall we see?' she asked it. She fiddled with the buttons till she found the playback, put her glasses on and watched the small screen. There were various files. There was footage of the Rocky Mountaineer, the long tourist train passing along the canyon line. Shots of two birds on a nest, eagles perhaps, which when she checked out the room window, she could see, far away on a platform on top of a pole by the river's edge. Further back, scenes of a waterfall. More of the river. And further again, what seemed to be his journey up from Vancouver on the Greyhound, shot from inside the coach. None of it of great interest, and no interviews with anyone on the subject of Lyle or anything related, at least as far she could find. Maybe he'd already downloaded them.

'Not much to see there,' she said, and picked up her cell phone to check the time. 'What shall we do?' she asked the dog, who seemed to think it was a good idea to go for a walk. The room was still very hot despite the fact that it was now almost six o'clock, and it whined at the half-open door.

'Okay,' she said. 'Let's take a look downstairs, see if the innkeeper's around. If not, we can take a walk. Guess you must be feeling the heat, honey. And you've finished your water.'

There was no one at the desk, and no one on the terrace. No sign of Rick. He wasn't in his place. Then she heard the low sound of someone talking come from the room to the other side of the stairs. She went in, the dog still at her feet. Two men were sitting in what appeared to be a guest lounge, looking a little tired and scruffy. One had his back to her, and when the other indicated to his friend that someone had entered the room, they both turned to look at her.

'Hi,' she said. 'Have you seen Rick?'

'Ah, no, ma'am,' said the furthest away, the older of the two. 'Think he went out.'

'Are you guys the tree-planters?' she asked.

'Well, two of them,' the younger guy answered. 'The others are in their rooms, I guess. We just got back. Been a hard day's night.' Both men were looking at her strangely. She guessed it was the Sigourney Weaver thing.

'I'm looking for my friend, the Scotsman who is staying here,' she said. 'He seems to have disappeared. You haven't seen him?'

'Saw him the other night,' the younger guy said.

'How did he seem? I mean, what was his mood?'

'His mood? I dunno. Seemed fairly quiet. We were watching the hockey together.'

'I wouldn't worry,' the older tree-planter added. 'He's out a lot, hiking about, talking to people. I'm Bob, by the way, and this is Doug.' It was as if he was hoping for her to offer her name. When she didn't, he added, 'Nice pooch.'

'He's a bit fatigued with the heat. Anyway, if Rick comes back, tell him I've taken the lad here for a short walk. I'll be back soon.'

She went out of the room and heard their voices behind her.

'Nah, that's not her. She's too young. Sigourney Weaver must be like 60 plus now.'

'I dunno, man. These celebrities get all kinds of work done. They don't age like normal people.'

Rumours travelled.

She opened the front door and left the relative cool of the AC with Hero. The heat was a powerful wave. They crossed the highway and walked alongside the railway line for a while, where one long snaking CPR train of various trucks lay waiting silently for its signal to roll. Hot as it was out, a breeze was blowing through the canyon. She found herself staring up at the steep rocky wall opposite, and down to the huge river roaring by below. The scale of the scene was vast, and the tiny gathering of houses seemed so insignificant, it was kind of overwhelming.

Hero didn't want to hang about outside either, for whatever reason, so they made their way back to the oldest inn in BC. Inside there was no one around – even the two tree-planters had gone. So she filled the water bowl for her companion and went upstairs again. Hero settled down again, sucked of all energy by the heat, in front of the fan. She picked up Gil's handwriting.

'Let's see what happens to my Czech alter-ego Martina next,' she said to him. 'And maybe you'll have a role too, buddy.' She put on her pink-rimmed glasses and began to read again.

That afternoon, after a nap, he took a walk around the shops in the Kitsilano neighbourhood in the sunshine. Everything seemed gripped by a blue and white fever – cars displayed pennants, flags draped on balconies, people of all ages wore Vancouver Canucks shirts as their daily wear – even a stuffed full-sized brown bear in the window of a second hand bookshop he visited wore the colours. He struck up a conversation with the bookseller who explained that the Canucks were playing in the final of the Stanley Cup, hockey's top prize. On the sign above an old cinema on Broadway near where he was staying, the sign where movie titles were displayed read 'WE ARE ALL CANUCKS NOW' across the top. It was if the whole city had invested in this contest, as if it was a matter of deep civic pride and not a sporting trophy that was at stake.

She turned up outside his suite as arranged, rang the doorbell. When he opened the door, she was standing there on the doorstep dressed in a Canucks t-shirt, her dark hair pinned up, and a Canucks cap on top. She smiled, her brown eyes shining that golden way he'd noticed on the plane. The first thing about her that had impressed itself on his memory. Again he had the vague feeling he knew her from somewhere.

'Thought we'd walk,' she said. 'There may be drinking involved.'

Together they set off through the suburban streets, passing house after house in a subtle variety of wooden styles. She asked if he'd slept and he said he'd had a couple of hours.

'Feel alright?'

'A bit tired. But that's normal. With the radiotherapy.'

'I nap too,' she said. 'Every afternoon.'

As they walked, side by side, it struck him that not only was she as tall as he was but their legs too matched perfectly in length, so that their strides seemed synchronised. They did indeed seem twinned. Radiation twins.

'I can't get over you and I having cancer at the same time,' she said, as if picking up on his thoughts.

'Well, lots of people did. Do. That's not so strange. But meeting the way we did, with the prospect of an air crash, it feels like we're fated in some way.'

'To have met?'

'To share something.'

'What?'

'Well, let's start with the hockey. Tell me about it. What's going on.'

So Martina explained, the Vancouver Canucks were 1-0 up in a best of seven series against the Boston Bruins, trying to win their first ever North American ice hockey championship, the Stanley Cup – the end goal of a long winter season and more than a hundred games. Tonight was the second match in the final. She turned out to be a big hockey fan. It was a hugely popular game in Czech Republic and a lot of Czechs played in the NHL, she said. He explained to her that in Scotland it wasn't all that popular, and was hardly played at all, though he could remember that when he was a boy the BBC used to show live games from the British League, featuring teams like the Fife Flyers and Murrayfield Racers, so he knew the rudiments.

She took him to a packed pub on 4th Avenue where everyone was glued to big screens, positioned throughout the roof at different angles to maximise viewing. A few people she knew welcomed her to their table, and she introduced him as a stray Scotsman she'd picked up on the way home from Calgary. They squeezed into a space next a man she called Alex.

Martina explained to him, over the hubbub, that for Vancouver this competition represented proper and full participation in the affairs of the continent. This was a young city even in North American terms. The stray Scotsman didn't really understand all the rules, or the commentators' jargon. He tried to follow the play, but it was so quick.

'I can't see the puck half the time,' he said.

'Watch what the guys are doing, follow the players, not the puck,' Alex said, without taking his eyes from the screen. Martina too was entranced. Her face lit up when the Canucks attacked, glowered and grimaced when in defence.

It turned out a very tense match. The Canucks finally managed to win 3-2 in extra time, or what they called overtime here. When the puck found the net, the place erupted, just like the football terraces he remembered from his childhood. Except with high-fives and chest bumps. Martina did a little dance of joy. She and her friends had hardly spoken since the start of overtime till the goal went in and victory was secured, but a lot of beer was consumed and the stray Scotsman had eaten his first plate of poutine, on their command, in the interim.

Alex looked hugely relieved, as if he'd lived through some mortal combat. 'Five to go and only two more wins required,' he beamed around the table, but after the elation had passed and the pub quietened down he grew worried. 'But I remember 1994,' he went on. 'I was just a kid. The disappointment and the riots that followed, man...' The emphasis on the final word stretched out significantly. That year, he continued, against the New York Rangers, they'd been 3-1 down in the series, then won two games to level at 3-3 so that everyone thought the momentum was with them, but they lost the last in New York by a single goal. And after the game ended, a frustrated crowd began to gather downtown in Vancouver, and it all went sour. A man fell from a street lamp and police on bicycles tried to escort paramedics into the crowd. Some people got rowdy, attempted to take a bicycle from one constable, the police retreated and warned them to disperse. When they wouldn't, the riot squad appeared and a full-scale pitched battle began. Shops were broken into and some of the angry fans looted what they could. Around 200 people ended up in hospital.

The way Alex described it, the trauma was obviously still lingering, like a shadow from youth that wouldn't disappear, but took the shine from the hope that this time it would be different. It was a salutary warning that nothing could be taken for granted. Although Vancouver had been the best team throughout the main season this year, Boston was a tough opponent with a good old goaltender, and he was anxious.

The pub slowly emptied and the stray Scotsman decided he should go. He stood up, and began to say his farewells to his new hockey chums, and to Martina.

'Are you going?' she said.

'Yes, I want to head back.'

She stood up next to him and leaned close. She seemed quite drunk, though he wasn't sure just how much they'd had to drink in the midst of excitement. 'You're not leaving without me,' she said, whispering so no one else could hear. 'My dates don't run out on me.'

He wondered, was this a date? Was she serious? Then she smiled, a little drunkenly, took his hand where it dangled at his side and squeezed it.

'I have to look after him,' she said to her friends. 'He's a sick-hearted Scotsman.'

Outside, it was still quite light, and they walked step for step along a quiet backstreet. She was swaying about a little, hardly sober, as she walked.

'I have to get home too,' she said. 'My dog is waiting for me. He needs a walk.'

'Your dog?'

'Yes. Hero.'

'You call him Hero?'

'Well, as a puppy they called him Milo but I never liked that name. Always reminded of the kid in the Phantom Tollbooth. So I changed it to Miro after the painter, then it became Miro the Hero, and then just Hero.

'Hmmm. You live in this direction?'

'More or less,' she said. 'I'm going to see you safely home first. It's my duty.' She smiled. 'After all, we're radiation twins.'

'We are indeed,' he replied, as she took hold of his arm again.

She held onto him all the way up the steps to the door of his lodgings.

'I want to see where you're staying,' she said, and she followed him inside.

While he switched on the lamp and drew the curtains, she flopped onto the bed, her forearm across her forehead.

'Wow,' she breathed. 'That was some match.'

He stood and gazed at her lying there, this beautiful stranger who had sprawled herself across his rented bed, her long legs stretched out, her eyes closed, her dark hair splayed over his pillow. She didn't move for what seemed ages. Was she falling asleep? Should he pull a cover over her?

He felt quite drunk himself, though at least the room wasn't spinning. He lay down next her, side by side, not touching, staring up at the ceiling in the gloomy lamplight. Then her hand took hold of his, her scent was rich and close, unavoidably attractive. He wanted to kiss her, but she flinched as if she'd been burned.

'We're twins,' she said. 'My Scotch friend.' She stood up, swaying slightly. 'I have to go. My dog is waiting.'

He lay there, silently berating himself as she fumbled drunkenly with the latch, opened the door and let herself out. He heard her footsteps clatter as she went down the wooden stairs outside, and slipped away into the darkening night.

'Hmm,' she said, and took off her glasses. She lay back on the bed, his newly rented bed. The dog Hero lifted his head, looked at her with his blank black-eyed stare, the one that seemed capable of seeing into her soul. 'What?' she said. 'It's just a story. It wasn't like that, I didn't do anything.' The dog leapt up on the bed next to her and she put her arms around his thick furry mane. 'You know you're my boyfriend.' Hero nuzzled at her neck and she laughed, but her hand went to cover her breast as he lay down heavily next to her, his paws on her chest. 'Don't be jealous,' she told him, as she ruffled his coat, and he licked her face.

The rumble of an engine outside made her sit up. Not the thunderous screech of the train like earlier, more a truck, by the sound of it, maybe more than one. She went to the open door and listened. If it was Gil, she'd better put his writing away.

As she closed the drawer, she heard the little bell ring as the inn's front door opened, and people came in, more than one or two. She heard their footsteps and their voices as they seemed to make their way to the terrace, so she opened the room window to eavesdrop.

Rick's now familiar eastern tone drifted up. She didn't catch what he said because of the noise the others were making. There seemed to be quite a crowd. She heard the clink of glasses, laughter, loud voices, then the squeak of steps on the staircase, and a knock on the half-open door. It was Rick.

'Any news?' she asked.

He shrugged his shoulders. 'Maybe. I went over the bridge and spoke to a few people in town. Seems Mr Johnson went out hiking early this morning. One of the First Nations guys, Big George Wakem, saw him heading up the highway to the north.'

'Did he say where he was going?'

'Said he didn't ask him. But he looked like he was headed somewhere important. George called a couple of the band, and they're spreading the word. Seems your Gil saw one of the elders the day before yesterday and she told him about a few places he might like to see, connected to Jimmy Lyle. We haven't been able to get hold of her yet, but George is here right now. He's downstairs on the terrace if you'd like to speak with him. And just to warn you, so is all his family…'

She was momentarily surprised but nodded. 'Sure,' she said. 'I'll come down.'

But Rick stopped her progress at the door, taking hold of her arm. 'One thing,' he said, 'If one of the kids happens to call you Ms. Weaver…'

She interrupted, 'What did you tell them?'

'I might have said you were the woman from Alien. I was just kiddin them.'

There was quite a little gathering downstairs on the terrace. When she appeared under the adobe archway, they all got up and, one by one, shook her hand politely. Rick introduced the patriarch first, George, and the patriarch introduced his family, and each almost curtseyed or bowed like she was royalty as she moved along the line and they said hello. Seven in all, Big George who was indeed big, his wife, her sister, George's two grown up sons, one large like his father and one not so, and a couple of their kids, George's grandchildren, all spread over the terrace. Too many names to remember.

They'd kept the best seat for her and Hero too was deemed royalty. The kids especially made a big fuss of him, wanted to know what kind of dog he was and where he came from.

'So Rick here says you're worried about your friend, the writer guy from over in Scotland,' George asked, when everyone had settled down. 'We met him across the river in Valhalla the other night, didn't we? Nice fella.' His wife and sister in law nodded.

'You workin on a film about Jimmy Lyle?' the smaller son asked.

The tall woman glanced at Rick, who was listening, a curious smile on his face. 'No. Gil, that is, Mr Johnson is just doing some research.'

George nodded. 'He said that. Was asking when we met. He was a good man, Jimmy Lyle. My father and him were big friends.'

'So maybe you'll be bringin a film crew up here sometime soon?' the bigger son inquired.

She frowned again at Rick. 'Come on, I want to be honest with you all, I'm not who you seem to be thinking I am,' she sighed, looking around the gathering, smiling.

Big George chuckled. 'Course you ain't.' And he winked at the company. His family all grinned, nodding as if they were in on the secret. She stood up quickly, was about to contradict them, but her head began to spin with the heat and tiredness after her long drive, and she felt a bit dizzy. When she recovered her balance, she said 'Honestly, I can tell you no film is on the horizon. It's just Gil… Mr Johnson who wants to find out about your Jimmy Lyle. Right now, I'm just worried that he's okay. Because he's been ill, you know. Very ill.'

'Would make a good film,' the bigger son said.

'Rick said,' Big George nodded. 'You think he may be intendin to do away with himself? Jump in the river?'

She shook her head. 'You've said too much, my friend Rick.'

'Hey now,' George's wife said, 'It's alright, honey. You got worried about him. Everybody does about them they love.'

Love? What did she know? It was disconcerting, their familiarity, this kindness. She looked down at her dog, lying comfortably in the arms of two strange children who were petting him like one of their own. Hero peered up at her, seemed to smile, then lay back down, enjoying those little hands rubbing his neck fur.

At that moment the phone inside the motel began to ring. Rick got up and went to answer it. She flopped back down into her chair and the two women soothed her with words she couldn't quite make out as she tried to hear what happening on the phone. Then Rick reappeared.

'George,' he said, 'It's Billy for you.'

'That'll be word, betcha,' George said, getting up.

She listened as George took the call, ummin and ahhin as the caller, whoever he was, talked. When George's lumbering frame reappeared in the doorway to the terrace, she heard him say, 'We better go look for the Scotsman, boys. Billy says somebody saw him headed up the Echte Valley, thinks he must've been looking for Jimmy Lyle's old cabin. It's a long old way, he may be stuck up there somewhere.'

George's two sons stood up, the bigger and the smaller, ready to leave.

'Where's that at?' Rick asked.

'It's a place. Secret place to us. It seems Pearl told him about it when he went to see her, and he must have decided to go try find it for himself.'

'I don't understand,' the woman who had given up trying not to be Ms. Weaver said. 'Who's Pearl?'

'She's one of our elders. Your guy saw her yesterday. She was tellin him what she knew about Jimmy Lyle. Guess he must have decided to try and go seek out the place he lived.'

'You mean he's out there somewhere in the wilderness? Where?'

'It's a sacred place to us,' George's wife said. 'Secret. Always has been since way back. But Jimmy Lyle built a cabin up there for him and his wife, lived there maybe ten years, long time ago now.'

'There's a trail in. The cabin is still there, but it's a long way and nobody ever goes there much now,' George's wife's sister offered.

'We'll take the truck, go look,' George said. 'He's probably somewhere on the trail.' He turned to the rest of his family. 'You all stay here. Me and the boys will find him. Come on now.'

Big George and his two big sons left. Ms Weaver laid her head back on the chair. She felt tears well up. 'I knew it, I knew something was wrong. I told Rick. Didn't I?'

George's wife's sister patted her hand. 'George will find him, honey. You'll see. They'll find him and they will bring him back. It'll be okay.'

'But anything could have happened. He doesn't know anything about anything. He could have met a bear, or wolves or...'

'No, not here,' one of the children piped up. 'No bears here. Worst thing is rattlesnakes.'

'Ssssh,' George's wife scolded. 'That's enough already. Don't you frighten the poor lady.'

But Ms Weaver's calm had disappeared. She pictured the wandering Scotsman surrounded by all the wildest, most dangerous creatures she could imagine, and a rattlesnake shaking its tail, springing at him while he stood transfixed, not knowing what to do. She stood.

'It's lovely to meet you all. You've been so kind. But I'm going upstairs now,' she said, on the point of tears. 'Call me as soon as you hear anything, will you? Come on, buddy.'

Hero reluctantly left his two new best friends and followed her up the staircase to room 14. There she lay on the bed again, her head still spinning a little at first, then after a while, once she'd recovered her poise, she opened the drawer of the bedside cabinet and took out the handwritten story she'd concealed there earlier. It seemed more precious now, more a communication to her from him, and whatever qualms she had harboured about reading it were gone now. She needed to know how he had felt about those days in Vancouver. Felt it was her right. She turned the pages, glancing over what she'd already read, until she found the place where Gil woke up the morning after the hockey. She settled herself on the bed, propped up by pillows, and tried to read, but her eyes kept drifting to the window, the fading violet daylight slowly disappearing, and her ears were primed for the slightest sound of Big George's truck returning.

How long would it take them to get there, to look for him? Would they make it before it was dark? And if not, and he was out there all night, would he survive? She should have gone with them. She should have insisted.

Then her mind drifted back to the fact that he had spoken about killing himself. Was this the way he'd chosen to do it? At Lyle's cabin? Had he set out with no intention of coming back? Was he surrendering to nature in the way he'd talked about surrendering to the cancer? Maybe there was some clue in the journal.

He slept a drunken half-sleep, restless with dreams he couldn't recall when he woke. Something about Egypt, the incest of twins, something he'd read somewhere lingered, but he couldn't place it. He couldn't even place himself at first, waking as he did in this strange bed. He checked his phone. It was almost mid-day. No calls, no messages. He turned over, feeling a little nauseous, remembering the poutine he'd eaten and the beer, the fumbled embrace when he'd overstepped the boundaries. He thought he should do some work, maybe at the main library downtown, if he could bear the bustle of people and traffic. There was comfort in being amongst books. But when he got there he found himself persuaded by the need to look through Lyle's photographic archive and he began to note down titles of significant images for future reference. The descriptions he took to be Lyle's own handwriting.

36242 Indian graveyard July 1916 - Single cross standing near corner of short wooden fence. "Indian graveyard ½ mile west of Cloud Falls on north side of river. Very picturesque about 20 - 30 years ago, all woodwork being painted in bright colors, fences surmounted with carved figures of birds and symbol of sun, moon, blankets, guns, baskets etc. Graveyard now neglected and all overgrown with rose and other bushes. Condition: negative in poor condition.

36245 View from Coyote Sweathouse Bluff July 1916 - Scene across river showing bridges and railway tracks. "View across Thompson River from Coyote Sweathouse Bluff. Looking up Nicola River at mouth showing part of east slope of slaka 'heaped up' mountain and some rounded hills or buttes in distance. When snow goes off these in spring (April) there will be no more frosts down in the valley and it is safe to put out tender plants. Indians and whites watch for this." Condition: good

26265 Hunting camp - Large canvas tipi with smoke flaps. Snowshoes, hunting equipment and animal carcass next to tipi. Cloth stretched over pole. "Taken during absence of hunter, tipi, snowshoes, deerskins, venison and two deer not yet cut up." TsEkiextcin Valley fifteen miles north of Cloud Falls. Condition: good

39754 Woman Digging Roots 1917 - Profile view of "Kokowatko" or Kaukuwatko 'sage brush water' woman of Potato Garden Band digging roots of Erythronium Grandflorum (yellow adder tongue lily) showing method of loosening soil with root digger. Sack slung around her waist. Mount Botani. Condition: good

39758 Cooking Sticks 1917 - Thirteen cooking sticks for cooking meat before the fire. Each had been used for this purpose at the same time. Indians must have killed deer in this place and cooked a lot of meat to eat while camping overnight. The remains of their fire was to the left of picture but there were no signs of tents having been pitched. Party must have been large to use so many sticks at once as indications were that the sticks had been used late last fall. When Indians left they stuck the sticks in the ground in a line all pointing the way the party had gone. Not usual to use these sticks for the latter purpose, Upper Skonkon Creek Valley near Botani July 1917. Condition: good

30609 Camp for Washing Gold 1915 - Roughly made shelters of canvas and a few poles on rock beach of Thompson River. Used by Indians washing for gold. Condition: original negative broken and repaired, unclear image

30611 Favorite method of Washing Gold 1915 - Woman standing on platform at edge of river carrying burden basket on back. Condition: good

30612 Woman washing for Gold - Woman kneeling on the rocks at river's edge with platform behind her washing the clean up out of the sluice box in a gold pan. Condition: good.

30995 Inga Lyle Horseback 1915 - Profile full length view of little girl on horseback. "Horse equipped with woman's riding saddle, saddle blanket and saddle bags, also baby carrier, horsehair bridle and halter and eagle feather horse necklace." Condition: good

23161 Coiled baskets of Cedar Root 1912 - Three tiers of baskets showing different sizes, shapes and decorations. "Coiled baskets of cedar root showing different imbricated designs. Including a basketry rattle, three birchbark baskets, one juniper bark basket, one elaeagnus twine basket with horsehair carrying strap. Cloud Falls band Nicola Division. Condition: fair

The list of photos went on, but her concentration was short. She flicked through pages of notes till she found another scene featuring her alter-ego, a description of the day she took him to meet Pauline Johnson. He seemed to have passed over the moment he first met Hero, how naturally they got along. And for some reason, he'd called him Henry.

The dog-walk involved crossing town to a park she called Pacific Spirit and the traffic was heavy. He wanted to say something about the night before, but the silence between them felt comfortable, as if they could co-exist without interacting, so he stayed quiet. Finally, she pulled up at the entrance to Squamish Trail.

'The park is huge,' she said, 'acres upon acres of land between the city and the university at the end of Point Grey. There's lots of trails. This is one of our favourites, isn't it, my lad?'

Henry was very happy to be off leash in the cool air of the forest. He busied himself rooting around in the undergrowth, disappearing and then returning to them as they walked, naturally in step, as if their strides were synchronised. An odd sense of ease spread over him, a deep companionship. Did she feel it too?

'I come here every day, before my nap,' she said after they'd walked in silence for a distance. 'Ever since the cancer. It's been a kind of healing balm, my time in the woods with Henry.'

'I read an article a while back,' he recalled. 'It was about some Japanese scientists who'd been studying how human beings respond to being in the forest, how their bodies react. They have a name for it, shinrin-yoku, if I remember correctly, which means something like greenwood bathing.'

'A kind of cleansing?'

'I suppose so. A way of getting rid of all the noise and clutter of life. And this,' he said, gazing around him at the huge conifers that stretched off into the distance, 'is a wonderful place to bathe.'

'Isn't it? But you know, these trees are quite young. All of this was logged. There's only a few old growth left, though you see the remains quite often. Look, over there.' She pointed to a vast decaying stump, like a giant anthill or a termite mound, or something sculpted.

'Looks like something of Gaudi's. But that's quite sad,' he said. 'To think of all those ancient trees cut down.'

'I guess. But the forest keeps on growing. Even fallen trees are nurseries for new shoots. See?'

Again she pointed into the crowded wood, and he saw an old decaying trunk lying horizontal that had sprouted three separate saplings from its core, which were now flourishing.

They walked on, in easy silence, as Henry roamed, till she called the dog over and put his leash on.

'He met a coyote here one day, not so long ago. Disappeared on me. I don't take any chances now.'

'The call of the wild?'

'I guess,' she laughed, 'But he wouldn't survive long out here, my poor lad.'

The trail wound on, uphill and down, a snaking route through the forest. She seemed to know her way well, and he simply followed. After a while, she let Henry loose again. She peered up at him as she undid the leash from the collar. Her brown eyes caught a beam of sunlight through the canopy and shone golden for an instant as she held his gaze. It was a look of intimacy.

'About last night... you know, when we were lying on my bed...'

'Were we? I don't remember. I must have been very drunk. What happened?'

Now that she had posed the question, he lost courage. If she really didn't remember, maybe it was alright.

'It's nothing, then. I just thought...' but he lost the thread.

'Don't,' she said. 'Don't think so much.'

As they walked on, side by side, step for step, he wondered if she really didn't remember, or if she was simply being kind by pretending to forget. Perhaps it didn't matter either way, as long as they could still be together without awkwardness. They came to a clearing, where she stopped and gazed upwards to the little patch of sky.

'It's amazing, but trees don't grow over the top of one another up there. They seem to sense the others and leave space. There's a name for it – crown shyness.'

'Really? Crown shyness? I like that. It's quite poetic.'

'Isn't it? If only people were as polite, the world would be a happier place.'

He looked at her, wondering if that was a warning, but she didn't give anything away. The trail began to circle back on itself. Though he had no idea where they were, he could sense that much. Henry's roaming became a gentle tired trot at her heels, and he panted.

'I have to go out of town tomorrow,' she said. 'I've arranged to see a friend over on Bowen Island.'

'Ah,' was all he could muster.

'It's weird,' she went on. 'I feel very close to you and we only met a couple of days ago.'

'Well, I'm right here beside you,' he joked, to lighten the mood.

'Will you still be here when I get back?'

'I've got three more days. Four more nights.'

'I'll see you again, then. We can do something. Maybe have dinner?'

'I'd like that. It would be good to talk more. I feel like I hardly know anything about you.'

'Well, you know I had cancer. You know that I'm a translator. I'm Czech. You know that I moved to Canada when I was young. And now you know Henry. What else do you want to find out?' Something in her tone meant he sensed she had a secret core to her being, that he would never come to know her inner self. Her mystery would remain impenetrable. So he didn't answer.

The sound of traffic signalled the end of the trail. As she clipped Henry's leash on, she asked 'What will you do?'

'You mean while you're away?'

'Yes. And afterwards.'

'Well, I'll spend more time in the library, I'll visit the city museum and the museum of anthropology, I'll try to get a better picture of Vancouver and BC in Lyle's time. I'll check out the bookshops. After that, I'm going to catch a Greyhound bus up the canyon to Cloud Falls and stay in what the website claims is the oldest inn in British Columbia, see what I can find out. From there, I'll go on to Merritt where Lyle lived later, then I'm going to visit a man who lives up north of Kamloops.'

'Wow. So who is this guy you're going to see?'

'I know him as a client. He's bought books from me. His family came from Scotland a few generations back. He's a Scot who has never been to Scotland.'

'So you've never met then?'

'Not yet. We've corresponded. His name is George Gordon Fergusson. He's a very knowledgeable man and he knows about Lyle.'

'Ah, your man Lyle! So that's quite a long way, if it's north of Kam-loops. Maybe not so easy to get to?'

'I checked. The Greyhound does stop on the highway nearby. Gordon will pick me up.'

He went to get into the wrong side of the car, a brief reminder of how unfamiliar this world was to him. The prospect of heading into the interior suddenly took on a more ominous complexion, as if he was about to enter the wilderness, heading off in search of Kurtz. 'That is, if I ever get there,' he added.

As she squinted over her shoulder to see if it was safe to pull out, she glanced at him curiously. 'What do you mean?'

In the passenger seat he sighed. 'I don't know, it all seems a bit crazy. Coming here, thinking I could write this book. I'm barely over the radio-therapy. And I'm not sure I have the will to make it happen. Or the ability.'

'Having dark thoughts again?'

'I always have dark thoughts,' he said. 'I'm Scottish.'

She laughed, but glanced at him with worried expression. As she drove him back to his lodgings, he thought to himself how meeting her had changed things. He'd come with a vague intention, a hope against hope that he might find his way, become the writer he'd always dreamt of being, that somehow the new setting would allow him to leave behind the ennui, the sense of futility that he'd lived with for so long. And it had, for those short hours spent with her. Without her, it was just him and his shortcomings, his sense of inadequacy, his poor sick heart. He had come in search of a story, one he imagined was about a man who'd lived a century before. A story that involved pioneers and Indians. What he'd discovered in these few short days had changed all that. He no longer saw the trail ahead with any clarity.

She had become the story. His guide.

The light was fading fast outside the window now. She got up and crossed the room. Hero raised an ear but didn't wake. She could still see the shape of the canyon wall against the sky but it seemed close to darkness, and lights in the town beyond the river were being switched on. The torrent continued to roar through the dusk, a constant she had quickly become acclimatized to. But there was still no sound of George's truck returning, with or without the lost Scotsman. She won-dered how much more daylight they might have to find him.

Instead, she had his written account of the time they'd spent together in Vancouver. But it wasn't what had really happened. Some of it she remembered, some of things they'd done, even some of the words that he'd put in her mouth, but the names were wrong, the details were wrong. If she had become the story, he had told it his way and it wasn't how she'd have done it. His story.

All the same, she was intrigued. It was like she'd stumbled on the inner workings of his mind, days afterwards. She lay back down for a while on the bed, staring out the window at the darkening sky. Did she really seem so impenetrable to him? She'd felt more herself with him than anyone for a long time, because the cancer bond they shared had made it possible to talk about what they'd been through. She felt for the scar under her bra, the line of hardening tissue once so intrusive and alien, now becoming part of her, her familiar, as it slowly healed. A defining mark, still painful.

The way he'd told the story, she seemed so upbeat, so positive, but that wasn't really how she felt. She'd thought about dying too, just as he had, had thought it through, in case it happened. Who would take care of Hero, who would get her books, her paintings, her clothes. What little money she had to leave. What she wanted for her memorial. All that was necessary. But this sullen sick-heartedness of his wasn't helpful. He had to understand that. And if she laughed and joked and made light of things, that didn't mean she didn't feel the void near at hand. It was her way of coping. Otherwise, it was desolation.

A knock on the door called her back to the present. It was Rick, with some sandwiches and a cup of tea.

'No news?'

'Not yet. But I think they should be on their way back now. According to what George's wife said, it's not so far. At least not in a truck.'

She thanked him as she took the tray. 'And if we're wrong about where he was heading for?'

Rick shrugged his shoulders. 'They seemed pretty sure. And the clue in his diary. You still reading that?'

She didn't reply, but turned the questioning back on him. 'Why did you tell them downstairs I was Sigourney Weaver?'

Rick grimaced. 'I didn't. I just said you looked like her. Then I had a joke with one the kids about Alien.'

'Well, just don't mention it again.'

He nodded okay. 'What should I call you then?'

Her pursuer, the man whose texts she was ignoring, flashed into her mind. She didn't want to be found, she wanted to be incognito. 'How about Martina?' she said. 'I'm getting used to not being me.'

Rick looked at her oddly, as if wondering what she meant. Then, as if realising it was a false name, he winked. 'Ok-ay, "Martina". I'll see you later.'

After the dull salad sandwiches, she fed Hero his supper and then went back to the notebook. There seemed to be one last episode to follow, and she thought she could guess what it would be. She may as well read it while she waited. But just then, a low rumble outside attracted her attention. She thought for a second it was Big George, but as the sound grew and the little inn seemed to shake, Hero leapt up and began barking loudly, and she knew it was the CPR, another long train heading out through the Canadian wilderness, carrying trucks full of whatever, to wherever they had to go.

'Ssshh, Hero,' she said, petting him. 'It's only the railroad. It'll be gone soon.'

But soon took a while to come, and the barking went on. She crossed to the window, gazed out again at the panorama of river and mountain, still just visible in the gloom. The little town was all lit up now, a tiny constellation deep in the canyon's shadow. If they hadn't found him by now, it could be too late.

Two days passed, much in the manner he had imagined they would before he left Edinburgh. He went to the museums, the bookshops, he took notes, he bought a few unusual local titles to post home. He ate alone. He functioned. He even wrote a book proposal, which could be sent to publishers or agents. Vancouver was a less welcoming yet less complicated city, knowing that she wasn't there. It was more as he had anticipated, strange, yet not so, as what he did was familiar, even if the location was new. But all the while he was aware of his phone. He kept it in his jacket pocket at first, as he thought it might buzz at any moment, just a small message to say *i'm back! c u soon* or something. But when that didn't happen, he started to keep it in his bag, further from his person. And he began to feel calmer. His aim was steadier. His focus returned. But he wasn't happy. The 'friend on Bowen Island' took on a haunting form. Of course it was stupid to feel that way. For years he'd been free of any involvement. But some things are involuntary. He missed her. He cared, ridiculous as it might seem, himself just a skin-covered skeleton with a bright red neck. He'd believed a part of him had died last winter, the one that was capable of caring. His mantra through the worst of the illness had been a simple 'I don't care', a pain-numbing repetitious pattern of syllables spoken over and over again, till he believed it was true. Yet now it seemed his capacity for love had refused to die despite the winter's hardship, had lain dormant waiting for the sun's return. He vowed to be careful, to remember how precarious the situation was, to do what he'd come to do and not be distracted. And then on his last day in Vancouver, before he was even properly awake, his phone did buzz, a brief and simple message.

Back in town. Wnt 2 meet?

His fingers had replied before his mind had time to remember his vow. *Sure!* Some things are involuntary, he thought. Mostly the promise of pleasure subverts the will to refrain.

The morning sky was heavy with cloud. Mist covered the mountains and it seemed like it would rain at any time. He watched out the window of his suite until he saw her car appear and park in front.

'Hey,' she said as he got in. 'How's Mister Sick Heart?'

'Good,' he answered brightly. 'Been busy with research.' He didn't say, all the better for seeing you, though it was true. 'How was your trip?'

She didn't respond immediately. She seemed subdued, less chatty, rather preoccupied. There was no Hero on the back seat, as he'd hoped there would be.

'So where are we going?'

'Siwash. Remember?'

'Ah yes,' he said. It was Thursday, then. He'd lost track.

She drove down MacDonald and turned on to the shore road.

At last she said, 'I feel I can you tell you this, Gil. I know we've only just met and I hope you won't think bad of me.'

'Why should I?'

'I went to visit a man I've been seeing.'

The words made her start in surprise. She threw the journal down onto the bed, causing Hero to sit up and stare at her quizzically. This had not happened. And yet, it had, but in another way. She would never blurt out something so personal as that. Whatever Gil was writing wasn't her. And yet he'd stumbled on something true in his fiction. She began reading again.

'That's no crime,' he said, though he felt it should be.

'No, but... it's complicated, as they say.' She let out a deep sigh. 'He's married.'

They approached Burrard Bridge with views over the harbour. The line of cars was slow. From there he could see Bowen Island in the distance clearly, she'd pointed it out to him the other day. Now it was the place her lover lived, and it seemed the heart of the darkness crowding in on his peace of mind. His vision clouded. The mist seemed to be in his head. 'I see,' he said. But he couldn't. He wanted to say, don't tell me any more, but she carried on.

'I knew he'd never leave his wife. He told me that at the beginning. I guess I got too attached. He's a writer. A very well-known writer, at least in Canada. A brilliant man.'

He wanted to ask who this "he" was, to map the coordinates of this brilliant rival who had covered the sun and brought the mist, then to find a way of undermining that place.

'Anyhow,' she went on. 'I ended it. I had to. It had turned toxic. Ever since my cancer. When I got the diagnosis, he just seemed to freeze.' She glanced at him as she drove, as if to chart his reaction. There was no golden thread in her eyes, they seemed dark and impenetrable. 'I'm telling you because I feel you'll understand. We're twins, after all,' she smiled, as if relieved.

He was struggling to assimilate the information. She'd been having an affair, got in too deep, then came the cancer, and her brilliant lover had withdrawn. Now she'd abandoned hope of carrying on. What could he say, to make a happy ending of it?

She sighed. 'I don't know about you, but I've sort of lost faith in my body.'

'That's an odd expression.' It was all he could offer in response. Rain began, little spits at first, covering the windscreen, then it grew heavier until it was lashing down. The wipers had to work hard to clear the glass.

'You're shocked?' she said, half a statement, half a question.

'No,' he said, scoffing. 'There's not much can shock me these days. Too long in the tooth. You're a very beautiful and charming woman. You must have a long queue of men waiting for you to call.'

She laughed. 'Well, maybe once upon a time. But that isn't how I feel. You know, when you stand in front of the mirror.'

'I never stand in front of the mirror,' he said. 'Far too frightening a prospect.'

'You're not so bad. A bit thin, maybe.'

'I am a red-neck,' he joked, and stretched his chin up. 'At least, I have a large red rectangle on my neck, thanks to the radiation. And it will never fade, apparently.'

Off the bridge, they hit more traffic and got stuck as she tried to cross town. At a set of lights, she turned to look at him. 'When I look in the mirror, I see the scar and what it tells me is that I am vulnerable.'

'I suppose I do, too,' he said. 'Anyway, I hope you're not too sad, after all that?'

'No, not now. It was over months ago, even before I was diagnosed. I just hadn't realised it. So I've done my crying. I just had to see him, to let him know. I was very unhappy for a while. I sometimes wonder if that had anything to do with getting ill.'

He nodded, mumbled a maybe. He was thinking of his own unhappiness, how it drove him to drink and smoke, to live an unhealthy life. The connection was possible, if indirect, the context.

She put his story down and took off her glasses. She was thinking of that long wait at the restaurant on the island, she the great writer's translator, he a well-known personality there. She was thinking of the awkwardness of everything, the pretence that had once been so thrilling now reduced to faint embarrassment. How he'd arrived half an hour late and slid into the private booth next to her, averting his eyes. He'd brought a manuscript with him, presumably as an alibi, though they'd long since finished work on his last book. How he had taken her hand under the table and asked if she was all right, was she coping, did she need anything? She knew he meant money, when all she really wanted was his companionship, the way it had once been, his mind and the brilliant things he said. Had he taken advantage of her somehow? Maybe. Maybe it had been mutual. She had needed his comfort, his wisdom, his encouragement. He had taken her to places and introduced her to people she wouldn't have met otherwise. But all he could offer now was a wad of dollars.

And now it seemed so sketchy, so shady compared with Gil's love-story. The feelings she had harboured could never fit inside that version - the half-eaten meal, the unspoken farewell, the ferry she knew would be her last, the long drive back with so many tears in her eyes she could barely see the highway, and the painful sleepless nights that followed. None of that could ever fit in Gil's story. Yet still he'd intuited something about her in his fiction. Why had she felt so strong a desire to tell him? She sighed and reached out to hug Hero, pulled him closer on the bed, then put on her pink-rimmed glasses again. She picked up the journal, and found Martina back in her car again with her strange new Scottish friend in the passenger seat.

As she drove along the shore road, the rain stopped as suddenly as it had started. A little patch of blue began to appear in front of them. They passed the Sylvia Hotel, scene of various literary doings she told him about.

'Are you fit for cycling?' she asked suddenly.

'I think so,' he answered. 'As long as it's not too arduous.'

'It's just that cycling the shore wall is the best way to see the park. It's perfectly flat, and we can get to Siwash Rock that way.'

He agreed, so she parked and took him into a bike rental shop, where they were sized and helmeted. The bike boy noted they were exactly the same height, and pulled out two identical cycles. Once underway, he followed her for a couple of blocks to the gates of Stanley Park. He remembered they'd been here the first night, that first tour, where she showed him the Burns statue gazing out over this Pacific harbour, as the yachts lay furled, sashaying slightly on the swell.

The bike track did indeed run flat along the shoreline, round the park, one way. She rode confidently through the crowd-tide of people all flowing in the same direction, cyclists in one lane, overtaking joggers in another. Skateboards and blades cut in and out. He felt enmeshed at first, but as the crowd thinned its way into the park, each finding its own speed, it was easier. She stopped and watched as he took a photo across the fjord towards the docks opposite, where a blue-hulled giant freighter seemed to lie waiting for cargo, next to a great mound of yellow, perhaps sulphur.

A signpost pointed towards 'Lost Lagoon'. He remarked on it as he pulled level with her on the cycle-track. She smiled, recited: 'O the Lure of the Lost Lagoon, I dream tonight that my paddle blurs, The purple shade where the seaweed stirs. I hear the call of the singing firs…"

At that moment, a blade-runner went past and she hesitated. When their wheels aligned again, she added, 'In the hush of the golden moon.'

'Who wrote that?' he asked.

She laughed. 'I'll show you soon. That's the surprise.'

He patted the cross bar. 'Thought that was this boneshaker.'

At the touristic totem park, where great colourful poles huddled together behind their fence like zoo captives, they stopped a while.

'They seem out of place here, somehow,' he said, meaning the enclosure, the tourist branding, the showiness of it all.

'Ah, not so,' she answered. 'They're very much at home here. This was a sacred place long before Lord Stanley called it a park.'

And of course the poles stood proudly, however incongruous the goings-on in front of them, the posing and the snapping. They were magnificent in their ability to ignore their present-day ignominy, were shameless and challenging, aware of their power. So he took photos, the same images, the same visual mementos of their brave stand as all the other visitors that day did, and every other day, while the poles stood patiently, too large to fit the photo frames properly.

She was already onto the next part of her guided tour, and came to a stop by the railings. 'That's Deadman Island, see.' She let go the handlebars, pointed a sleek arm outwards, across the water, in an arc that touched the land's extent. 'Long before even Scots arrived here, there was war between the people of the north and those of the south. So they met here, on this island, to resolve their dispute.'

'A bloody battle?'

'Not so much. More a sacrifice. They were here a long time, facing one another. Skirmishing while trying to reach some kind of settlement. Slowly the people of the north gained the upper hand. Finally, the south threatened to kill all their prisoners and then fight to the end. Their terms for avoiding slaughter involved the safe return of those prisoners in exchange for young warriors, who would then be killed in place of their wives and children and so on, who would die if they fought to the end. The men of the north agreed to be sacrificed. So they were slaughtered there.'

'Deadman's Island?'

'The Island of the Dead Men.'

They cycled on, past the replica Little Mermaid that the city fathers of Copenhagen had objected to, so that flippers had to be added, went under the great bridge to North Vancouver where the traffic bisecting the park passed overhead. Again he stopped to take photos of something too big to frame. The ambition of it all seemed too much, and all in just a hundred years, to make this great teeming city.

They passed along a section of the cycle-way which had been blasted out of the rock face, and faced the waves directly. For a minute, he was reminded of that east-facing part of the road round Arthur's Seat, where the rock had been cut through. But here the path did not look down on the quiet freshwater sanctuary of Duddingston Loch, but out to Pacific deep-water. All very far from the old grey city of the north. And then, as the road curved to the left, circling back towards downtown, a structure came into view, beyond the seawall, a tower of some kind, but with a tree growing out of it. He stopped to take a picture and saw through the zoom that this was natural, a stack, an outcrop.

'So here we are. Siwash Rock,' she said, when he caught her up again. She had dismounted, taken her helmet off and her dark hair blew gently across her face as the sea wind swept up the narrow approach to Vancouver's inner harbour. 'Remember the story?'

'Sure,' he said. In fact, he had written about the Four Men. His mind envisaged a breed of northern giants, like Norse gods, but native to these shores, these gigantic landscapes of mountain, forest and fjord, and these men of the north seemed to follow him, as he cycled after her rear wheel, along the coastal track, then up a sharp brae.

He found the climb hard going, and she had to wait for him. Seeing him pant, she suggested a stop, so they ate hot-dogs from a stand, on a bench overlooking the sands where day-trippers frolicked.

'I was trying to picture Captain Vancouver sailing up here, back in, what was it, the 1790s, seeing that rock. Giving places their English names,' he said.

'The names of his officers – Burrard, Bowen. I can't recall them all.' She took a bite from her hot-dog. 'These are quite good,' she said. 'I wouldn't normally eat them.'

'But as you're a tourist guide for the day?' She shrugged and smiled, then took another bite. 'You know,' he went on, 'The thing that strikes me now is how the native natural world is all still here, mixed in with the new – with the city, with that funny little statue of the mermaid you pointed out, with that massive bridge. But the stories you've told me, about Siwash and the all that, people know them, they're still told?'

'Not so much.' She put her head on one side, considering. 'And all the names are wrong. You know, the biggest of the misnomers are those!'

She waved at the grand mountains across the water. 'They're called the Lions, recumbent like Trafalgar Square supposedly. But in the local story they are sisters who married the enemies of their father so that there could be peace between them, after a long and bloody war. They insisted on it. So those are really The Sisters, symbols of peace, not king carnivores.'

'So it is all still here,' he said again, gazing around him, chewing his hot-dog. 'That history.'

'Not all, but yes, still here. Your Scots-built-Canada theory is not so strong in that light.'

He wasn't sure how they had reached agreement, or even what the exact point of debate was, but it seemed they had, as she dumped the last bite of hot-dog, got back on her bike and beckoned him to follow, saying over her shoulder, 'The surprise is this way.'

Up again they went, into the woods and he followed her wheel carefully across the rough track till it joined tarmac and arrived at the entrance to a scenically situated restaurant.

'One of the most expensive in Vancouver,' she said, as they watched a large black Mercedes drop a party outside.

'I'm not sure I'm dressed for it,' he answered. 'And didn't we just eat?'

'Don't be silly. We're not here for that. This way.'

She pushed her bike a little off the path, and under the leafy frock of a great pine tree, crossed the brown-needled floor to a large stone. On a branch above, someone had left a little votive offering in the form of a canvas bag tied up with blue ribbon. Inside the bag were the remains of burned stalks.

'Sagebrush,' she said. 'Sacred.' He sniffed the air, the scent comingling with the sappy aroma from the conifer grove. She edged around the rock and emerged again in the light, to the side of the restaurant. Now he could see that it was a large statue, a memorial rough-hewn so that the stone appeared to contain the form, not constitute it. Close up, it appeared like some mountainous cluster of bluffs and cliffs, yet echoed a human form – on what might have been the mountain's head was lightly carved the relief profile of a woman in what was once called 'Indian costume.' It was a strong face, slightly scarred by some eruption in the stone. On what might have been the mountain's knee was carved:

E Pauline Johnson 1861-1913
And to the side:
ERECTED IN 1922
BY THE WOMEN'S CANADIAN CLUB
OF VANCOUVER B.C.

'Ah, Pauline Johnson,' he said. 'My kinswoman.'

'Oh my god, I hadn't thought of that. You're both Johnsons.'

'Wasn't she called 'double-life' or something?'

'I'm impressed you've heard of her. Yes, she called herself Tekahion-wake. That was her stage-name.'

'In the second hand book trade, you come across everything at some time if you're in business long enough – if you're good, you scan and sample, retain the details. Often you don't read too much of anything, as that slows you down, unless it's really good, or something you're researching. I've sold her book 'The White Wampum'. A 1st edition, published London, 1903. Good price. But I haven't really read her. I didn't associate her with Vancouver, though,' he went on. 'I thought she lived in the east?'

'She was from the east, Mohawk, but she retired here when she gave up the stage. She died a few years later, but in those last years here she published a series of what were like dialogues between herself and her tillicum, a local chief called Old Joe Capilano, where he told her the First Nations' stories about this part of the world.'

'So she translated these into English?'

'It's more than that. They're really charming. You'd have to read them. Anyhow, after she died her friends collected them up and published them in a book called 'Legends of Vancouver'. It's a classic here.'

'You seem to know a lot about her?'

She smiled, then looked down, and her dark hair fell about her face. 'Well, for me it's personal. Our first Canadian Christmas, after we emigrated, my mother gave me an old copy, from 1920. She said she hoped it would help me learn English, and that I wouldn't feel so homesick if I knew some of the stories of our new home. Because stories make a place meaningful.' She stopped, as if her mother's presence suddenly materialised in her mind. 'I don't think she ever read it herself,' she went on. 'Her English wasn't very good then. Still isn't. So anyhow, the stories I told you – badly – are in a way, both hers and Pauline Johnson's to me. Or rather, her tillicum's.'

He circled the statue, taking photos. It seemed rather overgrown, as if the trees had surrounded her, drawn her back into the world of nature she'd come from.

'Must have been very strange for you, emigrating – and quite hard to adjust?'

'For sure – no carp in the bath for one thing.'

'Sorry?'

'It's a Czech thing at Christmas. Carp.' She laughed, but he could tell from the way she crossed her arms and turned slightly away that this wasn't something to pursue, at least not now.

'What's a tillicum, by the way?' he asked, instead.

'It's Chinook, you know, the trade lingo they developed here. Means friend.'

He smiled. 'Nice word. So are we now each other's tillicum?'

'I think we are, yes,' she said, nodding in that distinctive way he'd noted, as something quite definite she did on the moment of decision, having considered and affirmed. 'More than that, actually. Radiation twins.'

And then, out of the woods, a figure appeared, walking slowly towards them. At first glance, she might have been some sort of spirit, dressed in grey with long white hair braided to her waist, a holy woman. She moved towards them quickly, but barely seeming to step. She halted at the canvas bag of sagebrush.

'Seven years, and I didn't know she was here,' the woman said as if addressing them, though her eyes were unfocused, dark and wide. Then she seemed to drift on, away again into the trees.

'Who or what was that?' he said, as the spectre departed.

'A woman who knows what Tekahionwake means,' was Martina's reply.

'Was she real?'

'Worlds are overlapping,' she said. He wondered what she meant, but she didn't elaborate.

They rode back to the park entrance through the Lost Lagoon, a weaving path by great reeds, and bird-life everywhere – ducks and other water fowl he didn't recognize, some like herons he did. He'd got used to the bike, to cycling, it felt the most natural thing to be doing, here with her, this woman he'd met. He pulled alongside her where the path was clear.

'Say those lines again?' he asked. 'Tekahionwake.'

"O the Lure of the Lost Lagoon?' That verse?' She composed herself, spoke slowly as they cycled: 'I dream tonight that my paddle blurs, the purple shade where the seaweed stirs, I hear the call of the singing firs,' she recited, then prompted him with a look.

'In the hush of the golden moon?' he finished.

She nodded, 'Good.' She smiled. 'You have been paying attention.'

As they left the bike shop, he almost stepped out into traffic at the pedestrian crossing, but she pulled him back by the arm just in time.

'My god,' she said, 'Be more careful. I swear you have a death wish.'

'I guess I do,' he laughed. 'Or did. Since the cancer. But don't we all, subconsciously? Isn't that what old Freud thought?'

And then the walk sign lit.

She took him to Joe Fortes, part of his tour, she said. It was a Vancouver institution, this restaurant, named after one of the early city characters, a black lifeguard who had patrolled the beach at Kits for decades. Her mood had soured again and he wondered if she was processing the end of her affair. But after a few sips of wine, she brightened a little. He told her what he'd done during her time out of town and she seemed interested. That helped to focus his mind on the next adventure. In the morning he'd be on a Greyhound, heading into the canyon, to Lyle country and Cloud Falls. The prospect excited him. He'd studied the place from afar, knew quite a bit already of its history, and he was keen to see it in reality. But the idea that this was their last day in Vancouver together didn't please him, and he told her that.

'We'll see each other again,' she said. 'We're radiation twins. Maybe on your way back? Anyway, doesn't pay to look too far ahead. Let's go for a walk after this. Hero's been waiting patiently at home since morning.'

She parked outside her apartment block and went inside while he waited, to re-emerge with an eager Hero pulling on the leash. This time she drove to Jericho Beach and they walked through the park down toward the shore, but she led him away from the beach to a hidden meadow where lupins and sweet peas and purple vetch grew in great quantity. It was almost a little bit of Britain and he surmised what had been there in the past, if it was an early settler's garden run wild, pioneers bringing seeds from home to plant in the colony. But he sensed she was far away in her thoughts. They did not walk side by side, in step. She seemed to want to stay a pace or two ahead or behind, fussing over her dog.

They circled round through the park, past a little lake where she said she had once seen a beaver, but there was no sign of the famous rodent, once the prize of trappers right across the land, and hunted almost to extinction. He remembered Grey Owl, the Englishman who had pretended to be a native, and who championed the protection of the beaver in his hugely successful books until he was exposed as a man from Bristol, and they spoke of him for a while. She hadn't read his books, but knew of him through a recent film.

Across the water, the great freighters lay at anchor as before, but a different lot, in different places. The mist still hung over the mountains and for some reason he was filled with gloom, thinking this was possibly the last time he'd walk here with her. He could see Bowen Island to the west, and wondered what thoughts that sight spurred in her mind. Maybe he was sensing her mood?

At a bench, strategically placed to occupy the perfect viewpoint, he noticed the little plaque read 'Goodnight Irene – I'll see you in my dreams'.

'That was a favourite song of my mother's,' he told her, suddenly transported back to Edinburgh, to the old phonograph and the dusty 78 records his mother and father had collected. The version they had was by The Weavers, though he knew now it was Leadbelly's signature tune.

'What song?' she asked, distractedly.

So he explained, and sang it, at least the parts he could remember. The chorus and the verse that went 'Sometimes I live in the city, sometimes I live in the town. Sometimes I take a great notion, to jump in the river and drown.'

She looked at him intensely, those golden brown eyes piercing. 'You and your death wish,' she said, quite angrily. 'I've heard enough of that. Aren't you grateful to be alive still, after what you've been through?' She walked on with Hero, staring into the distance, until they reached her car again. When she dropped him off outside his lodging, she said, 'If you'd like a lift to the station tomorrow, I'll be happy to oblige.'

He thanked her, strangely elated at the thought he'd see her again in the morning, even if it was only for a few minutes. He gave Hero a furry hug, and turned to her. She smiled ruefully and kissed him on the cheek.

Ruefully, she thought? Who uses a word like that these days? His writing was annoying her now, it was prying and personal. She almost felt like disposing of it. What right had he to be using her in this way, making a fiction out of her life?

She heard the rumble of a truck outside, put the journal back where she'd found it, and went to the room door. Hero leapt up and joined her.

The little bell on the latch door downstairs rang, and she heard a commotion, George, his sons and waiting family, Rick's voice, everyone talking at once. She checked the room behind her, pulled the bed clothes straight, lifted her handbag and went downstairs with Hero, then stopped on the mezzanine landing, to see what was going on. She caught a glimpse of Big George and his son trying to fit through the front doorway while helping Gil to walk, his arms round their shoulders.

George was saying, 'Easy now, easy fella,' while Rick called out, 'Set him down here.' George said, 'Seems like he's twisted his knee. Plus he's been out in the sun a mite too long. Maybe got a touch of heat fever.'

'Where did you find him?' George's wife asked.

'On the trail in like we thought. He says he found the cabin and was on his way back when he fell. But I don't think he could have…'

'Mr Johnson? Bert?' Rick said. 'You okay?'

The figure now slumped in the chair Rick had brought nodded slowly.

'Can I get you anything? Whiskey?'

Again the figure nodded.

'There's a friend of yours here. Come all the way up from Vancouver cos she was worryin,' George's wife's sister chimed in.

The Scotsman spoke for the first time. 'A friend?'

'Martina,' Rick said. 'At least I think that's her name.'

One of the kids started giggling. 'She's the lady outta Alien really.'

'Sshh now, don't confuse him. He's in a bad way,' George said. 'Where is she anyways?'

'Here I am,' came a voice from stairway. The tall brunette woman in purple stepped slowly down, with the grace of Sigourney Weaver. Her collie followed obediently, stopped when she did. The Scotsman, his face red and bloated, tried to see who it was.

'What are you doing here?' he breathed.

'I came to rescue you from yourself,' she said. 'And so you're still alive, I'm glad to see.'

Gil looked anything but aware - like she might as well have been a hallucination brought on by the heat – and his exposed skin was painfully burned. After the whiskey Rick brought made him feel like throwing up, the assembly decided he needed immediate rest, so George and his sons carried him upstairs to room 14, where they laid him out on his bed. They pulled up his shorts so they could see the knee. It was certainly swollen. And the exposed parts of his skin, his fore arms and thighs, were lobster red. At least he'd been wearing a wide-brimmed Western hat to save his head and neck.

'I'll think I'd better go get some cream for those arms,' Rick said.

'There's some here,' George noticed. He picked up a bottle of Avon sun-cream from the bedside table, squirted a lump on his huge palm and began to gently massage his arms. Johnson recoiled in pain and the shock brought him to himself again. 'Where did she go?' he said, looking around, slurring his words. 'Is she really here?'

She was outside in the darkness with Hero, walking along the railroad under an arc-light, while the dog sniffed about among the tumbleweed. She was singing, softly, 'Irene, goodnight, goodnight Irene,' to nobody. Then she turned on her heel, called Hero to follow, and went back inside the oldest inn in BC.

Upstairs she went, towards room 14, from where the groans of the Scotsman emanated. She stopped in the doorway. Big George had given over masseuse duties to his wife.

'That's no good,' she said. 'He needs to be in a cold bath.' They all looked up at the tall figure in the doorway, her dog's face poking in beside her legs. 'Have you got oatmeal, Rick?' she added.

'Oatmeal?' the innkeeper asked, surprised. 'Sure. Why?'

'You put two large cups of oatmeal into a cold bath, give it a good stir, and put him in it. My grandma told me.'

'Oatmeal?' came the pained voice from the bed. 'You're going to put me in a bath of porridge?'

'It's a treatment for sunburn. Very soothing,' she said. 'A twenty-minute soak.'

'Are you serious?' Rick smiled. 'A Scotsman in a bath of oatmeal.'

They were all grinning now, all except the patient himself.

She gave Rick an unamused grimace. 'Just do it, will you please?'

'Okay… One porridge bath coming right up,' Rick said, squeezing past her at the door.

'The rest of you, many many thanks for all you've done – George, you and your boys probably saved his life. But he needs to be alone now.'

Big George looked down at her. 'Ms Weaver, it was you. If you hadn't come all the way up here from the city, we wouldn't have known he was out there until it was too late. You and Rick raised the alarm. You're the hero in this movie.'

Slowly, the ad hoc medical team filed out, leaving her and the dog alone with the figure lying on the bed, who still had his shorts on, but was otherwise naked. His arms and legs, his torso almost white, he looked like coconut ice candy. She could even see the outline of his sandals, sketched white on pink across his feet. Across his neck, redder than the rest, was the radiation rectangle he'd spoken about. She picked up a towel and dropped it on the bed next to him, telling him to take his shorts off, and turned her back.

Rick came in with a large jar of oats, went into the en-suite and turned the faucet on. 'It won't be ice cold,' he called through. She appeared in the door on the bathroom behind him. 'The water in these pipes is kinda lukewarm because it's so hot out.'

'Not too much,' she said, as he tipped in the oatmeal and stirred it up with his hand. 'Gil,' she called, 'Can you make it to the tub?'

A groan emanated from the bed. 'This is daft,' he said.

'It's a cure. My grandmother used it,' she replied. 'Come on, now.'

He managed to get up, towel tied round his waist, and staggered through to the tub. She took his upper arm, above the red where the t-shirt had offered some protection, and pulled the towel away.

'Hey,' he protested.

'We're not looking,' she said, eyes closed.

He lowered himself into the murky water with a deep sigh.

'How's it feel?' Rick asked, from behind them.

'Surprisingly good,' he said, lying back until only his head protruded.

'Okay, twenty minutes. No more,' she said, as she ushered Rick out. 'If you stay in too long, it'll lose effect and only dry your skin out even more.'

She closed the bathroom door.

Rick stood looking up at her, his face alert with the events of these strange hours. A day when drama came to his sleepy little town in the canyon.

'I've got a room ready for you,' Rick said. '17', and he handed her the key. 'It's not the best, I'm afraid, but it's all I got right now.'

She thanked him as he left, then threw the key on the bed and sat down heavily in the armchair, on top of Gil's discarded clothes. Hero came over and laid his chin gently on her knee. From inside the bathroom came the sloshing of water.

'Don't drown,' she called, stroking Hero's head. 'Not after all the trouble we've gone to.'

There was no response.

'You alright?' she called again, louder.

A weak voice sounded from the hollow chamber. 'Mm-hm. Good porridge.'

'You're not supposed to eat it,' she said, then laid her head back and relaxed for the first time that day. The phrase, a fish out of water came into her mind. That was what he was. A salmon that had come to the shallows and stranded there, trying to make headway in an alien element, not understanding where the water had gone and why flapping its tail no longer propelled it. She closed her eyes for a moment.

She woke with the noise of another train passing, and Hero's barking. Gil was lying on the bed, with just a sheet pulled over his candy-striped body, in the light from a bedside lamp. He seemed to be awake too. He had a little smile on his face as he looked in her direction.

'Talk about local atmosphere,' he said, as the room seemed to shake.

She yawned and stretched. 'What are you looking so smug about?' she asked.

He turned his head slightly in her direction. Grinned.

'Have you any idea how much trouble you've caused everyone?'

He didn't reply, but turned his gaze to the ceiling.

'It was worth it,' he said quietly. She could barely see him in the gloom. 'For what I wanted to find. What I was meant to find.'

'What are you babbling about?' she said, sitting up, rubbing her temples.

'Did you ever read 'Journey to the Centre of the Earth'?' he asked.

'Jules Verne? No. Why?'

'The explorers are guided by the carved initials of Arne Saknussem.'

'What're you talking about?' she said. 'Can't you speak plainly for once?'

'I found his initials.' He pulled out his camera, switched it on and flashed through the photos he'd been taking. 'There,' he said. 'Look.' It was a close up of the wall of a log cabin, or seemed to be to her. Then the batteries gave out.

'Is this the place? The cabin? Well, I'm glad this wasn't all for nothing. But what were you thinking, setting off into the mountains on foot? You weren't having dark thoughts again, were you?'

'I can't describe it. Just had this feeling, I had to go. I didn't know why. But I'll be alright. I'm feeling better.'

'You're pumped full of painkillers. That's why. Wait until they wear off. Listen, you should get some sleep, rest. Rick's given me a room.' She looked around her. 'Did you see a key on the bed?'

'A key? I don't know.'

'I put it on the bed, I'm sure. Maybe it fell down.' She stood up and started searching the floor in the gloom. 'Mind if I put on the main light?'

'Wait. Hang on, there's something I want to ask you,' he said, 'if you're not too tired?'

'Well, I guess I can wait a few minutes,' she replied.

'I was thinking, you drove up all the way up here for Vancouver? Why?'

'You didn't answer my messages and I couldn't get hold of you. And then you sent that postcard with that thing about jumping in the river. And I just had this feeling. Something was wrong.'

'Wow. Instinct?'

She smiled. 'Twinstinct. Isn't that what they call it?'

'Seriously, though, that was quite a thing to do. And I'm very glad you did.'

She sat down on the end of the bed, still in the half-light. 'I may as well tell you. I was going to in the morning anyway. I read your journal. I was worried about you after the postcard you sent. I knew you'd gone missing, so I was searching the room for some clue, and you'd just left it laying there on the desk with this mysterious message no one could understand.'

'What message?'

'About the sacred valley.'

'Ah yes. Anyway, I'm flattered to have a reader. What did you make of it?"

'I wasn't too happy about you using me for a model for Martina.'

'Don't worry, it'll never be published. I'll never finish. I never do.'

'Another great beginning? But why did you make her Czech?'

'Just happened. I suppose it's a subconscious homage – I love Czech writing. Hrabal, Škvorecký, Kundera. Kafka of course.'

'And what makes you think you could pull that off? Do you know anything about Czechoslovakia?'

'I don't know. I just started, in Vancouver. It's what came out. I didn't expect it would grow the way it did.'

'Huh… okay, we can talk about it tomorrow. We both need to get some sleep. Before the next train pulls through. Now where's that key?'

She switched the light on, dazzling them both for a few seconds, searched the carpet, looked under the bed, but no sign of it was to be seen.

'You could always sleep here,' he suggested. 'It's a pretty big bed.'

'I may have to,' she said. 'But it won't be very comfortable for us.'

'I don't know. I'm pretty tired. I'll be comatose in a while.'

She searched around for a bit longer, then gave up.

'Wrap yourself in that sheet, then,' she said. 'That way I won't accidentally touch your blisters.'

So she switched the light out, slipped off shoes, and got down on the bed beside him. There was a light top blanket and she pulled that around her, though it was very warm in the room. She lay for a while, unable to sleep. He was absolutely still next to her, and she thought he'd dropped off, but then he said, very softly, 'You're restless?'

A voice came slowly out of the darkness. 'You know that bit of your story where Martina goes to Bowen?'

'Yes.'

'I told you I was going to visit a friend. And that scene you made up, in the car where she tells him about breaking up with her lover...'

'I just thought it would be more interesting that way. If she had a famous Czech writer for a lover. I suppose that was the point where the fiction began to take over.'

'What would you say if I was to tell you that I did go to see a guy?'

'As you put it in the New World... Huh.'

They lay in darkness that hot summer night, windows open but still feeling the heat of the day, the gentle breeze providing some kind of relief. The sound of the great river rolled on, incessant and untroubled. The Scotsman had not been carried away in its powerful rippling currents.

Finally she spoke his name, questioning whether he was asleep. He said no, he felt as if he was burning up. After a while, she spoke again, asked him if she could read the book proposal he'd mentioned in his journal. He said yes, of course, he'd welcome her opinion, it was on his laptop. She got up and went over to the desk in the corner of the room, where the pile of books belonging to the innkeeper's absent wife was just visible. She lifted the lid of the laptop and the light shone over the carpet towards Hero who, exhausted by the heat, lay sprawled at the foot of the bed. He told her the password was *Olomouc* – the town Martina came from. The home screen appeared, a few icons and apps. She saw 'Book Proposal' and another word file, 'MacLeod Falls Journal', and asked him what the second was. He said it was the story of his time here. She could read that too if she liked. So she clicked on the icon for the proposal. At first glance she could see his terminology was all wrong - probably offensive. No one said 'native' any longer. But she began to read it all, interested to know about this pioneer who her friend was so interested in.

A BOOK PROPOSAL
A study of the life and work of James Alexander Lyle
by Gilbert J. T. Johnson

James 'Jimmie' Lyle's life is remarkable in many ways. He married a Native wife and was inducted into the N'laka'pamux tribe, becoming a trusted and valued friend who went on hunting trips with his adopted people. By chance, a visiting German ethnographer, Dr Franz Boas, happened to call at Cloud Falls where he met Jimmie. It was this encounter that began Lyle's scholarly work, though his formal interest in the Native way of life predates Boas's arrival. By that time Lyle was fluent in a number local Native languages, had corresponded with a local expert and written an essay on the 'Carrier Indians'. However Boas was in a position to employ him in this work and provide him with certain essential materials, as he did a number of other people in the Pacific Northwest. At Boas' prompting, Lyle's adoption of new recording techniques pioneered by such as Edison allowed him to amass an amazing library of Native songs on wax cylinders, besides much priceless collecting and documenting in the fields of photography and material culture.

Franz Boas (1858-1942) is himself a most interesting figure; indeed, he has been called the 'Father of Modern Anthropology'. Whatever his status, he was undoubtedly a very influential man in the field, whose reach stretched as far as Margaret Meade and the young Claude Lévi-Strauss, and his meeting with Jimmy Lyle was crucial in his early career as it gave him access to an intimacy with Native people he had previously struggled to attain. As he records in letters to his wife at the time, meeting Lyle renewed his faith in the fruitfulness of his fieldwork.

For Lyle, this encounter proved to be the beginning of a career which continued till his early death from cancer in 1922 at the age of 58. Lyle's early work for Boas culminated in the publication in 1898 of a large collection of N'laka'pamux stories, with an introduction by Boas, published as a Memoir of the American Folk-Lore Society. In the coming decade he published a number of other key works in the field, and by 1913 was becoming something of a legend amongst travellers in these remote territories. As one contemporary commentator phrased it:

> From the Customs officers of two nations to the humblest Indian child, Lyle's word is our passport, and his presence greeted. He not only knows all the Indian guides, but has trained many of them.

In addition to the work he did for Boas, from 1911 he also worked for Edward Sapir in the Anthropology division of the Canadian Geological Survey. By the time of his death, he had amassed a considerable output: 2,200 pages of ethnographic text in 42 published sources, and a further 5,000 unpublished, and a great array of artefacts, photographs, sketches and wax cylinder recordings. But unlike Boas and his ilk, Lyle lived amongst his subjects and was struck not only by the myths and wonders of the Golden Age then disappearing, or even the ravages wrought by the European presence in the form of illness or strong drink, but by the malaise which had struck the very soul of the native people:

> The belief that they are doomed to extinction seems to have a depressing effect on some of the Indians. At almost any gathering where chiefs or leading men speak, this sad, haunting belief is sure to be referred to...

So, while Lyle's work as an ethnographer is of great importance, it is his engagement with the contemporary political situation facing the Native peoples he lived among that marks him out as a personality worthy of greater investigation for me. Even while Boas and his ilk were locating their Indian subjects as hunter-gatherers in a pre-contact Golden Age, their subjects were targets of aggressively assimilationist policy. Out of the large number of ethnographers working on the Pacific Northwest field, Jimmy Lyle was the only one who confronted that reality.

Strangely perhaps, Shetland plays a part in this politicization. After the death of his wife Lucy from tuberculosis in 1899, and prior to his second marriage in 1904 to a woman of Dutch descent with whom he had three children, Jimmy Lyle made his first and only trip home, where he met and conversed with the writer and early Socialist J.J. Haldane Burgess (1862-1927), a fellow Lerwegian and his near contemporary. Lyle was then able to give a name to the impulse and the action he hoped may assist the Natives in rescuing their fate from the oblivion the more negatively minded among them felt was inevitable.

Back in Canada, by November of 1902 he had become a member of The Socialist Party of British Columbia and was contributing to the journal 'The Canadian Socialist.' It was a time of great ferment in the Province due to increased pressures by white settlers and too many restrictions placed on fishing and hunting, and in 1903 some of the tribes began to ally and organize to deal with these issues. In 1906, these groups sent a delegation of three to England to discuss their concerns with King Edward VII.

Lyle's role in all this is somewhat mysterious, but he was certainly of great importance. He records in 1909 that "the Interior tribes insisted upon my attending their meetings and helping them with their writing. Thus I commenced to act as their secretary and treasurer..." Subsequently Lyle was regularly in correspondence with government officials in both Victoria, the provincial administrative centre of BC, and Ottawa, the national capital. As evidence of his increasingly important function, the key letter setting out the Native case presented, at Kamloops, BC on August 25th

1910, to Sir Wilfred Laurier, then Premier of the Dominion of Canada, is an elegant and heart-felt plea. It is by no means without dignity, and is signed "Yours very sincerely, The Chiefs of the Shuswap, Okanagan and Couteau or Thompson tribes – Per their secretary, J.A. Lyle." And in January of 1912, when a delegation of nine chiefs representing the Thompson, Okanagan, Shuswap, and Lillooet peoples, and calling themselves 'The Indian Rights Association of British Columbia', travelled to Ottawa make clear their concerns in the presence of then Premier Borden and his Cabinet, Lyle travelled with them as their interpreter.

Indeed, in these early years of the 20th century, Lyle put himself at the service of the Native people's struggle for rights, as delegate, interpreter and secretary in their dealings with the Canadian state, even to the point of neglecting the duties for which Sapir had contracted him in favour of this political work. Today, in Canada, his memory is still cherished by the Native population of BC, as evidenced by the following record of a meeting that took place in Kamloops in 1999. Seventy-eight years after his death, about 100 people – both white and native – filled the Community Centre one afternoon to salute Lyle's efforts to explore, record and promote the culture of the N'laka'pamux nation. The ceremony opened with a song by the Morning Star drum group, the national anthem and a prayer by Joan Anderson, an elder from the Cloud Falls Indian Band.

> "Today is a powerful, good day," said Devlin Mutch, chief of the Cloud Falls band. "Even now we are relearning the songs he recorded and trying to bring them back into our culture." Cloud Falls band member Bill Mutch, 85, shared memories of Lyle with the audience. Having met the Scottish scholar in 1919, he was able to draw on personal and family tales. "This was known as Lyle's country... and at the last, big meeting a Vernon chief did this great war dance. Lyle said 'You dance very well but that will never win your country back.'

As I hope you'll see, Lyle's is a remarkable life-story. I appreciate you taking the time to read this outline and I trust it may interest you sufficiently to warrant further correspondence between us.

Yours sincerely

PS – I append a chronology of exploration and settlement of the province up to and including Lyle's times, to which I intend to make in-depth reference throughout the proposed book. I appreciate that not everything here listed may be relevant to the final text, however I consider it to be crucial background which may help you to place this proposed book appropriately in your forthcoming catalogue. Indeed, I would welcome any advice on what the reader may wish omitted.

APPENDIX

A Chronology of the History of Exploration and Settlement of the territories known to early European voyagers as 'New Caledonia'

1592   A navigator from the Venetian-governed Ionian isle of Cephalonia, Ioannis Phokas, in the pay of the Viceroy of 'New Spain' (Mexico) returns to Acapulco from a second commissioned voyage north along the Pacific coast in search of the entrance to the fabled but as yet unknown sea route between Atlantic and Pacific Oceans, claiming to have found it, with a large island at its mouth, at the latitude of 47 degrees North. The rewards promised to Phokas (known in Spanish as 'Juan de Fuca') fail to materialize and he retires to Cephalonia, but rumours of his discovery circulate and the mysterious 'Straits of Annian' enter nautical lore.

1596   An English sea-captain Michael Lok (Locke) attempts to enlist Phokas in the service of Queen Elizabeth I, but nothing comes of the plan. However, Lok's account helps to establish the idea of the mysterious straits as a rediscovery waiting to be made.

1670   The 'Hudson's Bay Company' is granted a charter by King Charles II, giving it a monopoly of trade throughout the watershed of all rivers flowing into Hudson's Bay. This territory becomes known as 'Rupert's Land' in honour of the king's cousin Prince Rupert of the Rhine who is made the company's first governor, and it covers an area of 1.5 million square miles, over one-third of contemporary Canada, but significantly does not reach into the province known today as British Columbia. The Pacific Northwest remains 'terra incognita'.

1759   An expeditionary force led by Major General James Wolfe, a native of Westerham in Kent who had distinguished himself early in his life during the suppression of the 1745 Jacobite 'rebellion' and subsequently spent eight years garrisoned in the Scottish Highlands, attacks the French stronghold of Quebec City. Amongst Wolfe's troops are a number of Scottish highlanders, of whom he writes in a letter, 'they are hardy, intrepid, accustomed to a rough country, and no great mischief if they fall.' After a long siege, Wolfe's forces are finally triumphant in the famous 'Battle of the Plains of Abraham' on the 13th of September, though their young commander dies in the field of battle. The fall of Quebec leads directly to the fall of Montreal, so ending French control of the country. Wolfe becomes an icon of the 'British Empire', posthumously dubbed 'the Conqueror of Canada.' At this time, the 'Pacific Northwest' still remains an unexplored and uncharted territory without established European claim, occupied by a great number of different indigenous peoples with developed cultures isolated from the rest of the world by the 'Rocky Mountains' and the 'Pacific Ocean'. However, many Europeans believe that the western entrance to the 'Northwest Passage' lies somewhere along the coast through the 'Straits of Annian' of de Fuca. How little is known of this territory in the 18th century in Britain is well-illustrated in the popular fiction of Jonathan Swift, who locates his land of giants, 'Brobdingnab', somewhere in the north of the region, claiming it to have been 'discovered, A.D. 1703' in map produced by Herman Moll c.1726.

1763   A 'Royal Proclamation' is issued on October 7th by King George III following Great Britain's acquisition of French territory in North America at the end of the 'Seven Years' War'. This proclamation forbids all settlement west of a line drawn along the Appalachian Mountains. However, it ensures that British laws are applied in 'Upper Canada' after 1791, and that British cultural customs are adopted, in order to attract British settlers.

1774   The people of Haida Gwaii ('Queen Charlotte Islands') go out in their great carved canoes to meet Juan Josef Perez Hernandez, a trader instructed by the Spanish Crown to take possession of land by erecting large wooden crosses on shore, during his voyage of exploration northwards along the Pacific coastline. After welcoming the strangers in peace, the Haida trade with them for two days but will not allow the Spanish to set foot ashore.

1775   Captains Juan Francisco la Bodega y Quadra and Bruno de Hezeta approach the Pacific Northwest intent on claiming sovereignty for the Spanish Crown. On the shores of Salish territory in 'Washington' state, Bodega erects a cross, but Quinault warriors attack and kill the landing crew.

1778   Captain James Cook leads a British expedition to the northwest coast. Unable to locate the 'Strait of Annian' as described by Lok's account of de Fuca's voyage, Cook dismisses it as a fabrication. Instead, he anchors off the coast in Nuu-chah-nulth waters, which Cook names 'Nootka Sound', and during a month of trading the crew acquire the pelts of several sea otters that later attract a high price in China. The fur trade that develops brings vessels from Spain, Britain, the United States, France, Russia and Portugal to the coast, and eventually leads to the virtual extinction of the sea otter.

1779   The 'Northwest Company', a rival to the Hudson's Bay Company monopoly in the debated territories, is founded in Montreal.

1782   The first smallpox epidemic to reach the lands of 'Cascadia' spreads overland from New Spain and goes on to kill one-third of the indigenous population, mostly in Salish territories. By 1840, smallpox, influenza and other diseases have claimed the lives of between 65 and 95 percent of indigenous populations in the area.

1787   The 'Imperial Eagle', captained by Englishman Charles William Barkley, finds an inland passage which corresponds to that described by de Fuca, and Barkley names it 'Strait of Juan de Fuca' in his honour.

1789   As the value of the sea otter fur trade grows, Spain and Britain struggle for control and sovereignty over the Pacific Northwest. The Spanish seize British ships and lands which the British believe rightly belongs to them. They kill Nuu-chah-nulth Chief Callicum and imprison British officers. Still further north, an employee of the Northwest Company from the Scottish Isle of Lewis, Alasdair MacCoinnich ('Alexander Mackenzie'), follows the course of the river known to the Dene people as Dehcho in the hope that it would lead him to the Pacific, so establishing a 'Northwest Passage', but finds the Dehcho river empties into the Arctic Ocean. It is rumoured that he 'named' it 'Disappointment River' as a consequence, though subsequently it is given the English version of his surname, 'MacKenzie.'

1790   Spain and Britain sign the 'Nootka Convention', under which Spain surrenders land taken and pays restitution for acts of violence against the British. They agree to equal trading rights in 'Nootka Sound.'

1791   Spanish explorers Juan Carrasco and Jose Maria Narvaez navigate the Straits of Juan de Fuca. They mistake the lowland estuary of the Fraser River for an inlet of the sea, which they name 'Canal de Floridablanca'. Meanwhile, a British expedition led by Captain George Vancouver who had accompanied Captain Cook on his earlier voyage, sets out from England commissioned with the task of exploring the Pacific, sailing east around the Cape of Good Hope.

1792   On April 29th, Vancouver's ships enter the Strait of Juan de Fuca, under orders to survey and map every inlet on the mainland coast as far north as Alaska, 'naming' numerous features as they progress – for instance, his 3rd lieutenant Joseph Baker sights a great mountain, which is therefore called 'Mount Baker'; another lieutenant Peter Puget explores a sound, henceforth 'Puget Sound'; another peak is named after Vancouver's friend Alleyne Fitzherbert, 1st Baron St Helens – 'Mount St Helens.' Meanwhile, Captain Dionisio Alcano Galliano has sailed north from New Spain in search of the 'Canal de Floridablanca' using Narvaez's chart and on arriving realizes that it is in fact the estuary of a great river. A few days later, on the 13th of June, Captain Vancouver enters the same waters, sailing past a headland which he names 'Point Grey' in honour of Captain George Grey, his friend. Vancouver then names 'Burrard Inlet' in honour of still another friend, Captain Sir Hero Burrard. Then, on June 22nd, Vancouver unexpectedly encounters Galliano and party at 'Point Grey' and, to his mortification, finds that the Spanish have already 'discovered' and mapped the coastline of the Straits thanks to the voyage of Narvaez the previous year. Nonetheless, British and Spanish crews collaborate on further surveying, before retiring to Nootka Sound for the winter. Vancouver and the Spanish commander Juan Francisco Bodega y Quadra agree to call the great island in which Nootka lies 'Quadra and Vancouver Island', later shortened to 'Vancouver Island' when Spanish influence wanes.

1793   Following a trip back to Britain to study the latest developments in longitudinal science, Alasdair MacCoinnich determines to make another overland voyage in search of a trade route to the Pacific. MacCoinnich travels in the company of his Gaelic cousin, Alasdair MacAoidh ('Alexander MacKay'), two native guides and six French Canadian indentured servants or 'voyageurs', and a dog, simply called 'Our Dog.' MacCoinnich reaches the Pacific Ocean at Q'urnk'uts ('Bella Coola') in Nuxolk territory. In 1801 a map of his journey is published.

1803   Nuu-chah-nulth wit-wank (warriors) led by Chief Maquinna attack the 'Boston', a British vessel in Nuu-chah-nulth waters, after the ship's captain insults him during trade negotiations. They burn the ship, killing all but two crew. European ships do not approach 'Nootka Sound' for two years following.

1805   Simon Fraser, a partner in the fur-trading Northwest Company and a man of Scottish descent, establishes the first trading fort in New Caledonia, 'Fort McLeod', in Tsek'ehne (Sekani) territory, which is then rapidly followed by others. Within two years the company builds forts St. James, Fraser and George in Dakelh (Carrier) territory. Fort St. James becomes the centre of government and commerce in the emergent interior territory then becoming known as 'New Caledonia' because of the number of Scotsmen involved in exploration and trade.

1808   The Musqueam people prevent Simon Fraser from entering their territory when he attempts to find a viable trade route to the Pacific Ocean by navigating the great canyon south from New Caledonia. He is forced to retreat up the river that later took his name.

1811   The 'Tonguin', a US ship in Tla-o-qui-aht waters, is captured and the crew killed after its captain insults a Nuu-chah-nulth chief by throwing furs in his face during trade negotiations.

1821   After long competition for dominance, the Northwest Company and the Hudson's Bay Company agree to merge. The British Crown grants the Hudson's Bay Company exclusive trading privileges with indigenous people in all the areas of North America claimed by the British.

1825   'Fort Vancouver' is established at the mouth of the 'Columbia River'. Great Britain and the United States struggle for control over the debatable lands in 'Cascadia'.

1828   Dakelh ('Carrier') Chief Kwah leads an attack on Fort St. James after Hudson's Bay Company employees attempt to capture and execute Dakelh-ne men thought to be guilty of killing two Hudson's Bay Company traders a few years before. James Douglas, the future provincial governor, then assistant chief factor at Fort St. James, is taken prisoner but let go after negotiation.

1829   James Douglas is transferred to Fort Vancouver. He is later promoted to Chief Trader in the Hudson's Bay Company.

1835   Traders learn from Kwakwaka'wakw people of coal deposits in their territory at 'Beaver Harbour'. Douglas sends a ship from Fort Vancouver to explore and take ownership of the territory if the claims prove to be true.

1843   James Douglas establishes 'Fort Victoria' on 'Vancouver's Island.' As Hudson's Bay Company chief factor, Douglas assumes Crown authority there, and begins dividing Indigenous territories for European settlement.

1844   Quw'utsun' ('Cowichan') warriors, led by Tzouhalem, attack Fort Victoria.

1846   Great Britain and the United States of America sign the 'Oregon Boundary Treaty', establishing a border along the 49th parallel which cuts across Indigenous boundaries in Cascadia. Britain claims 'Vancouver Island' and the mainland north of the 49th parallel, so asserting sovereignty over what would ultimately become known as 'British Columbia.'

1849   James Douglas establishes 'Fort Rupert' to begin coal-mining in Kwakwahwakw territory. Douglas aggressively promotes the development of mines all over Vancouver Island, which becomes a recognized British colony. Queen Victoria then leases it to the Hudson's Bay Company on the condition that the company promotes colonization.

1850   Richard Blanshard becomes the first Governor of the 'Colony of Vancouver Island'. James Douglas begins to negotiate agreements with Kwakwaka'wakw, Saanich, Snuneymuxw and Songhees/Lekwungen,

Sna-Naw-As, Scia'new, T'Souke and Malahat peoples now displaced by the Colony. Written records state that the Indigenous signatories surrendered their territory forever in exchange for small reserves and residual hunting and fishing rights. However, oral record indicates that these agreements actually reaffirmed Indigenous ownership, but allowed for peaceful European settlement within their territories.

1854   The last of Douglas's treaties is signed, affecting the coal mine in Snuneymuxw territory at Nanaimo. Text of this treaty is subsequently lost, while oral record persists.

1858   The focus of exploitation and colonization shifts from Vancouver Island to the mainland when over 30,000 prospectors, mainly from California, make their way into the 'Upper Fraser Valley' and 'Fraser Canyon' after reports that gold has been discovered in the river. European and American speculators attempt to sell land near Fort Langley, provoking Douglas to declare without authority that these lands belong to the British Crown, prior to the actual constitution of the mainland 'Colony of British Columbia', which nonetheless follows rapidly, the name being selected by Queen Victoria in preference to the term in use, 'New Caledonia', on grounds that the French Empire already has a such-named colony in the Pacific. Douglas resigns from the Hudson's Bay Company to become governor of the new colony. Great Britain grants to him sole authority to allocate land to settlers and to establish Indian reserves. Britain deploys Royal Engineers to build roads and to bridge rivers, to survey and map, to plan settlements and fully establish the United States-British Columbia border.

1859   Governor Douglas issues a proclamation stating that all land, mines and minerals in the Colony of British Columbia belong to the British Crown; he sets out arrangements for land auctions, road-building, ditching and working of gold claims, and declares that the capital for the Colony will be 'New Westminster', to be situated at Skaiametl, the main Kwantlen community in Sto:lo territory. Douglas dispatches an Indian agent into Nuu-chah-nulth territory to induce people to abandon their traditional ways, and to regulate the sale of liquor. The Indian agent disappears, presumably killed by the Nuu-chah-nulth.

1862   As the Fraser Canyon gold rush reaches a disappointing end, news of deposits discovered in the 'Cariboo country' creates a new fever. Over 10,000 miners travel further north into Dakelh ('Carrier') territory through the canyon. Construction of the 'Cariboo Wagon Road' from 'Yale' to 'Barkerville' through Tsilhqot'in and Dakelh territories begins.

1862   Infected European migrants bring smallpox to Fort Victoria, initiating
        an epidemic. Vaccinations are dispensed, but the disease spreads when
        infected Indigenous people are forced to go back to their original com-
        munities from the colony where they have been living. During the two
        years of the outbreak, over half the population in native communities
        die throughout the two colonies.

1864   *James Alexander Lyle born in Lerwick, Scotland, 18th April.*

        The Tsilhqot'in attempt to halt the spread of smallpox into their terri-
        tory by stopping the construction of the Cariboo Wagon Road. Three
        Tsilhqot'in men, twelve road workers and six settlers die in the conflict,
        but within a few weeks an army of 100 colonists track down and arrest
        eight Tsilhqot'in chiefs. Tried for murder under British law, six are hung.

1864   In response to repeated Indigenous resistance, before his retirement
        Governor Douglas sends a surveyor, William McColl, to determine what
        ought to be designated 'Indian land' in the central 'Fraser Valley', and
        the outcome is the marking out of a number of reserves, some as size-
        able as 9,000 acres. When Douglas retires, Frederick Seymour becomes
        Governor of the mainland colony, but refuses to recognize the legiti-
        macy of such large areas. Seymour appoints Joseph Trutch as 'Chief
        Commissioner of Lands and Works for the Colony', and he assumes
        responsibility for Indian land policy. Trutch publicly denies the existence
        of Indigenous rights, reduces the size of existing Douglas reserves, and
        sets a new reserve allotment formula at 10 acres per family. Thousands
        of Sto:lo and other Coast Salish peoples travel to New Westminster on
        Queen Victoria's birthday to protest against the extent of immigration
        into their territories, though they express satisfaction with the reserves as
        initially established by Douglas. Oral records among the Sto:lo suggest
        that Seymour responded with a promise that one third of the proceeds
        from all land sales in the Fraser Valley should be taken by the colonial
        government, the second third should be given directly to the Sto:lo, and
        that the final third should be set aside for the governmental provision
        of education and social services for their people. In the same year as the
        Sto:lo attempt peaceful settlement of their grievances, Nuu-chah-nulth
        wit-wank board the British vessel the 'Kingfisher' in Clayoquot Sound
        and kill the crew. Britain deploys two naval ships, ostensibly to capture
        those responsible, but once in Tla-o-qui-aht territory, the ships begin
        shelling, destroying nine villages and killing 13 Nuu-chah-nulth people.

1866   The colonies of island and mainland are united by an Act of Parliament.
        'New Westminster' becomes the official capital of the united colony of
        British Columbia.

1867   'The Dominion of Canada' is established by 'the British North America Act'. Under this Act, Canada asserts jurisdiction over 'Indians and Indian lands'.

1871   British Columbia becomes part of the Dominion of Canada, and the Canadian government assumes jurisdiction over Indian affairs in the new province. It incorrectly assumes the 1763 Royal Proclamation to secure the surrender of Indigenous territories has been applied there, and the Terms of Union guarantee a reserve policy specified to be 'as liberal as that hitherto pursued' by British Columbia, so approving Trutch's reduced 10 acre per family allotment without knowledge of Douglas's earlier policy. The earlier colonial department is replaced by 'The British Columbia Lands and Works Department', but its task remains to survey, map and administer land. The position of 'Commissioner' in this new department is politically powerful, due to the opportunity to grant land as patronage. The Canadian government publishes 'A Schedule of All Indian Reserves in the Province of British Columbia' but a number of reserves are omitted.

1872   Israel Wood Powell is appointed 'Indian Superintendent' and attempts to allocate more land for reserves. The Canadian government supports his recommendations and requests that British Columbia should adopt an 80 acre policy. British Columbia agrees to a 20 acre standard but reneges on this agreement. Powell stops laying out reserves in protest.

1872   Thousands of Salish gather outside the 'Land Registry' office in New Westminster to demand recognition of their territorial rights. The Gitxsan close the Skeena River to colonists. The provincial government mounts a military campaign to reopen the river.

1873   The 'Federal Department of the Interior' is created. A 'Board of Commissioners' is set up to administer 'Indian Affairs'. The Salish and Tsilhqot'in peoples deliver a petition demanding compensation for land taken by settlers. Fifty-six chiefs sign, asking for reserves containing 80 acres per family in accordance with the federal government's recommendation, noting settler encroachment and previous poor treatment. They threaten to appeal to the Dominion for arbitration if the Province does not respond. It does not.

1874   The Salish organize a protest rally, drawing people to 'New Westminster' from communities along the 'Fraser River', the mainland coast and the interior. British Columbia passes a new 'Land Act,' so consolidating all previous land legislation, which authorizes the annexation of Indigenous territories and sets 'Indian' reserve allotment at 20 acres

for every head of family regardless of family size. The Canadian government again requests that the province adopt an 80 acre standard.
British Columbia refuses, so Canada disallows the 'Land Act'.'

1875   The Dominion government passes an order in council recommending
        that the BC government allot 80 acres of land to every Indian family of
        five persons. BC refuses, asserting that not more than 20 acres of land
        are required for each Indian family. A revised BC Land Act is passed,
        setting the 20 acre Indian reserve formula while providing 160 acre
        land grants for individual settlers free of charge.

1876   The Indian Act consolidates all previous legislation regarding Indians
        and Indian lands in Canada. Over time, the Indian Act is amended to
        prohibit cultural practices and public assembly, to confine Indians to
        reserves, and to prevent the pursuit of land claims. While the Indian
        Act asserts Canadian jurisdiction over Indigenous peoples, creating
        "Indians" and "Indian reserves," it signals some governmental recog-
        nition of Indian lands and of the distinct position of Indigenous people.

1879   The Nlaka'pamux assemble at Lytton to discuss their land rights. A
        new political structure, consisting of a head chief and 13 councilors is
        proposed to deal with the colonial governments and the Nlaka'pamux
        request that their system be recognized under the Indian Act.

1880   Construction of the BC portion of the Canadian Pacific Railway (CPR)
        begins, contributing to increased immigration.

1883   Railway lands in BC are transferred to Canada to help pay for railroad
        construction costs. The Railway Belt is a 20-mile strip of land on either
        side of the railway line totaling nearly eleven million acres. An additional
        3.5 million acres, known as the "Peace River Block," is transferred to
        replace land already taken up in the more populated sections of the prov-
        ince. The Railway Belt and Peace River Block, including all Indian reserves
        contained within these sections, remain under federal control until 1930.

1884   *James Lyle arrives in Canada.*

1885   Canada enacts a potlatch ban. Every Indian engaging in a potlatch or
        Tamanawas (spirit) activities is deemed guilty of a misdemeanor, and is
        subject to imprisonment of up to six months in jail. Uslick, a Sto:lo man
        from Chilliwack, is the first person arrested under this law. Three Tsimshian
        chiefs travel to Ottawa to express their concerns about land rights. They are
        the first Indigenous delegation from BC to take their protests to Ottawa.

She scrolled forward. The list went on for another ten pages or so,
entry after entry, hardly a year missing from the chronology. It was

impressive research, but it was far too much to take in, there in the darkness of the canyon night, so she scanned the remainder looking for more mentions of Lyle.

1894   *James Lyle meets the ethnographer Franz Boas.*

1899   *James Lyle's wife dies.*

1909   Secwepemc, Okanagan, Nlaka'pamux and St'at'imc leaders meet in Cloud Falls and form the Interior Tribes of British Columbia. James Lyle, a local ethnographer, is recruited to translate their concerns and demands to Canada and BC.

She scanned forward again. The list of names and treaties, of tribes and protests, went on and on, right through the First World War years, an astounding catalogue of history she knew little about. Her Scottish friend had certainly done his research. But it was too much to take in piecemeal. An overwhelming sense of injustice towards First Nations people came over her at that moment, and it was tinged by a kind of settler guilt. Although her family had nothing to do with those actions, had been in no way involved in the British colonization, her very presence here in the province seemed to implicate her, as she flash-read incident after incident in the Indian Rights movement's history. The last page came into view.

1921   Indian Agent and Justice of the Peace William Halliday orchestrates a major RCMP raid on a Kwakwaka'wakw potlatch at Mamlillikulla (Village Island). They arrest 49 people and confiscate all sacred regalia, masks and other items. Twenty-six people are imprisoned and all artefacts are sold off to public and private collectors. The Kwakwaka'wakw join the Allied Tribes.

1922   *James Lyle dies in Merritt.*

She closed the file. In the light from the laptop, she looked at the sleeping Scotsman, lying wrapped in a white sheet, an echo of the shroud she'd saved him from. Where had he come from, bursting into her life like this, waking her from the stupor that had hung over her life since the surgery and the radiotherapy, that dreadful listlessness she had endured till her trip to Calgary? Suddenly she was elsewhere, in a world she did not know. Except of course she did. She was not the same person she had been. Except of course she was.

She clicked on the icon entitled 'MacLeod Falls Journal'.

Second Dance
'The Walking Scotchman'
(Slow Waltz)

The pioneers in this movement will conquer the territory not with arms in their hands, but with the gold-rocker, the plough, the loom, and the anvil, the steam-boat, the railway, and the telegraph. Commerce and agriculture, disenthralled by the influences of free institutions, will cause the new empire to spring into life, full armed, like Minerva from the brain of Jupiter. Its Pacific ports will be thronged with ships of all nations, its rich valleys will blossom with nature's choicest products, while its grand rivers will bear to the sea the fruits of free and honest labour.

R M Ballantyne, *Handbook to the Goldfields*

HE WATCHED AS the coach wound its way ever further into the interior, and into an ever steeper gorge surrounded by mountainous slopes and wild forest. Familiar though it seemed from the Highlands of home, the Scotsman was amazed by the scale of it all, despite the fact that he knew where he was going, had read and prepared, had studied maps and guides. He knew that for centuries this territory had been the place of the N'laka'pamux, who moved through the canyon and the valleys surrounding according to season, prey and natural crop, until finally they found themselves fenced in by the land grants given to the invader by the invader's government. The N'laka'pamux knew where the gold they brought to trade at the white man's fort could be found on the bars and spits of the canyon shores. The company traders learned from them, prospectors followed in huge swarms.

In the 1860s, the 'Couteau Indians' resisted. When miners raped two of their women, they found the culprits, cut their heads off, floated them downstream to the miners' camp. Then, it was the wild frontier. Now, in the summer of 2011, the Scotsman stepped off a Greyhound bus from Vancouver, into the baking heat of noonday at a settlement they now called Cloud Falls – though he knew it had once been MacLeod's Falls. He knew a lot about it. He'd mapped it from a distance of 5,000 miles as well as anyone might scope it at that range. He'd google-walked the highway and the main street, but the backstreets and the hidden places were unknown. He knew the story of the old bridge he must cross to get to the inn. He'd made its history familiar, important, but now all that seemed strange because today the settlement he saw was stripped of story, and all appeared a tiny temporary structure among vast mountains, encamped alongside a great urgent river that could sweep it away in an instant, mere human scratchings in the wild.

He could see the inn where he was to stay on the far bank. It was supposedly the oldest in continuous use in the province, first opened as a glorified cabin, a roadhouse where travellers could wait till it was safe to cross the river on the great winched basket established by a man called Sigurd – which gave it its first name, Sigurd's Crossing. It had slowly evolved to its heyday as stagecoach stop before that trade was put an end to by the coming of the Canadian Pacific Railway. After the first bridge was built, the later town grew on the near bank, where there was a little land that could be farmed with proper irrigation and diligent care. It was there that Jimmy Lyle's uncle John Macleod had created his fiefdom, once known as MacLeodville.

He passed between a few houses, set back from the road, but his eyes were on the bridge. From a distance, the old structure reminded him of the Forth Railway Bridge, a fellow Victorian wrought iron creation, though the span and the scale was very different. The bridge was sturdy, a belt and braces design made to resist annual floods. The sensation, that great notion he'd had in Scotland during those weeks of cancer treatment, that peculiar vertiginous urge to jump swept over him.

He stepped onto the great wooden planks – the rail was high but not a deterrent, and the river was moving rapidly, still carrying melt-water from the high mountains. The flow wasn't smooth – rapid wave crests caused by hidden rocks appeared to want to flow upstream, but were constantly frustrated by the current. He leant over the barrier and watched this turmoil churning below, a vast silvery grey soup of silt. He knew that while the river was narrow up here in the gorge, it had a seasonal urgency sufficient to carry away any engineer's designs, that it had done so once, before this structure was erected. The current would sweep all debris downstream, as it had the headless miners back in the day.

The breeze blowing down the canyon was warm yet still refreshing on his back after the stale air of the coach. He felt a little flashback to Vancouver in the early morning, before she dropped him off at Pacific Central, him telling her about John Buchan and his last Canadian book, as they'd waited in the lines of traffic. This would indeed be a good river for the drowning of a sick heart, unlike the shallow Almond at home he had left behind almost dry, its submerged rocks revealed. That was a lowland river with too gentle a name for tragic drowning. Here at Cloud Falls in New Caledonia, there would be a poetry about it. But he resisted, carefully walked the line between the lanes to the far bank where the inn stood, safe above the floodplain.

From there he could see properly the mountainous crag above the town which John MacLeod had dubbed 'Arthur's Seat', because it reminded him of Edinburgh's volcanic heart. It was in some way similar, but steeper and more forbidding by far.

A giant railway track ran alongside the highway as he walked, lugging his bags, and a train of trucks announced the Canadian Pacific he knew from the old song, their livery and logos giving a micro chain geography of Canada, with place names decorated here and there by graffiti.

The inn came into view, reminding him of one old photograph he'd got from the BC archives that had shown the inn in its prime, in the halcyon days of the stagecoach. It was only a thumbnail that pixelated when zoomed, but the hotel looked so freshly constructed the viewer could almost smell new-cut timber. Upstairs windows were raised, but the blinds drawn. Next to the stagecoach, a man in white shirt sleeves stood arms aloft, as if ready to give the signal to depart. Another held the bridles of the first of two pairs of horses. On the coach, three ladies in long dresses pulled headscarves tight around their chins, as if afraid their bonnets would fly off once the coach got under way. Two old longbeards sat by the opened inn door, watching the show, while another bearded figure stood closer, slightly off-balance as if in mid-step, staring right down the camera lens. It was a picture of pioneers establishing timetables, routes, routines, of a desire for connection, for swiftness.

The key was waiting for the Scotsman on the reception desk as he'd been told it would, with a note from Vince the proprietor to say he'd be back at 5pm. It was tagged 'Room 14'. He made his way upstairs, lugging baggage, thinking of the list he'd made before he left Scotland in his notebook – a kind of guide, but one that took no account of how the journey felt, of the dead weight of things, of who was met or missed and how that diverted. Still he'd got there, and the room was clean, a tiny sanctuary from the road. The windows looked out across the river to the town on the far bank.

Once inside, he unpacked his gear and fixed tripod to camcorder, and plugged in the laptop so that he could lie on the bed and watch the image while he controlled the remote. The village across the river was too far off for clear images, present only in a rough blur. Still he could see wooden settler houses well spread out, but not much seemed to be happening. Further to the right was the bridge he'd crossed, the mad rush of water only a grey glistening without definition. Panning left, the land on the floodplain below came into focus, and his zoom lens found a nest on a platform atop a great wooden pole, where the electricity line crossed the river. He sat up so he could see the image more clearly, adjusted focus. There were two large birds flapping around among a pile of sticks and branches. One seemed to be pestering the other by flying up a short distance, then dropping down on to the back of that sitting, hopping around as if to tell it that it must move – go fishing!

It was a nest, and yes, he saw they were indeed ospreys – another strange coincidence to his mind as it sought for meaning, a little bit of home that had nested here. For forty years, ospreys had avoided Scotland where they had been persecuted to extinction. The last recorded chick preceded the First World War, so when in 1951, a pair nested in the Highlands – not reintroduced, but naturally – it was a big story. He knew it well. The countryside and the way of life had changed so during the intervening years, but here was something of the old world that chose to return – the Fish Hawk. After the long years of war, it was a hopeful tale, somehow, and a pilgrimage for those who had the means. It was a trip his mother and father first made together sometime in the later 1950s, north from Edinburgh on the old A9 to Boat of Garten in their Vauxhall Vesta. He wasn't with them, was still a toddler so he'd stayed with the next door neighbours, but he remembered their monochrome photos, so when he zoomed in on this Canadian pair among twigs at the top of their tall pole above the river, strung round with heavy wires, he zoomed into his own past.

The sight triggered memories of where he'd come from and suddenly he found himself back in the old country, glad that he'd had those months with the old girl before she died. Though it was the cancer that drove him back to live with her, it was fortunate because it turned out to be her last months, and she needed him – perhaps they had needed each other? And as his mother began to unravel, he began to heed her words in a manner he hadn't done in many years, because among the nonsense and the senile rambling she would sometimes say something that made his ears alert. It was as if she'd taken some kind of truth serum, and the silences she'd previously imposed on her early life melted into a form-less lucidity over which she had no control. When she spoke during these times, it was not as if to him, but to some unspecified other she felt was listening, or perhaps judging, some presence to whom she felt the need to justify her deeds. Her speech in those moments – the two of them in the little kitchen of the cottage she'd made her final home, the old stove lit and her chair at its side, him at the table – was the voice of her childhood on the estate where her father was once gamekeeper, and her mother a maid at the castle. Braid Scots.

He never knew how present she was at those times. The trigger seemed to be stillness, the warmth of that stove, maybe the singing of the kettle or the aroma of the tea that she habitually stewed in the pot at the edge of the hotplate. But he couldn't manufacture the circum-stance. Maybe there was something in that room that reminded her of the old days? She would only talk when she felt ready and what con-stituted readiness he could never quite establish, though he knew the main ingredients and could sense when she was in a mood to begin. But he was aware he had to sit still, almost fade into the mirk of the unlit room, to become a shadow without form. Then she might, of her own volition, start to talk a little about the events and the people that had stayed with her, even into her eighties, as she wandered mentally. He had realised, after a while, that if he spoke English, he would rouse her from her distant reverie, she would become aware of the present again and lose trace of the daydream. But if he sat quietly, still in the gloom, she would talk, and if he asked a question in Scots, she didn't seem to realise who he was and would sometimes answer, though she took little direction. Sometimes he was able, briefly, to turn her monologue into a one-sided interview, and ask her questions he wanted to. Yes, in the gloom of fading light at Kirkliston one evening, he asked his mother, in the voice her senility trusted: 'Why did ye merrie Dad, an him a wid-ower that muckle aulder than ye?' And she had answered, 'I only loved wance.' And he knew that to be true, his mother's wartime sweetheart had a special private place in their bungalow even when his father was still alive. It wasn't a shrine, but he existed, this dead flying officer hero, in little glimpses, a subtle manifestation of his imagined glory, and his father accepted that, for some reason. He knew, as a child growing up, that this dead stranger was still with her – and was even present then in Kirkliston, a few months from the end – while his father she seemed to forget latterly, as if the sixteen years of their marriage had melted away or had never really been, in the catalogue of her romantic life, all that tangible an object.

He remembered, lying there on that hotel bed five thousand miles from home, in the intense heat of the day, the cold grey city all those years ago and how his mother's hair went white around the time his father died. She was much younger than his father, and she soon had it done in the latest style, and with her new black and white Coco Chanel clothes, silk headscarves, and a little lipstick, became both older and younger than before – because she was a young widow, because she was no longer living with a husband a generation older whose fashion sense had always been at best Edwardian. The farm girl was very much the woman about town for a few years. Her young son became her companion. She took the driver's seat and the boy became her navigator in passenger seat.

When he rose from this hypnagogia, the astral plane gave way to an evening far from the grey city of his memory. Although the river roared, the village beyond was at peace – a barbecue plume rose from somewhere among the scattering of buildings on the far bank. The houses sat secluded in tree-lined lots. He gazed through the zoom on his camera, scanning over it. No sign of people out front, just, he imagined, the whirr of the sprinklers he could see, the hiss of summer lawns.

He left the baking chamber of Room 14 and went downstairs in search of his absent host. There was no one on the desk - he rang the bell as instructed but no one came, so he went outside to see if anyone was there. It was like a western ghost town.

He walked across from the inn, beyond the highway, to where the railroad corralled the line of stationary CPR rail trucks he'd seen earlier. It was so long that it ran out of sight around the bend. But nothing pointed as far back as Sigurd, he of the original crossing, the pioneer American who was the first to drag a hawser over the river and fix up pulleys to transport the gold-hungry strangers headed up-country. He'd built a sizeable business in logging and trade further down the canyon, until his partner died young in a brawl, and left Sigurd sickened of the country. So he moved back home to Washington state and founded a town there instead. In Sigurd's Crossing he'd left his name for a while, till it became MacLeodville, then MacLeod Falls, and finally, simply Cloud Falls.

Looking back at the inn, the Scotsman wondered if it was really, as the Gold Country brochure suggested, the 1862 building. It wasn't the shape of the one in the picture archive, not from this angle, but an adobe structure. It was built like the one further along the road to the south, the original community hall built, he knew from his research, in 1907 in the cement and stone architectural style that Archibald Clements – at that time known as "the owner of Cloud Falls" and perhaps the man responsible for the name change – had learned about on one of his many excursions to Mexico. Clements' family had come from Cornwall, had emigrated to Ontario in 1855 when Archie was three, settling later in Alberta where the family grew up. Young Archie moved west to what was in the process of becoming the city of Vancouver, when he was old enough to strike out on his own. He bought up property cheaply, and profited as the conurbation grew rapidly after the CPR chose it as the terminus for its great transcontinental adventure. At one time or another, Clements had owned the Hotel Regent, the original Pantages Theatre, then the Theatre Royal, Billie's Poolroom, Hastings Rooms, and many buildings on Columbia Street. And after making his fortune, he moved north into the sunny interior in the 1880s, and then up the canyon property by property, until he acquired the estate of Jimmy Lyle's uncle, John MacLeod, who had died suddenly.

The original Morton's hotel, Clements had promptly closed in favour of a newly built one near the railway line, higher up the riverbank by some hundred feet or so, with hollow cement blocks and stonework suitable for the dry climate. It was just as well, as the old hotel building was swept away two years later in a flood that also carried off Sigurd's original crossing. So the Scotsman was fairly sure his current residence was the 1892 structure, not the one from thirty years earlier but part of Clements' Mexican-inspired dream, built long after gold fever had been dispelled by disappointment.

Whatever its history, in 2011 it was a pretty little terracotta-coloured building, quaintly charming even, like the set for some old Western movie, sublimely framed by the great rocky crown of bare mountains louring over the valley floor. A quiet spot even with the river's roar, were it not for the railway monsters that passed, pulling their chain of squealing and grinding slave-trucks.

When he went back inside, he could see through the open door that a little group had gathered on the terrace, and he was immediately the object of their scrutiny, the stranger in town, the greenest of horn. He went to ring the reception bell again but the absent host appeared from among the gathering, smiling, before he could do so, welcoming 'the Scotchman'. Before the guest could ask, Vince said sorry the wifi wasn't working, that they had no cell phone reception either, and when the Scotsman asked about dinner, Vince explained they 'don't do food any more – long story, wife went back to Ottawa.' The only place to eat was Colette's – over the river, next the store.

The Scotchman said he knew where Colette's was from all the googling he'd done in Vancouver. Vince offered a beer, as if he owed one for not telling him sooner about the wifi or his wife. Vince was talkative. As he handed him a cold lager from the cabinet, he said it had seemed like such a good idea, opening a vegan restaurant up here to make use of all the local produce. They both wanted to get out of the city, and she'd always been interested in this part of the world, had written her thesis when she was in college about the native basketware of the region, but when she got here, it was like the reality didn't live up to what she'd expected, she couldn't actually settle.

'Yes,' the Scotchman said, 'I can understand. It's a long way out up here, from Vancouver.'

'Ottawa, we came from,' Vince corrected. They thought it would be good for their kids, but then there was the business, the way it tailed off. Especially after Colette opened her place across the river, nearer to the highway. 'So anyway, just six weeks ago, she walked out, went back east. What's a guy to do?'

The Scotchman headed out, digesting this impromptu confession, the fact that he had no connection to the outside world, back along the highway and its companion rail track to the old bridge. The roar was as it had been earlier, a micropolyphony of cluster notes comprised of river rapid splash and thunder. He thought of the old song, the title of Ken Kesey's great novel about the dysfunctional logging family to the south of the US border, but he didn't give in to the screaming urge to join the cacophony. Another sound emerged, and he saw a second railway line on the opposite bank to the CPR ran along the bank. He hadn't seen it earlier, so intent had he been on the getting over the bridge itself, hauling luggage.

So he crossed again, as the line of rail trucks ran noisily underneath him. He was keen to see the little town properly, without the weight of his luggage, and he knew that Colette's was the last remaining building from the days of the great orchards, when apples and pears and other fruit bearing the stamp of Spark's Orchards, the Royal favourite, left Cloud Falls on the CPR for the world in great quantity. The BC archives had a photo from back in the 1880s when Jimmy Lyle's uncle John MacLeod's little empire was in its pomp, before he fell on hard times and Archie Clements came north with his wallet full of Vancouver dollars and bought everything up. There were no settler houses then, just two perfect avenues of acacias planted to stretch from his grand wooden ranch house and its great barn, over to his large emporium store. Like the inn, brave hopeful structures right on what was then the frontier of the settler world, now all gone except the apple store.

The Scotsman knew the birth of the Cloud Falls orchards was in essence MacLeod's one brilliant idea – a system of artificial wooden channels to carry the fresh water that fell from the creek in the hidden valley above, into the plain of thirsty sedimentary soil that had accumulated over millennia at the fork of two great rivers to the north. How those flumes he had his workmen build, to carry water from the falls, had profited those who followed, the Spark family who took them over when the pioneer died, and ran a successful business right up until the Second World War. But now all that was left of that enterprise was this one little wooden building, by the end of the bridge, which was now open as a restaurant – Colette's. He stood a while in front of it, and took a few photos. The front garden had some tables and chairs, and there was a newish porch over the door, but otherwise it seemed much as he imagined it had done, back in the day.

No one was around, though it was now supper time. The door was tricky to open, so a woman came from behind the counter inside to help, not Colette, he discovered, but Dorothy, who was welcoming, interested and talkative. He asked but she didn't know anything of Jimmy Lyle. She'd only moved here a few years ago when she retired from teaching. Colette's was very homely, plain aside from a little stage built into the far corner, where a mike-stand and a single amp were tucked away and a few posters illuminated the Cloud Falls music scene, regular shows hosted by Colette herself, who seemed proud to wear a fringed Stetson and to be able to introduce the country stars of the canyon. He imagined her entrance, in bouffant wig maybe, swishing the curtain back and stepping confidently through, to take the mike and give folks a song. Except there were no folks there that evening, only the Scotsman, waiting for the house special stew.

It was welcome home cooking, his first proper meal of the day, and he ate in silence, leafing through his Gold Country guide. Afterwards he thanked Dorothy as he paid, and left.

Outside, he went round the back of Colette's to find the general store. It turned out it was just another door into the same building, though this side had an original apple-shaped advertisement from the days of the Sparks' orchards, a great board with red paint peeling but still proud. *Purveyors to the Throne*, it said.

Again, it was Dorothy who greeted him. She apparently had just stepped through from the kitchen while he'd trekked around the outside. The stock was fairly minimal – a yellow-pack low cost range, tins and a few newspapers, drinks in a cooler. She asked if he was still hungry, as he went to pay for a few snacks and bottled water.

'No,' he answered, 'like I said that stew was really good. But what I really was looking for was sun-cream. That sun is really hot. But you don't seem to sell it?'

'No,' she said. 'But yeah, it's desert sun. You want to be careful walking around this time of year.'

Crossing the river again in the gloaming, he walked quickly over the bridge to the safety of the shore, and turned back towards the inn, his eye firmly on the white line down the middle. By the rail track, where the long train still hadn't gone anywhere, a CPR pick-up truck was parked astride the rails, its tyres replaced by rail wheels.

The driver nodded as the Scotsman approached, wound down the window and smiled. 'Just passing through?' he asked.

'Staying at the Inn,' the wanderer answered. 'Quite a train you have here.' He nodded at the long line of trucks that stretched out of sight.

'Yeah. She's a mile long, this'un. I'm Ken,' he said, offering a hand through the window. The Scotsman shook it, introduced himself.

'So what brings you here, Bert? Fishing?'

So he explained the mission, that he was from Scotland, asked if he'd heard of Lyle, but CPR Ken shook his head slowly, gazing down the track ahead. 'I heard it was a great place once upon a time, though, Cloud Falls,' Ken said. 'But there's nothin much here now.' He said his home was down the canyon in Boston Bar, and it was his job 'to make sure one end of the train talks to the other.'

The inn was suddenly populous as the Scotsman opened the door. Noisy even. Groups of people, two and threes, sat on the terrace, drinking as the daylight faded, smoking and laughing. But there was no one at the desk. He rang. A woman dressed in t-shirt, pantaloons and sandals came bouncing in from the terrace.

'Hey,' she said. 'So you're the Scotsman? Bert, right? Afraid Vince is not here right now.'

'Ok. I just wanted to ask about breakfast.'

'Yeah, sure – it'll all be out here. The tree-planters usually come down around five thirty, so it may look like locusts passed through, but just ask for anything you need. Vince will be here in the morning. I'm Rosie, by the way.' She gave him a quick smile and retreated to the terrace.

A tv chattered in the lounge, so he went through to see what was going on. In the half-light from the set, a man sat watching some nature show turned and nodded. The Scotsman saw at a glance that there was quite a library in one corner of the room, and went to look. It was mostly flotsam of the kind you might find in any place where holidaymakers leave a half-read novel they didn't like enough to bring back home, or some hardly-used guide to the locality they no longer needed, but in the corner was another layer, older books, what the trade called 'Canadiana', among them many local publications even he'd never heard of. He ran his eyes quickly over the titles, making a mental note – *Indian Myths and Legends from the North Pacific Coast of America, Our Tellings, Skookum Wawa, Travels in British Columbia and Alaska,* by Newton Chittenden. Vince had said his wife had studied this area. Maybe these were hers?

'You know anything about these books?' he asked of the tv watcher.

'Not much. But if you want to read anything, you just take it. Vince doesn't mind.'

He took a few books upstairs, things that might be useful, and began flash-reading them in the way that years in the second-hand book trade had trained him to do. He noticed that Chittenden's book was published in the same year the young James Lyle arrived here, 1884. It had no index so he flicked through it looking for some mention of Cloud Falls, then remembered at that time it was probably still called Sigurd's Crossing. And so he found it, so comma heavy as to have cost the printer extra ink.

"Mr. John MacLeod, an old time resident, owns a fine property and ranch here, upon which, in addition to excellent grains, vegetables, apples, cherries, plums, and berries, he has grown, this season, grapes, which, he says, the Marquis of Lorne pronounced equal to any raised in the Dominion."

Chittenden had also written a brief memorial to the first pioneer, the man whose enterprise preceded even MacLeod's. At "Sigurd's Crossing" it said, the population was "32 whites and 130 Indians, with 5 general stores, 3 hotels, one Indian Church of England and one school", and principal industries were "fruit growing and farming. The road crosses the great mud slide, or moving mountain which a railroad engineer said was sliding toward the river at the rate of eight feet a year. How to build a railway over this changing base is a problem the engineers are trying to solve. I am well acquainted with Wayne Sigurd, who immortalized himself, and made a fortune here, in the days when the Cariboo was rolling out her fabulous wealth, by ferrying over the armies of gold hunters rushing northward. A man of remarkable energy and exceptional ability, he rode into this country poor, on a mule, and out of it in good style, a few years later, worth his thousands, added to them by successful operations in the West, invested all in California, flourished, became banker and Mayor of the most beautiful city on the Southern coast, and then, in the general financial crash of 1877, turned everything over to his creditors, like a man. The place is now quite a little village, and being situated at the entrance to the Nicola country, will always prosper..."

At the end of the verso page was an advert:

The Best Accommodations for Man and Beast.

JOHN MACLEOD'S

MACLEOD'S FALLS,

B. C.,

Native Flower Seeds,

and English Gooseberries,

a Specialty.

At that moment, the video camera clicked itself off. It had reached its limit and shut down automatically. He got up, downloaded the files onto his laptop and set it up afresh, then watched the footage from the time he was out, 4x zip-by-speed. Trucks and other vehicles passed intermittently on the new highway while Cloud Falls lay bypassed. Every so often a snaking train slid along the far riverbank, the CNR line as opposed to the CPR on this side, running long and slow through the settlement, truck after truck. What looked like coal, and containers with legends in Chinese or Japanese from the orient, which was really occident here.

To the left of the shot, the ospreys danced, fast-forward – one leaving and returning. It became clear, watching for a while, that one was the giant chick and the other its mother, that the chick couldn't yet fly. Then video dusk fell at equatorial speed, a mobile darkening meld of hues of grey and mauve, and soon after black, footage cut out.

He lay on the bed, stomach full of Colette's stew, thinking again of the ospreys back home. He remembered that the name 'Boat of Garten' had puzzled him as a child. How could a place be a boat? And he remembered his father explaining how the boat was originally a ferry at Garten, across the river Spey, and that was how the name came to be. And it struck him that this was the Boat of Sigurd - his ferry, a crossing.

Drifting into a light sleep in the darkness of New Caledonia, listening to the river's roar with the image of his crossing it, not jumping, a vision of his father woke him sharply, drowned in the sump in that garage of his, his wee kingdom in Duddingston, the dark oily pit below, the sump where he'd go with his spanners, his head-torch on, dressed in his old army boiler suit, washed so many times it was slowly turning from khaki to beige. He remembered how once as a wee laddie, curious, he went down there and the dark streaks of oil on gathered rain shining in the torch beam looked like the lochs of some alien planet. He'd wondered if sometime his father would simply be swallowed – never come in from the garage when his mother called him for supper. The dream he'd had was of that dread.

Then a noise began to emerge out of the river's unchanging rush, a groan of metal shot through with shrieks slowly rising higher until the pitch was painful. Room 14 seemed to shake and he realised that CPR Ken and his truck had done the job, the train was off, shouting to itself loud enough to keep even the most exhausted tree-planter awake. And it went on and on, a mile long, filling the darkness, somehow terrifying and ushering an intrusive attack of painful cramped self-loathing – it came from nowhere but he suddenly felt he was as good as dead, a cancerous creature whose active existence had been hollowed out, almost empty, a shadow of the self he might have been had he not spent his life learning about other people, their adventures and heroic acts, gathering books and packaging them for still other people, a conduit through which lives and deeds of others passed, an observer when it came to the active. He had only lived in his head, retiring, shy and sensitive, a grown up child whose imagination ranged the world, engaged in all kinds of wonderful adventures. His parents' home in their pleasant suburb encouraged that, they were reserved and mostly silent, the house was filled with raw material for imaginative exploration – the library his mother and father had gathered between them, throughout their adult lives. So he'd learned to read early, knew a great deal about the world without ever having travelled, could answer questions on 'Top of the Form' to his mother's delight, but he voyaged without moving. From the first time he read *Gulliver's Travels*, that children's edition illustrated by Arthur Rackham Santa brought when he was six years old, his mind fixated on the strange and distant, and his studies followed accordingly, fascinated by the Wild West, cowboys and Indians, the dark heart of Africa, India and the East. But he wasn't a traveller, the family never went anywhere outside Britain, the car trips that his parents were always taking rarely even crossed the border into England. He would sit in the back while his father drove and his mother navigated, the big Bartholomew's road atlas open on her knees. Driving, touring, was a thing they shared, that brought them together, while he was in the back seat, elsewhere. He was always a reader, came to know a lot of stories about the world, yet in reality all he knew was books, and in a way, that's the adult he became, sitting in the back seat of life, reading about faraway places, about the past. Of the present, the real world beyond the pathways of his narrow Edinburgh routines of auction, house clearance, bookshop and pub, beyond the columns of newspapers, he really knew very little. Maybe, in contrast to his safe childhood, his reading emphasised the aspect of terror in the unknown, simultaneously stimulating a desire to know and a fear of not knowing. His parents were afraid of the world, they'd lived through wars and foreign places were full of enemies to them – perhaps his parents' caution made him overly timid and afraid, of taking risks, of love, or accident and death.

But the cancer changed everything. Something like that shifts a person's perspective in the most fundamental way. He'd felt a kind of wild ecstatic need to live while he still could, do what he could while he could, though of course what he could do was more circumscribed by the illness, and the treatment. Something in him that wanted to live had driven him to book that flight, to make his way to the airport, to board, fasten seatbelts and soar. To cross the fabled Rockies, so long a magical name is his gazetteer of knowledge. Sitting in his mother's little garden after she died, watching the planes as they flew in and out of the airport, he had realised that if he was going to die too, which he was sooner or later, he should at least experience a little life first.

And then there was the puzzle of his father, who'd died when he was still so young, who had seemed very old, as old as his classmates' grandfathers. He didn't come to collect his son from school very often as he was mostly at work, and when he did, he waited at the corner, wouldn't talk with other parents. He could be quite affectionate some-times, but he was always distant. Affection meant he might ruffle his son's hair, say 'That's my boy' when he got a question right or a good report card, which he invariably did, but never did his father praise him with what might have been called an exclamation of delight, no matter what his boy did. It was more as if he knew that was what he ought to say. His father was preoccupied, he had his cars, and his cars were all. His cars he could control. He could fix whatever went wrong.

Or so it had seemed. Now, forty years later, after the involuntary disclosures of his mother's dementia and his rummaging through her effects after she died, he knew that his father was born in Lerwick in 1884, to a widow in her thirties, a woman whose husband had been drowned whilst fishing from an open boat, who lived in the Shetland town until she herself died a very few years later. From the Scotland's People website, he knew that his father had then lived in what was the town poorhouse for a while, cared for by his maternal grandmother. They were both on the census of 1891 at that address. He knew that he had enlisted in Leith in 1912, that he became a motorised vehicle driver and that he was ultimately the personal chauffeur of the Earl of Angus during the war, that a driver then meant mechanic too. He knew that, when the Armistice came, he was offered the opportunity to continue as the Earl's personal chauffeur, but chose instead to emigrate to Canada. And he knew, as of a few months ago at his failing mother's stove-side, in the dusk while the tea pot bubbled, that his father came here to Cloud Falls. Or so the story seemed to go.

Lying there in the stifling warmth of the canyon night, windows open in the hope of channelling the cooling breeze the river brought, he found himself wondering if he could even be sure of what he thought he knew. He tried to think back to when his father was alive. Although he was old, he was a kind of royalty in their parish, as he drove the big van for Jenner's after they opened their depository on the edge of town, and everybody knew he'd been a general's driver in the first war. He, his son, was proud of him in a roundabout way, not for what his father was whilst he knew him, but for what he had once been. He remembered when he died, how his mother sold the over-sized spotless Standard and the ageing Bentley, and bought a little sports car, an MG, second-hand – only two seats, one for her, and one for him, 'her boy'. She went to work for Jenner's too then, in accounts. They really were like royalty to some, or it felt like that, those first few years. They were proud of Jenner's, the best shop in town, proud they had found a way to be safe and sound, to ultimately buying a house, having a car, and finally having a child.

He thought about his mother's home territory in the green farmland of West Lothian. They often went to visit Grandma and Grandad. But Shetland, his father's birthplace, always remained foreign to him. His father, whatever his experience of it was, didn't talk about it. He didn't seem to have any interest in it, which might have alerted him, if he'd been older, to something unhappy, deeply buried. His father's voice, as far as he could recall, had the sibilance of Edinburgh's softer accents. If anything, only the faintest hint of islands remained. Now he knew that his father had come from Shetland as a boy, orphaned, but as a child he'd wondered what had happened to his father's family, his other grandparents.

So it was a surprise when one day, soon after the funeral, he had to go with his mother to meet his father's cousin, a woman he hadn't known existed. And it hardly seemed possible that she should be alive, she was so frail and old, so foreign, so Shetlandic in her ways and her speech, despite living in Leith. That was the first time he'd ever visited a proper old tenement, such a narrow dark staircase with people living on top of one another in such proximity. It seemed to him it must be a den of thieves, the kind of Dickensian underworld he'd read about, and he watched from the old aunt's top flat window, worried that someone might make off with their car and leave them stranded there.

He slept fitfully, waking intermittently, but morning came, his first in the interior. Still half asleep, he sat up and gazed out the window. The sun hadn't risen high enough to light the canyon floor, but the very top of the mountain opposite was lit with a dazzling yellow glow, while the grey river seemed to babble a foreign language. And then he noticed, in the grassland on the floodplain below the inn, a woman was walking, looking around her carefully, stepping, stooping – picking berries maybe – so he switched on the camera and zoomed in. She moved slowly with a light-footed grace, dark hair covering her face from view, and he felt centuries swirl around her red-patterned skirt as it swept through the shrubs. He laughed. It was a tartan check.

Further to the left, the ospreys caught his eye, wings folded on their nest, that awkward huddle of sticks. He zoomed in and behind them, across the scrubland at the very edge of focus, he noticed in the distance what must be the Indian Church referred to in the guide – and behind that, barely visible on the far side of the river, the glint of something he guessed was the waterfall that John MacLeod gave his name to – the wrong name, of course, like all of the settler names. He decided to go there after breakfast. He had it in mind to taste the water he could see cascade down the canyon wall in the distance.

As he showered he went over in his mind what he knew about MacLeod. He had settled here in Cloud Falls around 1870, was first listed as the settlement's 'Toll collector and Telegraph Operator' in one of the province's early directories he'd found. By the early 1880s, he owned most of the property on the north side of the river, and in addition to his orchard, he operated a general store, had an interest in a greenhouse, a stable, and the Morton House Hotel. MacLeod's was one of first seed houses in western Canada, selling them in little brown paper bags with his name stamped on them. It was, for a while, quite an enterprise.

When he had dried himself off, he switched on his laptop to check a note he'd made in Vancouver, from the archive of *The Colonist* newspaper, a report that said: "MacCloud Falls is growing fast, and what with rival stores, hotels and railway enterprise is becoming quite a busy, bustling depot. 'MacCloudville' begins to assume quite the appearance of a small town, and presents a constant scene of business and enterprise. Mr. MacCloud's new store looms up grandly, being a building some eighty feet long by thirty, two storeys high, and having projecting dormitory windows along the roof. Importing directly from Canada and Great Britain and appointed agent for a number of influential firms, Mr MacCloud eminently deserves to be considered one of the most enterprising and successful merchants of this upper country."

The name was wrongly spelled throughout. He knew MacLeod was an Aberdonian whose father had been a shopkeeper in quite a poor quarter of that old city where he sold tobacco, whisky and essentials. After his father died, young John, then in his mid-twenties, appeared to have taken his share of what there was to inherit and set out for California, where there was gold to be found and fortunes to be made. He knew from some brief memoirs published in *The Colonist* shortly before MacLeod died that he had arrived in Victoria from the USA in 1859 where the pioneer spirit then building a new colony contrasted greatly with the decaying old town of Aberdeen he'd left behind. From the eloquence of his prose in those memoirs, it was easy to imagine the fine descriptions the émigré had sent home to his sister in Scotland, the one who had gone to Lerwick from Aberdeen as a schoolteacher and married a shopkeeper by the name of Lyle, who then had a first-born son called James. What tales of the wild frontier the émigré uncle must have told in his long letters to this Shetland family, sufficient indeed to turn a young boy's head and cause him to follow into the Gold Country himself.

He clicked on the portrait of John MacLeod he'd found in the BC archives. It wasn't dated, but he seemed quite young despite his full beard. Humour winked out from the lines around his eyes, eyes that gazed out at slightly different angles as if perhaps he squinted. A kindly quality too, but focused in scrutiny of something, the camera, the photographer, or something deeper maybe, an internal purpose, the fulfillment of a vision. His forehead was broad and his nose promi-nent, though the flash of the photo had obliterated some refinements of his features. He wore a checked jacket and a white cravat. In his breast pocket, almost lost in the corrupted image, was a pressed white handkerchief. This was the image of a man in his prime, confident of his schemes, the kind of picture he might have sent home to some pro-spective spouse or adoptee he was trying to persuade to join him on the frontier, the face of someone who was profiting from life in some satisfying way. There was nothing in his face to say he was a Scot, par-ticularly – northern European, perhaps, but he could have been English, Welsh, Irish, French, German or Dutch or Scandinavian, or whatever.

He could not be sure, but guessed this was the uncle who the young Jimmy Lyle joined in 1884, the man whose optimistic gaze had looked at this place in the long canyon's scope, had gauged its natural qualities, and foresaw in his waterfall the source of irrigation for the ranch he would establish. Had he at any point wondered about the rights of the native population to the land he staked? There was no evidence he had. But his adopted heir, his nephew, surely did later.

There was no one around in the dining room when the Scotsman went downstairs. The evidence of the tree planters having passed through was there in crumbs, banana skins and dirty dishes, though. Vince came through from the kitchen and greeted his guest, who asked about the books in the lounge as he filled his plate from the cold buffet. Vince told him they belonged to his absent wife, but didn't seem inclined to talk this morning as he had the night before. Take anything you want, Vince said. It's no skin off my nose. He made his apologies, said he had work to do and left.

The Scotsman ate quickly, packed a few things to take with him in his rucksack, and headed out into the thin morning sunlight, direct rays still to cascade over the ridge of crags. He crossed the empty Highway 8 in front of the inn towards the CPR rail-lines, where a fresh train of trucks stretched out of sight southwards, waiting for the hour when Ken got the message to make them roll. For now nothing moved in the CPR universe, except softly tumbling tumbleweed rolling slowly in a gentle breeze, infused with a scent – sagebrush, maybe.

He set out along the road in the direction of the falls. Up ahead, a small wooden sign bore the legend: CLOUD FALLS COMMUNITY HALL built 1907 by A. Clements. The numbers 3641 descended in a column beside it. The doors were locked, but the blocked-up windows had personalities – figures painted on boards, sharp black silhouettes on whitewash. In one was the outline of a man and a woman in what was clearly intended as native dress – with the schematic, in white on the man's torso, of a spindly bird, perhaps an eagle. Above them a black sun concealed an air-vent. In the next window, a portly Western couple stood face to face, their profiles sharp below the point where two Stetsons met. In a third was a woman in a tight bodice, a bustle, a three-feathered cocked hat – and in a small skylight above the door, a black silhouette cat.

He nosed around the outside. On the gable of the little hall was a commemorative wall of plaques, little brick-like tiles highlighted by means of relief, set into the plaster so that the names they bore protruded, but none at a height of more than four feet, as if perhaps the hands implanting them had belonged to children. He counted 77 – some he knew of, such as SPARK Jessie, the orchardist, her early-departed husband SPARK John, LYLE James, MACLEOD John, with CLEMENTS Archie, died 1922, above, as if denoting how he had superseded the early pioneer. And then there were names he didn't know: BILLY Stage George; GOGLIN Ernie; MUTCH Forrest and Bill; WONG Ying Yee; BERGERON 'Honest Paul'; SWARK 'Potato' Joe and Sarah. They spoke of a mix of cultures here among the good folk of the cross-ing – they did not mark graves, but were mementos of lives and deaths, surrounding their benefactor, the Vancouverite of propertied means who had installed the first power plant, and brought electricity to his hotel and to the citizens of the town he renamed Cloud Falls.

The Scotsman had read the story of how, in 1898, Clements had returned to Europe with his wife where they attended the World Exhi-bition in Paris and saw the latest horseless carriages, how he placed an order to have one of these vehicles shipped to him, how when it arrived more than three years later, he and Mrs Clements cruised down the two roads of Cloud Falls that led nowhere outside the town in this beau-tiful 1902 Wolsey with copper-coil radiator, high in the saddle with lamps on the side, and how the townspeople craned necks to capture a glimpse of this miraculous engine.

He walked on. The 'Indian church' he'd read about, and had glimpsed from his room through the zoom, stood at the south end of the village with only a little graveyard between it and the junction of new highway with old. Around it was an area of cabins, timber corrals with automobiles at various stages of decomposition. One cabin adver-tised, in a loose hand, Antiques.Art.Tools for Sale, around which lay an array of rusty barrels, hoses, wheelbarrows and other metal devices whose purpose was mysterious to him. A face looked from a small side window and the Scotsman realized this was the reservation, a tiny tri-angle of land in the middle of this huge canyon, fenced off and fenced in. This was a portal to Lyle's time, the long sore question of land rights that had preoccupied him in his later years, when he acted as secretary and scribe to the local chiefs.

The path to the church ran through the reservation, but there was a wire fence on either side, between the two. The church was amongst its congregation here but separate from it, and worse for wear. Its timber-tiled shingle walls were spotted with lost or splitting squares, the squat bell-tower sat like some shaggy mushroom cap waiting to open – all seemed less man-made than forest-given, and looked aban-doned now. The bell was still where it should be and the cross at the apex too, but there was a raven perched on top, admiring the panorama, unmoved by the transformation of tree to wood church to spirit house. He knew that the missionaries had come early to the province, of different hues and temperaments yet all driven to convert and civilize by that peculiar sense of superiority the self-convinced carried with them like a beacon. Little churches like this were the places where that boundless holy spirit focused its energies, where it was corralled, not allowed to roam and manifest in sun or moon, or beast or plant. These four square walls sent up a heavenly aspiration, from this reservation for the spirit, led by missionary voices. Multiple generations of ravens had seen them come and go, had sat crowing on the roof while they sang, and had cawed out a parting greeting when they left.

He stood and took the vista in, as this raven was doing. Beyond the actual reservation, in the distance the woman he'd glimpsed through the zoom from his room was gathering her berries at the river's edge, bending down while, behind her, the settler community lay across the river, and behind it again, dwarfing all, bare rock mountain with only the occasional tree clinging to what little soil there was. On the other side of the path that divided sacred from secular stood a sky-blue-painted, low-roofed building with a handwritten sign – CLOUD FALLS BAND OFFICE. The sign bore the same schematic of a skinny black eagle he'd seen on the window of the old community hall. Someone had blocked off the double-door wheelchair access on the end and a kind of porch was being erected in the middle. Someone seemed to be making a new home out of the old Band office.

The land looked different on either side of the pathway, as if an invisible border based on polarised perceptions of the world existed here, as if two separate histories defined themselves along this path. One recorded 150 years of attempted settlement, of enterprises small and large, successful for a time such as the orchards; the other, centuries of moving a little here, a little there, depending on the season, but never really leaving, just moving with the natural changes, successful because of that, until it was fenced in here, next to the little church and the graveyard by the highway. The graveyard was surrounded by a low fence, now in disrepair. The soil was stony desert dirt, heaped up to cover graves. The Scotsman lingered at the gate, but didn't go in, he'd save that for another day, but he could see the names on some of the nearest graves, surnames that matched some of those commemorated on the wall of the hall along the road.

So he walked on, eye drawn to the waterfall that MacLeod had used to irrigate the poor land and bring fertility. To get there, he had to cross the river again, this time on the new bridge, the one that carried the highway around Cloud Falls, bypassing the little town that had grown there. The footpath to the side of the highway was broad, the balustrade high and he felt no urge to leap. Crossing the river, the falls came into view in marvellous fashion. It was quite miraculous how it emerged from the canyon wall, as if some Old Testament prophet had struck the rock with a rod to bring it gushing forth. He knew that it was really the outflow of a hidden creek at a point where the canyon wall had slipped, yet still it seemed a wondrous thing that this pure water should be falling so extraordinarily from the dry desert slope. It wasn't only the fact that it was water that made it marvellous, there was plenty of that in the river, it was that it was able to be harnessed that made it so precious. The great river was too wild, too unpredictable – no man-made system could have survived its moods back in MacLeod's day.

He clambered down the giant quarried rocks that supported the new bridge on the far side, and met the old track beneath that headed along the riverside towards the falls, walking away from the settlement and out into the wild. The road went uphill at the side of the cleft in rocks from which the water spilled. Up close, it was a powerful flow, a drop of maybe a hundred feet. He could get near enough to dip his hand into one of the pools below, to taste that pure water, and the coldness surprised him. A small hut had a sign to say that this was the local water supply and should not be tampered with. This was the lifeblood of the community even now, though MacLeod's flumes were long gone.

He walked up the track, beyond the waterfall. The town receded into the distance, and the scale became that of mountains and canyons, not people and buildings. From high up he could see beyond the bend in the river, southwards. He sat a while and mused on this place. Here, away from people and their engines, the landscape was closer to Lyle's time. He imagined him arriving here, a lad from Shetland in a land just about as different as possible from the one he first knew. Lyle grew up by the sea with the salt tang on his lips, a low-lying place without trees where people huddled in ancient stone houses and eked a meagre living from a tumultuous ocean and diffident unyielding soil, where nothing grew big and the only giants were the storms, the crumbling cliffs. Here, far from the ocean, deep in a mountainous canyon, the river was master. He knew little of how it felt to live beside this torrent, but he understood how it dominated, how it was the highway in the days when the white men first came from the north, the Hudson's Bay Company's explorers in search of a trade route to the Pacific.

When Simon Fraser and his men first sailed through this territory in a great canoe, down the river that now bears his name – another wrong one – the N'laka'pamux believed them to be the Ones they knew from the stories, the Ones who were predicted. Fraser, they believed, was the Sun, his companions the Moon and Coyote. These strangers went on to build forts and trading posts, where the Nicola River met the Lower Thompson they called it 'Little Forks', and 'The Grand Forks' where the Nicola joined the Coldwater river – naming and claiming.

And that was how it was between the two peoples, for half a century, until the Gold Rush. Then the whites came from the south, hordes of them, mad for a strike. The canyon was over-run. Douglas's government in Victoria tried to control it, but the flood was already in full spate, and the fever had to run its course, no intervention was possible, so swift was the contagion. And within a decade, the prospectors had moved further north, though their supplies still passed up the canyon by barge and trail.

He began his walk back towards the town, thinking that nothing is ever really lost to us as long as we remember it, and that maybe that's what he was doing here, trying to remember, not only these lives, but the lives of those whose child he was, whose offspring he was. And even more than that, he was trying to find out what they'd forgotten, or perhaps had never known, to piece together the story.

He clambered up the rocks from old trail to new highway, and as he stood on the new bridge again, musing on the history of this place, a gentle roar approached from behind, growing ever louder, overlaying the river's now familiar tones. At first he thought it was a truck, one of those North American giants he'd seen from the Greyhound, but as it got nearer it sounded more like some kind of swarm. Turning, he saw a crowd of motorbikes, big machines, a biker-gang, come rolling onto the far end of the bridge in formation.

As they passed, deafening him, a sense of power emanated – men and machines, conquering the landscape, an echo of Sigurd and his mechanical pulleys. A fleet, a posse, a chapter, of chrome and gas, of mirror and shades, cruised by. He had the camera in his hand and, as the bikers streamed away to the other bank, he took a picture as the last two bikes passed. The guy nearest raised his gloved middle finger and when the Scotsman checked the picture on the viewer, it was perfectly focused in shot. Otherwise it was a flock of shades, a herd of leather, a shoal of shiny chrome roaring up the highway, issuing a collective roar that echoed through the canyon. The air shimmered heat as the vision passed. Streaky gas exhaust fumes hung above the asphalt as the last bike rounded the bend and disappeared.

The roar slowly faded and then the river's rush emerged from where it had been hiding in the engine noise, almost a hush now by comparison. That gloved middle finger, a greeting, a beckoning, a threat, hung in his mind. He seemed to have no choice but to follow, like a child who had seen the circus pass through town for the first time, both scared and captivated by the strange glamour of the chapter's procession.

The great highway he'd travelled aboard the Greyhound the day before, he now walked, keeping to the kerb. For a while it was quiet, and then a large crimson truck passed, a Ford with the legend FX4 OFFROAD on its rear wing. A couple of guys sat in the back, leaning against the cab, and they stared at him, said something and laughed as the truck pulled away. It struck him how walking here in the interior, where trucks and cars and bikes were essentials, must mark a person out as odd, as some poor demented creature not capable of operating a vehicle.

Here, where he wore sandals, shorts and a baseball cap, gear he'd hoped might help him blend in with the locals, walking alone along the highway was enough to show him to be a stranger. It was a thing not done. Even the great rocky face of the mountain they called The Chief seemed to frown down at him, quizzically.

Despite that, walking along the highway meant he could see over the bypassed township below, and at that slow pace he could study it without appearing to spy. But it was getting pretty hot as the sun finally rose above the canyon wall. There was a kind of motor graveyard at this end, where a beat-up yellow school-bus, a few small lorries and trucks were jammed in together just below the riverside railway embankment. One lorry at least seemed to have been moored there, its box trailer concreted into the ground, and he reckoned none of them were going anywhere again, other than slowly down into the shallow desert soil, atom by atom. Another shack had accumulated a forest of pipes and hoses and ladders around its entrance, topped off with an impressive display of antlers nailed above the door, and at the far end a long trailer home had a large Canadian flag planted at its side, though it hung as if wilted and hid its maple leaf. Another low prefabricated building had a rough hand-painted sign which read:

Community Spirit

includes everyone

use at your own risk

It didn't look as if anyone had taken up the invitation in a decade or so.

The grey asphalt of the highway with its white and yellow lines stretched out ahead of him. He kept walking, passing a small garage business set back from the road at the foot of the mountain, old cars and trucks lined up outside. He took some photos from the road but didn't stop. He kept on, past an abandoned motel, a fragment of punctured tyre, a triangular yellow road-sign with the black outline of a very upright Stetson-wearing tractor driver who seemed joined to his vehicle at the waist, like some weird centaur.

In the heart of the settlement, the houses looked better maintained, their painted wooden exteriors glistening in the sun. And then, rather incongruous amongst the squared-off settler dwellings, he spotted a bunch of bound poles emerging from the apex of a canvas triangle, the unmistakable top of a tipi. This time he stopped to take a photo and, using the zoom, was able to make out the pattern on the cloth, a single purple stripe above a circle of roundish white shapes. When he studied them, he recognised the sequence of the lunar cycle as the moon grew slowly from new towards full. Below that, on a base of white, a shape that could have been a branch or an antler seemed to support the moon. It was a smart design, tasteful muted greys and pinks. The tipi looked altogether contemporary and relatively new.

He walked on. Another sign appeared, this time a yellow square with the silhouette of a ram and the words CAUTION BIG HORN SHEEP NEXT 4 KM, but he kept walking, half hoping he'd sight one of these fabled beasts, feeling the heat of the day begin to burn his neck. The thought of a cool drink began to nag at him. He knew there were a couple of places, a motel and a pub, and the image of a beer took tempting shape in his mind. In the distance he could make out a sign, and as he approached he saw that it said

RUMOURS
BEST FOOD IN THE CANYON
BREAKFAST $6.49

A couple of cars were parked at the side, a big old Cadillac with a sign behind the windshield that invited OFFERS and a Mercedes, but when he tried the restaurant door it was locked, and a small sign pinned there said CLOSED. No explanation or indication how long it had been closed, or whether it was likely to open again. The image of the waiting beer faded a little, his throat was now on fire like it had been during the days of the radiotherapy. A picture of a giant ice-cream cone teased him. But another sign on a long, low, almost window-less log cabin surrounded by a timber fence a little further down the slope towards the town offered fresh hope:

VALHALLA
PUB

Below the main sign, someone had added a smaller improvised one that said 'GO CANUCKS GO!' Ice hockey fans, obviously.

The log cabin looked as if it was open, as if it must sell beer, and so he made his sweaty way down the road off the highway towards the township. The car-park came into view, and there he saw the motor-bikes that had passed him just an hour or so before, now parked up, a mass of chrome and leather, a herd of frozen steeds tethered obediently outside a saloon. There must have been thirty of them. So this was where the chapter had stopped their roar. Here, where the beer he now fetishized could be obtained, and him in this strange garb, the clothes he'd thought would help him blend in, with his camera slung over his shoulder. He smiled, thinking of the gloved finger, but he was so thirsty, so overwhelmed by the heat of desert noon, he headed towards the door.

He pushed the heavy solid wood. It swung slowly open on gloomy interior walls of undressed logs, and the sound of heavy metal, deep voices talking and laughter spilled out. But the bare wood had been highly decorated by an array of pictures and memorabilia. It was a shrine to all things motorcycle, as gaudy inside as the outside was plain. As he looked around the cavernous timber walls seemed to spin away, opening a chamber that seemed much bigger than the frame. The chapter were sitting and standing around a group of tables in front of a corner stage, above which hung a giant screen showing a music video. It looked like ZZ Top.

On a raised dais along the far wall, a perfect motor machine stood above all on the altar of worship in this temple to the god of rides. The chrome gleamed in a spotlight that shone down from above, and the red leather seat looked plush and moist like flesh. The handlebars, if that was what they called them here, stood high and proud, like the horns of a bull or a bighorn sheep, but horns with large mirrors. On the side of the bike, along the gas-tank, a glistening logo spelled out Harley Davidson.

Below and around this impressive shrine, the gathering of bikers drank lager beers, while a young waitress in high heels and short skirt distributed pizza which they hungrily scooped up from the giant chrome platters she bore towards them from the bar. At first no one looked around as he entered feeling half-naked and completely out of his element. He didn't cross the floor of the cabin, but sat on a stool at the far end of the bar by the door. He took off his cap and waited. The barmaid, a matronly woman wearing glasses, was pulling pint after pint of lager, and talking loudly to her customers as if they were old friends. He couldn't hear what they were saying over the sound of MTV, or whatever channel it was that dominated the big screen, but the sound of loud guffawing carried across the length of the long wooden bar to him. A middle-aged man with a long blond pony-tail emerged from the back carrying still more platters of pizza, which he set on the counter, from where the girl took them to the waiting hungry.

From his vantage point, he stole glances at the company and noticed they were far from a rough, scarred crowd. Their leathers were clean, new-looking, and those who'd shed their outer skins revealed t-shirts that looked neatly pressed. The badges and chains that decorated their gear were brightly polished, their tattoos artistic, not the kind a biker might have carved into his arm in some fit of frenzy. It seemed as if even their scars might be delicately sewn.

At last the matron finished pulling pints, and acknowledged his presence with a nod. 'Be with you in a minute,' she called over. He nodded back and smiled, began fiddling with his wallet, desperate for liquid.

'So, what'll it be?' she asked, finally.

'A beer, please.'

'Molson?'

He didn't know what that was, but answered in the manner he was getting used to. 'Sure.'

She wasn't fooled. 'You British?'

He shook his head. 'No, Scottish.'

'Scottish?' She smiled. 'My grandfather was from Glasgow!'

'Really? Seems to me a lot of people who settled here were Scottish – you, know, from place-names and so on.'

'Sure, a lot of Scots came out to BC. So what brings you up here?' she asked as she set the longed-for glass of beer in front of him, and waited for his answer, although there was already a queue at the far end of the counter.

He took a long draw from the glass. It was ice-cold. Perfect. 'I'm researching a story.'

'You a writer?'

'Sort of, yes. I'm staying over at the inn for a few days.'

'So what's it about?' she asked again. A few voices called out to her, but she dismissed them with a gesture of her hand.

'A man who came out here from Scotland in 1884. James Lyle. He was quite well-known around here at one time.'

'Hmmm, name's familiar, not sure why. Listen, as you can see, we're a bit busy here right now, but if you want to stop by in the morning I'll be free to chat then. I'd like to talk about Scotland with you. My great-grandmother was Marjory Kennedy-Fraser.'

'The song-collector?'

'You've heard of her?'

'I certainly have. Her song settings were very popular once upon a time. I think I may have a few records somewhere back home.'

'Really? That's great. Listen, stop by here in the morning, around 11. I'll ask around about that guy, what was his name?'

'Jimmy Lyle.'

A leather-clad customer called to her from the far end of the bar. 'Hey Marie, get yer sexy ass down here and serve your real customers.'

She shouted back, 'At least this guy's a gentleman with some manners!' Then, to the Scotsman, she said, 'Okay, I'll ask if anybody knows about him. I'm from Alberta myself, we've only been here around eight years. But maybe some of the regulars will have heard of him. What was it he did?'

'He did a whole lot of different things. Came out to work on his uncle's estate to begin with, but then he sort of went native, as they used to say. Married a local woman, one of how do you say it, the N'laka'pamux?' He tried to wrap his tongue around the pronunciation as best he could.

Her face changed a little at that point, the welcoming smile a mention of Scotland had brought seemed to disappear. 'Your guess is as good as mine,' she muttered. Marie's expression was hard to read. 'Jimmy Lyle? And he lived round here when?'

'From 1884 until around 1915.'

'Guess that's too long ago for anyone to remember him then,' she said. The chapter began baying for her attention, so she turned away, heading back to their end. He lifted up his glass and drank down the rest of his Molson's thirstily. The noise level was rising and the pizza was almost demolished. One or two of the bikers had fastened their attention on him now, and he felt their interest grow in a none too welcome manner. His knobbly white Scottish knees poked ridiculously out of those stupid shorts as he sat on his barstool. How could they bear to wear so much leather in these temperatures?

Just as he was draining his glass, Marie called over from where she was pouring still more lager. 'Hey, by the way, if you wanna drop by later tonight, we're having a special on food for the hockey match. 8 o'clock puck down. It's Stanley Cup finals. First time the Canucks have got there since 94. Everybody's really stoked about it.'

'Well, I'll see. Looks like it may get a bit rowdy here later.'

'These guys? Na, don't worry, they're pussies. Be long gone up the canyon by then, anyway. This is just a stop-off for them. A pizza and a beer, then they're gone. Tonight it'll just be the locals, and there's more than enough room for you. Besides, you'll get a chance to talk to a few people about your story.'

He thanked her, said he just might do that. As he got down from the barstool, he took another look around the timber walls of the cabin at the array of bike memorabilia. 'Amazing place,' he told her. 'I must have a proper look around when I come back.'

'Sure,' she said. 'The guys often bring us stuff, you know, bike-stuff, photos. We get people from all over. Next week, if you're still around, it's the big canyon burn-up.'

He didn't know what she meant, but she'd said it as if everyone should know. It sounded as if it might be some sort of bonfire, maybe for midsummer. She pointed towards the door. 'Winner gets to do one of those.' He looked in the direction she indicated, unsure what she was talking about, but before he could ask she had gone off to serve another leather-jacket, a big old man with a grey handlebar moustache.

Outside the bright sun was a shock and his eyes took a half-minute to adapt. When they had, the waiting herd of chrome beasts hadn't moved, but they seemed less potentially aggressive, less fierce now that he'd seen their riders close up. That gloved middle finger, maybe it was just for the camera. He moved through the bikes, admiring the engineering and the aesthetic without really understanding either, but it reminded him his father had once owned a motor-bike, back in the days before he could afford a car. He'd seen photos of it, but the where and the when, the detail, was a mystery. And now, with his mother gone, how would he ever know? Maybe there would be something written on the rear of the photos? Sometimes she had done that, particularly in the early days when they were first together and touring. Just a name or a phrase, like 'Boat of Garten – ospreys'.

His reverie was broken by the sound of a train on the far side of river. The little town of Cloud Falls lay between him and it. His highway walk had carried him north of it. The pub was the last building. As he stepped from the shadow of the log cabin, the sun caught the exposed skin on his neck again and he realised he really would have to get some sun-cream somehow. Maybe there was somewhere he could try besides the store? He thought he'd ask there.

As he walked down the road back into the town, he noticed the street sign read Acacia Avenue. This must be those acacias Lyle's uncle John planted back in the 1870s, along the road that ran from his new store to his new house. They looked old enough, all gnarled by the desert extremes, some had clearly either died or been taken down, for the avenue now had a lot of gaps. But the scent of what remained was strong. He wondered if the people living here today such as Marie even knew why the acacias were here, how an old Scots pioneer had laid out his plans for a fruit farm, complete with beehives, and the aim of exporting acacia honey, all to be carried away to the south by the marvellous new railroad that came to course the canyon's length and on to Vancouver.

The station at Cloud Falls was long gone now, but as he walked along Acacia Avenue he began to whistle 'Canadian Pacific', that Hank Snow song his country & western loving mother used to sing. He could picture the album cover even now, the dungaree-clad singer with red neckerchief, smiling puckishly, dwarfed by giant railroad wheels behind. Strange how these random childhood images persisted while so much of note was forgotten. The chorus came to him – Canadian

Pacific, carry me ten thousand miles. Or was it two? He supposed two
was more likely.

He knew the last spike on the railroad connecting eastern Canada
with the new province of British Columbia had been driven close to
here. Widow Spark had written about the sense of hopeful occasion
that everyone felt for the new colony and its prosperity, when at last
the dream of Lord Strathcona was fulfilled and the tracks reached the
rapidly expanding new city of Vancouver, where the immense wealth of
natural resource that land and sea had to offer would shape fortunes
far more lasting, in a manner a deal more gracious than the greed for
gold that had first tempted white men up the Fraser Valley and into the
canyon. But that was all book learning, things he'd read 5000 miles
away. He'd studied all he could, but this was detailed reality that no
remote preparation could prepare him for.

The burning sun on his bare neck was not virtual, some digital
version of sunshine. He suddenly felt exhausted, like a wave of the
fatigue the radiotherapy had caused hit him. He felt weak, just a little
ginger-haired dot, walking around pointlessly going nowhere, realising
his own folly for smoking all those years, the futility of this mad adventure he'd set out on. Maybe he wasn't even going to write the book.
Cancer hadn't changed him fundamentally. He felt like the same 'fool
boy' his father sometimes used to chide.

Yet there had been so many peculiar coincidences, so many clues
that seemed to draw him here, even right up until meeting the woman
on the plane. And however tiny he felt in relation to this landscape, it
was sublimely, wildly beautiful here, the way the river swept through
the canyon, the way the scrubby slopes rose to the scarps above, to the
great mass of rock that crowned it all. It was exhilarating. So he pushed
the doubt away.

Dorothy was in the store. She reckoned it was just possible that
Sally in the Post Office would have sun-block as she was the local
agent for Avon, if he called by her in the old school. So he bought
some more bottled water and set off in the direction he'd been given,
walking deeper into the little huddle of settler houses musing on the
thought of Avon calling on any of them here in the canyon. The town
seemed deserted as he strolled down the road in the hot sun. No one
sat on porches, no life showed except a couple of fairly fierce dogs that
growled and barked as he passed. Luckily they were chained up and,
though they pulled at the extreme of their tethers, could not escape.

The old school turned out to be the long low prefab with the community spirit sign he'd seen from the highway earlier. Sally's post office was a small vestibule, probably once a cloakroom, with a kitchen in rear. A desk had been fashioned in the wall, and here he found the Post Officer, a little old grey-haired lady with half-frame glasses reading a magazine. She looked up lazily at first, even a little displeased at being interrupted, and then, as if adjusting her vision and noting he was a stranger, seemed interested.

'Sun-block?' she said, when he told her Dorothy had sent him. 'Oh! Well, let me see.' She got down off a tall stool, revealing just how tiny she was, and rummaged in a cupboard. She brought out Avon product after Avon product, and finally emerged with a squeezable tube, which she proudly placed on the counter.

'Now let me see, with tax, that's nine dollars straight. You just passing through?' she asked, as he pulled out his wallet.

'I'm staying at the inn for a while. I'm interested in a man who lived here long ago, that is, back around the turn of the century – the last century, I mean.'

Old Sally's eyes lit. 'Really? Now who might that be?'

'A man called Lyle.'

'Ah!' she said. 'Jimmy Lyle.'

It was the first positive response he'd had since he got there.

'You've heard of him?'

'Well, sure. He was a friend of my father's. I don't recall him myself, but my father sometimes talked about him. So what makes you so interested in Jimmy Lyle you've come all the way up here, and from Scotland too, I think from your accent?'

'You're right, I'm from Edinburgh. He's a relative of mine, I think. And I'm thinking of writing a book about him, his life.'

'Well, the people you should really talk to are Hesther and Kyle. They live in his old house, down by the river. You've maybe seen it? The one with the tipi out back? At least, that was one of his houses. He lived other places round here too, I believe.'

'I saw the tipi earlier, yes. So, this Hesther and...'

'... Kyle.'

'Are they interested in Lyle?'

'Oh yes, Hesther knows a lot about him. They're not from here, you understand, they only just moved over from the island two years ago.'

'The island?'

'Vancouver Island – anyways, when they heard his old house was on the market, and they just upped sticks and bought it. That's how keen they are on Jimmy Lyle.'

Although this seemed encouraging, there was something in the tone of her voice that suggested to him she didn't altogether share the new arrivals' enthusiasm.

'So, could I call on them, do you think?'

'Well, maybe, but they're not always around. They travel all over the province to these gatherings, you know... other people like them.' Again, there was hint of something like disapproval in the way she spoke, this sweet little old lady with her half-frame specs who kept the Post Office going, and perhaps the gossip mill too. He was curious. Villages all had sides, their local versus incomer tensions too. But 'people like them' seemed a heavy nuance. He had to ask.

'So what kind of people are they?'

'Oh, I don't mean nothing, but I hear they're involved in what folks on tv sometimes call the alternative lifestyle. If you know what I mean.' She seemed to wink at him. What exactly could she mean?

He wasn't sure how best to enquire, so he said, 'I suppose having a tipi in your garden is a bit alternative. Do they live in it?'

'No no, Hesther is a healer. A spiritual healer. She uses the tipi for her sessions.'

Again, something in way she spoke that last word seemed dismissive, if not outright disapproving. Sessions – in a tipi! Like it was some form of occult practice, and Post Office Sally couldn't frank it with her rubber ink-stamp of approval.

'So how long are you staying for?' she asked.

'I'll be here a week or two, I think. I'm Bert, by the way. I want to see the places Jimmy Lyle lived, talk to people.'

'Well you know, Wednesday is free soup day here in the centre. You'd be welcome to come along, and you'll get to meet Hesther and Kyle that way too, because they're the ones who make the soup.'

'Free soup day?'

'Well, it's not just soup, there's bread and salads and sometimes people bring cakes and things they've made. It's a new idea Kyle dreamt up, to try to bring the community together a bit. These days people don't mix the way they used to do. It was a great place here once upon a time, back in the days of the Spark lady. She was Scottish, you know. She and her husband had a huge fruit farm, orchards all over the place and they grew all kinds of things, though apples were the main crop. She even won prizes for them at the Empire Exhibition in London, and the King of England himself asked for Widow Spark's apples. It's all in her book she wrote when she was old. I think I have a copy somewhere if you're interested?'

'Actually, I've read it. I've got a copy back in Scotland. It was very interesting,' he said.

'Well then, you'll know she knew Jimmy Lyle very well, they even came out here together along with her husband – they were to work for his uncle, John MacLeod.'

'Yes, that was all very interesting. She didn't have too much to say about Jimmy Lyle in her book though.'

'Well, why would she? It was her book, after all. Anyways, you can see her place from here, just across the school field there.' She pointed through the window behind her towards a row of wooden houses.

'I didn't realise her house was still standing,' he said, peering out. She seemed pleased to be able to tell him something he didn't already know and came round to the customer's side of the counter, then took him over to a bigger window in the schoolroom wall, so she could point out exactly where it was.

'It's in pretty bad shape right now, I'm afraid. I tried to get the community interested in preserving it, because it's local history and dates right back, but so far we haven't managed to do anything. Seems it's owned by some of her great-grandchildren down in Vancouver and they can't agree on who should get it, and so nothing happens. They don't even come here now to take care of it, so every year it's a little closer to being a ruin. It's very sad when you think of everything she did for this community. But you can't tell the young folk, they don't want an old house like that, they want it all modern, open plan or whatever they call it. Not the kind of house I grew up in.'

She seemed to drift away into some memory or another. 'I remember her,' she said after a while. 'Not clearly though. It would have been when I was around 5 or 6, just before she gave it up at the beginning of the war. A very small woman, but always well-dressed and busy.'

He thought then of his father, and asked if she had ever known a man by the name of Johnson, a young Scotsman who had lived here for a while in the thirties, but she shook her head and said no. Her eyes were narrowed behind her glasses, her forehead lined, as if searching through some vault of memory.

'I'll try to come along to free soup on Wednesday then, as you say. And thanks for this.' He put the Avon sun cream in his bag. 'So glad you had some. Had no idea the weather would be so hot up here.'

'What?' she asked. She hadn't heard a word he'd said, so deep in the past had she been.

'I said I'll see you on Wednesday for free soup, then?'

'Oh no, I won't be there. The Post Office is closed on Wednesdays. But I'm very pleased to have met you, Mr...?'

'Johnson... Bert Johnson.' he told her.

'And you're from where, did you say?'

'Scotland. Edinburgh.'

'Ah! A lovely place. Or so I believe. Not that I've ever been to Britain. But no doubt we'll be meeting again at some point if you're staying a while. You could come for supper some evening. I'd like to hear more about what you're writing.'

'I haven't really started the writing properly yet. This is just research, you know, taking notes and that sort of thing.'

'Ah well, still, I hope we can have another chat. I have a lot more I could tell you about this place. Things not written down in any book. The secret history of Cloud Falls, you could say.' And she winked at him again, behind her half-frame glasses, and chuckled to herself as if sucking on some very juicy little secrets that she might just be prepared to share. 'I'm Mrs White, Sally, by the way.' And she offered him a delicate little hand, covered in liver spots and slightly arthritic, the skin loose across thwarted bones. He shook it gently and she chuckled again. 'I'm very pleased to meet you, Bert. I can tell you're a historian like myself,' she said.

'That I am, Sally. I love nothing better,' he told her, as he opened the door to leave.

He lost no time in applying the Avon sun-cream once he was outside, so soft and soothing to his burning neck and arms and legs, then wandered over the school playing field towards what he now knew to be Widow Spark's home. It was sadly dilapidated, as Sally had assured him it was. The white paint was peeling off everywhere, and the picket fence around the garden was broken down and missing in places. Weeds grew up through decking which looked rotten here and there. The shutters across the windows hung loosely skewwhiff, as if the hinges had given way. From the side gutter, a small tree had sprouted to quite some height. He didn't dare go too close, as he felt sure Sally was watching and would certainly disapprove of any sacrilegious entry into the sacred sanctum of the widow's ground.

Instead he simply stood for a while in the shade of a cottonwood tree, taking photos and thinking back over the little memoir he had ordered from the bookseller he knew in Victoria, how delighted he'd been to get the package and read the testimony the old fruit farmer had recorded in her twilight years. The book had been quite a success in the province, from what he could find out. It represented a glimpse of those years now lost in the early settlement of the interior, when the imperial connection to the old country was still very strong, and it was valuable record of the struggle of those pioneers to turn the natural wilderness to productivity. She described her life in Aberdeenshire, where she had worked in a school, the classmate who had fixed his mind on her when he was still a lad and came back home when he had established himself in British Columbia, with the determined aim of proposing, marrying her and taking her back out with him. He was an orchardist to trade, who had been one of the men contracted to erect the telegraph system to the coast, and when the gang brought wire to MacLeod Falls, he met Lyle's uncle John, a fellow Aberdonian who had taken on the post of telegraph operator there. With MacLeod's dream for his estate, the plans for orchards and so forth, it seemed like a fated encounter, so when the telegraph job was over, he headed back up the canyon to work for MacLeod, and set about the task of making the dream a reality. MacLeod had the vision to bring the water from the falls to irrigate what otherwise was an impossibly barren stretch of desert, but he was no orchardist. Without John Spark's skill, the plan would never have worked so well. But work it did, and by the time Spark returned to Scotland to seek the hand of his sweetheart, MacLeod had expanded his premises and his ambition accordingly. He had persuaded a nephew of his to come out to join him, a young man who would inherit, as MacLeod himself had no heir. And all perhaps would have been well, had the lovely young Scottish bride not caught the eye of the proprietor, to the point where he would find excuses to send her husband off somewhere so he himself could seek her company. Scandalous, potentially, though Widow Spark in her memoirs made it perfectly plain that nothing unsavoury ever took place, despite his attempts. But maybe there was more to tell, rotting in the timbers of this old settler house in the desert of the canyon, secrets which the widow had kept but the post office lady knew and wanted to share with the right listener, a historian like herself.

Cool now, thanks to the shady embrace of the cottonwood tree, and soothed by the power of Avon, he took a swig of water and headed back into the sun. It was after 1pm and he thought it was time to cross the river again, to return to the inn, to write his journal and take a siesta in the faux-Mexican adobe of the oldest operating hotel in British Columbia.

He found a partly shaded path along the CNR line, and strolled along thinking back to the week he'd spent in Vancouver, and the woman he'd met. He couldn't work her out – at times so open and friendly, so funny, so affectionate and even sexy that last night when they had smoked a tiny reefer she'd produced from her pocket as they walked through the balmy late night air after the hockey, when she came to his room and lay on his bed. But then when she picked him up the next morning to take him to the Greyhound, she'd been so distant, so formal, like a stranger again, as if he was a cold caller she hadn't the time nor the desire for, as if the intimacy they'd shared had never happened. Everyone had moods, different sides to their personality, but in her case it was as if she became a different person, could switch from one to the other without the slightest prompt or warning. Not that it really mattered. He wasn't in any kind of state to get involved with anyone, he knew exactly what he was, a cancer survivor whose remaining hair was falling out, and whatever attraction he might have held for women was long diminished. He'd accepted that, those long months living alone at his mother's place after she died, observing his face in the mirror every day.

Yet she stayed in his mind, and wouldn't depart. They had connected, they were cancer twins. Some people just couldn't cope with proximity to the illness, as if it was contagious, as if they'd fall victim just by being in the same room, just as some others came forward with offers of assistance, people who'd never been that close, as if they'd been summoned by the need to minister to the sick. Who knew why, and what distinguished them? Some he had loved and valued had disappeared completely from his life. Some he didn't really know before had become confidants, had shown him love, a side of themselves he hadn't intuited.

But she, this woman he'd met, seemed to do both, according to some mysterious mood pattern. She was there, close, caring, then absent, lost in her own mind, whatever the reason.

In this great wilderness, where human beings held the barest hold on the little space they'd cleared for themselves, all that seemed fairly irrelevant. Here was the river, the bridge barrier easily surmounted, and certain death below. He stepped onto the planks and stared down at the violence of water current. No long drawn out psychodrama of hope frustrated, no desperate need to prove anything, no one to please, not even oneself – and no more mother. Just the inevitability of a swift release. It would be easy. He only had to lift himself up onto the iron rail and then lean forward. In a matter of seconds, the impact would kill him. In no time his earthly remains would be miles downstream. If he was found at all, he'd be unrecognisable. Just a battered, bloated body. Perhaps headless, like those miners found long ago.

And was that why he'd come here, at a deep level, subconsciously, because of a death wish like she had suggested? Not really to try to write the book he'd always dreamt of writing, but just to find a good place to die. His own Sick Heart River. Maybe. He placed both hands on the iron balustrade and eased himself up until his feet were off the concrete and his weight was evenly distributed above and below, the tipping point. It would be easy. And for an instant he was almost falling, before something, some instinct seemed to halt him, like a force grabbing his ankles and pulling him back. He fell to the wooden floor of the bridge, sweating from the heat of the sun, and felt some internal source burn him, from the core of his being outward.

In his mind he had been ready, had been so since he came to terms with the diagnosis, but his body refused to fall. For some reason it wanted to live a while longer, despite the prognosis, despite the depression that had clouded everything. There was a curiosity. So he got to his feet, and walked on to the end of the bridge, the urge gone. His feet seemed to have decided, his legs too. Maybe it was as simple as that – what the body wants, it has to get. The body wants to cross, not jump. The mind follows, eyes perhaps glancing at the great river below wistfully, but the great notion fades, step upon step.

He made his way across safely, walked along the rail track, head suddenly void of thought. Back at the inn, there was no sign of Vince and still no wi-fi. He helped himself to one of the raisin bran muffins and put a loon in the honesty box. Then he heard the sound of a woman's voice and a dog bark echoing from upstairs, and went to investigate. Piles of laundry lay outside bedroom doors and from one a voice sang some song he didn't know. He knocked on the open door, a little Yorkshire terrier came dashing towards him barking, and the young woman he'd met the day before looked up suddenly from her task of changing sheets, dyed pink hair straggling round her face.

The terrier growled at him. 'Don't mind her, she's just frightened,' she said. 'Are you looking for something?'

'I was looking for Vince. He said he was going to fix the wi-fi this morning, but it's still not working.'

'There's never been wi-fi here,' she laughed.

'Never?'

'No. Not in all the time I've been working here anyway.' She looked him over. 'You a writer or something?'

He nodded. 'That's pretty cool,' she said. 'I write poetry myself. Not that I've ever had anything printed but you know, it's good to do it. Helps me make sense of how I'm feeling and stuff.' She finished tucking in the sheets and scooped the dog up into her arms. Its little doggy face poked out, no longer growling, but secure. 'So, you been out exploring the metropolis this morning?'

'A bit,' he said. 'I walked down to the junction with Highway 8, and then back along the highway on the other side of the river.'

'Not so much to see, I guess?'

He smiled, recollecting the people he'd met. 'Oh I don't know. I ran into a biker gang over at the Valhalla. That was quite exciting.'

'Oh yeah, I saw them too when I came over to work. But those guys, they're not real bikers. Just weekenders, you know, vacationers, suits up from Vancouver or Seattle, doing the canyon in their expensive leathers. They pass through here all the time, sometimes stay here at the inn. Now I could tell you all about real bikers. When I was younger, like sixteen, my guy – my ex, actually – me and him rode all over Canada, out east, up the Trans Alaskan, and down to the states. Route 66. Those were real road trips, I can tell you. Some of the scrapes we got into, wow-we. Kinda fun though. But he turned out bad, and so I ended up here in little old Cloud Falls living with my mom. And Tyler here. Isn't that right, my little precious?' She lifted the Yorkie up level with her face and planted a kiss on its hairy mouth. Little ribbons twisted into her hair gave the dog a doll-like look. It was hard to square this baby sweetness with a biker girl past.

'So, anyway, no wi-fi?' he said. 'And no mobile signal?'

'Mobile signal?'

'Sorry, I mean cell phone.'

'Ah, no. Fraid we're a bit cut-off up here. Landlines only. You get used to it, I guess, though sometimes I just take such a hankering to be off on a bike again. Specially this time of year.'

He left Tyler and Rosie to wrestle with more bedsheets and duvet covers, and went downstairs into the lobby. Out on the terrace, the evidence of smokers and coffee-drinkers sat on the tables. The stink from the ashtrays made him glad he'd stopped, but all the same he felt a wave of regret when he thought about all the mornings he himself had spent with coffee, cigarettes and a good book, and a sudden rush of desire for a smoke gripped him. It was a feeling he got from time to time, like a vacuum would suddenly appear in his lungs, the memory of something that should be there but wasn't any longer. Like a lost lover, whose toxic presence was once everywhere, whose absence felt both sad and welcome.

He lay on the bed and prepared to write his journal. Down below the inn, he saw the river constant as ever, and the ospreys nesting on the pylon platform. Only the giant chick was there, stepping from taloned foot to taloned foot, as if waiting impatiently for something. The village on the far side seemed more familiar now. He had learned a bit, knew there was a single tipi in the back garden of Lyle's house where a kind of alternative group gathered, that little old Sally kept the post office, the community spirit and the gossip running in the shutdown school, and that gangs of weekend bikers called into Valhalla for beer and pizza in the shrine to Harley Davidson, run by the greatgrand-daughter of Marjorie Kennedy-Fraser. And he had learned that old Widow Spark's house, which must be the oldest surviving dwelling since John MacLeod's original one was gone, was slowly returning to wilderness. He had walked the perimeter, seen the falls where the magical transformative water came from, the Indian church, the reservation, the highway that now bypassed the settlement.

After he'd written his journal, he decided to go to Valhalla for the big match as Marie had suggested. Up here in the canyon, though it was a five-hour drive from the city, the hockey fever seemed just as strong. While he made ready, the huge rocky crag on the opposite side turned the most brilliant roseate shade, and then a slow tide-line of dusk rose up from the river in the valley floor until it covered the whole of the canyon.

It was just after seven in the evening and the sun had long dropped behind the canyon wall by the time he headed out from the inn, this

time wearing long trousers and jacket, clothes a little less conspicu-
ous. It was quite cold now, and the canyon wind blew as ever. Yet if
he looked up, the sky still glistened with an opalescent amber light
above the steep crags. Crossing the bridge came easier – no urge to leap.
Curiosity had won this battle, and he stood a while mid-course trying
to pick out planets. But the ecliptic was hidden, the canyon bowl just
too high.

He walked along Acacia Avenue and up the slope to Valhalla. The
gleaming polished motorbikes that had filled the car park earlier were
all gone, and a few dusty battered pick-ups and cars had taken their
place. The promised locals, presumably. Inside the timber cavern, only
four or five tables were occupied so far – a couple of groups of varying
ages, that could have been families, and some of the tree-planters. The
big screen was showing the pre-game. The expectant crowd, however
few in number, was just as intense and anxious as the crowd he'd been
a part of that night in Vancouver for the previous match.

Marie looked pleased when she noticed he'd taken up her invitation, and poured him a beer without his asking, though she didn't stop
to talk. He settled down at a table on his own, just behind the group of
tree-planters from the inn, who acknowledged him briefly with glances
or nods. The tension really was, as the talking head on-screen said,
palpable.

Marie brought him the beer and a homemade pizza bedecked with
pepperoni and vegetables, and set them both on table with a flashing
smile. Then she straightened up, put her hands on her hips she shouted
'Go Canucks Go!', not at him or indeed anyone, just an involuntary
release of energy. The little crowd of cheerleaders yelled in response,
not quite in unison, as if badly rehearsed. 'Go Canucks!'

As the pundits went through the pre-game, discussing the various
players and their talents or failings, he was watching the crowd more
than the screen, intrigued by these local faces. Perhaps that one family
of different generations all wearing Canucks caps were First Nations,
members of the N'laka'pamux band, even relatives of Lyle's wife? Their
features were not unlike hers. There was a patriarch, a man of maybe
sixty or seventy, of wide girth, at the heart of the group. Beside him a
much smaller woman of his age. Then, around their table and another
beside that, a group of three younger men and two women of their
age with children on their knees. On the floor at the feet of the grandmother, two small boys of six or seven were playing some computer

game on a hand-held screen, and glancing up every so often to see if the match had begun. Whatever it was they were playing was every bit as intense as any hockey game could be, their little faces contorting with alternating expressions of pleasure or annoyance.

Some of the tree-planters were there too, this tribe too taking on a peculiar and unexpected mystique, from the remains of their crack-of-dawn breakfast he discovered scattered around the dining room in the mornings and the exhausted expressions they wore as they dragged their tiredness around, like weaklings or invalids moving through the shadows of the inn for a brief hour in the evenings, before presumably they disappeared upstairs to sleep the sleep of the righteous in preparation for yet another crack-of-dawn start. Most of them seemed quite fit and young, but it was clear that work was heavy even for them, though a couple of the older ones wore that seasoned look of experience and seemed to have perfected the art of the tree-planters' day, whatever that entailed. These older men looked like grizzled 60s survivors, back-to-the-earthers of the kind he remembered. At the table in front of him was the one young lad he'd spoken with briefly when he found the library back at the inn. Close up, he had an intense look that reminded of DH Lawrence, face angular, expression slightly forbidding. With him, a jolly slightly boyish girl he'd also glimpsed around the inn, and an older woman who seemed to be enjoying her food more than the hockey.

He decided to strike up conversation and leant forward just enough to let them know he wanted to be friendly.

'So this is going to be quite a match, then?' he said.

DH Lawrence didn't turn around as he replied, his eyes fixed on the screen. 'Sure hope so. 3-0 and we could all breathe a bit more easy.'

'I hope Timmy Thomas gets chased off the ice,' the girl said. The woman busy eating pizza looked up for a moment and grunted her agreement. That was the goaltender for Boston. He'd learned that much in Vancouver, that Thomas was Boston's top-performer and had almost kept the Canucks out in the first games.

The camera went to the Sedin brothers, the Swedish twins whose combination play had been so much a part of Vancouver's successful season so far. One of the other tree-planters shouted out 'Go on Hank! Go on Dan!'

DH Lawrence glanced briefly behind him at the interloper. 'So you like hockey?'

'I'm intrigued. It seems everybody I've met since I got to British Columbia is focused on this.'

'Yup, pretty much. Never won it before. We nearly did in 1994, went all the way down to last game. Real heartbreaker.'

'I was eight, watched it with my dad,' the jolly girl said.

'Vancouver will never win the Stanley Cup,' said the disinterested eater, lifting another slice of pizza. 'Never have, never will.'

'Now that's where you're wrong. Vancouver has won the Stanley Cup,' one of the older guys at the next table said.

'Not the Canucks, though,' said DH Lawrence.

'No, but it was a Vancouver team. Back in 1915,' he went on, addressing the outsider and the disbelieving, 'there was a team went by the name of the Vancouver Millionaires, only been going for two or three years, and they won the cup. Swept the series against the Ottawa Senators 3-0.'

'He's right,' another voice confirmed. 'The Millionaires won it.'

'Yeah, but that was like a hundred years ago. I mean now,' the pizza eater grunted, her mouth full.

The outsider found his imagination captured by the sound of that team, the Millionaires. It made him think, as mention of that word always seemed to do, of his mother's favourite cake, so called millionaires' shortbread. It was one of those memory reflexes he welcomed, as it brought a warm fuzzy feeling of days now indistinct in the kitchen of childhood. The Vancouver Millionaires – a loud and proud name for a new team, representing a new city, a new province even. And of course that was back in Lyle's era, when he was still well, still working. It was a strange tangential connection that seemed to reach back through the decades and join this moment to that.

As the puck drop approached, a few more people came in and settled in front of the screen. Marie and her man filled beer glasses and the cabin got ready to roar. The opening action was tense and both sides were giving it their full physical presence. Lawrence explained what was at stake in this third game was control of the series. A 3-0 Canucks lead would make Boston's task almost impossible, while a win for the American team would give them momentum. About five minutes in, the scores still level but Vancouver pressing hard, one of their players hit a Boston guy really hard and he fell to the ice, pole-axed. The cabin erupted as Rome, the offending Canuck, was given a major penalty, and left his side a man down for 15 minutes. Boston pressed hard to take advantage and a hush of anticipated disappointment fell over the cabin. As each attack was repelled, with the Canuck goaltender standing firm, a cheer of relief arose. At the end of the first period, the score was still tied at 0-0. It was a tense match, ill-tempered and brutal, and the mood spread to the small crowd sitting in the isolation of the canyon pub. The false Lawrence's staring eyes burned with passion worthy of his doppelgänger as he complained about the penalty. Hockey was getting too soft, he seemed to be saying. Hits were a part of the game. People got hurt. That was how it was.

In the second period, it all went bad for the Canucks. Eleven seconds in, Boston scored, and fifteen minutes later they were 4-0 ahead. The Canucks goaltender, who everyone referred to as Lou, looked shaken. The match was surely beyond them. The outsider could feel the anger and disappointment of the fans around him. He tried to care, and did with the mild enthusiasm of someone who didn't really know what was going on or why it mattered so much, and he sensed that his confused presence was becoming unwelcome.

At the end of the second period, all the tree-planters but false Lawrence got up and left the cabin, complaining that they had to get up at 4am. Maybe he should have left with them, but there was a spectacle unfolding here in front of him – somehow involving him – that felt compulsive. He felt sure that Martina would be watching it too, back in Vancouver, and he'd liked the feeling that they were sharing something, despite the distance between them.

False Lawrence sat glaring at the screen, listening to the pundits discuss Vancouver's collapse, and the penalty incurred which seemed to have proved so decisive in the match. The outsider's slightly vacant confused expression seemed to annoy him, as did the fact that the group of First Nations at the next table seemed to be carrying on with their chatter and laughter, despite the tragedy unfolding in the match. He kept glancing over at them as if he really wanted to say something, to tell them to shut up or get out.

Marie brought them both another beer. 'Cheer up,' she said. 'It's not over yet'. False Lawrence scowled at her. She seemed not too unhappy at the score – presumably she'd profited regardless, and was reckoning up the tabs mentally as the game wore on. No one in the cabin cared enough or was angry enough for the solitary tree-planter remaining, and when the third period began it was just one foul after another, the players battling as if the incident in the first period had been the first act in a war. Boston scored again before Vancouver managed one, but then it was disaster after disaster for the Canucks. In the last ten minutes, the Bruins scored another four goals to end the match 8-1 up.

The outsider didn't know if that was as extreme an outcome as it would have been if the same score had occurred in a football match at home, but the face of the guy in front of him said it all. Finally, as the pundits gave the statistics on how long it was since a team had won by that margin in the play-offs, and how all the penalty minutes compared with other years, false Lawrence slapped a banknote on the table and got drunkenly to his feet, glaring at everyone in his way as he stomped towards the door. The expression on his face said he was looking for a fight, but was unlikely to find it here in the canyon tonight. Marie came over to clear his table and smiled at the stranger.

'Some people just can't take a loss,' she said. 'So you wanna come talk to some of the people over here? They might know about that guy you're interested in. George's folks have lived here forever.'

He followed her over to the table where the family group sat talking. They didn't seem too despondent at the outcome of the match, they were laughing and joking about something.

'George,' said Marie, attracting attention of the patriarch, 'This is the fella I told you about earlier. He's here from over in Scotland. He's looking to find out about a man who used to live here about a hundred years ago, a relative of yours, is that it?'

The stranger from Scotland nodded, said yes, he had been a relative most probably, judging by what he knew, but he was still trying to work out exactly how.

George, a big man with a black ponytail pulled back from a balding brow, leaned back and smiled, revealing a chequered line of teeth, gaps where some were missing, and gold in other places. 'So he lived here in Cloud Falls?' he asked in a deep voice.

'Yes, from about 1884 until sometime around 1915, I think. He was about eighteen when he arrived here. His uncle had an estate and a store. John MacLeod.'

'Ah, you mean Jimmy Lyle, don't you?'

The response was so ready, and so definite after having met with such vagueness so far when his quarry was mentioned, that the Scotsman laughed.

'Yes I do. James Lyle.'

'Well now, Jimmy Lyle was a great man, I believe. A great friend to our people, and to all the native people of British Columbia.'

'So he's still remembered?'

'Remembered and honoured. Just last summer, the band erected a memorial to his memory.'

'Really? Mind if I sit down?' the Scotsman said. They pulled up a chair and he joined the company. Marie had gone back to the bar. She glanced over as she washed through a few glasses, watching and maybe eavesdropping too.

'Yes. It was 100 years, you see, since the time when all the chiefs of British Columbia gathered here to sign a paper that was presented to the Prime Minister at Kamloops. They came here because of Jimmy Lyle, because he could speak their language well and they wanted him to write down their words in English. He was a very clever man, could speak a lot of different native languages. So last year, when it was one hundred years since that, the chiefs gathered here again and we had a ceremony at the new gathering place up past the reservation. You seen that?'

'No,' Bert said. 'I didn't know about that.'

'So what brings you here? You seeking after your ancestors?' the woman sitting to George's right said.

'This is my wife, Amber,' George offered. 'I didn't get your name.'

'Bert. Bert Johnson.' He shook them both by the hand. 'I suppose I am in a way, seeking my ancestors. Most times it seems like it's the other way round, people turn up in Scotland from Canada, looking for their people.'

George nodded. 'Well, Bert, if you're interested I think you should really talk with one of the elders. I don't know all that much about Jimmy Lyle, you see, but there's some do.'

'How long are you here?' Amber asked. She seemed a little suspicious to the Scotsman, not as open as George seemed to be.

'I'll be here a while. I'm staying over at the inn on the other side of the river.'

'And you come all the way here from Scotland? To find out about Jimmy Lyle?'

'Yes.'

'He must be pretty important over there.'

'No, not really. Not as important as he should be.'

'So you are going to make him famous or something? Marie said you were writing a book.'

'Well, we'll see. At the moment I'm just finding out as much as can, you know. And I wanted to come here and see for myself what this place was like, not just read about it in books.'

'And what do you think so far?' Amber asked.

'I think it's about as far away and as different as anywhere could be from where Jimmy Lyle grew up.'

'Where was that?' George asked.

'He came from a little island way out in the middle of the Atlantic Ocean. No trees, high winds and pretty cold.'

'Ha, yes, I guess it is pretty different then. And you from there too?'

'No,' said the Scotsman. 'No, I live in a city. Edinburgh.'

By the time the stranger got out of Valhalla that night, they'd drunk a few beers together and had struck up a friendship. The hockey game seemed far distant, almost a memory of another day altogether. George had promised he'd take Bert to the new memorial just as soon as he could arrange it, and Amber who had finally come round to trusting him had invited him to supper that Friday. The Scotsman said goodnight to Marie as he left. They had a meeting scheduled for the next morning at 11, when the pub would be quiet and they could talk. She seemed slightly cooler towards him, he thought, as he wandered towards the bridge.

The moon had risen above the canyon walls and the strip of land with the little village glowed eerily. Gloomily, even. Across the CNR track, the river shimmered silver as it rippled southwards, incessant and unfaltering. He wheeled onto the bridge and began the crossing. There in the distance, leaning over the balustrade, was a figure, smoking. The faint scent of marijuana, then not so faint, but pungent. It was the false Lawrence, who had stormed out of the pub earlier after the Canucks' collapse. Had he been waiting?

The echo of his footsteps sounded loud in hollow moonlight and the smoking loiterer turned to watch him approach. Closer the Scotsman got, one heel toe after another, as on he went.

'Hey…' The greeting wasn't threatening, just a Canadian drawl that sounded stoned or drunk or both. 'I was waiting for you.'

'Waiting for me?'

'Sure. Just watching the river and smoking up.' The Scotsman was only a few steps away. 'They're taking all the man outta the game, buddy,' the loiterer drawled. 'A hit like Rome got binned for, that's a part of the game, always has been.' He shook his head, drew on whatever it was he was smoking so the tip lit like a firefly. 'That was just wrong. Sometimes guys hit each other. It's what they do.' He shook his head sadly, as if he had lost some close relative and couldn't quite fathom the harshness of fate.

'I suppose so.'

'You suppose? You suppose so? I'm telling you, man, it's a part of the fucking game. People get hit, people get hurt. That was just wrong, that penalty.'

The Scotsman stopped a few feet away from the tree-planter. He was shaking his head, gazing down at the river. Then he straightened up and held out the burning smoke. 'Want some?'

It was a reflex to reach out and take it. For so many years he'd thought nothing of sticking a burning cigarette or a pipe or even a joint in his mouth, but since the cancer it seemed as if it was a little bit of hell, tempting and damning. Would it be construed as an act of ill-will if he refused? So he took it, the reeking joint, no more than an inch long and put it to his lips. Pure grass. The wisp of the aroma rose into his nostrils, the in-draw caught his throat and he coughed. That was enough to break the loiterer's mood, and he laughed.

'Not used to it, are you?'

'Not really.'

'You don't need much then. That's pure BC bud. It'll knock you out.'

And suddenly the threat was gone and his new companion put his arm around his shoulders. 'Come on, my little Scotch buddy. Let's head back to base camp.' He gave the joint back and they carried on over the bridge, beyond the point where jumping would be easiest, and along the bank on the far side, past the long line of CPR trucks waiting for the signal to take off to wherever in this vast country they were bound.

'So what is it you do, this tree-planting?'

'Plant trees, man. What else? We go in where the loggers have been clear cutting and we plant as quick as we can. The more we plant the more we get paid.'

'All day every day?' His new buddy nodded. The Scotsman felt a rushing in his mind, a euphoria he vaguely recognised but hadn't experienced for a long time, as the effects of the smoke seemed to bend his thoughts into new and unexpected shapes. It was a long time since he'd been stoned, and never had such a little quantity hit him with such force. Hit, he thought. Hits are part of the game.

'I'm just earning some money here. I'm a student at UBC in Vancouver. It's tough work if you're not used to it, but I been doing it for a while now. Some guys work at it all year round.'

'But there's no trees round here. I mean, it's desert.'

'No, not round here. We're working about 100km north of here. We just use the inn for a base cause it's cheap but better than camping out. You wanna see some of the places people work. Just a bit of old tarp in the middle of a swarm of black flies. This is luxury by comparison.'

They reached the inn where the little neon sign still burned. But the lights were all out in the rooms upstairs.

'Shit,' the false Lawrence said. 'It's late. I'm wiped. Fucking hockey.'

'You've got an early start?'

'Up at 4. In the truck by 4.30. Breakfast as we go. On the hill by 5.30.'

He pushed open the front door and the Scotsman followed. He let out a big sigh and turned to climb the stairs. 'Name's Doug,' he added, holding out a hand.

'Good to meet you, Doug. I'm Bert. Must be hard work.'

'Sure is.'

As they parted, Bert smiled. 'By the way, did anybody ever tell you look a lot like the young DH Lawrence?'

'DH Lawrence? Who he?'

'A writer – an Englishman.'

'No, can't say anybody ever told me that. Was he any good?'

'Yes, he was good. So it's a compliment.'

'Okay!'

The Scotsman watched him wearily take the steps upwards, and went into the lounge. A single standard lamp was lit and he sat down under its arc. The room seemed to morph and sway, tending to lurch away to his right, but the books on the shelves were old friends and they stayed put. He fixed his attention on them. The titles on the spines were like an anchor to a familiar world, even though many were unfamiliar volumes, Canadian writers he'd never heard of. And then he saw a DH Lawrence – a little Penguin Travel Library edition of 'Mornings in Mexico'. He pulled it off the shelf and leafed through it. He'd read it long ago as a youth, when he'd had a few months of Lawrence passion. A passage caught his eye:

Now the white man is a sort of extraordinary white monkey that, by cunning, has learnt lots of semi-magical secrets of the universe, and made himself boss of the show. Imagine a race of big white monkeys got up in fantastic clothes, and able to kill a man by hissing at him; able to leap through the air in great hops, covering a mile in each leap; able to transmit his thoughts by a moment's effort of concentration to some great white monkey or monkeyess, a thousand miles away: and you have, from our point of view, something of the picture that the Indian has of us.

He sat with Lawrence for a while, not so much reading but thinking. He'd read it before, yes, long before, yet somehow it was still with him, the mood if not the exact words. That yearning for somewhere beyond he'd ignored for so many years while his Edinburgh life piled up volumes he bought and sold, a mountain now of printed paper which he'd tried to scale but never quite did as it grew faster than he could climb. An unreached peak, much discussed during a life spent in pubs, punctuated by conversations with men and women who shared his passion for the written word, who'd fallen like him for the illusion that this eternal literature, this deathless prose, was what life was really about. His mind had travelled the world, had settled briefly in one place or another, following in the tracks of different writers whose imaginations had grasped his attention for a while like DH Lawrence, were captured and bound by the printer's art, but he hadn't gone anywhere. Not Ranamin, not Mexico, nowhere.

Only a day and a half had passed, only a matter of a hours since he stepped off the Greyhound, yet already this strange place, deep in the heart of British Columbia, hidden away in the canyon, no more than a scattering of houses between the highway, the railway, the river and the other railway, already it was opening up to him and showing him that the history he had studied, the books he had consumed, the lives he had sought out, all was still here – buried and decaying maybe, but still it was here, all its atoms, the rocks and water, the timber houses and the iron bridge, where trucks and bikes and hockey games were mere transients, travellers passing through the timeless, electrons spinning. The dead were still alive, the memories still active, the quantum heart still spinning, however elusive and hard to find in the quotidian.

God, he was stoned.

To gather his thoughts, he focused on his quarry, Jimmy Lyle, embracing the culture of the local people, the way of life, their stories and their deep beliefs, of how he'd sought out the culture he knew was dying and tried to give it a shape, a form in a different way, that would at least acknowledge its existence, and that it had once been the way of life here, the only one.

Was that all a falsification, a translation into English of a Macphersonian type, that palatisation of the dying Gaelic culture of the highlands of Scotland for the drawing rooms of Edinburgh and London, of Paris and Vienna, a romantic myth of primitive savagery which troubled young yellow waist-coated Werthers in faraway cities could swoon over, before they borrowed the pistols of a rival and blew their sorry little brains out? And he thought of Franz Boas, collecting up the sacred artefacts, even the skulls of the tribal ancestors, to be shipped off to whatever museum or university was paying his expenses, wasn't he just another Burke and Hare clone, profiting from the trade in the name of science? Those white monkeys with their trickery and technology had had their way with the others, sent them off to be educated and Christianised, to rob them of what they decreed brute natures, dressed them in the mode of the time, filled their heads with another set of stories they couldn't understand because they were foreign, never to be naturalised. Those white monkeys, of which the Scotsman realised he himself was one, had brought their settled ways, had built their permanent houses, had converted untilled soil to prodigious productivity, but even that was gone now.

In the eternal scale, the great orchard, the little station carrying away the fruit and honey to the tables of the grand, even the churchgoing congregation, seemed no more than the merest spike on the timeline that ran on through the centuries as full and relentless as the river itself. They were all passing through, carried along on the stream, the carrying stream as Hamish Henderson termed it, a cavalcade of busy business that bloomed occasionally but always returned to desert when the flumes broke, or the timber rotted or the iron girders rusted down to what they wanted to be, to what creation always inclined, the entropic, the shapeless, the identity-free. Whether it was called Arthur's Seat or The Chief, or whatever name the old indigenous culture had for it, the mountainous rock that seemed fixed and motionless above the little town was itself shifting imperceptibly, slowly eroding, grain of sand by grain of sand, and it too would be gone one day. All things must pass through.

The grinding screech of rail-truck wheels rose to fill the air again, bringing an end to his stoned meanderings. The little inn seemed to shudder with the noise. Ken, the CPR linesman, must have spoken, given the okay for the long line to depart along the river, heading for the mountain passes that would bring it to the next halt, to disgorging and uncoupling, to be filled again, to wait a signal, to move on, always on. He wondered about the tree-planters, whether they woke and cursed the interruption to their well-earned rest, or if the fatigue of a day on the mountain was so great that they didn't even hear it.

The great forests were gone, and a billion seedlings set in the clearing in their place. The white monkey magic. He felt dizzy at the thought, seemed to be rising above the land, high into a cartography of satellite imagery, mind racing, twisted into a new shape by travel, by strangeness, beer and the joint of BC bud he'd shared with Doug, who was not Lawrence, not of Arabia or Ranamin or Nottingham, but a student from Vancouver. He rose and staggered upstairs, where he lay on his bed and watched the footage of the ospreys again, the giant chick's reluctance to leave the nest, the mother – or was it father – hopping on and off its back, trying to shift it.

His mind was still racing, not quite able to sleep despite the fact he'd walked a fair bit and had felt the full heat of the day, so he put more sun-cream on, thinking, discomfort and unease aside, he was feeling something, his curiosity awoken by the unfamiliar, he was alive after all, in spite of himself – how does someone survive when the world turns against them, when people you love die or leave, when your work becomes irrelevant and even your own body begins to destroy you, cell by cell?

He had done it, this far at least, by numbing himself, by ridding himself of all emotions, detaching from all the people and things that had previously given him a sense of who he was, or had brought him pleasure. Moved away from the life he led, closed the bookshop, sat through the long days in his mother's house in the country, no longer even reading, till she was gone too. He had shut down everything but the essential, a little food, sleep and minimal exercise, surprised himself by how reduced a life could be. Until he found his father's Canadian photos. And now he was here, in the place itself, eighty years later, stoned and beginning to feel again, to lose the numbness, to care. Like the way a finger feels when it gets too cold and then begins to warm, or how an arm comes back to life slowly after you've slept the wrong way and cut off circulation, a seeping of blood to the isolated part. In this case, the isolated part was his soul, or his psyche, the seele of Freud.

And the woman he'd met, who'd swept into this narrow numbed world like a tornado for a few short days, before she drove him to the station to get on the Greyhound in Vancouver that morning, and set him on the next stage of his quest. Could he really care about her, after everything that had happened, after all the loss and the shutting down he'd had to do? He tried to picture her, to see if the image would stir him.

She was tall and slender, in the way that Slavic women often are, but not the White Goth type that the Ottoman sultans had so prized as wives. No, she was dark, another stock, her eyes such a deep brown until you looked closely, and then the gold showed, emerging like a circular aura of sun from deep wooded shadow. He could picture her, feature by feature, if not an entire conjuring. Her nose smallish, ever so slightly squint, but a good shape, certainly not too elfin. Her lips quite thin but shapely. And her chin strong, somehow confident. But all of that was obscured by the memory of her smile, and that alto laugh. And she had seemed kind, empathetic, most of the time at least, until she did that Garbo imitation and wanted to wander off alone.

He sat up. No, it was folly. He couldn't get involved, he was a cancer victim, it could recur at any time. He had to save himself as much trouble as he could, keep life simple. But then, if that was what he was meant to be doing, why was he here? His mind danced with pictures of her, merging into some weird fragmentary slideshow of images from those days in Vancouver. Hockey and bears in Canucks shirts, her stretched out on his bed, stoned and giggling at nothing, walking through the huge trees up at Pacific Spirit where she'd taken him, pretending a long tangle of seaweed was her tail at the shore as dusk fell, cycling round Stanley Park, eating oysters on the roof at Joe Fortes. And then that dark stare, when her eyes would turn completely opaque and she'd withdraw, as if he'd done something terrible, or come too close to knowing her, as if she'd given away too much of herself in some way or another, as if she'd crossed some invisible boundary of self she'd set for herself. It seemed there was more than one of her, as if she was multi-faceted, a cut stone glinting as she spun and moved. That morning, when he'd left Vancouver bound for a place she'd never been, had never even heard of until he mentioned it, had she really been tearful and upset? It seemed so unlikely, the whole encounter. He might well have dreamt it all.

In the darkness, his senses sharpened till the sound of the river below seemed to boom out a barrage of drumming, and the little moonlight creeping into his room became more than enough for him to see the furniture. The wardrobe, the single straight-backed wooden chair, the long fitted desk and the pile of books he'd gathered there, the tripod with the video camera pointing at the osprey nest. His suitcase and backpack, the evidence of his transience, of just another nameless figure passing through. Except he wasn't just another. He knew now there was a story here, and he was going to tell it, if he could. At last, he'd write his own book, not simply buy and sell the books of others. That would be reason enough not to jump.

Lying there, his mind drifted to the shop door in Edinburgh. It must be filthy now, unwashed, covered in street grime. Bill posters will have pasted and top-pasted the news of coming festival shows all over the front. If he was there, he'd light the little stove, and welcome bibliophile, browser, potential shoplifter even. But no. That life was gone. The door was locked. He could not conceive of the forces that held him there for so long, any more than why, so suddenly, they should have ceased to apply. But in a world city of literature, as Edinburgh is, there are many ways for a literate person to make a living. In his time, he'd done most of them, starting as a book hound, back in the days when he was still a student in need of some extra money. It began with a chance find, at the bottom of dusty cardboard box of old cinema magazines, in a charity shop full of the detritus of lives undocumented – a perfect 1st edition of the translation of Remy de Gourmont's *The Natural Philosophy of Love* with Ezra Pound's introduction, bought for a pound and sold for £50. He wanted to keep it, but needed the cash. After that, he was hooked. The city then was home to quite a few of them, walking the old streets hunting through second hand shops and jumble sales, in search of their gold-dust – hawking finds where they could. They grew to recognise each other, figures laden down with tell-tale bags bursting with rectangular corners, even acknowledging one another with a faint nod as they passed, but where they went and what they found was guarded as zealously as the old-timer's stake in the gold rush.

His stoned mind drifted through his past, telling himself the story of his life in recap, as if he needed to understand how it was he'd got to this point. He remembered the excitement of opening the impromptu bookstall, two mornings a week in a basement at the university, selling on less valuable acquisitions, set-texts to students like himself for a few pence, much cheaper than they cost in even the second hand bookshops. How he got to know the real bibliophiles, young professors like Ronnie Jack and the aspiring, got to know the kind of thing they wanted, and made it his business to find that. How, by the end of second year as an undergraduate, so much time was taken up in this hunt that he dropped out. It was a compulsion, a book fever, but much as he loved reading, he couldn't be bothered with the academic game. Yet he continued to hang out with his university friends.

He remembered the wee flat he first moved into with Zack from his course, and how his mother protested against his leaving home. How Zack had moved in with his girlfriend and, because he could afford the cheap rent, he didn't go through the hassle of finding someone else. He needed the space, was gathering more and more books – every day seemed to bring home another carrier bag full. But it wasn't simply about making a living. He genuinely believed – still did – that he was rescuing something of eternal value, making it available once again, to those who appreciated the quality that lay within the covers. Slowly, that little flat had filled up. Piles upon undocumented piles, although he began with the earnest intention of cataloguing everything, the more he acquired the more diverse and confusing it all became. Within a year it was beyond him, and he had simply tried as best he could to remember what was there and what he'd sold on.

His mind went to the MacQueens, how, after he sold them the Pound, he'd slowly got to know the strange old couple who ran the second-hand bookshop down the street, and used to sell on to them whatever he could. They didn't pay much, but he had learned a lot about what was valuable and what was not, just from what they chose to buy, and after a while they took a shine to him and he'd spend hours in the back-shop, drinking tea and talking trade. Their thing was modern 1st editions. How they became like parents to him, or perhaps the grandparents he never really had, and finally he started to work there. It made perfect sense to take over the shop when they decided they'd had enough, and wanted to retire. For a while he just ran it for them, but the longer he was working there the more it started to feel as if it was actually his, and after a particularly good few months when he was lucky enough to get his hands on three outstanding collections, he bought them out. They were happy to have a lump sum, because they weren't doing much business any more.

And so the bookshop became his life, his work and his passion. He got to know writers and collectors through that little shop, they all seemed to pass through at some point or another. Ian Rankin as a young student, studying Muriel Spark, McCall Smith when he was still a lecturer and hadn't made his name with the No 1 Detective Agency used to come in from time to time, and he believed he once bought a lot of Beat generation books from Irvine Welsh, though he had no idea who he was back then. Jo Rowling he met, back in the days when she was spinning out her first wizard tale in Nicolson's cafe. Those and hundreds of would-be writers who bought and sold books. His shop was a point of exchange, where literature was dusted off, given a wipe, revalued and re-shelved, awaiting the next hungry mind.

But the times he loved best in the bookshop were those midwinter afternoons, when the fire was lit and the shop cosy, the dusk descended, when he'd sit with whatever book he was reading while the world hurried by. Yellow glow heaven – leerie as a lamplighter, the script unlocking worlds and minds he'd never know. It was why he never travelled, he had so much to read, so many places to fly to imaginatively. The world was in that bookshop, the cosmos too. Sometimes, if the book had really gripped him, he'd lock the door and draw the blind, pour a whisky and carry on – another chapter, then another, until the paraffin ran out and his feet got cold. But the evenings, when the lights were lit, when friends and characters, writers and ranters, used to gather! It brought a smile to his face, there in the canyon night. Ah, that was another life, back then. Edinburgh was full of pubs where writers gathered, and it seemed he knew them all – though he was never in foreground, he was a face that everyone knew but couldn't name. The book guy, who sat at the feet of the great, helped others edit magazines and books, to organise readings, watched as contemporaries rose to prominence. Applauded them. And yet, and yet, some take it all far too seriously. Writing and all that. A lot of the books he handled were simply curate's eggs, with something to commend but faults aplenty. Out of all those that passed through his hands, more than a few went to the tip, the pulper, irredeemably worthless as text, object or art. He never felt good about dumping any book, though, always had a sense of the effort that went in, the author's pride, even in the more worthless. The would-be writer inside empathised. Deep down he knew where that ambition was rooted, it was his mother's doing, and he remembered when he was nine, how he gave his mother a poem he had written at school about an otter. He had never seen an otter, except in books, but it was his first proper poem, employing what he had learned, through imitation, about metre and verse. 'The Otter' became an instant classic in their bungalow – she framed and kept that poem on the mantelpiece in the sitting room, told him he would be a proper writer one day, that he'd publish books, as if it was the highest of vocations, and books were gold.

What a notion to plant in an impressionable lad's mind. This strange currency of books had insulated him from life and led to his retreat, until the outside world and its reality was submerged always in a fog of words, of minds, ideas distant from the street he lived on. Until the towers of titles, threatening to fall, were threat enough to drive him out to Sandy Bell's, to the whisky, to the music and the warmth. And the writing of his own became a fading myth. But now he was writing – words at least, though not much about Lyle, more about his past and all so fragmented.

As if in an echo chamber, he heard again her voice in Vancouver. 'So live. Write!' And at last his stoned mind gave in to sleep.

Hot and sweaty, he woke on top of the covers he'd kicked off in the night. His mind seemed to bear the traces of his dreams, a raccoon he thought he'd seen, a text message he'd had, and her. She'd been there. All night, with him, though she was far away and he had no way of contacting her, no signal for his phone and no internet.

Out the window, nothing seemed to have changed in the little town, though the sun was now slowly sending a descending tide of light down the far side of the canyon wall. On the nesting platform, the osprey chick was alone, a giant baby crouched as it was the day before. He switched on his laptop, checked the time and saw that he'd slept late. From below, the clink of dishes suggested breakfast might be over, that the tree-planters had long since headed off to their mountain. He dressed and went downstairs. Vince was in the lobby, carrying plates and cups to the kitchen.

'Ah, there you are!' he said. 'Wondered what had happened to you this morning.'

'Slept late,' the Scotsman answered. 'Any chance of a coffee?'

'Sure! And I've got something for you. I thought I remembered seeing these over at the recycling plant. Someone must have pulled them out of the garbage.'

From behind the reception desk, Vince produced two magazines printed on a cream paper, monochrome only. 'That's your man there, isn't it? James Lyle?'

And it was. The Scotsman took them and leafed through, as Vince set the coffee machine in process. The magazines dated from 1995, published by the Nicola Valley Museum.

'I read them earlier,' he said. 'Kinda interesting. I had no idea we'd had such a famous resident out here.'

'These are like treasure, Vince,' he said. 'I had no idea they existed.'

'Well, I guess you wouldn't over there in Scotland.'

'How far away is this museum?'

'It's over in Merritt, where the recycling plant is.'

'What kind of thing does it have?'

'You mean exhibits?'

'Yes.'

'I don't know. I've never been there. But you know, Merritt's a big old cattle town, in the middle of cowboy country. So probably a lot of stuff about ranching. Local history, settlers, First Nations.'

The Scotsman sat with his coffee on the terrace. It was getting very hot even this early. The two museum magazines contained a number of memoirs, and most interesting of all, a transcription of Lyle's diary from 1910. Not a great deal of detail, and little description, more a log of what he'd done. A few illustrations showed his tiny meticulous handwriting. Reading through, what was noticeable right away was how mobile he had been. There were constant references to catching trains, down to Vancouver or up to Merritt, and it seemed that Cloud Falls had been far from isolated back then, with a regular passenger train service up and down the canyon. He'd even been over to Victoria on the ferry to consult with experts at the university, men whose names the Scotsman thought he recognised from his research, but couldn't place without access to the internet.

When Vince reappeared from the kitchen, where the sound of the dishwasher resonated, the Scotsman thanked him again, then asked whether he'd made any progress with restoring the router. Vince winced a little. 'Ah, no. I'm sorry about that. I was going to ask the man over in the village who deals with the local connection to take a look at it today, see if he can get it working.'

Just then Rosie and her little Yorkie came in, and Vince, glad of the distraction, got up and left.

'Hey there,' the former biker girl said, on seeing the stranger again. 'You good?'

'I'm good,' he said, adopting the phrase.

'How are your investigations going?'

'Good too. I'm going round to interview the woman in Valhalla in a bit.'

'Marie? Don't think she'll know much. She's only been here a couple of years.'

'Eight, she said.'

'Eight? No, don't think so. They sorta keep themselves to themselves over there. Got their own customers, you know. Trans-Canada Highway drivers like those weekend bikers you said you saw.'

'Anyway, she asked me to call in. Her grandfather was from Scotland.'

'Well good luck with that,' she said, and she and her dog companion headed off upstairs.

He sat reading the two magazines Vince had fished out of the garbage. They really were treasure, full of the kind of detail he could never have found at home in Scotland, the kind of culture that went under the radar, printed locally and disposed of as readily as any newspaper might be, when the reading is over and the time for clear out comes. It was a little miracle that his disorganised and eccentric host should have found them and brought them to him. And there must be a third, at least one more, number 1 in the series.

It was a kind of book hunt, the sort of quest he'd been doing since he was an undergraduate about to drop out in favour of the easy money he could earn. But here he was far from the familiar world of Edinburgh's narrow streets where print culture was ancient, woven in, like mortar between the stonework, or seemed to force itself like dandelions from between every paving stone. Out here there was little he knew, and little he could do to find the tracks. But perhaps in Merritt, where the magazines had been printed, perhaps at the museum he'd find out more. He rose from the table and went to his room, added the magazines to the material he was gathering, and wrote for a while, the story of the night before.

An hour passed, and when he checked his watch again, it was time to head towards Valhalla. He wasn't sure what to wear, it was so hot, and yet his skin was still sore from the day before. Loose shirt and trousers seemed wise.

Crossing the bridge once more, he hesitated at the place where he had leant over the balustrade the day before. The urge was gone, he really didn't feel like jumping now. Instead he carried straight on to the other side, past The Apple Store, along Acacia Avenue, up the hill into the empty car park.

The bar was empty too. He stood for a moment, looking at the odd marks on the wooden floor. Marie must have heard the door, because she appeared from the back, wiping her hands on a towel. 'Ah, the Scotsman! You made it,' she said. 'Looking at the signatures?'

'Signatures?'

'On the floor. Every year after the burn-up, winner gets to sign the floor inside here.'

Then it clicked. 'You mean these are tyre marks?'

'Sure! Winner gets to bring their bike in here and sign the floor.'

He laughed. 'Must reek the place out, surely?'

'Yep. Takes about half an hour to clear, before anybody can come back in,' she said.

He pictured the scene, the bike-beast revving and roaring, the front brakes holding it, the back tyre spinning and melting till it was soft enough to leave the skid mark. The grinning faces of the bikers waiting outside to see how skilfully the rider could make his mark. Not really signatures as such, just crazy black rubber squiggles.

'So you want a coffee or something?'

'Ok. Thanks, yes.'

'I saw you talking to George last night,' she added, as they crossed to the bar. 'He able to tell you anything about your guy?'

'A bit,' he answered. 'Said there was some sort of new memorial to him here they'd erected last year.'

'Here?'

'Somewhere round here. You haven't heard of it?'

'No,' she said slowly, holding her hands up, palms out. 'But then I don't hear much of what goes on with them.'

The word 'them' hovered in the air, unresolved. He sat on a stool as she disappeared around the back again, presumably to fetch coffee. His eyes came to rest on a small sign pinned to the wall next to the till. WALL OF SHAME, it said. He read the names casually, not really paying attention, until he spotted one that was familiar. It was the chief's, the band leader. The man he was hoping to meet, whose calls and emails may be waiting somewhere in the ether he couldn't access.

When she came back bearing two cups, she sat down next him on the customers' side of the wooden bar. 'So, good old Scotland,' she said, with a smile. Close up, he noticed her frown lines. 'You know, I've

been over there a few times, when I was younger. We went all over –
Glasgow, where my cousins are. Edinburgh. Stirling too.'

He hesitated, didn't say that wasn't really 'all over'.

'My mom was very proud of being Scottish. She had this whole
language she used to speak to us when we were kids if we were naughty. I still remember it, even though she passed on ten years ago. She used
to call me a wee bissim. Or a blether when I talked too much. I miss
her voice sometimes. Though I guess if it hadn't been for her passing,
I wouldn't have been able to buy this place.'

'It's quite a place,' he observed, looking around at all the biker
memorabilia.

'Ain't it just? You know it's the biggest log cabin in BC? We've
had over 500 bikers stop here on the annual Hot Poker run up to
Kamloops.' A broad pride showed on her face as she leant back on her
barstool, and took a sip of coffee. 'Quite something, eh?'

'It is,' he agreed. But his curiosity was headed in another direction.
He took a mouthful from his cup. 'I wanted to ask you about that notice,'
he said, pointing at the sign that had caught his eye, the wall of shame.

'That?' she said, frowning. 'That's the people who aren't welcome
here. Why do you ask?'

'I couldn't help noticing that one of the names is the same as the
head of the local band?'

'It is,' she said, slightly puzzled. 'It's him. He's one of the four bad
chiefs in BC.'

'Why do you say that?'

'He's holding the town to ransom over water is why.'

'Water?'

'Sure - says that the town's water supply comes from Indian land.'

'It comes from the falls, doesn't it?'

'Yup. Over on the far side of town.'

'MacLeod Falls?'

She looked at him oddly. 'You mean Cloud Falls, don't you? You
seen them?'

'I walked up there yesterday. But they used to be called MacLeod
Falls. The man who gave his name to them was Jimmy Lyle's uncle.'

'The guy you're writing about?'

'The very same. A Scotsman.'

She took another sip from her coffee and stared at him for a while.
He could see her mind doing some kind of assessment on whether

he was telling the truth. Then she said, 'No I didn't know that. So he named the falls after himself?'

'It seems so. He bought a big estate here, back around 1870. It was him who planted the acacia trees along the road here. He was the one who began the orchards.'

For a moment, she seemed unsure whether to believe him, as if wondering who this stranger was, wandering into her domain, telling her things about it she didn't know. Then she shook her head. 'No, that was old Mrs Spark, I'm sure it was.'

He nodded. 'Yes, she and her husband did run the orchards, for many years, but they worked for MacLeod at first. It was MacLeod who brought the Sparks out here from Scotland. And it was him who first brought the water from the falls. He had a whole complicated system of irrigation built that ran all the way down here to his fields.'

She registered surprise, and so he told her in outline what he knew, of the early settlement in the place she now lived, of Lyle and the Indian Rights movement, his uncle and his schemes. When he was done, she drained her coffee cup and frowned at him, then gave a snort and laughed.

'Well, you have been doing your research. Guess old Macleod didn't have anybody telling him he couldn't help himself to the water back then. Or that he couldn't call it his if he wanted to.'

The phone rang and his host got off her stool to answer it. He thought then about the thesis he'd read in the UBC archive, written by one of the local band who was now a lawyer in Vancouver, which had focused on the water rights issue. He remembered the opening chapter and the story she told there, of being out with her father in their truck one day, heading up the slope away from the reservation, and coming to a locked gate across a path that was traditional – how her father had backed up, and then charged the gate, which had crumpled in front of the cowcatcher. It seemed these old tensions ran as deep now as ever they'd done. He'd come here on the trail of a story he'd thought was history, yet it was clear now that nothing was resolved and that the struggle Lyle had engaged in was still ongoing.

He wondered if he should press the point and try to find out more about Marie's feelings, but decided against it. He had to remain open, impartial, and not make assumptions. The case of the rights of the N'laka'pamux was clearly not resolved even after a hundred years. He wondered, would Lyle have stood with his friends the Indians against his fellow white settlers, even his fellow Scots like Widow Spark? Or had there been a limit to his sympathy? From what he knew of him, he would have sought some equitable solution, something to benefit all, if that was possible when a resource like water was so necessary to all. But wasn't it a paradox that people should be squabbling over water from a little waterfall when a great river roared past, only a matter of a few yards away?

'You know, I'm supposed to meet this chief here,' he volunteered, when she hung up the phone.

'Here?' she queried. 'Surely not here?'

'No, not in here exactly. Just sometime while I'm staying. But I can't pick up internet or phone messages.'

'Ah okay.' She shrugged. 'Word'll get around. Just you rely on the bush telegraph. If he wants to see you, he'll find you.' She probably didn't intend to sound racist, but her attitude smacked of a deep distrust. Then, as if she could read what he was thinking, she added, 'I got nothing against them, you know. Some of them, like George and his family you met, I get along fine with. They're good friends of mine.'

The contrast between the beautiful multicultural city he'd spent the week before exploring and this little back-country village struck him then. In cities people can live in their own ethnic groups, maintaining their own cultures and observances without friction, but in a place like this there is no avoiding the other. The divide between indigenous and immigrant, even the native-born, seemed palpable here.

'So,' she went on, 'What is it you want to ask him about? The chief?'

'Jimmy Lyle,' he answered. 'I want to know what they, you know, the First Nations people think about him now.' She didn't respond. It seemed he'd lost whatever intimacy their Scottish commonality had gifted him. He had become complicated now, someone not entirely straight or trustworthy, someone who knew too much. He could see it in her eyes as she lifted the coffee cups from in front of him and made gestures towards having work to do.

'Westering Home,' she said, suddenly, her face brightening.

'Sorry?'

'That was the song, my great-grandmother's greatest hit. You know it?'

'Yes, I do remember it,' he replied. He wasn't at all sure that it really was written by Marjorie Kennedy-Fraser, but if it was one of her family myths, he wasn't about to disabuse her of the notion right there and then.

'Whistle the tune, then?' she said, in plaintive tone, as if she herself had forgotten.

So he did. He began to whistle it and, as he did, fragments of words began to crystallise from his childhood memory. He began to sing. 'Westering home with a song in the air, light in the eye and it's goodbye to care, laughter o' love and a welcoming there, isle of my heart my own land.'

Her face was suddenly a picture of childish delight. 'Oh yes!' she exclaimed, 'I remember it now. My mother used to sing it to me. Sing it again!' And so the two duetted, those four lines he could recall. And when it was over, they both laughed heartily.

'I believe it was based on an old Gaelic song about the island of Islay,' he said, getting his breath. 'Maybe that was where your family first came from?'

She hesitated, frowned, thought for a moment. 'I don't think so. I never heard of that – Islay?' Her eyes glazed, turned sad, as if the song from the old country had let some tide of regret sweep in from beyond the walls of her biker shrine. The look of the little girl who had sung so sweetly disappeared from her face and she grew pensive. 'Y'know, I really wish I'd asked my mother more, you know, about Scotland and all, while she was still alive.'

These words set him thinking just that. He grimaced. 'My mother died six months ago,' he said. 'So I know exactly what you mean.'

'It's a tough loss,' she said. The bossy matron of bikers seemed long gone at that moment. 'There's so much I don't know about the family. Never will now.' But then, as if she caught herself slipping into a despondency she desperately wanted to avoid, she smiled. 'You know the other song she used to sing to me? Marie's Wedding?'

It was clear from her pronunciation that she identified with the girl Mairi who she almost shared a name with. 'I do,' he said. 'A very popular song in Scotland to this day.'

'That one I can sing,' she said, and she did, doing a little dance step while holding the edge of her pinafore, out to either side. It was a little incongruous, there in the land of Harley Davidson and ZZ Top, but he applauded.

The interview ended quietly, quite naturally. The awkward moment that had occurred, to do with the local chief and the struggle for water rights, had passed away easily in their singing, so that when he stepped across the bike-tyre signatures and pushed open the heavy timber door, she was there at his side, nodding and saying she hoped he'd come by again. She had a lot of things her mother had left her and she hadn't really known what to do with them, hadn't really thought about them until now, if he wanted to have a look. He promised to call back sometime.

Outside in the blazing sun, leaving the cool AC air that was gathered in the darkness of the cabin, the noonday heat was overwhelming. He felt himself begin to sweat before he'd even crossed the car-park. He took the Avon sun-cream from his backpack and squirted some on his fingers, then massaged it into his neck, and spread it over his bare arms. Already they were red and beginning to freckle, as his skin always did, rather than tan evenly. A few more days of this and he'd be one big freckle, his pink Scottish skin blistered and sore. He had to find some shade, and soon. Walking down towards the old acacia avenue, where the remaining trees offered some respite from the desert sun, he understood properly why water should be the cause of dispute here. The dryness in his throat caused him to catch his breath and swallow uncomfortably. It was like those days when he was having the radiotherapy, when he'd wake in the night in agony, reaching for the painkiller by the bedside and drink it down as if it was some lifesaving antidote.

And yet here it was, the Thompson River charging through the canyon at great speed, billions upon billions of gallons of the stuff just there, yet out of reach. He felt a strong urge to try to find a place where he could get down the bank, to at least dip his feet in the cold water, but the current was too swift and the swollen river had covered whatever shore there might be when the waters were lower. He would be swept away in seconds.

And he remembered again the story he'd read from 1858, the year John MacLeod left Aberdeen for the New World, of the headless bodies of French gold-miners that were carried downstream to Yale, where they circled in a great eddy next to the miners' camp. How they had been decapitated by the people then called Couteau Indians by the whites, the very N'laka'pamux people Lyle came to live among twenty years later. The dead miners were rapists, their victims women of the tribe, and so the Couteau men took revenge. How back then, white settler and 'Indian' hardly knew anything of each other. Native people who had never left the canyon and the lands around it saw only a few ragged miners on their traditional lands, and meted out their own natural justice to the criminals. So they floated the headless bodies downstream, towards where the whites were coming from, a silent message that there was a different way of life upriver, a different set of values which would not condone that kind of brutality. How the white gold-miners looked upstream and thought much the same, that brutality which could behead a white man would not be tolerated.

The Scotsman found himself a shaded spot overlooking the river, and fished the book with the story from his bag, to remind himself of the details. While many of the more timid miners left the region, frightened off by the fearsome reputation of the 'knife' Indians, others stayed – hardened Civil War veterans who had come north from the Californian gold rush demanded immediate justice, and organised the more belligerent into a small army to march upstream and teach the Indians a lesson. Six regiments were assembled. One faction, formed mostly of southerners under the command of a Captain Graham, wanted to exterminate the enemy wholesale, but the largest group, led by Captain Snyder, favoured pacification. Snyder insisted distinction be made between war-like and friendly, and that messengers be sent ahead for natives to display a white flag as a sign of peace if they did not want to be harmed. The ragged army marched up the canyon to Spuzzum, one of the few crossing points, where 3000 panicked miners had gathered, unable to move in any direction for fear of what might await them.

Snyder's company crossed to the east side of the river, while Graham's group carried on up the west. The former met with no resistance and sent messages ahead, to the Indian centre at Camchin, that they wanted to parley peace, but Graham's men destroyed everything in their path, food caches and potato fields, although they found few natives to revenge themselves upon. Then one night, a rifle fell over and went off in the middle of Graham's camp and, thinking they were under attack, they began shooting each other in the dark. Only a handful of men survived.

At Camchin, the leaders of the N'laka'pamux and their allies were holding a war council. The N'laka'pamux war chief tried to incite the warriors to wipe out the white men once and for all, but the Camchin chief Cxpentlum had established good relations with the governor, James Douglas, and he argued for peaceful co-existence. Unwittingly, Snyder marched his men into the middle of this perilous situation. If

they'd known thousands of warriors watched from the mountains surrounding, they might not have been so bold, but according to Indian
custom they had a right to speak. So, through their translators, they
told the assembled council that, if war began, thousands more white
men would come to fight. The white men demonstrated their modern
rifles, saying that if it came to a battle their countrymen would finally
kill them all. The Indians had only a few old muskets and carbines. Six
treaties had been made that day, none of which survived, dealing with
the peaceful co-existence of the white incomers with the natives, and the
working of the imagined goldfields.

Musing on this, he made his way back across the bridge, past the
CPR lines, with the intention of spending the afternoon writing. But
back at the inn, he found there was a note awaiting him on the front
desk. It was from George, the man who he had met the night of the
hockey match. Written in a sloping hand, it said he was invited to meet
an elder of the band, someone who George said knew about Jimmy
Lyle, at 3pm in the band office, if that suited him, in the new community centre in the town – the mysterious new building with the giant eagle
schematic he'd seen when he first got off the Greyhound.

So after grabbing a bit of lunch from the cold cabinet Vince had
directed him to, he set off again on foot, walking back the way he'd
come, wondering just how far he had tramped already since he got to
Cloud Falls, how many times he'd crossed that bridge without jumping.

When he reached the band office, the scale of it impressed him.
He'd seen the old office on the reservation on his first perimeter walk,
a wooden shed broken down and neglected, but as he pushed open
the door of this new building, the scent of the 21st century met him.
There was something symbolic about its position too, not on the
margins of the town in the reservation, but here in the heart of it, half-
hidden among the settler houses. This new community centre with its
imitation-wood flat-pack furniture seemed a little odd, but then what
had he expected, that they would meet in a tipi and pass around a peace
pipe? Or some ancient darkened log house where the walls had eyes,
like something out of a John Buchan story or a Boas essay? Instead he
was shown into a cleanly minimal office of the kind to be found all over
the so-called western world.

The elder was a small white-haired, sallow-skinned woman dressed
in a white cotton sweater, trainers and well-pressed denims. She looked at
him curiously through rim-less glasses, as if her dark eyes were questioning

his very presence here in the office of the band - the 'Indian Band', as they still styled themselves. But she held out a tiny delicate hand in greeting, and they made their introductions. He looked around him. In the windows were stylish stained glass images that spoke of their specific situation – a rattlesnake, coiled, its tiny yellow eyes staring threateningly; a coyote, neck upstretched, howling presumably; a heron wading in a blue stream. And above the elder's desk was the magnificent mounted head of a bighorn, the kind of sheep he'd read about, those that roam wild in the mountains around Cloud Falls. This specimen had been a beauty, its huge proudly held head framed at either side by grand curving horns that twisted round on themselves in perfect symmetry.

'He's quite a fella, isn't he?' she said, following the line of his gaze. 'Big old ram, he was.'

'I suppose he would have been a prize,' he smiled.

'I guess,' she said. Her face seemed to remain expressionless, her voice monotone. Was he even welcome here? He couldn't tell from her manner. 'I don't know,' she went on. 'He's been around the Band Office for as long as I can recall. And I've been around a long time. We just moved him up here from the old place.'

'This is pretty new here, this centre? It's very smart.'

'Sure, just four years old.' She gazed around the office too. 'Yup, it's sure a big improvement on the old one,' she added, but again her face gave away no emotion. 'So George said you've come over from Scotland because you want to know about Jimmy Lyle. How come you're so keen on finding out about him?' she asked.

'Well,' he began, feeling that he was the one being interviewed, 'I believe he's a relative of mine. I've sort of known the story all my life, of this man who went off to British Columbia. I remember an old magazine my mother had, with a story in it about him. 'Friend to the Indians', it was called. About how he married a local woman and learned to speak the language, and then helped the Indian Rights movement. And it always fascinated me. I thought one day I would write about it. I wanted to see where he lived for a long time, to find out if anyone here still remembers him. So here I am.' He smiled warmly, hoping that her ancient reserve might ease.

She didn't respond to the smile, but nodded gently, as if she seemed to accept the reasoning. 'Wasn't so strange for white men to marry native women back then. Country wives, they called them. Didn't mean they had any rights, though. Most stayed where they were, if their husband went back home. But Jimmy Lyle, I believe he was a good man and, sure, we still know what he did for us. I only just remember him a little, but my father, he knew him well. They were big friends.'

He was shocked. 'You actually remember him? How old are you?' It sounded impolite after he'd blurted it, but her expression registered no offence. It seemed barely possible that anyone from that era would still be alive, but he supposed it was, just.

'I'm ninety-nine,' she said, with a little touch of pride in her voice, and seemed to wink from behind her glasses.

'Wow,' he breathed. 'That's amazing.'

She didn't respond to that, but carried on talking about Lyle. 'I do remember him, yes, at least a little. I think I was about eleven when he died. Course he'd moved over to Merritt by then, so he'd be close to a doctor, cause he wasn't too well for a long time, but he'd still come back here to see my father on the train. When there was still a station. The CPR doesn't stop here anymore. CNR neither.'

'It seems strange, these big railway lines here, and no station.'

'Well, I guess so for a stranger. It's just how it is. Now everybody drives. And with the new highway, nobody really stops. Just pass on through.' She looked right though him again, her face impassive, but her words seemed friendly. 'So what can I tell you, Bert? What are you so curious about?'

He tried to choose words carefully. 'I suppose, what I want to know is, how do local people feel about him now. I mean, your people – the N'laka'pamux. How do you say it?' He wondered whether he'd even pronounced the name correctly.

'Okay, sure. I understand what you're asking.' She slowly pushed her chair away from her desk and took from a drawer a copy of Jimmy Lyle's book, his account of the culture of Indians of the territory which Franz Boas had published. 'You ever seen this?' she asked.

'I have a copy. I've read it,' he answered and the elder smiled for the first time. Her eyes twinkled behind her frameless spectacles. She waited for more information, so he went on, 'I know he wrote a lot about the traditional way of life, the stories he heard. And I do understand that these days, a lot of the writing done by settlers in English back then is considered to be – well, the term is appropriation – like, what right did these Europeans have to take the native stories – I mean, First Nations – translate them and claim to be doing them justice. To

be telling the truth. Because every story loses something when it's translated, doesn't it?'

There was long pause while she appeared to be considering her
response. When it came, the sentences were punctuated by further
sighs, further pauses. 'There's some people who object to that, you're
right… and it's true what you say, a story is different when you tell it in
another tongue… every storyteller has their own versions, they kinda
tweak it, like they say today… to suit themselves or who they're telling
it to… Jimmy Lyle was just working from memory, writing down what
he could remember, he had no tape recorder like people today, and so
he kinda pieced together the stories from different versions… That was
what old Professor Boas wanted…'

She looked at him to see if he knew who she was referring to, and
smiled again when he nodded to assure her he did.

'So we don't know, when we read Jimmy Lyle's book, who told
him what…' she said, and smiled slightly ruefully, as if reflecting on
those lost voices, people like her father who had been one of his source
informants. 'But you know, Jimmy wrote a lot of things down, not just
stories, but all kinds of folklore, things that we would have lost otherwise. There's not too many people around now to ask how things used
to be, and not many who can really speak the old language. So Jimmy
did a lot, saved words even, medicine, ceremonies. All these things we
later lost. Or would have done, if he hadn't written what he did.'

He nodded. She seemed to be opening up to him. 'You've heard
about the residential schools, I guess?' she went on.

He nodded again, thinking there was something regal about this
little old lady, a grace, a presence. 'Some, yes.'

'Well, when they took us away there, we weren't allowed to use
our own language. They gave us new names, new clothes and all, tried
to teach us new things to believe in. All the old knowledge, that was
supposed to be forgotten. I remember that well.'

Again, he felt that incredulity he'd had when she told him her age.
'You were at a residential school?'

'Sure. We all were, just about. From age four. Me and my two
brothers. It was a hard place for little kids. And you know they used
to beat us? Just for speaking our own language? It was a cruel, cruel
place. Cruel people. We were abused, all kinds of ways. Some of the
kids never recovered from it. Broken for the rest of their lives, spirits
crushed.'

She stopped, gazing to the stained glass image of the rattlesnake in the window, lit by the sunshine outside. He looked too, as those little yellow snake-eyes seemed to shine with an impenetrable foreign quality, an opaque enmity which spoke only of hatred, of ill intent and possible death. He felt himself, in his white-skinned complacency, to be culpable somehow, and searching for some way to say he understood, cleared his throat. 'You know, back home in Scotland, in some places it wasn't so different. In some parts, like the northwest where people had a different native culture, Gaelic as we call it, or in the north like Shetland where Jimmy Lyle came from, where the people had once been part of Norway, their native tongues were suppressed. Kids were punished for speaking, like you say. They were seen as barbarians by people in the south.'

'Huh,' she said, for the first time lost for words.

'One of the things I've been wondering about is whether he, Jimmy as you call him, saw what was happening to native culture here and recognized the same imperialist British policy as he'd witnessed back home, growing up.'

She seemed to breathe deeply, to relax at this, as if understanding that this visitor wasn't simply some white settler's descendant or distant cousin, but someone who had some parallel experience, who was offering some kind of insight into Lyle and his life.

'I didn't know that about Scotland, that there was natives there too,' she said, after a while.

He wondered how much she needed to know, whether to embark on a historical lecture, to explain the effects of the aftermath of Culloden on the culture of the Highlands, the repression of Gaelic and the breaking up of the clan system. Maybe it wasn't quite the right moment. Or even all that relevant?

'Oh yes,' he said. 'There were natives there – still are. Though it's not quite the same, you know. In Scotland the natives don't really look different. It's more a matter of culture, of language. Not so obviously racist.'

'I see,' she said. 'I'm kinda curious now. If Jimmy Lyle was a native in his own country, that would explain a lot. But he did kinda look different from the other white people, and he seemed to know how things were for our people. At least that's how I understood it, from my father. Seemed to want to be useful, you know, writing down what the people wanted. You know about the letter to the premier of Canada they wrote?'

'I read about it. About a hundred years ago, wasn't it?'

'Hundred and one years now. Jimmy Lyle was the one who wrote it down. The chiefs all came here, told him what they wanted it to say in their own language, and he turned it into English. They presented it to Laurier. We had a ceremony last year, on the anniversary. The centenary. We built a new place, up to the north of the town, near the reservation. For meetings, you know. Jimmy Lyle was mentioned. We even put a plaque up to him. You should go see it. It's beautiful. Cedar wood, but in a modern design.'

This was still news to him, though George had mentioned something about it. He hadn't known, even imagined, that Lyle had been so recently on the lips of people, that the centenary had been celebrated. 'I'd like that,' he said. 'Whereabouts is it, exactly?'

The elder took a little slip of paper and drew a rudimentary sketch of the river and the town, with the two bridges, one old one new, then marked a cross where he would find the memorial. He realised that there were two reservations, one to the north he hadn't known about, and asked where else he should go, what other places she could recommend that had to do with Lyle's life here. She thought for a while, as if scrutinizing him again, wondering could he be trusted.

'You could go to his wife's grave, maybe?'

'Lucy?'

'That's what the missionaries called her, but her name was really Antko. Her stone is in the Indian graveyard by the old church. Right in the corner. It's a big one. Jimmy Lyle put it there.' She stared once again at the stained glass in the window, her black eyes full of something very deep, a pool of night, he thought. 'Course you know, to us, it was Antko who was the important one. Like I said, Jimmy wrote things down, but it was her who made all that possible. She was a very special person. My father used to say she was a wise and patient woman. And it was a great loss when she died, to Jimmy Lyle and everyone. Just 33 years old.'

Again she drew on the little map. 'Then I guess you'll want to see the houses he lived in.'

'Houses? More than one?'

'Yeah. He lived in a few different places. One he built, down by the CNR line, that's near here. There's a couple live there, very keen on

Jimmy Lyle's writings about plants. Then he was up at High Ridge after Antko died, when he married the Dutchwoman.'

He pointed to the photo on the cover of the book, where Lyle was in Stetson, looking like a proper cowboy, his fair hair longish with a moustache, his native wife by his side, and the big dog in the foreground. Her hair was tied back and she was wearing a smart western dress. He had on a fringed buckskin shirt. The black dog curled at their feet, panting.

'Where was this taken?' he asked.

'Ah, that's the cabin they lived in, in the early days.'

'Is that still around?'

'It's a ways off from here. Up in the Echte Valley, back from the highway. Not so easy to get to. Echte valley is a kinda sacred place for us. The cabin's hidden away. They lived there for years, before Jimmy Lyle met Boas and started making himself some money out of all that. That's when he built the new house down by the railway.'

She pushed her chair back from the desk and stood up. Such a small woman, but such an intense regal presence.

'It's not where the white folk think it is,' she said, looking out the window, her back to him. 'They think they know, but it isn't there. That's another cabin, not theirs. Theirs is a way further back, up the trail.' She turned and smiled at him. And did she wink, conspiratorially?

He didn't have time to consider, as a shouting began outside the office. He couldn't hear what exactly was being said, but one loud voice seemed to dominate. Suddenly the door opened and a striking figure filled the frame, a younger woman whose thick gloss-black hair was the antithesis of the elder's neat white. She wore a short jacket with a bold native design imprinted, like the work of the Haida Gwaii artists he'd seen in Vancouver. When she glanced at him sitting there, black eyes flashing, he thought she could be Elvis's sister.

'Deeanna,' the elder said. 'I'm busy. What is it now?'

'I wanna put this poster up. Gilly says I have to ask you.'

'What's it for?'

The intruder became a little defensive. 'A meeting.'

'Let me see.' The She-Elvis came into the room, her boots clicking loudly on the tiled floor, and presented a sheet of paper. He couldn't see what was on it. The elder read it through, then handed it back. 'I can't put this up here, Deeanna. It's going to cause a lot of trouble. You know that.'

'Yeah, I know that. But I'm puttin them up all over town, anyways.'

'Chief is going to be mad.'

'I don't care. It's time somebody spoke up. And I'm not frightened of him, there's nothing he can do to me that's worse than what's already happened.'

The elder glanced at him again, as if unsure whether he should be hearing this. She made an apologetic gesture towards him.

'Look,' he said. 'I can come back if this is an awkward time for you.'

She nodded, thanked him, showed him out, explaining briefly that Deeanna was her god-daughter and that she'd had a difficult time in her life lately. She'd just moved back to Cloud Falls. He nodded too, said he understood and that he hoped they'd meet again soon. She suggested he take a look around the centre – down the hallway was a framed copy of the claim of right and the pledge they'd signed last year on the centenary of the original that he might be interested in seeing, and other stuff too, maybe. He was welcome to look around.

He found the claim of right, facing the renewed pledge, both beautifully framed. On either side of the text of the 1910 claim were two feathers, presumably eagle by their size. The left hand one was beaded to display the number 1910, and the right 2010. On the opposite wall facing was a list of signatures of chiefs who had signed in 2010, the nations they represented appended. He read the text:

'We the undersigned chiefs and representatives of the following indigenous nations gather together with the above signatory indigenous nations to honor the Spirit and Intent of the original Wilfred Laurier Memorial and to honor the efforts of our ancestors in the past 100 years to find a Just and Lasting resolution to the Land Question.'

It was astonishing to see something he had thought was history so recently revisited and presented in this way. He'd read the original text before online, but hadn't known it was still so current as it obviously was, the 'Land Question.'

Bemused by this realisation, he walked on down the corridor and stumbled into an empty meeting room where hung four large Canadian government posters, each showing the life-cycle of a different salmon – Cohol, Pink, Sockeye and Steelhead – from smolt to returning adult, the prize awaited by beast and man alike. He gazed at the tracks of their migrations across the north Pacific to Kamchatka and Japan. It seemed barely possible that life should persist with such determination.

Then behind a whiteboard, standing in front of the far wall, he noticed the corner of a painting. Dark, sombre blues, with flashing sheet lightning. He peered behind the board and, to his shock, recognized it as a portrait of Lyle's native wife, Lucy, whose name he knew was really Antko. It was a large canvas and he tried to pull it out from where it was hidden but couldn't easily. Instead he squinted at it, as she squinted at him from within the image. It was a portrait he recognized from the photograph on the cover of the book he'd just been looking at on the elder's desk. She was wearing the same full-length western dress buttoned up to the neck, almost scowling at the viewer. It was hard to see but he knew it was a good painting, the balance and choice of colour, the composition.

The likeness to its subject was remarkably good, but what was most striking of all was what had been omitted. The old photograph showed her and her white settler husband, with their dog, in front of their domestic abode, the cabin in the sacred valley. In the painting, it was simply she, Antko, a woman alone against a background of what appeared an ultramarine night lit by shafts of moonlight or even lightning. The image had an elemental quality, robbed of its domesticity – only the quaintly remaining buttoned-up dress suggested wife and homemaker. Had she been robed in some buckskin, or a painted blanket, it would have looked less odd, but the painter, whoever they were, had at least stripped her of the inherited identity, as wife to the Scotsman, Jimmy Lyle. He pushed the whiteboard out of the way to see it properly. The signature in the bottom left corner was 'Deeanna'.

Outside in the warm air, he decided to look for the Indian graveyard the elder had told him about, to see if he could find Antko's stone. The one that Jimmy Lyle had placed there, way back in 1899, long before even the claim of right. He walked along the river to the new highway bridge till he came to a pathway lined with purple flowering alfalfa on the other side, the one that led to the old wooden church. He pushed the little metal gate open and it creaked as he did so.

A black feather spiralled to the ground at his foot. On the top of a tree-trunk electricity post that steadied and stayed a half-dozen heavy wires, a single raven pivoted, tail dipping, bobbing. He took his camera from his backpack and zoomed in until he could see the sunlit arc on the curve of its beak, and its talons gripping the trunk stump. Behind it, in frame, the hulk of the mountain they called 'The Chief', and thundering through the canyon, the Thompson River's urgent melt-water, though it was now late May, the mile-long trains of the CPR.

Behind him, in the Cloud Falls cemetery, Antko's stone was tall among unmarked graves, small wooden crosses and barely detailed stones. In the scrub of sagebrush and purple alfalfa, among the sandy grit and leaves, lay the scorched remains of old bouquets, some the handmade twistings of local plants, some floral, decorative and bought. Her grave was the last, in the corner furthest from the settlement, edging close to where Highway 1 split from Highway 8, the stone text hidden from the stream of drivers even in the north lane.

A block of bare concrete, spotted with lichen, held the upright slab in place. That too seemed concrete, but had a plastered exterior in which were imprinted the words

SACRED
TO
THE MEMORY
OF
ANTKO
beloved wife of
J.A.LYLE
Died March 2, 1899
Aged 33 years

And as he approached he saw, part covered by the brush, beneath the English text, in italics, these words:

Tcuk aks kazuzems

It must be the N'laka'pamux tongue, opaque to him, but the old voice of this territory, veiled and hidden. Closer, on the ground he could see a wreath, quite a recent one, though bleached in the desert sun. An array of roses and dahlias, and another smaller flower he didn't recognise. If they were different colours once, now all were one shade, a very faint lilac-white, like beautiful flower bones.

He felt an intruder here, among these personal gestures, these venerable reservation houses and sheds across the fence, the tinder-like wooden church on the point of tumbling down across the field. Yet the elder had told him to come here, so if someone was looking suspiciously from one of the windows, he was here with her authority. Maybe phones had already rung, the news might already have travelled, of the stranger in town from Scotland?

He thought he'd like the raven's feather to be a sign of acceptance, and maybe of intention - what he knew in Shetland people called a 'penn', a quill to write with. It seemed to fit his hand, a perfect implement for ink, once cut. But then it was just a feather, about five and a half inches long, sleekly perfect, so that its many jet-black silky fibres formed something more than their distinct parts, a comb of common function, a tiny part of the raven's essential nature – to be feathered, to fly.

He picked a sprig of purple alfalfa blossom, and placed it on the concrete base of Antko's stone, between the gnomic N'laka'pamux inscription and the somehow very British floral wreath. He thought again of that shared portrait with husband and dog, outside the cabin where they'd lived in the hidden valley, recalling the strong face, almost scowling at the photographer, her dark gaze seeming to penetrate the camera's lens, to joust with picture-taker's own. Only the dress seemed alien - Lucy's, perhaps, that other self, the Christian name given to her by the missionaries. There was no mention of 'Lucy' on this gravestone, here on the corner of Highway 8 and Highway 1, where the road split for Merritt or Cache Creek. No mention of God or angels, even. Whatever was sacred about this spot was sacred because of Antko's memory.

He made his way out of the cemetery and closed the white gate, put his hands together in a momentary gesture of prayer by the wire fence. The path to the church ran through the reservation. Missionaries first, organised resistance much later. When the funeral party carried Antko's dead body from the stoop of the little wooden church to the furthest corner of the graveyard, early in March 1899, there was no Band office.

He wondered who was there, at that funeral in the last spring of the 1800s: Antko's relations, no doubt, and of course Lyle himself. But did the better-off settlers come to this ceremony on the edge of town – the wee Scottish Widow Spark, mistress of the famous orchards, or Mr Archie Clements, the man of property, who had built the Inn and the community Hall? Old Sigurd who gave his name to the first regular crossing of the river, who himself died later that year? Sigurd's Crossing it was called, once upon a time, this flat-banked canyon just below where the Nicola River joins the Thompson. The N'laka'pamux had other names for all.

He closed his eyes and tried to imagine that procession – he could visualize the church, quite new back then, perhaps the paint job fresh, but the pall-bearers led by the widowed husband, that *cheechako* who'd married the *klootchman*, they remained indistinct. He could picture a slow solemn walk past the settler graveyard to the furthest corner of the other, and imagine the English voice of the preacher, saying what must be said, the different tongues spoken as mourners parted again, to go to where they must go – their side of the tracks. N'laka'pamux, Chinook. French, English. Mandarin, Scots, all drawn here to this huge isolated valley, the wintry river ripping past, full spring still distant, a strange array of people intent upon making new homes. And the Cheechako Lyle, finally alone at home, her presence suddenly absent among her things, did he speak distractedly to himself in the dialect of his native Shetland? The English of his education? Or in the language of this canyon that she had helped him learn?

Tcuk aks kazuzems – what could it mean? So many secrets, it seemed. The elder had told him no one outside the Cloud Falls Band really knew where their cabin was – the white people thought they did, but they were wrong, the place they thought it was wasn't near as far away as the cabin Lyle had built for his first wife. That was much deeper in the valley, hidden. But knowing this, there was nowhere else he wanted to go more. Yet he was excluded. As he wandered back along the highway, towards the inn again, he wondered about the task of telling the story of another person's life – any other person – the difficulty and the ethics of that. For all the knowledge he might gather of their life, the historical detail, even if he was to learn the native language, he, like Lyle, would be limited by not being one of them, and could only speculate on the deep selves that underlie actions. Yet the raven had given him its pen, as the elder had seemed to approve, he had taken up the commission, and put it in his backpack. He was there in Cloud Falls at Antko's grave, over one hundred and eleven years since she was buried, looking for her, Jimmy Lyle, and their tangled stories.

It was getting late by the time he reached base. He had walked, for a second day, round and around Cloud Falls in the heat, but today he'd got deeper, much deeper in. His feet were swollen and sore so he bathed them, then began writing the story of the day. He'd eat at The Apple Store later. Once more over the bridge. It was only then he realised he'd forgotten to ask the elder if she had ever known his father.

The Apple Store was empty of customers when he went in. Dorothy appeared from the rear and welcomed him like a friend. He said he'd got the sun cream from the Avon lady like she'd suggested.

He was tucking into the special of the day, a chicken fricassee, and chatting with Dorothy when a large Chrysler truck pulled into the parking lot outside at speed, coming to rest just outside the window by the table where the Scotsman sat. The cowcatcher on the front filled the window like prison bars. From the cab jumped a swarthy man, a stocky figure that moved with a muscled assurance. He nodded as he passed the window, opened the door briskly, cast an expressionless glance over at the woman behind the counter, and strode over to where the stranger sat.

'Chief Mutch,' he said, offering a rough strong hand. The Scotsman put down his knife, reached over and shook it. 'I'm Bert,' he said. 'Bert Johnson. I'm sorry, I haven't been able to pick up messages since I got here, so I don't know if you've been in touch?'

The chief looked in a hurry and didn't respond directly to his question, but gave a shrug of no importance. 'Called along the inn, they told me you were down here,' he said quickly, and sat down opposite the eater before he could be invited. 'Spoke with the elder earlier. She said you two had a good meeting today.'

Bert leaned back from his half-eaten plate. 'Yes, it was good. She was very helpful. I had no idea she had met Jimmy Lyle. She must have been quite young.'

'Just a little kid, I guess, yeah. Listen, I'm sorry, but I gotta go down to Vancouver for a meeting otherwise I'd take you round myself, show you those places you were asking about. Be good to talk a bit too. The elder says Jimmy Lyle was a native back in Scotland. I didn't know that.'

'Well, it was a bit different from the situation here. But yes, he was in a way. I think he identified…' He didn't finish his sentence, as Chief Mutch glanced again at the counter where Dorothy was silently polishing things, ears flapping.

'So you're writing a book about him, then?' he said, still watching her.

'Well, I'm just researching at the moment. Taking notes. I just wanted to see the place he lived for myself, and talk to people, see if he was still remembered at all. And I was amazed when the elder told me that you'd had a commemoration last year.'

Chief Mutch turned his attention back to him, and frowned. 'Not of Jimmy Lyle exactly. You know about the Laurier memorial?'

'I do. I saw the framed text in the community centre.'

'You know, Lyle was important, of course he was. But the story isn't really about him, not to us. And I guess whatever you're writing won't really....' He hesitated. His dark-eyed stare was intense, challenging, without the slightest flinch. The Scotsman could feel that he was a powerful presence, a poker-faced, possibly overbearing leader, a chief like the mountain above, leaning over the settlement, seemingly resolute and immoveable.

'I can't say what I'll write. Not yet. But I know what his role in the memorial was, that he wrote down what the chiefs wanted.'

'Yeah. He was their scribe. And that was important. But for us, the story is that all the chiefs in BC came here, from all over the province. Some of them travelled for days to be here. That was historic. You know why?'

'Why what?'

'Why they gathered right then?'

The Scotsman shook his head, then shrugged. 'Land rights?'

'Sure, but specifically the provincial government suddenly decided to cut the amount of reserved land. No reason, no warning. They reckoned the Indians didn't need it so much. That was why the chiefs all travelled here.' He glanced again at the polishing audience. 'Not much has changed since your Jimmy Lyle's day.' Chief Mutch smiled. 'Your plate's getting cold.'

The Scotsman shrugged. 'I was finished anyway.'

'You sure?' His eyes flicked around the café. 'Listen, I gotta go,' he said, 'But first I'll tell you a little story. Maybe it'll help you when you come to write your book. It's about when I was a boy and I used to go out with my father in the truck. We would drive about, all over this territory, N'laka'pamux territory. We'd set traps and we'd watch to see how things were growing, what water was in the streams, how the snow was melting. Cause out here water is key to everything. And this one day we came to a big old gate, with a padlock on it right across our trail. The gate had a sign too, a sign that said Private Property with the name of some company, I can't recall exactly what it was now – JPD or PDJ or something. Now, under Canadian Law this company owned the land, but under N'laka'pamux law, it was ours and always had been. People had been going through that territory for centuries just like we were that day. But there it was, a big old metal gate with this lock on it. Well, my father just backed up our truck, geared down and drove straight through it. The lock was bust open. We closed the gate behind us, and carried on. And it stayed like that. The so-called owners never went there, so they never knew. We just opened that busted gate and shut it again after us every time, and nobody ever came to repair it. The shiny new sign just got old and fell off. The Canadian government still thought that company owned it. We knew they didn't.'

His eyes had been glazed, as if remembering his childhood and his father, but as he finished his story, Chief Mutch looked up at the Scotsman and grinned in a toothy twisted way. He had heard this story before, or rather had read it, in the thesis from the UBC archive.

'Absentee landlords,' the Scotsman ventured in response, 'We have them in Scotland too. They think they own places, and try to keep the people out with their fences and signs. They use these estates for forestry and they farm deer for hunting. Their rich friends come up on hunting trips.'

The chief grinned again. 'Well, maybe Scotland isn't so different then. Listen, like I said, I'd take you round, show you things, but I got a meeting down in Vancouver. How long you staying?'

'I don't know yet. Maybe another week. Maybe more, it depends on how things go.'

'Maybe I could arrange for someone to take you round? You don't have a truck or a car or anything, do you?'

'No, I'm on foot.'

'I heard that.' He smiled again, as if the Scotsman's peregrinations had been the subject of a joke or two in some circle or another.

'I like to walk,' he said, 'I see more that way.'

'Well, okay. But out here in the sun, it's not so good.'

'Nothing's that far, though, I'm never out too long. Tell me, though, I want to know more about Lyle's cabin. The elder told me it was in some secret valley.'

The Chief's demeanour changed at the mention. He frowned, leaned forward a little. 'She told you what?' he said, his voice a little lower in tone.

'She told me it was in a secret place no one knew except the band. That another place had been mistaken for it and nobody had ever corrected…'

The chief interrupted. 'She told you that?' He glanced over to the counter again. Dorothy was still dusting off glasses. If she was really eavesdropping, she was doing a good job of cleaning at the same time.

'I want to know if I can walk there. Or is it too far?' the Scotsman asked.

Chief Mutch pushed his chair back. 'That's not really a place you should go.'

'Why not?'

'You'd need a truck.'

'So I couldn't walk there?'

'It's not so easy to find.' He glanced at his watched. 'Listen, I gotta go, drive down to Vancouver.' He stood up, glanced again at Dorothy, who this time acknowledged him with an awkward grin. 'Wait till I get back, will you?' he added, and then he was gone, out the door with the same spin of speed he'd arrived with. His stocky frame seemed to spring up into the cab of his truck. He started it up and swung out of there as the gravel crunched and the dust rose.

When he paid, Dorothy seemed to want a little information, but the Scotsman's mind was on what had just happened. It was a whirlwind encounter and not at all what he'd hoped for when he first made contact with the chief. He'd seemed abrupt, suspicious, although not outright unfriendly, and even if it may have been that he was just in a hurry, it left the Scotsman feeling, for the first time since he'd arrived, like an intruder.

Back at the inn, he went up to his room. He hadn't bothered with the video, so there was no footage to check. It seemed the tree-planters had already all retired, and he drifted off to sleep in the heat of the evening, his mind still full of the brief exchange with the chief. In the hypnagogic state, reality morphed into dream, and he felt himself borne across deserts on the gentle breeze above the rush of river water. A figure appeared on the edge of consciousness. An elder who wanted answers from him, sitting by a fire. So you want to write my tellings down, she asked, in her own tongue, which he seemed to know. And in English? In the dreamy firelight, he averred. And what kind of word is that, averred, she said? Could she read his mind, or had he spoken out loud? Have you forgotten who you are? I am your great-grandson, he answered. Never forget that, she told him. Or you will forget yourself. She poked in the fire. The flames had burned a tiny bright-lit cave into the embers, and here she placed the point of the poker, turned it, causing the unburned fuel to fall into the heart of the blaze. The light from the fire was all the light she had. He couldn't see her face clearly, but he could fill the detail into the darkness, the tight skin stretched across her cheekbones, her small round nose. Her bright eyes twinkled amongst the wrinkles. She had kept him when he was a small child, and had always told him stories. In her tongue – she knew a little English, could still recite 'Lord Ullin's Daughter' which she'd learned at school in 1890s under pain of severe punishment. The literal.

A chieftain, to the Highlands bound, Cries, "Boatman, do not tarry! And I'll give thee a silver pound To row us o'er the ferry!"– "Now, who be ye, would cross Lochgyle, This dark and stormy weather?" "O, I'm the chief of Ulva's isle, And this, Lord Ullin's daughter…

Parrots can do that, she says. A story stops changing when you write it down, she says. It's like it dies, just becomes dead sound. The stories I tell, they are alive and changing all the time. It's never the same. He thought he knew that, that every time she told a tale, it was different. He remembered Tami Nori, the child's game from mythical Shetland his father used to play with him when he was very young – A'll tell de a story aboot Tammi Nori, if du winna spaek ida middl'o'it. And then she was gone, and he slept.

The next day he woke feeling sore and tired. He felt he'd had too much sun, had walked too far, had pushed his physical being beyond what post-radiotherapy fitness allowed, so he stayed at the inn, writing. He wrote his journal, and then carried on with the story he'd started about his time in Vancouver. That seemed to flow far more readily than his scratchy attempts to record the world of 1899, or the mind-set of the man he wanted to write about.

The day was hot again, so he had both windows open to channel the canyon breeze through, past his desk. And at last, he found he was really writing – words came quickly, almost too quickly to write them all down. Vince came up to his room, and seemed to want to talk, but the flow was too strong to stop. He had his host bring him some soup and bread at lunchtime, so he could carry on. He thought he wouldn't stop as long as inspiration lasted, but after eating, after writing for some six hours, he went to lie on the bed, feeling exhausted, but happy.

He woke to the sound of the tree-planters returning, as they always did, around four o'clock. Their day started before dawn, but it finished early too – only so much bending a person could do on any one day, he supposed. He heard a few make their way upstairs but a group went out to the terrace below. They were talking animatedly, as if carrying over an argument started earlier. The reek of tobacco and pot rose with the sound.

He realised they were discussing the First Nations situation. Apparently one of them, who sounded like the older man from the hockey game, had read some article out to the others on the drive back to the inn. The Scotsman went to his window so he could hear more clearly, then switched on the video camera so he could record what they had to say, though the image was just the same slow-moving panorama of the village across the river and the steely glint of the stream.

'I completely get it,' the older man said, 'The First Nations were treated unfairly and horrible things happened. But are they gonna hang onto that victim status for the next twenty generations, or are they gonna do away with the reserves, get over how they were treated and get with the programme?'

A woman's voice sounded. 'Maybe Canada can start by paying back all the money owed from the use of their land and resources. Then maybe repay the funds stolen from them and spent on projects that were not for First Nations.'

A third voice, Doug, the false Lawrence's interjected. 'Why is eliminating reserves even considered a solution? If you take away reserves, there's nowhere left for them to call home. There'll just be Canada, a country that obviously doesn't respect the native population or the history of the people.'

The woman picked up his thought. 'Canada can't hide genocide. What needs to be addressed first is the underlying racism and ignorance. Today's problems will never go away until Canadians address that.'

The older man spoke again. 'Yeah, it's funny with all the money reserves get – maybe it's time to disband the chief and council and let the government do it. The way it is, they're the only ones that benefit, while other people suffer like they lived in the third world.' Doug scoffed, but the older guy was adamant. 'So how about elimination of the reserves and joining the rest of the country in the 21st century? Can't apologize forever. Paying taxes would be a good start also...'

The woman gave a snort of condemnation. 'Native people never put themselves in the position of reserves and not paying taxes to the government,' she said angrily. 'The British commonwealth and the church put them there. What you don't seem to understand is that everybody except the aboriginal peoples are actually immigrants to Canada. This is their land we've been enjoying while taking advantage of them, while raping the land of its resources.'

There was a brief pause, the clink of glasses or bottles. Then the older man spoke again. 'Okay, I'm gonna ask the obvious question here. The on-reserve problems, are those not the responsibility of the bands to fix using the money the federal government gives to them? I'm not trying to be ignorant, I'm just not sure what can be done, other than giving them their allocated money and they stretch it as far as it can go.'

At that moment, the argument ceased altogether and the company fell silent. The Scotsman wondered what had happened. Then a new voice spoke, one he thought he recognised as the painter of Antko's portrait, the elder's troubled god-daughter, Deeanna, who had burst into the office at the community centre. Her voice was commanding, loud and impassioned.

'Who the fuck gave any of you so-called majority people the right to judge anyone? The bloody system is set up to continue to kill off First Nations! What you mean is join the rest of the country, and be a white person, in a white system. Don't waste words, just state it – be white.' He heard a rattling sound, and the scraping of chair legs, as if people were moving around. The older man started to say something in protest, but she cut him off. 'You should educate your mind, your spirit, and your mouth. Simple like that. Teach the truth about the times from first contact on. The glorified history books in Canada are full of prejudice and lies. You see us as parasites and yet the new immigrants, they get far better treatment. Teach the kids the truth. To asshats like you with the boring old get-over-it-already, I say every time we get together and make an effort to raise awareness and a call to action for change, you turn to us and say "You again"?' The older man was about to respond, but she blocked him, speaking louder still and he was quiet. 'You know what needs to happen, indigenous people need to take back treaty lands and control education to grade twelve and make new indigenous universities that promote our ancestral knowledge and values, connect to our histories before and after contact and become one nation and be recognized as a nation by the United Nations. When you have a government that continues to legislate laws and bylaws to steal our traditional lands, our children, our culture, our language, and even distort Canadian history to pacify most citizens so they can be blissfully ignorant. What most Canadians don't seem to grasp is the fact that aboriginal people have been raised on decades of crimes against humanity, committed by the government of Canada and the church.'

She stopped at that point. It was a breathlessly eloquent outburst. No one spoke for a long spell, then someone applauded, a single person's hand-clap that filled the vacuum. He couldn't tell whether it was intended as ironic by the sound alone. Finally he heard the antagonist of earlier say, 'I sure don't want be disrespectful, Deeanna, but the problem seems not to be federal funding. According to what I was reading earlier – I'll read it you, what it says in the paper here – "in Attawapiskat reserve, the federal annual funding was around 31 million for 1500 living people. So for a four-member family, the annual funding was $80,000." Maybe the problem is who controls the funding in those reservations?'

The Scotchman heard a loud decrying laugh from Deeanna. 'Thinking that more government can solve the problem is like asking your rapist for marriage guidance,' she said. 'How about giving us the same rights you have, how about treating us like people instead of a hindrance to society? How about putting as much effort into finding our lost and stolen people as you do others?'

The older guy snorted. 'Typical. First Nations people do not want to be equal or assimilate because they think they have been displaced. So they want hand-outs cause they think they have been treated badly. Well, I say get off your horses, assimilate and work. Some of your leaders have bucks coming out of their ears. The bucks are not getting distributed to those that need it.'

Deeanna's reply was simple. 'When it comes to running reserves, we need more women chiefs.'

The tree-planter woman gave a little squeal of affirmation. 'Yeah,' she said. 'Put more women in as chiefs. When women are in charge, tribes get taken care of.'

'Maybe the government should start closely monitoring the corrupt reserve Chiefs. There are groups of First Nations people who are blossoming – why can they not learn from and apply the fundamentals of those communities, who are effective and creating wealth,' the antagonist went on.

Deeanna laughed. 'To come even remotely close to a financial remedy, each First Nations person in Canada right now would need the equivalent of what a good fertile hundred-acre farm is worth. That's trillions in total, I reckon.'

'Quit blaming others, I say. Lots of reserves in Alberta are doing very well, but it takes hard work. Let them go do the hard work, I say.'

There was a pause. Then false Lawrence spoke. 'Dood, you have no idea about the history or how this country even functions, what money goes where and where it comes from,' Doug said, and laughed. 'You read one article, suddenly you're an expert.'

The Scotsman had heard enough. He wanted to be a part of this argument, he wanted to see the faces of those involved. Particularly he wanted to see this eloquent, angry woman who had painted the portrait of Lyle's native wife. So he left the videocam running and went downstairs, but as he reached the bottom, the inn door swung closed and, on looking around the terrace, he realised that she had gone as quickly as she'd arrived. The three pot-smoking tree-planters were out on the terrace alone, silenced by her intervention – Doug, the Lawrence lookalike student, the older man who'd told him about the Millionaires who was sitting with his boots up on the table in front of him, and the jolly girl whose name he couldn't recall, who smiled at him as he crossed onto the terrace.

'Hey, Bert,' Doug said, greeting him, looking less like DH Lawrence by day. 'How's the writing?'

'Okay, thanks,' he answered. 'I've been writing today. How was the mountain?'

'Same old. Dirty, back-breaking. You want some of this?' He held out a thick half-smoked joint.

The Scotsman shook his head. 'Thanks, anyway. So who was that I heard just now? The woman?'

'Deeanna?' he said. 'She's one of the Cloud Falls band. She's a bit crazy. Comes up here sometimes, gets drunk and shoots everybody down. Greg here likes to make her mad.'

'Don't mean no harm by it,' Greg, the older guy, said. 'Nothing wrong with natives. They should be treated the same as all Canadians, that's all. Nothing more, nothing less.'

'Deeanna's alright,' Doug added.

'Deeanna's great, you mean,' the girl cut in. 'She's smart as anything, just never had a proper chance. Fostered. Pregnant at fourteen,' she said, aside, as if for the Scotsman's benefit. 'I bet she was raped.' She took the quickly disappearing joint from Doug, and sucked deeply on it. 'Now that's what you should be writing. Her story, all abused women like her. And all the disappeared native women.'

'Disappeared?'

'Yeah. It's criminal, the number. And the authorities don't bother.'

'How come you know so much about it, Lydia?' Greg asked.

'I watch the news, Greg. So should you. But if you really want to know, I am one quarter native myself. My grandma Anna was Squamish.'

Greg didn't reply to this right away, but his facial expression registered some surprise. Then his eyes narrowed and he turned to Doug, and said, aside to him, 'What do you know, Lydia's part Indian.'

Doug sat up straight. 'If you wanna know, Greg, so am I.'

Greg seemed flummoxed. He began to speak, but no words came out. After a minute or two he stretched his arms out above his head and yawned, then stood up, saying he was going for a lie down. Doug looked tired too, and soon followed him upstairs, leaving the Scotsman with the girl, Lydia, who was smoking the end of the joint. It was the first time he'd been alone with her, without her tree-planting buddies.

'So you making headway with your project?' she said.

'Some, yes.'

'What is it about this guy that's so interesting to you?'

'His whole life, I suppose. But you know, the longer I'm here the more I think the story isn't just about him. I thought I was going to write a history book, but what I'm finding out is that the story is every bit as alive today. I mean, the work he did with the local Indian tribes back then, their claim of land rights, all that, it's every bit as relevant now.'

'Sure, nothing much has changed. Although at least now the Canadian government recognises them and pays some kind of lip service, but in fundamental terms, like land and water, in compensation nothing much has changed. And then there's a lot of people now, like me and Doug, who are part First Nations. We don't all look it, but we are.' She glanced at him, then stubbed the joint out in the overflowing ashtray.

'How well do you know this Deeanna?' the Scotsman asked.

'Some. Why?'

'She interests me. I saw a portrait she painted, over in the community centre. I'm sure it's a copy of a photo of Jimmy Lyle's wife, the N'laka'pamux woman he married.' Lydia didn't appear to understand. 'That's the man, you know,' the Scotsman added, 'I'm here to find out about. He married a First Nations woman.'

'Ah, okay.'

'So I wanted to talk with her. Deeanna.'

Lydia shrugged. 'I can give you her home phone if you want.' She pulled out her cell phone.

'You get a signal?' he asked, as she waited for it to start up.

She shook her head, no. 'Not here,' she said. 'Further up the canyon I do. It's useless down here.' She read out a number, which he copied down on the back of a Molson beermat.

'So I should call her?' he said, looking it over.

'Sure. She's great, a real woman warrior, is Deeanna. She comes down here a lot. Old Greg just doesn't get her, thinks he's being smart. But she could eat him up for breakfast if she wanted to.' She yawned. 'Listen, I'm gonna go lie down too. Give her a call if you like.'

She left with a smile to him cast over her shoulder, jolly Lydia. He waited for a bit, alone on the terrace in the shade. He wanted very much to meet this Deeanna, this woman warrior. She would probably take some time to get back home, wherever that was, so he waited for a while and then rang the number from the motel lobby payphone. It rang out and went to voicemail. He thought he wouldn't try to explain who he was in a message, he'd try again later. His nap had refreshed him and he wanted to get back to his laptop, to write some more of his Vancouver story. He worked late, didn't really notice dusk falling. Couldn't be bothered going out to one of the only two places in town to eat, so just got a club sandwich and coffee from Vince and wrote on, into the night.

Writing about Vancouver brought his cancer twin into the moment, and he felt the desire to be in touch with her, to see her smile again. Maybe he would on his way home. He had the little card she'd given him with her name and address. He decided to send her a postcard tomorrow, a picture of the river. Then he realised that this was the first time he'd thought about the return journey since he'd arrived. Had that great notion to jump in the river and die passed?

He woke to the sound of someone knocking on the door. He was lying naked on top of the bedclothes, no memory of when he'd stopped writing, no sense of how long he'd slept. His mind was still in Vancouver, somewhere in Stanley Park.

It was Vince at the door. Someone was on the motel phone, asking for the Scotsman. His first intuition was that she had somehow picked up his thoughts, had found the number somehow, but as he pulled on his clothes hurriedly, that seemed a little crazy. It could be Big George, calling to arrange that supper, or maybe Deeanna had heard he wanted to speak with her? But when he lifted the receiver, it was neither. It was the man who now lived in Lyle's house down by the river, and he was calling to invite the Scotsman to visit. The summons was particular – an appointed hour, as if he had requested an audience: 'Hester would be pleased if you could call on her today at noon at the Lyle house.'

The invitation was unexpected, but yes, he was indeed bidden to call on Hesther the healer. Only after he'd come off the phone did he wonder how they had known about him. Had news travelled some-how? If so, how? And the caller had completely circumnavigated small talk of the kind a stranger might be expected to engage in. Yet it seemed perfectly natural that they should call, and that he should go. Why hadn't he gone there before? They were the ones who knew about Lyle, from what he'd established so far. Yet, since the first day, when he'd seen the tipi hidden among the wooden colonial houses, he'd regarded it as a kind of cuckoo in the settler nest, an anachronism. He was searching for the unknown, for the forgotten where most of the townsfolk were concerned, but here was someone who presumably knew as much if not more about the object of his quest as he did, someone who had relocated to the canyon to live in Lyle's house. He felt curious, yet reluc-tant, as if meeting this healer might entail some loss, as if she might take from him an essential possession he had carried with the care he might have given to a passport or a plane ticket.

He knew the house well enough, directly across the river from the inn, on the road close to the CNR railway line, where once had been a station. He had zoomed in on it with the videocam, had walked past it more than once out of curiosity, but had never seen anyone around. A large spruce tree shaded the front, and various other shrubs hid all of the fence but the little wooden gateway. It had been built after Lyle had become something of a celebrity, following the publication of his study of the native people, and after his wife's death. From here, with the station more or less at the end of his garden, he was able to travel both up country to Merritt and Kamloops, and down the canyon to Vancouver, just by stepping onto a train, giving lectures and calling on fellow experts as far away as Victoria and so forth. His life was very different then from the buckskinned adventurer in the early photo, driving a team of horses, or the lad who had arrived from Scotland in 1884, green behind the ears.

The Scotsman set off ahead of time, walked down along the railway tracks. A long chain of coal trucks was passing. He had become
so familiar with the haulage he hardly noticed any more, these great
snakes of metal that shunted a slow route by, rarely stopping. They
seemed to have so little to do with the settlement itself. As he crossed
the old bridge, the sun was already hot. He was glad of the limited
shade where he could find it along the gnarled avenue of acacias. Somewhere in the distance a chainsaw started up, and a dog began to bark.
Within seconds, others joined in.

He opened the rickety little gate and went up the porch steps, into
the shade. The screen door was shut, but the window next to it was
open and he could hear the sound of music from inside. He listened,
trying to identify it, but the volume was too low. Something with a
tinge of native drumming, something incantatory. Or was that his own
expectation, projecting meaning on the barely audible?

No one had answered his hopeful knock, so he pushed the door.
It was locked. He sat down on the swing settee on the porch. He was
a little early, so maybe the healer wasn't quite prepared. But for what?

Then, out of nowhere, it struck him he was about to see a healer.
A flashback to the waiting room in the Cancer Unit where he had sat
among fellow sufferers, all nervously attendant on the wisdom of the
specialists. Some with scars where their faces should have been, some
still unscarred but marked by the familiar terror of the unknown, the
undone, the ghost of mortality flitting before them, intangible yet so
very present. Had he travelled so far, five thousand miles, only to sit
waiting under a spruce tree in the desert of North America for the wisdom of another kind of specialist?

It gave him a shudder, this reminder, of the fear he had sought to
evade by getting on that plane. But there was no escape, he knew – the
terror was inside him, just as the cancer was. He felt his red neck itch
uncomfortably in the heat, and pulled his collar up, to protect it as he
had been told to at the hospital. There was no forgetting. Maybe this
was why he had shied away from meeting this Lyle enthusiast, while
wandering around the town asking people who hadn't heard of him
what he meant to them?

The distant dog began to bark again. Across the river, on top of
the electricity pole, the nesting ospreys were doing their dance again.
He was too far off to see properly, but he could picture it, from what
he already knew of their habits, the young monster reluctant to fly, to

feed itself, the impatient parent clawing at its back. Then he heard a commotion from inside the house, and the door was unlocked. The Scotsman stood up and turned to see it creak open to reveal a small man of considerable years, whose long grey hair was pulled back in a ponytail. His features were handsome, his eyes seemed sharp-seeing. But what drew the gaze was a beautiful rainbow blanket slung around his shoulder. Whatever echoes of the cancer clinic may have been in his mind, the Scotsman quickly forgot.

'Gilbert,' the man said, before his visitor had a chance to speak, or wonder how he knew his full name, 'Come in. We're ready.' He ushered him into the house with a sweep of his arm as dramatic as his garb. The transition from desert sun to shady interior took a moment and, as his eyes adjusted, the Scotsman saw a room which seemed as if it must be unchanged since Lyle's era, judging by the colonial furniture. But he had no time to focus on this as he was shown into a kitchen equally antiquated, and then out of the house proper through the back door, down some wooden steps and into the waiting tipi. The whole process was so swift that he felt as if he had passed through two or three centuries in the space of thirty seconds.

The tipi was lit by the sunshine gently penetrating the cloth. The pattern of the moon waxing and waning he had observed from the highway with his zoom lens days before was now bright and clearly defined, as was the antler-like symbol that seemed to support it. Woven through the design were shapes which could have been animals, perhaps a bear, a wolf, a snake and a raven. But the Scotsman's eyes had no time to fully distinguish them as they were drawn to the figure sitting in the centre of the tipi, a similarly grey-haired woman with a multicoloured blanket around her shoulders.

In the centre of the tipi, below the smokehole, a fire of herbs smouldered, sending a thin spume into the air which seemed a mix of many scents he partly recognised, and some he did not. Was it sage? Was there cannabis? The music he had thought he heard when out front seemed to fill the space as did the aroma, and now it was clear, the swirling of a minimalist range of notes with an insistent drum beating across everything, then a voice singing very slowly a language he did not know.

'Sit,' the woman said. He looked for a seat, but there was none, so he sat cross-legged on the ground in front of her. She had her eyes closed, and breathed heavily through her nose, as if drawing in the air, as if smelling him. Again he couldn't help but think of the day back home in Edinburgh where he had gone to see the consultants, the radiographer and the laser expert who'd said he could treat the cancer but that he would destroy his vocal cords at the same time. He laughed inadvertently, then thought it may be construed rude and stifled it. But the woman and the man just smiled.

'You've come a long way,' she said at last, opening her eyes. The Scotsman tried to focus on her face but she seemed enshadowed by the strangely patterned interior, as if she was a moon mother face, among many. He could feel her stare though, emanating out of the darkness.

'Yes,' he said, 'Yes I have.'

'And you're searching for something very important to you, I feel that.'

The music stopped suddenly, dramatically. Was it the end of the CD or had some mystical force switched it off right on cue?

'You struggle with unseen forces, with doubt,' the woman said in a soft monotone. In his mind he thought, don't we all, but immediately had the feeling that these people did not, that doubt was not an issue in their minds; that they believed in whatever they believed in wholeheartedly, were at ease with shadows. 'And you've been ill. And you've suffered a great loss,' she said. The scent from the smouldering fire was overpowering at that moment, as it belched ever thicker white clouds into the apex of the tipi, where it was swiftly sucked out into the daylight beyond.

'All right.' It was a totally inappropriate response, but it was all his dry mouth could muster at that moment. He had walked into a house, expecting handshakes and introductions, but instead had been teleported from porch to yard, into some kind of séance in a darkened tipi. How could she know about his mother, his illness?

Then, from the shadow, the man who must have been Kyle stepped forward. 'Maybe Mr Johnson would like to hear about why we came to live here, Hesther,' he said gently to her. She looked up, as if her trance had been broken.

'Oh, yes, of course. I'm sorry. Gilbert, isn't it?' Her voice was then quite proper, quite colonial, though she looked like some native shaman or medicine woman. 'Please forgive me, I had the strongest intuition when I saw you. I forgot you're not here for that,' she added.

'Hesther is highly attuned, highly empathetic. Sometimes she feels things she can't quite control,' the ponytailed figure said in his low sonorous tone.

She nodded. 'Yes, quite often. It's a gift. It caused me much sorrow when I was young, but now with Kyle's help and the discipline of an ordered life, I am better able to make use of it. But you're here because of Jimmy Lyle, aren't you? You are a relative, we heard.'

'It's an honour to meet anyone of his family,' Kyle said. 'Hesther and I have been followers for many years.'

'Many years,' she repeated. 'It's what brought us together in the first place.'

'And it's why we moved here, why we bought his house. As soon as we heard it was for sale, we just got onto the realtor and said whatever it takes, we want that property.'

The Scotsman felt relief at this return to the norms of social inter-action, even if the three of them were still seated cross-legged in the tipi surrounded by incense-laden air in an isolated canyon five thousand miles from anything familiar. Yet it seemed quite ordinary, some-how, and the fact they seemed to know so much about him could be explained by the operation of the local grapevine, couldn't it?

'I see,' he said, but his mind was lagging behind the conversation, still curious about her intuition. It had disturbed him. What exactly had she felt when they first met? He felt he must know. 'When you say followers, what exactly do you mean?' he asked.

'Healers,' Kyle answered. 'Herbalists. You know he collected all kinds of information on the plants of the province and their uses by the First Nations? Ethnobotany.'

'If it hadn't been for Jim Lyle, who knows how much of that ancient wisdom may have been lost?' she added.

The Scotsman was surprised. 'I didn't know that, no. I mean, I've read his book, and there's some mention of certain…'

She interrupted. 'No, this wasn't published. But it was in his archive, hundreds of pages in note form. Kyle found it when he was a student.'

Kyle explained. 'We've dedicated our lives to finding the plants he recorded and developing the science, which hasn't been easy because so many of the names were only in the local tongue, and often Lyle himself wasn't sure if his notes were correct, if he had written it down properly. And so much of the information has been lost in the last hundred years, you know, within the band themselves, what with the residential school system and all.'

'There are very few fluent speakers left now,' she said.

'Less than twenty. And they are all pretty old.'

'These are treatments and cures that have been around for centuries, maybe longer. They don't stop being helpful just because the big drug companies don't know anything about them.'

The Scotsman nodded. It was very interesting, of course it was, but still he had the feeling that he must learn what she had intuited about him when he first arrived. But before he could find the words to ask, Kyle spoke up. 'Do tell us about yourself, Gilbert. Sally said you were interested in the history of the province, that you're writing a book?' So it was Sally Post Office who'd told them about him. Not some mysterious intuition. That explained some things. But not her knowing he was ill.

So he had to explain, once again that he had always wanted to know about Lyle's life here, that he was a distant relative. That he wasn't really a writer. They were interested, asked him all about Scotland, which neither of them knew much about, and in particular Shetland, the childhood home of their hero. He explained what he knew, and answered as many of their questions as he could.

'He was only a youth when he came here,' Hesther said. 'He didn't have time to live much of a life. Or am I wrong?'

The Scotsman realised that in this area of the great man's life, he was the expert. And he began to tell them the story of Lyle's family as he had researched it. They seemed to know little beyond their own sphere of interest, the ethnobotanical, in which they were secure in their expertise, and his own detailed knowledge of the birth of Cloud Falls seemed to surprise them.

The faint shadow of the sun on the tipi wall crept slowly round, rising as it did so in a gentle arc. At last silence enclosed them, and he was able to pose the question that had been troubling him. What exactly had she felt when he first arrived?

Hesther gave a gentle maternal smile, as if she had anticipated the moment. 'I sensed you have been very ill, that you're here looking for an answer to problems that have troubled you for a long time.'

'That's it?' His voice came out strangely, almost like it wasn't his. It all seemed a bit surreal. She merely smiled, her radiance palpable.

'If you like, I'll look deeper?' she said in same calm monotone. His throat felt very dry. So he merely nodded and she closed her eyes, reached out her arms to him.

'Give her your hands to hold,' Kyle whispered.

As she took his hands in hers, he felt a great heat surge from her into him, as if he was being invaded by some force. She began to speak, slowly. 'Your mind is full. Full of things that are irrelevant. Your body is weak. Energies are very out of balance. There's something in you – some fear that has caused this. You don't really believe you will be well, or find what you are looking for. It's as if you have waited for death, merely playing out time until it comes for you. But you have the power to make a difference to your life and to those of others, you are not so ill or so doomed that you cannot still do remarkable life-changing things.'

Through his dry throat he croaked, 'And will I?'

'That, dear Gilbert, is undecided. You are the only one who can make the changes happen, and you must want them enough to believe in the possibility. I can't tell you your future, that isn't my gift. I can only sense what you feel at this moment, and help you to see the obstacles in your way. I believe you have always had the ability to do remarkable things but your own doubt has led you to avoid the task. Until now.'

'Until now…' he repeated. 'I see.'

'How much do you really want to live? Ask yourself that. And when you have an answer, you will know what you should do, you will find the…'

She stopped abruptly. 'The what?' he coaxed. 'Find the what?'

'The road you seek.'

'To where?'

'Somewhere you never believed existed.'

Immediately the thought of the secret cabin, deep in the sacred valley, came to the Scotsman's mind. It was like a vision, the overgrown timber structure out of sight in what had once been a clearing, garden flowers now gone wild. He turned from the stares of his hosts, rubbed his forehead, slightly dizzied by the atmosphere, and the prospect of a road he suddenly felt he had to find, to believe in it. His knees seemed to insist he stood up, so he did.

'This house,' he said, 'This wasn't where Lyle lived when he was with his native wife, was it?'

'No,' Kyle answered. 'This house was built in 1901, after he came back from Scotland.'

He sat down again, the vision of the cabin not quite gone, but now spectral on the edge of his consciousness, a future destination, a peripheral yet fundamental belief. 'There was a cabin he lived in, one he built for his first wife. Do you happen to know where it is?'

Kyle laughed. 'It's a mystery. There is a cabin in the Echte valley near here, where he's supposed to have lived. But we're not sure that's the real one. The original is probably lost.'

'We don't feel it,' Hesther added. 'I'm sure it isn't.'

'The Echte valley? Where exactly is that?'

'Behind the falls,' Kyle replied. 'It's where the town's water comes from. There's a path up behind the falls you have to follow.'

'I'd like to go there, to see it for myself.'

'Then go,' Hesther said. 'Perhaps that is the path you need to find.'

Kyle showed him out, returning him to the tarmac road, with the railway lines in front. As he said his farewell, Kyle held his gaze for a moment and told him to be careful. The path was easy to lose, it was wilderness, and there were rattlesnakes and bighorn.

The Scotsman felt dizzy in the light and heat of the day. He sat for a while by the riverbank, unable to think. His whole body felt strangely energised, but his mind was blank. He got up and seemed to float slowly back to the bridge, crossed without once thinking of the jump, and made his way to the inn. Something pivotal had taken place, but he didn't know what, or how to process it. It was a very long way from the Cancer Unit in Edinburgh.

He lay on the bed in his room for a long time, motionless. It was as if his body was entirely at peace. Not a single muscle twitched. His mind, too, seemed calm. The breeze blowing the blinds was the only motion. A CPR train passed and the room shook with the noise but still he was unmoved. Then he slept.

The sound of the tree-planters woke him. It seemed as if they were very far away, almost in another dimension. He lay awake, as if paralysed. Rising took a great effort, but when he did, when he went and washed, he felt amazingly refreshed.

Out the window, he could see the berry-picker was in the field again, between the inn and the river, next to the reservation. He took his camera and zoomed in, trying to get a shot of her as she bent among the bushes. Something archetypal, from ages past, among the contemporary mesh of metal rail and wire – 'Native Woman picking berries', such as Lyle might have photographed, way back in 1910. But when he zoomed in, he realised he recognised her. It was Deeanna, the painter, the rebel, the woman he had nearly met twice, but hadn't. And he took it in his mind to go down there, to greet her in the field where she was. He put his boots on.

The field was not as it had appeared from the inn. A deep bank lay hidden, like a ha-ha, and he struggled down to the plain by the river. Whatever cultivation had once existed there had clearly been fairly haphazard and he had to stride through rough ground, a scrubby sparse woodland. The bushes where the woman was busy picking fruit seemed natural, not farmed. She was dressed quite differently now, it seemed, from the way she'd appeared in the centre that day, like a moody she-Elvis in her fringed jacket. She wore a yellow printed-pattern sari-like garment, and carried a loose cloth bag slung around her waist into which she placed whatever the crop was. Her thick black hair was pinned up somehow.

As he approached she looked up, as if sensing or scenting someone, straightened her back so to gaze at him and stood watching as he came slowly closer, like a deer waiting to see whether the threat was sufficient to warrant elegant flight. It was as if she might metamorphose in an instant to some spirit animal self and disappear. But the closer he got the more obvious it became that, whatever her spirit animal was, it was not inclined to flee. His steps slowed.

'Hi,' he said, from a few paces distance. 'I'm…'

She interrupted. 'I know who you are.' Her expression was non-committal, neither friendly nor unfriendly. But he felt as though she might eat him. 'You're the guy who's been asking about Jimmy Lyle.'

'My name's Bert. I wanted to talk with you.' He reached where she was standing, next to a spidery bush that shot long stems from its heart, hung with small red berries. 'What are you picking?'

'Salmonberry.'

He noticed the berry was not unlike a wild raspberry or a black-berry. 'Are they good?'

'Sure. Try some.' He picked one from the long stem that swayed in the canyon breeze. It was both sharp and sweet, subtle and wild. 'So you're writing a book?' she asked.

'These are good,' he said, and picked another. 'Well, I'm researching. Maybe a book, maybe something different, maybe nothing. I saw your painting – at least I think it was you? Of Jimmy Lyle's wife. Antko?'

At this, her expression brightened, her pose relaxed.

'It was you, wasn't it? Deeanna?'

'It was.' Her voice was gentler than he remembered it, from the two confrontations he'd witnessed. She too ate a berry, examining him closely as she did so. 'To me, he's not the story, she is. To us, she is the one who made it possible for him to write what he did.'

'I realise that now,' he said. 'I understand that nothing he did could have been done without her. Without cooperation.'

She nodded, accepting. 'The elder you were talking to told me you're like a native back in Scotland, like Jimmy Lyle was. I didn't know that.'

'He was, in a way. But it's not quite the same as here. There was, a long time ago, a real difference between peoples, certainly a different language, even a different way of thinking about the world, but nowadays I don't think many people really think of it in that way. Native or not. People intermarried, you know. Differences were lost. I'm not myself, really. I don't have much connection with that side of the family.'

'Don't you think it's important to remember those things?'

'Well, yes. Up to a point, I do.'

She put her head on one side and looked at him carefully, as if making an evaluation. A proud stare. 'The elder said you were alright,' she mused.

'Your godmother, isn't she?' he asked.

She seemed surprised. 'How do you know?'

'She told me. She's an amazing woman. And ninety-nine!'

'She sure is. A survivor.' Another long stare followed, weighing things up. Then she said, 'I guess you may be alright. Wanna walk with me a bit? There's a place down here by the river where I like to sit.'

He nodded, and she led him down through the scrub of bushes, past the occasional salmonberry plant where she stopped to pick a few to put in her bag. The roar of the river grew louder as they approached. About a hundred yards away was the electricity pole on which the ospreys had their nest.

'The river is high right now. Snow melt up the high mountains,' she said.

They reached a small crook, an indentation in the flow, where a great flat boulder had refused to give way to the pummelling water as the earth around it had done. She walked carefully out onto its table and crouched down. 'This is a good seat, out of sight,' she said. 'Come, sit.' He clambered up, joined her there. She was staring deep into the eddying flow. 'I always used to come here when I was a girl. If I wanted to get away from the family,' she said, without looking at him.

'You grew up here then?'

'Sure. On the reservation. Me and all my brothers and sisters, in our tiny house.' She grimaced at the thought. 'Left soon as I could, though, before I was really old enough. Caught a Greyhound down the valley to the city with my boyfriend. I was thirteen, he was sixteen. We ran away.'

'Wow,' he said. 'That sounds brave.'

'We were just kids, didn't know what we were doing. Ended up on the downtown eastside. You won't know where that is, but it's in Vancouver. Like skid row to my folks. It was nothing we had ever seen before. He got a bed in a man's hostel, I had a place across the road. Through the day we hung out together. Then one day I was out front of the hostel waiting for him to come out, and I looked around me. I saw one guy on the nod with heroin, another raking through bins, and then a little old native lady came by, pushing her trolley. You know, one of those supermarket trolleys, with everything she had in the world in it. She could have been my grandmother easy, cause I never knew them, they both ended up down there too. And then I heard this voice in my head, whispering, saying Deeanna you need to get out of here, you are too good for this, you need to do better than we did, for all of us.'

'A voice?'

'It was my grandmother whispering. I'm sure of it. One of them, one of the grandmothers I had never known. She was telling me to leave, to go back home before it was too late for me, like it was too late for her by the time she realised.'

'So you came back here?'

'No. The very next day we got caught, put into foster care. I didn't come back here till around four years ago. But I didn't go back to the downtown eastside either.' She opened the bag she was carrying, full of salmonberries. 'Want some more?'

He picked a few out, asked, 'What changed?'

She shrugged. 'I always felt this was home, that this was my band, my people. My place. Always tried to stay in touch. Even though I thought I couldn't live here again. I only came back when my father died. Then the house was empty. At least empty of living people. It's still full of all their ghosts.'

'All?'

'My brothers. My momma. And him, my father.'

'They don't sound like happy ghosts that are easy to live with.'

'No, they're not. They're not at peace, not at rest. No more than they were when they were alive. I grew up with violence. It kind of haunts you forever after. My family was not a happy one.'

'Where are they now?'

'Three dead. One in prison. One in the US. But me, I am a grand-mother.' Her mood shifted then, and she smiled. 'Yep. Just thirty-nine years old and I got me a little granddaughter, two years old. So you know, I try, I try to be positive. But it's hard at times.'

He took a few more berries from the open bag that lay on the flat rock between them. 'What about your painting? I really thought the one I saw was good.'

'I don't have a chance to now. Back when I did that, I had a place to work. I was living with this guy who was kind of an artist, used to make things for tourists. He sort of recognised my ability, helped me develop. Most of the time I made the things he wanted me to make, so we could sell them, but he knew a lot about art, not just native designs, he'd studied a lot himself in the public library. He encouraged me to try. But he was evil with liquor and would beat up on me. Finally, I had to leave. And I left everything I'd ever painted with him, except that one picture of Antko. I'd given it to my godmother before. The lady you met that day at the centre.'

She was gazing out over the frothing river, the maddening current, towards the village on the far bank. 'I used to do pottery as well, but I couldn't get my wheel or my kiln. He wouldn't let me. So here I am. Back home again, the black sheep. Even my godmom says she doesn't like me.' She laughed at that, as if it was intended to be ironic, but it was a bitter sound all the same, full of hurt and loneliness. The Scotsman looked at her as she sat there, staring at the river's incessant turbulence, this strong-willed determined person who had been thrown around in the midstream of her life, her talents unnourished.

'Anyway,' she said, 'Why am I telling you all this? This isn't the story you want to hear. It's not about your hero, Jimmy Lyle.'

He scratched at his developing beard. He hadn't shaved since he had begun to write. 'Maybe not, but like you said, maybe the story I came here to find was the wrong one. I didn't expect…' He hesitated.

'What?' she coaxed.

'It's hard to explain. But I suppose my ideas were all very romantic, you know, this tiny wild west town where once upon a time my ancestor came, where he found his way and learned to hunt and speak the local tongue, how he became a great man, expert in all the native culture.'

'Some of that is true,' she said. 'But what it doesn't tell is who made it possible for him, who taught him those things.'

'I'm learning that.'

'What made him different from all the other settlers who wanted to learn is that he had the help of a remarkable woman, who could persuade her people, especially other women, to talk with him, to tell him their stories and sing their songs.'

Suddenly, across the distant rock face of The Chief, the shape of an osprey materialised, flying quickly towards the nest on the top of the pole. It hovered for a moment, then disappeared out of sight on top of the platform.

'This place is incredible,' the Scotsman said, more to himself than her.

'I guess it is,' she answered. 'Certainly wherever else I went I never felt like I do here, even though I wanted to get out of here when I was a kid. But now I know it wasn't the place, but the situation. The place, this river, these mountains I have always loved.'

Her tone was so earnest, he didn't for a moment doubt her sincerity. And the thought of the secret valley occurred to him.

'Tell me,' he asked, 'Where is the Echte valley?'

He felt her stiffen in mild surprise. 'Why do you ask?'

'I want to see where the cabin is, where Antko and Jimmy Lyle lived back in the early days.'

'How do you know about that?'

'Your godmother told me. She said that no one but the band members know where it really is.'

'She told you that?'

'She did, yes.'

'Huh,' she said, and gathered up the bag of berries. 'She must really have liked you. But why do want to go there? The house he built is right here in town, and you can see where he lived later up at High Ridge.'

He sighed, looking for the right words to explain. 'It's a feeling that I've had, the longer I am here, the more it seems to me that I have to go there, to the cabin. Like it is the source. And what you've said about her, Antko, being the key person in his life confirms that. I want to see where they lived together.'

At that moment, the gentle wind that blew through the canyon seemed to rise, and the berry bushes, the scrub grass bent over in response. Without any warning, she too jumped up from the flat rock by the river's edge, her long yellow dress crumpled around her, as if summoned by something he could not sense. Her dark hair had worked itself loose from the hairpins that held it, and it fell around her face, veiling her expression momentarily.

'I have to go,' she said, fastening it up again. 'I'm sorry.'

'Okay, but will you tell me about the cabin first?' he asked.

She was silent for a long while. He felt his smile slowly slip, caught in the snare of her stare. Finally she said, 'You shouldn't go there, I don't think it would be right for you to do that.' The warmth he had felt emanate from her as she'd told him about her life had now disappeared, blown away by the canyon wind, maybe. Something had spooked her, whatever it was he didn't know, and she wasn't about to explain.

He sat on the flat rock watching as she wove her way up through the bushes, away from the riverbank, up the slope in the direction of the little reservation next to the Indian church, where the old blue band office could be seen at the top of the rise. He was thinking of her life as she had described it, running away from the canyon for the city, brave and hopeful at first, not knowing the scale of the world she was about to be plunged into, then plucked out of skid row for foster care as a prisoner, leaving foster care to become the dependant assistant to a maker of tourist art, a frustrated bully when drunk, while all the time that proud individuality she had expressed in the painting he had seen was repressed, kept down by the circumstances of her life.

She was a remarkable woman, just as Lyle's wife had been, wrestling with the strictures that bound her. And had Antko done the same? How had the frontier world of the 1880s regarded her, how difficult had it been for her to flourish, as the Indian wife of the settler Lyle? In her day, she must have been every bit as much of a rebel. Maybe that was why they had retreated to the secret cabin, away from the gossip of the little town and the tumult of the great river.

Glancing up the slope, he saw that the figure in the landscape was gone. Now only the wind, the river, the looming shadow of The Chief and the faint smell of sagebrush were with him. After a minute or two he wondered if she had really been there at all, or had she simply been some spectre, some spirit which had appeared to him briefly? Truly a 'native daughter'?

He had to go. He would go, to the secret valley, to find the sacred cabin.

Third Dance
'Country & Western Capital of Canada'
(Square dance)

SHE CLOSED THE lid of his laptop and laid it aside. Her furry companion raised his head and together they left the ginger pink man to his slumber.

Outside, the moon was high above the canyon wall, just beyond full, filling the gloom with a faint glow, and laying highlights on houses and ridges. They walked, a leash connecting them, along the road by the multiple railtracks, past the waiting trucks with their insignia and graffiti. Down the bank to the far side, the rolling river. And the old bridge up ahead.

So she'd been right, he had thought of jumping in, as she'd intuited. She pictured him now, lying there on the motel bed, wrapped like a mummy in a white cotton sheet, except with his little pink face poking out and its gingery beard growth. A bearded baby in swaddling clothes. Safe. She laughed.

And she stopped, gazing slowly from the southern canyon's turn beyond vision, to its northern equivalent. The town was defined by those twists in the geography, like the twists of candy papers.

'Weird, isn't it?' she said to the dog. 'A little guy reading books five thousand miles away has given this place a history for me.'

The dog didn't disagree. He simply sat by her feet, watching the moving water, his upper lip giving the occasional tremble of a suppressed bark. Then she turned back towards the inn and he fell into a trot by her side. She walked on, past the inn in the other direction until she came to the old community hall, with the silhouettes painted on its boarded windows. Somehow she could see them more clearly by moonlight, not just as decorative outlines, but as memorials of a kind to the people who built this town around the ferry crossing, the pioneers. And among them were the local First Nations, pushed to the edge of town and their reservation.

Of course she knew all that. It was so deep in her understanding of this world that she barely noticed it. But here, it was all too plain, too starkly bare, too foregrounded, and Gil's writing had given these silhouettes names and faces, had animated them. Round the side she found the little clay nameplates he'd mentioned. It was too dark to read them, but she ran her fingers over the relief of some, feeling them.

Hero suddenly stiffened, sniffing. He seemed freaked by something, something that had been there and left its scent. Out there in the dark was the wild. These little nameplates were meaningless to it. The enemy.

They walked until Hero had found a spot to relieve himself, then strolled through the moonlight back to the inn. The night was cold and she didn't want to catch a chill.

She wished she could find the key to her room, which was lost somewhere in Gil's bed, so she went upstairs to his room again, thinking she'd find it if she felt her way over the bedclothes. She heard sounds of residents stirring, the tree-planters no doubt, rising for another day on the clear-cut mountainside.

Gil was still asleep, wrapped in his sheet. She began feeling around the bed, in the hope of finding the lost key. Daylight was just starting to seep into the canyon gloom. She could see a rim of light edging the very top of the rocky crag opposite. Gil grunted, tried to turn, but was restrained by his wrapping. Then his eyes opened, as if sensing her gaze, and his expression seemed pain-free.

'How are you feeling?' she asked.

The little pink mouth opened. 'Like the singing detective,' it said.

'Who's he?'

'Famous tv drama in Britain.'

'Ok. Maybe didn't air over here.'

'Anyway, it doesn't matter. I'm alright, considering.'

She indicated the laptop with a flick of her thumb. 'So I've read your writing. The story about the Scotsman in Cloud Falls.'

'Oh yes? What did you think?'

'It's quite good.'

'*Quite* good?'

'Yes. There were parts I didn't understand, Scottish things, like what's an Aberdonian, all that detail…' She sat on end of the bed.

'Well, it's only a journal. I may never make anything of it.'

'I appreciate that. But you've fictionalised yourself, written it in the third person?'

He unwrapped himself from his cocoon slightly, examined the skin on his arms. 'It was as if I had to. It's strange being the alien, the outsider. I don't think I've ever felt that, at least not like this. It seemed easier to get some distance that way. And 'The Scotsman' is what everyone seemed to be calling me here.'

'Is it true? I mean, all those people, are they fictional too? Hester the healer? That Diana?'

'Deeanna. I suppose so. In part. A lot of it is what happened. Or a version of it. Some of it, at any rate.'

'You seem to be making everything so difficult for yourself. And the reader too,' she observed.

'Hah,' he sighed, 'Writing is difficult. At least for me. Why else do you think it's taken me this long?'

She stood up and stepped to the window where the video camera pointed towards the houses on the far bank, just beginning emerge from night. 'Has it occurred to you that everything you've written since you got here has really been about yourself, not Lyle?' She could see the osprey nest quite clearly now, on top of the electricity pole, the giant chick crouched there, wings folded.

'Meaning?'

'Well, it seems to me that it's not Lyle you're searching for, but yourself. Or some part of yourself you've lost?'

'Very perceptive. But it's not just about me, there's the people I met. And you're in there too.'

'No, I'm not. Some idealised female character based on me, maybe. But it's certainly not me.'

He laughed, then breathed in through his clenched teeth, as if it was painful to do so. 'You're my muse. And my only reader.'

'I don't want to be your muse. I don't want to be anybody's muse,' she said irritably, as if this idea was somehow irksome to her. 'And I don't want to be put on a pedestal. You really know nothing about me.'

The slow creaking of a distant CPR train began again. It grew gradually to its deafening peak. Hero started barking and, for a few minutes, conversation was impossible. As it finally began to wane, she turned from the window. Through the opening, they could hear the tree-planters downstairs on the terrace.

'Ouch,' he said suddenly, and fished underneath him, pulling out the room key.

'Ah, at last - that's what I was looking for.' She took it from his outreached hand and stood up. 'So I think I'm going to go for a sleep now. If I can.' She crossed to the door. 'You really feeling okay?'

'Yes,' he said. 'I'm tired though. I think I'll sleep late too.'

She found her way to the room and unlocked it. It was quite pokey, not nearly as nice as the one Gil had. But the sheets smelled fresh and so she slipped off her clothes and got in. Hero leapt up on the bed beside her. Her eyes closed and she saw the story of the wandering Scotsman play out in a blurry series of fragmented images as she drifted into unconsciousness.

It was after eleven when she woke. The room was hot, unbearably so, and Hero had gone to lie by the door where there was a small gap at the base. She got up, dressed in the same clothes as yesterday – she'd brought so little with her – and went out into the hallway, which was only slightly cooler. Gil was awake when she tapped on his door. She peered into the room where she'd sat for most of the night, reading his story.

'I'm taking Hero for a walk, maybe seek out this restaurant you wrote about and have some brunch. What was it called, 'The Apple Store'? Or did you make that up too?'

He grinned, 'Maybe… but you'll find it.'

'Want to come?'

'God no.'

'Well I'll see if Rick or Vince or whatever his name is will bring you some soup or something?'

'I really couldn't eat.'

'You'll have to, sooner or later.' His pink face surrounded by the white linen looked ridiculous, like she was having to feed a giant-sized baby.

The baby-mouth opened. 'Not right now, though. I just need to rest. Another porridge bath would be good though.'

'You really are a damn fool,' she said, and smiled. 'I should drown you in porridge and be done with you. Come on, Hero. Time you had breakfast.'

After she'd fed him, she drove along the road from the inn, her dog on the passenger seat panting, slowed down at the community hall where she saw the silhouettes painted on the boarded up windows and the little name plaques on the wall she'd run her fingers over in the night. She passed the reservation, the graveyard and the Indian church, all described in his journal, and turned onto the new highway, towards the bridge across the river. In the distance she caught sight of the waterfall, Cloud Falls itself. Or MacLeod Falls, as it had been. She passed the garage, the truckstop Rumors which was still closed, and turned into the town, pulling up outside the restaurant he had called 'The Apple Store'.

She took Hero on leash to do his business. Walking along the side of the road by the river, she felt the hot sun burn her neck, and thought that the whole tour had taken just a few minutes. It was the kind of little town in the interior she'd have driven past without giving thought to, why it was there, who had founded it and when, or who lived there now. It was just another bypassed community clinging to life as a stop-off for drivers. Yet once upon a time, she now knew, it was a key river crossing, a place where settlers had built up businesses, where fruit had grown in abundance. A place where the wandering First Nations had been fenced-in and Christianised. Whatever strange instinct had driven her here, she had no reason to rush back to the city now. She might just stay another day or two, make sure he was alright. The Scotsman may even want a lift back. She felt an odd duty of care towards him.

As she walked back along Acacia Avenue to the restaurant, she was aware of being watched. First curtains twitched, then a man appeared on the deck in front of his house and said 'good morning' brightly. Cloud Falls seemed to be waking up. Then, she spotted a dog running towards her on the old bridge crossing the river, followed by what seemed to be a young guy. Hero bristled and growled, but the other dog paid no heed, just darted past them in the direction of the restaurant, pursued by the youth, who gave her an awkward smile as he chased after it.

When she reached the restaurant, they were seated out in front at one of the tables under a parasol, the dog panting, the boy sweating. He gave her another goofy smile, as she sat down in the shade of a neighbouring parasol. Hero flopped under the table gratefully, carefully eyeing the running dog, while the boy, who was maybe around sixteen, eyed her.

A blonde woman came hurrying from inside the restaurant, wiping hands on her apron. She glanced briefly, disapproving, at the boy and his dog, then smiled warmly at the stranger.

'Well hello,' she said, 'Welcome to Cloud Falls. We're so pleased you're here.'

'Really?'

'Yes. Everyone's talking about you. And is this your dog? What a darling! What's his name?'

'Hero. But I think maybe there's been some mistake.'

'Why? We're honoured to have a movie star visit.'

She laughed out loud. So it was that again. 'I'm not really who you think I am,' she said.

The hostess took a second to process, then said, 'Oh! Of course. Sorry,' she said. 'I forgot.' She put her forefinger to her pursed lips and winked. 'Anyway, I'm Paulette and this is my little place here. Anything you need, just let me know. Special diet, whatever. It can be arranged. I know you film stars have your special likes.'

The woman who was not Sigourney Weaver stared at her host briefly, as if on the point of insisting. Then she sighed and said, 'Oh no, there's no need, Colette.'

'It's Paulette.'

So that was one thing Gil had changed, her name. Not-Sigourney wondered what else might have passed through the prism of fiction. 'Oh sorry, yes. Anyway, I just want some good coffee and a croissant maybe, with butter and jam, if that's alright.'

'Sure, that I can do. What kind of jam? We have a whole range of home-made preserves.'

'Hmmm. How about apricot?'

'Sure... um,' she hesitated. 'So what *do* I call you?' She winked again.

'Me? Ah, you can call me Martina,' the visitor answered. She may as well be Martina. Better than Ms Weaver, and she wasn't sure she wanted to give her real name now things were getting crazy. Why not just live the fiction for a few hours till she left, it may be easier all round?

'Okay, sure, *Martina*,' she said, and winked. 'I'll bring some nice cold water for Hero too,' she added, then turned back towards the restaurant. She caught sight of the boy, who was lounging on his chair, feet up on another, listening carefully. 'Feet down, please,' she ordered. He took his legs down from the chair and sighed. After not-Colette had disappeared inside, he said, 'She's my mom.'

'Ah, okay,' Martina nodded. 'I see.'

The boy sat watching her as she checked her phone. It was bar-less.

'No reception,' the boy smiled. She shook her head, but continued to scroll through the old messages.

'You makin a film here?' he said, after a while.

She looked up at him, his youthful face shaded partially from sight. 'No,' she said, exasperated. 'There's no film.'

Again he watched her. She felt a little uncomfortable under his gaze.

'I rap,' he said, after another silence.

She smiled. 'You what?'

'Rap,' he said again, 'You know. Like Eminem.'

She nodded, tried not to laugh. 'Okay...'

'Name's Declan Zee.'

'Hi Declan.'

'Nice dog,' he said.

Not-Colette reappeared with the coffee and croissant. 'Hope you're not annoying the lady,' she said to him. 'If you're gonna hang around down here, go in and do some dishes or something.'

The rapper snarled, whined 'Mo-om!' and slunk off inside. The other dog followed him to the door, but when it was shut out, it lay down in the shade and whimpered.

'You'll be eating here while you're stayin?' Not-Colette asked, 'Only I know Rick don't do meals any more, and I'm happy to cook whatever you like, if you let me know.'

Not-Sigourney smiled. Not-Colette was so sweet and keen to please. 'Well thanks, but I won't be here much longer. A couple more days, maximum, we'll see. My friend may be longer.'

'Ah, yes, your friend. You know what they're calling him round here?'

'What?'

'The Walkin Scotsman,' Not-Colette laughed, a weird high-pitched snicker. 'CPR Ken came up with it, he's the linesman on the railroad. Like the Flying Scotsman, famous old train in England, he said.'

'I see. Yes. That's quite good. Witty.'

'He's been wandering around interviewing people for the script, hasn't he?'

'He's not a scriptwriter, he's...'

The hostess interrupted. 'No, of course not, sorry. I forgot,' she said, and snickered again, then smiled a little smile of conspiracy. 'Anyways, if he wanted to see where Jimmy Lyle lived, back in the day, the old house up at High Ridge, well my brother-in-law has it now, the fruit farm and all, and he'd be happy to show you round. It's a bit of a mess right now cause his son's been living in it, plus he's put some of the pickers in it these last few years and they make a fine mess, but it's all still there, just as it was, you know, back in the day. Could be cleaned up easy. Nice location.'

The woman who wasn't Ms Weaver laughed, despite herself. So they were planning locations for the film already? What did she have to say to stop the rumour, or was it already too late? And would it really matter if she let it run? She sighed and smiled. 'Well, thanks. I'm sure my friend would like that. How do we get in touch?'

'Oh, he'll get in touch with you once I let him know. Maybe tomorrow?'

'Maybe. Mr Johnson isn't all that well. He got a bit too much sun when he was out yesterday.'

'Yeah, I heard that. Big George had to go pick him up, didn't he? But he's okay, isn't he?'

'Yes, he'll be good to go in a day or so.'

'He oughta know better than to be out walkin in the heat of the day.'

'He's from Scotland. They don't get much sun there.'

'Ah, okay.' The hostess thought for a moment, then said, 'Listen, if you're free, it's my Country and Western night tonight – that is, Dolette's, my *alter ego*.' She spoke the latter phrase with great importance, and pointed to a poster of a figure in a bouffant blonde wig with a pink Stetson on top, and a mother-of-pearl inlaid guitar round her neck. The apparition beamed out across the café deck. *Dolette's C&W Nights*, the banner text announced.

'And my brother in law'll be here, so you could talk with him then. Look in if you can, we'd be honoured.'

'Well maybe I will. What time do you serve food 'til?'

'Oh, there'll be pizza and wings and things all night, but if you want a regular supper then try to be here before the show, say around 7? Just let me know what you'd like, I'm happy to make it special.'

'Can I call you later, when I've spoken with Gil?'

'Gil?'

'My Scottish friend.'

'I thought his name's Bert?'

'Well it's Gilbert, really.' She popped the last mouthful of croissant in her mouth. 'Mmm, very nice,' she told her hostess. 'So this Jimmy Lyle, what do you know about him?'

'Me? Not much. Heard the name plenty, of course. Now, if it was George Jones or Willie Nelson...'

'But isn't he kind of famous round here?'

'Not that I know of. But there's one person who does know. She moved up from Vancouver, bought Lyle's old house down on the riverbank.'

'Sorry, now I'm confused. I thought your brother-in-law owned that?'

'No, that's another one.' Then she hesitated, frowned as if she was confusing herself. 'Guess he must have lived in more than one. Anyhoo, she's an expert, I heard. She's a bit...'

'A bit..? What?'

'She has a tipi in her yard. She calls herself a healer.'

'Ah!' Not-Sigourney said. So the healer was real. 'Yes, Gil told me about her. Tell me, is she First Nations?'

'No... at least I don't think so, though maybe she is come to think of it. I reckon she's more of a hippy. Goes out collecting plants, you know, all the traditional herbs and things. And she holds these séances or whatever they are. People come from all over. Anyway, she's the one who knows most about Jimmy Lyle. So I heard from old Sally in the Post Office. She's been here all her life. Knows all about the history. Your Scotch friend should go see her too.' She nodded confirmation, glad to be able to offer assistance to the great lady from Hollywood.

Not-Sigourney thanked not-Collette, and walked to the car with Hero, feeling the eyes of the restaurant owner watch her all the way. 'Remember tonight. Dollette will be so glad to see you!' she called. Not-Sigourney smiled back and waved goodbye. She stood a while by the car, as Hero nosed around. He was hating the heat. From inside the not-Apple Store, she heard the matron shouting something, and the moan of the rapper.

Back at the inn, she went up to Room 14. The door was unlocked but she was surprised to find Gil awake, dressed in a robe and at his desk with the laptop open. 'You look better,' she said. 'What happened?'

'I had an idea,' he said, from behind his glasses. 'Wanted to get writing.'

'Okay…' she said. 'I'll leave you to it.'

'Did you want something?'

'It's just I was down at Colette's place across the river and, you know what, she says you've got a nickname now.'

He didn't look up from the screen. 'What do you mean?'

'They've given you a nickname.'

'Who?'

'I don't know. The townsfolk, I guess. They call you 'The Walking Scotsman'.'

He hesitated, peered over his glasses at her. 'That's quite funny. But *the townsfolk*? Really? You make it sound like we're in some Gothic novel.'

They both laughed. 'Yup. I think we could be,' she said. 'Hope they don't come after us with a wooden stake. And here's something else for you – they think you're a scriptwriter and that I'm Sigourney Weaver. They think we're going to make a film about Jimmy Lyle or something.'

'Who?'

She was puzzled. 'Who what?'

'I mean, who is Sigourney Weaver?'

She stood open-mouthed. 'You don't know?'

'I may have heard the name. Why? Should I know?'

'Don't you watch movies?'

'Not really. At least not since I was young. Then it was Westerns mainly.'

'You've never heard of *Alien*? *Gorillas in the Mist*? *Ghostbusters*?'

'Heard of them, maybe… seen them, no.'

'You are an antique, Gil. It's amazing you even have a laptop.'

'Had to get one. Online sales in the book-trade took off and I wouldn't have been able to compete otherwise. Don't use it for much else. Not until now, at any rate. Suddenly I'm writing. At least, if you'd stop talking and let me get on with it…' he winked at her.

'Sorry I'm sure! Anyway, glad to see you're feeling better.' She turned to go, then stopped on the threshold, her dog at her knee. 'But when you're done and feel you can talk, I'd like to hear what happened yesterday. You were babbling on last night about finding some cabin with initials carved on it?'

'That's what I'm writing right now.'

'Ah, okay. Sorry.' Again she made to leave, but he turned to her with a theatrical sigh.

'Hey, it's alright, I'll tell you now. I suppose I owe you after you saved my life.' He winked again. 'May help if I rehearse the story before I try to write it anyway. Come in, sit down.'

'Okay.' She sat on the end of the bed. The heat-fatigued dog lay down at her feet, tongue lolling.

'It was, well, strange. I didn't really know where I was going. None of the band want to talk about the cabin, it's their secret.'

'I read that. Last night while you were sleeping. Tell me what you found. Where you went.'

'Okay. You see, there's this creek that flows into the river just south of the town. It comes out of the side of the mountain as a waterfall, it's really amazing.'

'I saw that this morning, yes.'

'Huh,' he said. 'You've been busy. Anyway, that water has supplied this little community since the first settlers arrived. It's cool clear water that could be easily diverted, not like the stuff in the river outside here, where the current is far too strong. It's all silty – and of course back then they didn't have fancy pumps and filters like today. But the falls was like a gift of gravity. All they had to do was channel it.'

'Yes,' she said, rather impatiently, 'I read all about that too. Get to what happened – you know, after the end of your journal.'

'All right. So anyway, I learned from the elder I spoke to that the cabin where Jimmy Lyle had lived with his first wife was somewhere in the hidden valley this creek flows out of.'

'I know that too.'

He put down his glasses and looked at her. 'You really are interested?'

She held out her palms to him and shook her head a little, as if to say isn't that obvious? 'Tell me what happened after you spoke with Deeanna down at the river. Assuming that actually happened?'

'You read all that?' he said, 'Huh.' He got up from his desk and went to window to look out. 'Okay, well,' he began, 'After I came back here to the inn, I studied a local map I'd found in the library, and worked out where the cabin most likely was. Actually there were two places it could have been, where there seemed to be a homestead. So the next morning I set out to look for it. I walked up the trail past the waterfall…'

'Like Kyle told you…'

'Yes, though his name isn't really Kyle, so I came to a fork in the track just at the shoulder of the ridge. I could still just see the southern edge of the town, the new bridge and the inn in the distance. And just as I was wondering which way to go, I saw this figure in the distance up ahead. It looked like a child, an Indian child…'

'First Nations,' she corrected.

'Yes, sorry, slip of the tongue. But the thing was, she or maybe it was a he, they were wearing what looked like buckskin and had their hair in a braid. It was like they were dressed as an Indian as they used to be, you know in all the old Westerns.'

'They were never Indians, not even back then.'

'I know that. I'm not explaining myself properly. What I mean is that it looked like the Hollywood cliché of what the aboriginal inhabitants of North America looked like. Does that make sense?'

'Not really. Why would anybody be dressing like that now in 2011?'

He laughed. 'Maybe they wanted to be in a film that doesn't really exist?'

'But wasn't this before I got here and all the Ms Weaver movie stuff started? By the way, remember to call me Martina here.'

He looked puzzed. 'I'm incognito,' she said after a moment.

'Anyway, I don't know why I saw what I saw, but I did. And this figure, young woman or maybe a young man, seemed to be signalling me to follow. So I did. By the time I got up to where they'd been standing, they had moved up higher still.'

'So this was like a trail?'

'It wasn't much more than a track. There were no tyre marks, no trucks had been up it, it was just hoof prints, bighorn sheep, I thought, goats or deer or whatever else is out there. And the further up I went the narrower it got.'

'And?'

'Well, when I got up to the top, I could just about see what lay on the other side. The waterfall came out of a hidden creek, on a much higher level than the valley here. You could see how the water was eating away at the rock that divided the two, the canyon below and this tributary, and that at some future point in time the divide would give way. It was a landslide waiting to happen, and there was nothing to stop it. And somehow I just knew that this was the sacred valley I'd heard about, hidden away above the town, the source of its water supply.'

'And?'

'Then I saw something moving in the sagebrush, quite a distance off so I could hardly see it clearly in bright sunlight, but I just knew it was the same figure who had helped me find the right path up the mountain side. Again they seemed to be waiting for me to follow, so I did. No sooner was I on the move, winding my way through the scrub, the scrawny bushes and the rocks, than they disappeared again. This place was like a pass between two glens...'

'Glens?'

'Scottish for steep valleys. When I reached the place where my elusive guide had last been standing, suddenly I could see the panorama of the secret valley. A perfect mountain loch in a kind of corrie...'

'Translation?'

'Em, like a small lake in a gulley in the mountainside...'

'Okay...'

'The sun was catching the rock face behind it, dazzling bright yellow with these blue or purple fissures cut into it in such a regular pattern, it almost looked man-made.'

She nodded. 'I noticed that too, how the canyon looks like someone carved it to a pattern. Driving up from Vancouver took my breath away. All the way from Hope we were climbing, climbing, and it just got more and more dramatic, didn't it, Hero?' Hero didn't argue.

'Yes, but this wasn't part of the canyon, it was a small side valley at a much higher elevation, like I said. You can't see it from the road at all. You'd never know it was there except for where the waterfall bursts through. And up there behind the waterfall is this amazing place, protected from the full heat of the sun because of where it is. It's so green and lush around the loch, it seemed like another country altogether. And the scale was smaller. Like Scotland.'

'So what happened?'

'That's the strange thing. I'm not sure. Not now.'

'What do you mean?'

'Well, as I was standing there, taking in the sight, about a hundred yards ahead, the same figure I had seen before, guiding me up to the pass, appeared again, on a small rocky outcrop above the path. And with them – she or he – was another figure in buckskin.'

'And?'

'I felt sure it was him - Jimmy Lyle. Because I thought I could see he was blond, not dark, under his Stetson, and he wore a fringed jacket like one he was wearing in a photo I have. In fact, I thought he looked exactly like he did in that photo.'

'But that's impossible.'

'That's what I'm saying... now it seems ridiculous, but at that moment I believed it really was him. And it didn't seem at all strange to me then. And I seemed to know that the young guide was his N'la-ka'pamux wife. That she had brought me up the mountain so I could see him there...'

Not-Sigourney sat quietly, Hero by her feet, her brown eyes seeking meaning from his, but her face otherwise expressionless. After a while she said, 'You were probably suffering sunstroke or something.'

Gilbert shook his head, his pink nose beginning to peel a little. 'Maybe. But it seemed very real. Or about as real as a vision might be. I'm not explaining this very well. Maybe you should just read what I've written?'

'Okay...'

'I'll scroll back to the beginning. Mind, it's not finished yet...'

'Sure.' He got up from the desk so she could sit down.

She read.

The trail turned back upon itself, and I found I was above the water-fall, a steep crevasse between where I stood and the place where it sprang from the canyon wall. A larch stood on one side, almost impossibly rooted between rocks, its trunk twisted in an attempt to defy gravity. Two old birches faced it, their trunks gnarled, leaves few, and yet they stretched towards the place where the sun might reach them, beyond the canyon shadows. From that viewpoint I could see the waterfall began not as a single stream but as two, joining as they fell, invisible from below, as the water vapour rising masked their merging. The mountain John MacLeod had called 'Arthur's Seat', because it reminded him of Edinburgh, from here looked quite different, though no less kingly. The sun was almost behind it, so that the slope of 'Arthur's Seat' was shaded darkly, but further on, where the canyon turned westward into the sun's rays, the rocky steep shone golden. Below, the narrow strip of green where the settlement was established lay shaded from the summer heat, a vague haze of verdure between mountain and river. Those were orchards once, watered by the flumes that John MacLeod had built, a matter of three miles or so, slop-ing gently down to the little plain formed who-knows-when by the land-slips whose origins could be seen quite clearly in hollows in the shadowed steeps. MacLeod Falls – I thought of how his history had been obliterated,

how the syllable that commemorated his effort, the great labour of engineering to irrigate the land below, that simple 'Mac', had been forgotten.
Now these were simply the 'Cloud Falls', a far more poetic name, like an
Anglicization of a native observation, those clouds of water vapour that
billowed constantly from the crevasse below. I followed the narrow path
a little further until I could see beyond the ridge, to the far side of the hill.
In the shadows a fleck of red caught my eye and I made out a figure sitting
on a boulder overlooking the waterfall. I stood watching as a second figure
appeared, clambered up to the very edge of the precipice above the falls,
where they stopped on a protruding rock that stuck out over the drop,
like a giant nose breathing in the vapour. The figure seemed almost to
float above the water in the clouds that rose from below. The noise from
the falls was deafening, but I fancied I could hear a voice, chanting, in the
midst of it. I was transfixed. It was a moment of sublime enlightenment,
and I felt somehow that these figures were the man I was seeking and his
wife. But how could they have been? They'd been dead for a century. They
were spectres at best, conjured by the heat and the mist, the sunrays' splin-
tering. And at that moment, it struck me that 'Cloud Falls' was exactly the
right name for this place. Even if everyone had forgotten John MacLeod,
even if the name was now a corrupted misnomer, it described the natural
phenomenon, a truth.

She looked up from the screen. He was sitting on the end of the
bed, lobster-red, and she couldn't help smiling. He looked quizzical.

'Is it funny?'

'No, it isn't that. I just thought of something else. Actually, it's quite
poetic. So what happened then?'

'I'm not sure. It's all pretty hazy after that,' he said. 'But I seem to
remember following them down the far side of the pass to their cabin
by the lakeside, and him pointing out my father's initials carved in the
timber,' he said, then frowned uncertainly. 'Or did I show him them?'

'Maybe we could go back there and see? I mean, not right now
obviously.'

'I don't know. I'm not sure I could find the path. Maybe I imagined
it all? Even if the initials were there, I couldn't be sure. Maybe I just
carved them myself? While I was sun-struck and delirious?'

'Do you think you did?'

'All I really remember is coming-to when George and his sons
found me. From the young woman guiding me to the secret valley until
the lights of the truck shone in my face, it's hard to say what happened.
I felt sure I'd found the cabin at first, but now I'm not certain. It seems

so bizarre, it must have been some kind of dream. But some of it did happen. If Lyle and Antko were illusions, what about the cabin? And the carving?'

She didn't say anything for a while, but got up and walked to the window, from where she could see the mountain. She didn't know anything about this 'Arthur's Seat' back in Scotland, but she pictured Gil walking up that great slope in the hot sun, here in Canadian canyon and thought again how foolhardy he had been. 'I think you're still a little delirious. You should rest,' she said.

He stretched his arms above his head and yawned. 'Maybe you're right. But I feel I have to get this down while it's fresh.' He sat for a moment, in thought. 'You know, thinking about it now, maybe it wasn't a vision. I think it may have been the painter I saw at the top of the waterfall.'

'The one who painted the portrait of Lyle's wife in your journal?'

'It could have been her, yes. With someone else.' He seemed confused, trying to work out what had happened to him.

'Okay, I'll leave you. But don't overdo things. Remember you're not a well man.' She turned and walked to the door. Hero got up and followed her. 'Oh, I forgot, there's something else – then I'll go, I promise. We've been invited out tonight to Colette's Country and Western night - no, not Colette, Dolette. You know, the Apple Store woman. Whatever it's called.'

'Her what?'

'You know, music, Country and Western.'

'Really?'

'I know you're not well enough, but…'

'Who says I'm not? I love Country music.'

'Gil…'

He laughed. 'And I want to see who's there… it's research.'

He did seem to be okay, she thought. 'And she says her brother-in-law who owns High Ridge where Lyle lived will be there, and that he'd show us around the house if we asked.'

'Wow,' he said. 'You're a fast worker.'

'It's easy when you have wheels, Mr Walking Scotsman. You're very lucky I turned up.'

'I suppose I am.'

'You suppose?'

'Okay, I am.'

She was about to leave him to his writing when a thought stopped her. 'One more thing. That healer in your story, the one who said you would find the road to the cabin – Paulette mentioned her.'

'Yeah?' But he wasn't paying proper attention, he had returned to his laptop, and was peering through his glasses at the screen. 'What about her?'

'What did you feel? Assuming it actually happened?'

He stopped and turned to face her. 'Hah, yes that happened. Strangest thing.'

'And you really felt different afterwards?'

'You know, I'd almost forgotten about that, what with the cabin and all. But yes, I really did, at least at first.'

'As if she'd healed you or something?'

'Ach, I don't know,' he said. 'I don't really believe in any of that. Away you go,' he said, 'We'll talk about it later.' And he went back to his writing.

'You sure you're okay?'

'Sure I'm sure.'

'You still look like a lobster,' she said as she closed the door. She went downstairs with Hero, thinking she'd like to see this healer herself. She felt like calling back to him, that even if he doesn't believe, maybe she does. But she wasn't sure if she did. What harm could it do, though?

It was hot again and Hero was feeling it under all that fur. She filled his bowl of water on the terrace and sat down in the shade. Her mind was confused by the twisted truth she had read and the real town she found herself in. Her life had suddenly lurched sideways, revealing a secret territory she had not expected could exist, and she was now standing on the threshold of travelling deeper into the country that had adopted her than she had ever been before. The history that Gil was uncovering held a strange wonder for her, and it was leading her into a past that was also very much present. It was a world beyond, a life beyond cancer, beyond her imagined death. Something they had both shared, and something that now bound them together. Where they were to go, what lay ahead, was impossible to predict, but she felt sure that she must travel this road as far as it went, this road she had not believed possible until a few days ago. Something in her had been freed and her worst fear quelled. It was like some part of her had died – a part of her that wasn't her but yet, at the same time, it was, which was in her but shouldn't be. She and Hero were travelling now, driving away from home and away from all of the past. And they had a passenger, a hitchhiker on the highway north, a pink man who bathed in porridge.

The majesty of the mountain across the river loomed over everything. In Vancouver, the mountains provided the backdrop against which city life played out. Here, the mountain was on stage, present, at the heart of all, that and the great grey river that raced through the canyon. Then she noticed, below the inn, a woman walking through the scrub, looking around her carefully and picking berries. Centuries seemed to flow around her as she brushed through the shrubs, her dark hair catching the breeze. Was it Deeanna, or the woman Deeanna may be in reality? Everything had the wrong names now, yet it didn't seem to matter. Behind the naming was an essence, and in the essence lay a kind of truth that was unchanged regardless of who told the tale and what names they gave. The mountain was the mountain, the river the river, the woman the woman.

The afternoon passed lazily. She read a little book of poems written by a local woman she had found among the innkeeper's wife's library, then decided to go for a drive around the town again, to check her phone for a signal. None appeared, and so there were no new messages from her lover. She felt a sense of relief, as if she had entered a safe space where he couldn't reach her, a space she needed badly at that moment while she tried to regain an emotional balance.

She stopped at the Indian graveyard to see Lyle's wife's grave, and drove on to the foot of the waterfall where she let Hero have a proper walk. It was amazing, the way it issued from the canyon wall and fell straight down, sending clouds of vapour into the air. As she passed the town on the highway she tried to spot the tipi among the houses. She felt annoyed at Gil for being so dismissive of the woman earlier. If this healer – whatever her real name was – could really heal, then it was a place she needed to go. But she couldn't see it – a truck passed on the opposite side of the highway and her attention was broken. Maybe there was something to what he'd said, about the benefits of walking, and seeing.

When she got back to the inn, Gil was napping. She woke him gently and told him if he wanted to go to the Country night, he should get ready. He did, and they were about to leave Hero in her room and set out on foot as it wasn't far, but Hero wasn't having it, so she decided he'd be happier in her car where it was familiar, and cooler in the evening than the little room.

By the time they arrived, the restaurant was already packed. Gil said he'd never seen anyone else in there before. Two seats seemed to have been reserved for them in the centre of the room. They shuffled through the crowd, nodding at eager faces they'd never seen who seemed to know them, and sat down just as the MC stepped up - had he simply been waiting for their arrival in order to begin?

'Ladies and Gentlemen – and the rest of you!'

The MC was dressed as a cowboy, complete with gun in holster and leather chaps. He wasn't someone they recognised, but she thought he resembled Burt Reynolds in his prime. 'It is my pleasure to introduce to you, our host for tonight, the one and only, your favourite and mine, the lady with the big…' Howls of laughter. '… Voice… our own queen of the canyon, the beautiful Dollette!'

Gil looked at 'Martina' in surprise, and they both burst out laughing as the formerly rather mousey lady who owned the restaurant entered stage left, now fully made up, topped by pink Stetson above a blonde bouffant wig worthy of the great Ms Parton herself, and wearing a tiny frilly pink dress barely concealing a push-up bra as she stepped up confidently in high-heeled leather boots. The band, a guitar player, a woman on an electric piano and a fiddler with some kind of drum machine at his side, played an intro. As she reached the mike, 'Dollette' pitched into a rousing rendition of 'I will always love you,' which she directed specifically at the MC, and when it came to the high notes she hit them true.

'Wow,' Gil said. 'The lady has a voice.'

Dollette was followed rapidly by another tribute act, or so it seemed. Who the man with the quiff in the white-spangled jacket was intended to be she did not know, but the song was obviously well known to the company, and it encouraged a chorus sing-along. Drinks were brought to order. She glanced at Gil. He seemed to know this song, with its down-home chorus… 'Canadian Pacific, carry me three thousand miles'… and she remembered he had mentioned it in his journal. As she watched him, she noticed he seemed changed in this atmosphere, this spangled fringed sequinned corner of the cosmos, his pink alien Zoidberg exterior penetrated by some force she didn't quite understand. He was singing along as if he belonged among these people in a way that she didn't.

'Who's he meant to be?' she asked, leaning in to make sure he heard.

'George Hamilton the Fourth,' Gil said gleefully. 'My father and mother had this record.' She smiled as if she understood, but she had grown up with Dvořák, Smetana and Janáček, with Brahms, Debussy and Ravel, with Bach, Mozart and Beethoven. This music seemed to be what her mother would call 'American hoakey'.

The transformation in the restaurant itself was as remarkable as that of Dollette. The lights were down on all but the little stage, and the room was filled with delighted faces, barely visible in the gloom. 'Sigourney' could feel eyes straying towards her, turning from the stage to glance at her as if she were really the show, the Hollywood star, the unwilling impersonator, and not these sequinned performers. And, truth be told, she had spent more than the usual time at the mirror that night, perfecting her look, the one that had stopped the staff in Bloomingdale's Manhattan in their star-struck tracks a couple of years before. She supposed she too was a performer. Like Paulette/Colette/Dollette she was undergoing her own transformation into a new space where she could make herself up like a fiction to suit the occasion. As a translator, she understood the process of transformation, but to be the transformed was strange. Unsettling, but somehow freeing.

She peered around the room, trying to see who was there. In one corner she could just make out Big George and his wife and family, who waved immediately when she noticed them. They looked as if they'd dressed up for the occasion – or was it for her benefit, the supposed Hollywood star, who was not 'Martina' or 'Sigourney'? In another corner she saw some of the tree-planters she had glimpsed at the inn, standing at the bar drinking, too cool to watch. They too acknowledged her presence. And could that be the woman from the Post Office Gil had written about, the little old historian lady with the glasses, smiling at her?

Meanwhile, as the applause for the George Hamilton IV tribute slowly faded, Dollette returned to the mike, her pink Stetson tipped back and hanging by a string around her neck so the full bouffant surrounded her face like an overgrown halo. With a 'Let's hear it for…', she roused a further round of applause for the white-jacketed singer, who was now retreating into the shadows.

'Now, friends, it's time for our very special guest – BC's own country star, a man you all know well from his records, who so kindly accepted my invitation to travel all the way up here from Vancouver to appear here tonight, even though he is in the middle of a tour. Especially for you, please give a great big canyon welcome to, The Entertainer himself, Mr Raymond Griffin!'

Gil glanced at her with down-turned mouth, an expression that said he didn't know who 'The Entertainer' was either. They both watched as a slightly built man with tan skin and the shoulder hunch of considerable age got up from the front row table. He took the mike with an assurance that spoke of many years gracing stages far bigger than this. The entertainer sang of Blue Canadian Rockies, of British Columbian pioneer homes, cabins in clearings and lovelorn hearts, and the audience were entranced. Though she didn't know who he was, she could recognise that here was a man at home among his people, a troubadour come back to familiar territory, singing about places and things his audience recognised.

She found herself gazing around her at the dimly-lit faces which were all now focused on the professional guest performer, not on her and Gil as before. She was looking for one who might just be the woman Gil had written about, the painter, the First Nations woman warrior he had described, the figure she thought she'd seen in the berry fields below the inn – Deeanna, he'd called her. She was hoping she would make an appearance, this artist and painter of the portrait, this powerful female character he had written – if she did indeed exist. He had been rather evasive about that. But there was no obvious candidate that she could see here. And if she really was as Gil had sketched her, she would not be inclined to hide in the shadows at this show, surely? She'd grab the microphone, and make some kind of speech. She might even sing some native anthem or another – but not 'O Canada!'

Just as 'Martina' realised how much she wanted this woman to exist, The Entertainer finished his third song with an impressive crescendo and a high yodelling finale. The applause was deafening. The Apple Store seemed to tremble. Dollette stepped onstage and embraced him. He sure was a star here, whoever he was. Dollette announced a short intermission, the chance for people to get another drink, and the lights came up. Suddenly, the crowd was revealed to one another, friends greeted each other, people began to mingle. Martina looked around her, searching for the face she imagined Deeanna to have – a female Elvis, he'd described her as – but she saw no one who might fit that image.

There were still plenty of eyes directed her way – or Sigourney's way – but less so than at first. She turned to Gil, whose face was an odd sickly yellow pink in the house lights, but his eyes were gleaming with a delighted boyish look that told her just how much fun he was having. She couldn't help but laugh a little, so glad to see her cancer buddy enjoying himself so. And if truth be told, so too was she. She laughed aloud.

'What is it?' he asked.

'Your face, lobster man.' And she was about to ask him if his fictional creation, the wild Deeanna, was here in reality when Dollette and The Entertainer approached their table. Up close, the singer looked much older than under the stage lights, at least old enough to be her father, his thinning hair coiffed to maximum volume, his skin stretched as if much work had been done, and stage make-up carefully applied.

'Raymond,' she said. 'These are the people I told you about. This is Martina,' – she seemed to wink at him as she said this – 'And this is the writer, Gilbert Johnson.'

'A pleasure, I'm sure,' the grinning star said. 'When Dollette here told me you were in town, I wanted to meet you right away. Drove up today. I'm a canyon boy, you see, though I ain't lived here for a long time. But I got songs, songs about it. Been writing about it all my life. You heard some just there.' He flicked his thumb at the stage behind his shoulder.

Gil was staring at the singer, smiling, his pink swollen skin in sharp contrast to the taut tan facing him. 'Great!' he said. 'We really enjoyed your set.'

'You did?' He was looking right at 'Martina', but obviously seeing Sigourney. 'That's great. You know, if you need a song written special, I can do that. I done film work before.'

Martina sighed, turned her eyes to the ceiling.

'"Ballad of Jimmy Lyle" has a ring to it, I was thinking," he added.

She was about to try to tell the singer to stop when she glanced at Gil and saw his grin. 'Sounds great, Ray,' he said.

'Really?'

'Why not?' Gil added. 'Sigourney' shot him with a glance.

Dollette laughed, not a Ms Parton sound at all, but her own nervous girlish giggle. 'I just knew you'd get along. Ray here is someone we're very proud of. He's written songs for all kinds of singers. Lots of hits, haven't you, Ray?'

'Sure. Listen, how about this,' he said, and his yodel-voice sang out – *Jimmy Lyle, Jimmy Lyle, his life was one great trial, but he just kept right on goin till the end...* That's what came to me driving up. Little refrain.'

'Great!' Gil said again, smiling. Martina just sighed and shook her head, and turned away. Over her shoulder, she heard Raymond ask if she was okay. She nodded towards the washroom, and left them talking. A little group of guys were on the threshold at the back door, some of them smoking, as she passed. One of them she recognised as a tree-planter from the inn. She smiled at him as she passed. 'Na, that's not her,' she heard him say, behind her. She looked straight at him, said, 'Thank you.' But as she carried on down the corridor towards the washroom sign, she heard another voice say. 'Yes, it is. She just don't want you to know, dood.'

She pushed open the door to the washroom, to see the pinkest room she had ever encountered. Dollette's personality had been expressed in full. Everything bar the mirror and the faucets were a shade of the hostess's favourite colour. Above the long mirror, a row of theatrical bulbs shone incandescence over the small space.

The single cubicle door was locked so she waited, studying her face in the mirror. It was true, she did look a little bit like Sigourney Weaver, particularly in profile. Particularly the left side. But how a whole town could convince itself she really was a film star baffled her. They must really want some drama in their lives.

As she stood there, gazing into her own reflection curiously, in the mirror behind her another woman appeared. Maybe she did look a little like a female Elvis, or a female Johnny Cash. Or was it Joan Baez she reminded her of? She sure looked like someone. She was a slightly bizarre sight, here in Dollette's shrine to the full blush of pink femininity. Her strong face, dark complexion and such jet black hair combined with such a determined stare, contrasted to the pink of the white woman, the white pink, the lobster skin of the alien, that foolish traveller she had adopted, the walking Scotsman. And there was strength in her shoulders. But when she turned there was nothing but a feeling, a fleeting figure passing and the cubicle was empty. Only a closing door to see. If someone had been there, they had left. She sat down on the pink padded chair in the pink washroom, her mind a mess. Who was she, after all, to be here now in this strange place? It was another Canada up here, and she did not belong.

Back in the room, she saw the woman from the washroom talking with Dollette on the stage. As she crossed to her seat, Dollette stepped up to the mike.

'Now folks, you all know we like to encourage new talent up here at The Falls, and next we got a treat for you. She's a Falls girl who's been away a long time, down in the city, but now she's come home again. And she's got a song for you, one you all know. Ladies and gentlemen, put your hands together for one of our own, Miss Dee Anne.'

As she sat down next to him. Gil said, 'It's her. The native woman I saw.'

'First Nations,' she corrected. 'And I know,' she replied. 'I saw her too. Just now. In the washroom.'

The band played the intro, the crowd murmured recognition. They knew she was going to be a country girl again.

'Buffy Saint Marie,' Gil said approvingly.

'Really?' she said, ironically, but he missed the tone.

'Yes, she's Cree. Adopted by a white family, then discovered her native roots when she was older.'

Martina smiled. 'Mansplaining,' she said, to the air in front of her, then winked at him. 'In fact, white mansplaining,'

Gil's pink face looked puzzled, then he caught on. 'All right,' he said. 'I got you.'

'Sshh,' she hissed. 'I want to hear her.'

The intro over, she began to sing. Her voice was not perfect, but it was strong and for the first time that night there was a real passion, not mere pastiche, in the sound that emanated from the stage. The crowd felt it, they responded, wanted to join in, to help her hit the high notes, as they became her chorus, singing along to a song they all knew well. Even the band seemed better, rising to the challenge as if thrilled to be part of the moment.

'Wow,' Gil breathed as she turned from the mike and, the spell broken, the band stumbled towards unrehearsed conclusion. Martina simply sat there staring at the singer, a faint smile on her face. The moment of triumph was brief. Dollette came to the mike, applauding daintily, her Stetson oddly squint above her blonde perm wig. But the singer wasn't done, she wanted the mike and wrested it from Dollette's surprised grasp. Confused words echoed as both spoke at once, but the audience heard the hostess say, 'No, the band don't know that,' quite clearly even without amplification. The singer ignored her and began unaccompanied, but Dollette unplugged the mike after a few words. For a moment they stared at each other, then the singer stepped off the front of the little stage and stormed out the door, bumping into chairs and tables as she went.

Gil turned to Martina, to make some comment, but she was already getting up, following the runaway's steps towards the door, slower and more elegantly. People looked on, surprised, as if wondering what bond could exist between them. A couple glowered at Gil, as if he might have an answer, but all he could do was shrug.

Outside, the singer was standing on the edge of the deck, her back to the door, the dark gloss of her hair fringed silver by the arclight above. Martina shut the door behind her and walked slowly across the wooden planks, her shoes clicking out a rhythm, until she stood alongside her. The woman didn't move to acknowledge her, she seemed lost in her own mind. In front of them, but hidden from view, was the great river, its constant rush loud in the evening's silence. Along the old bridge a string of lights flickered, as if responding to the motion below, or the breeze it created.

'You sang well,' Martina said, after a while.

No response.

'What happened in there?' she asked.

Finally the statue moved. 'I know who you are,' she said.

'Do you? I'm not so sure I do right now.'

'You want to make a movie about that Scotsman, the one who helped the BC chiefs a hundred years back.'

Martina laughed softly. 'No,' she said. 'That's just a rumour.'

'I met him. Your scriptwriter. I know.'

'No you don't.'

'You're pretending not to be who you really are, the two of you. But everybody knows. It's a waste of time. And a bad idea.'

'You're wrong. But anyway, lots of people here seem to think it would be a good thing. If it was real, that is. But you don't.'

'No.' She took a pack of cigarettes from her bag and lit one. The light from its tip glowed as she inhaled.

'Can I ask why?'

'You care? A big Hollywood star like you cares what I think, some poor Indian woman down on her luck.'

'I would never call you that. And I'm not a big Hollywood star.'

'It would be a big mistake.'

'I wouldn't do it.'

'I mean the film.'

'There's no film, no scriptwriter, and I'm just a woman from Vancouver. It's all a big misunderstanding.'

Then the singer turned to face her. The arc of light caught her profile and for a flash she was Elvis. She even curled her lip when she laughed and said, 'Wanna walk?'

'Yeah, why not. I was going to get my dog from the car here, though. He needs a run.'

She opened the door and clipped her lead to his collar.

'You can have him off leash, you know.'

'I don't trust him here. We're too close to the river. He's got a thing about running water. Maybe I should tell Gil, Hero?' The dog gazed up at her lovingly. 'Nah, he'll be okay a while, I guess.'

Walking along the riverside block lined by acacias, the singer spoke again. 'So where you live in Vancouver?' she asked. 'One of them big movie star houses on the shore at West Van?'

Martina was taken aback for a moment, then noticed the smile. 'Nice try. I told you, it's just a stupid rumour.'

'Okay!' she said, 'I believe you. Now I see you close up, I can see it. I saw you in the washroom looking in the mirror, and thought you could be her, but that was just your reflection. Now I can see you better.'

'So will you tell them, there's no film?'

'Who?'

'Whoever you have to, to put a stop to it.'

'If you want me to. But they won't listen to me. They'll go on believing what they want to believe, that one day this big movie star is going to rock up here with a million dollars for them. A million each.'

'I guess it's a pleasant daydream at least.'

'Let them dream, honey. It's kinda funny.'

Both burst out laughing. 'I guess,' she said again.

'I'm Deeanna,' the singer said. 'You?'

Martina who was not Martina, who was not Sigourney, hesitated a moment, then spoke her real name. 'Veronika.' After two days of being Gil's Czech muse and then a famous Hollywood actress, it felt good. Even though she'd never really liked the name her mother chose for her.

Hero wanted to water the roadside, so when they rounded the shrubs and the river shivered silver before them in the moonlight, they stopped.

'So why'd you come back here, Deeanna?' Martina asked. No answer came.

Instead, the singer suddenly veered up towards the bridge and, from its barricade, called out above the roar of the water, 'When I was a girl, I thought this was amazing.'

Martina called back. 'And now?' Her dog shook itself, then leapt forward, overtaking her, and pulled on the leash towards the bridge, so Martina followed.

'I still do,' Deeanna said.

'It sure is,' she agreed, as the vast moonlit water ran beneath her, a billowing fleece of river. Leaning on the rail, the scale of the stars so immense, the cosmos was huge and so they stood close, close enough to talk above the constant noise that wrapped them in privacy. Though the night was still, a breeze blew downstream after the water.

'It was always tough, though. The people. I never felt good as a girl growing up. And then when I started to develop, you know... I ran wild a stretch. Either the men wanted to fuck me or fight with each other over me. Sometimes with me.'

'What happened?'

'I got out. Ran away with a boy to Vancouver. But that was hell. Got put in care. Anyway, finally I met an older guy from the island and moved there to be with him. He was an artist - made sculptures, what they call traditional arts. I liked to be around him, his energy. I felt like I could learn from him. But he never let me in his studio. So I used to go in when he wasn't there, mess around. I started painting, though he didn't know. When I had something worth showing, I showed him.'

'And?'

'He laughed. But I knew I had something.'

Hero, who had been standing eyeing the water, finally could resist no longer, and leapt up. He emitted a long howl, maybe at the river below, maybe at the moon above, or maybe at something he'd heard. The two women looked at each other, both surprised by the passion of this creature's communication. And then, from very far away, echoing through the canyon to penetrate the rush of water, came a response.

'Coyotes hear you alright,' Deeanna said. She bent to ruffle the ears of the beast, as he listened far beyond her, bristling.

'Wow,' Martina breathed. 'Never heard him do that before.'

'Call of the wild,' Deeanna said, standing up. They listened as the river ran on. The breeze blew. The coyote was silent.

'How old were you?' Martina asked, after a while.

'When?'

'When you left?'

'Coming on fifteen... but I thought I was grown up. Got fed up with being treated like a piece of young native flesh.'

Martina laughed at the expression, but deep pain was manifest in the sigh that followed. 'You must have been beautiful. You still are,' she added.

Deeanna laughed. 'Ya I know...'

Veronika felt the breeze rise slightly, blowing her hair into her face. 'So what's it like, being back?' she asked.

'I don't take shit now. Men leave me alone. So it's better some, worse some. Changed some, stayed the same some. But you know, it's home. That's what I realised. And my culture. When you live outside a while, it becomes more precious. Now I want to learn more about it and pass that on, now I'm a grandma.'

'You're a grandmother?'

Deeanna laughed again. 'Shit. Feels like I've told you my life story,' she said, and stepped away. Veronika felt the distancing, as if the past had been closed off, and didn't pry further.

'You didn't get to sing the song you really wanted to, back there?' she observed.

'Hah,' the singer scoffed.

'Which was?'

Deeanna looked at her closely. 'Little bit more of Buffy, but political. Bury my Heart at Wounded Knee, you know it? Not Paulette's kind of thing.' She laughed again, scornfully this time.

'Ah yes, I do. I see the problem,' Veronika said. 'Anyway I'd better go back. My friend Gil, he's not well. You coming?'

The singer shook her head. 'I'm done there,' she said, and went to walk away across the bridge in the opposite direction. Then she stopped. 'I liked your Scotch friend,' she added. 'We talked the other day. I heard he got too much sun, didn't he?'

'Yeah, he did. You know, I want to ask you... he seems to think he might have seen you. He said someone was up ahead of him, at the top of the falls, showing him the way?'

'To where?'

'To the cabin.'

'What cabin?'

'The cabin where Jimmy Lyle and his wife…'

'Antko…'

'Where they lived when they first got together.'

'Ah ya… he asked me about that. But I didn't mean to show him. It was just a coincidence.'

'How come?'

'I was taking my daughter and my granddaughter there. Your friend just happened to see us, I guess. I thought he was following us so I tried to lose him. But he kept popping up.'

Veronika smiled. 'Seems you did, finally.'

'Good. It's not his business. Not his place. But I didn't mean him any harm. That's why I phoned George to let him know I'd seen him.'

'That was you?'

'Sure. I heard he was missing and phoned Big George.'

'Then you probably saved his life.'

'Not really. Anyway, I'm sorry. I felt bad afterwards, when I heard what happened. But we were going to Ankto's place. It's special to me. Like a shrine, maybe, to her memory. I was taking my daughter and her daughter there. I want them to know about her, to see where she'd lived.' She took a step back in Veronika's direction. 'Because it was through her that those things were written down. She was the one. Lyle was her scribe. That's why we have his book with all the old ways in them. It was her knowledge. Our knowledge.'

Hero began to pull on the leash, as if he'd seen enough of the river. Veronika held him back. 'And you painted that portrait of her in the centre?'

Deeanna gazed at her for a moment, there on the bridge in the moonlight, the stars bright above them. 'I gave it to the elders,' she said, 'But they haven't hung it.'

'Yet. I bet they will, one day.'

'Hah! We'll see. Anyway, I'm going. Home to the res.' She waved her arm towards the far side, took a couple of steps away, then said: 'Hey, I'd like to give you something. It's my card. If ever you want anything.' She handed Martina a business card from her bag. It was hard to see what it said in the moonlight, but the First Nations design was bold. 'For the movie,' she said.

In the half-dark, Veronika thought she saw her wink, before she began to skip away across the bridge, almost dancing, and then for a moment she was indeed dancing, spinning and circling, growing further away through the rigid square balustrades and the lines of shadow thrown by the moon.

Veronika walked back to the Apple Store, and put Hero back in the car. He was unwilling and she had to push his backside to get him to go in. 'Won't be long, lad,' she said. 'Promise.'

Inside, Gil was sitting in the heart of a gathering. The stage lights were off, the show was over and some people had left, but others had shifted tables to extend the circle. He looked tired but, when he saw her, seemed to leap up happily, as if in need of rescue. The company turned to view her, standing on the threshold. Here she was 'Martina', the incognito Ms Weaver again.

'I won't come in,' she said. 'It's late and I think Gil needs rest. As you know, he had a bit of an adventure yesterday.'

They people laughed, some in the know, others less so. Dollette appeared, or rather Colette. Or was it Paulette? The one without the wig, who was now de-Stetsonned too. Martina looked around. The company was already partly familiar, but there were strangers too.

From among them, Gil said, 'Sure. You're right. I am tired,' and there was visible disappointment in the faces around. She was the spoiler.

'I mean, we've all got work to do, right?' she said, and spread a smile. Of course, of course, work, they mumbled. Someone said, a film to make. Fruit on the vine.

'But you're comin tomorrow, right?' a tanned guy seated next to Gil asked.

The Scotsman answered, 'Yes. If that's okay? High Ridge, fruit farm. Where Lyle lived. About five miles…'

'Kilometres…'

'It's still the original house,' Gil said to her, beaming, as he moved through the crowd to her side. 'That okay?'

'Why are you asking me if it's okay?'

'Because you'll have to drive me.'

'Sure.' She shrugged, 'Why not?'

Hands were shaken, goodbyes said, thanks to the hostess. Everyone was Gil's friend now. It took an age to leave. A crowd came out to watch them drive off. At last the people went inside and they were alone in the car, with Hero in the rear seat, though his long snout poked between them.

'You seem popular in town,' Martina said, as she craned her neck round to reverse out. Her dog rubbed its nose against her cheek.

'All of a sudden I'm a celebrity.'

'Or a celebrity's scriptwriter…'

'I was thinking more about my epic adventure.'

'You mean going off into the wilderness completely unprepared and burning like a potato chip?'

'Haha. You mean crisp, I think. Anyway, where did you go so suddenly?'

'I took Hero for a walk. And I talked with the singer – you know, Deeanna, the woman you thought you saw that day above the waterfall.'

'Really?'

'Yes. We had a long talk.'

'What did she say?'

'I'll tell you over a scotch, Scotchman, back at the inn. I assume you have a bottle tucked away somewhere,' she said, glancing at him.

'I believe I do. The last of my duty-free. For medicinal purposes.'

'Of course. And of course it will help make your hair ginger,' she teased, as she turned onto the old bridge. As they crossed, the wooden sleepers that comprised the boardwalk beat out a rhythm under the wheels, and the image of the dancing woman leaving earlier seemed to her to flicker in the driver's headlamps, as they clattered over to the other bank.

'She'd make a great cameo for the movie,' she smiled.

'Who? Dollette?'

'No, Deeanna. Or Buffy, as she was tonight.'

He laughed. 'Buffy? Yeah.'

She opened her purse with one hand, and dipped inside. 'She gave me this.' She passed it to him, he turned the card over, and she switched on the interior light so he could read it, but the print was dark and hard to make out.

'Hmm,' he said. 'Interesting. I can't wait to hear more. You exchanged business cards?'

'Not quite. She gave me hers. On a bridge above a gorge in the moonlight.'

'Nice scene. Pan out over the river. Wonder if Dolly Parton would be down, as you say over here, to play Dollette?'

She laughed as they pulled up the bank towards the inn. She switched to full beam then. The highway was empty as they turned onto it, and nothing moved on the CPR lines. The headlamps caught truck after truck and the business acronyms, the graffiti signs and the wheels flickered past.

'I sorta feel like we're in a movie right now, don't you?' she said, as the inn appeared on the roadside ahead.

He laughed. 'Had that very thought earlier. So who's writing us, do you think?'

'Maybe that woman on the plane from Calgary, the one who kept watching us. I think she was a writer, and she saw a story in us.'

'So she went home and started writing this?'

'Yeah.'

'So who would play you in the movie?' he asked as they turned into the lot.

She looked over at him as she drove, fixed his gaze. 'Ahem… Sigourney Weaver?' she said, pointing at her face. Eyes back on the road, she added: 'You?'

'Dunno. If it's Hollywood, maybe Sean Connery with his hair dyed ginger,' he said after a minute.

She laughed out loud. 'Yeah, in your dreams…'

'And Hero? Who will play you?' he asked the dog's nose that was, as always, between them.

'Hero always plays himself,' she said, as she brought the car to a stop in front of the inn's neon sign. 'Don't you, lad?'

The dog raised his long nose higher, and nodded slowly.

The scotch was a bad idea. That was the first thing. And then, where was she, even? Tangled up in bedclothes and Hero. And Gil, again.

Daylight was streaming in the window. The empty glasses from the sink they'd used were on the bedside table, the Johnnie Walker almost empty. She lifted them and went to the en-suite, where she swilled them out, and looked hard in the mirror. Not a good idea. As she stepped back, she tripped over Hero, who had crept up silently from the bed.

'Okay, okay,' she said. 'Gimme a moment.'

Downstairs, the tree-planters had already breakfasted and gone. Even though it was only half past seven, it was already warm outside, so after Hero had relieved himself, they walked on along the road next the CPR lines, on past the community hall, and on down Highway 7 towards the reservation and the little graveyard, the very last triangle of earth in the town before the junction and the new bridge cut it. There was a breeze, a soft warm wind, and a tumbleweed blew past them, causing Hero to leap after it and pull her almost off her feet. Then came a truck, a huge thing hauling a cargo hidden under tarpaulin, and they stood at the roadside as it thundered past, and he went crazy, barking.

'They've got strange beasts up here in the interior, Hero,' she said to him as they walked on. 'So what happened last night, lad? I remember drinking whisky, talking and laughing about the movie when we were drunk. But not much afterwards. We probably just passed out, did we?' But Hero kept what he knew to himself with an impenetrably dignified stare.

She wanted to look at Antko's grave properly – not just from the car as she'd done the day before. It was right where he had written it, in the farthest corner of the graveyard, where the highway split in two. So that much was true at least. But would there have been any highway at all in her lifetime?

It was a good stone. Over a hundred years old and it still stood straight, it still bore its worded tribute clearly. And there were flowers, not recent, but the bleached remains. No doubt she had family, even if she didn't have children herself. Cousins, descended from her siblings. No doubt they came here sometimes. The women especially. Deeanna and others. It was surely a great thing to be loved in this way, so long after death, by people who knew what you'd done and respected it. Antko. Such a distinctive name, yet somehow overlooked by history like so many whose quiet actions made the future possible.

She walked back along the highway and went to her room, showered and put on the only change of clothes she had with her, her yellow cotton sun dress.

'Sorry,' he said, when she went to his room and knocked. He was barely awake. 'I think I passed out last night.'

'Me too,' she nodded. 'It was a busy day.' She didn't go into the room. Did he even know she'd slept there?

He yawned and stretched, rubbed his ginger hair. 'It's funny, since I got here I haven't felt the fatigue, you know, where I used to have to sleep every day, after the radiotherapy. But last night it hit me.'

'I think that was the whisky,' she said. 'And you're probably not through getting better from the sun.'

'No, I suppose. I feel really tired today. I want to do things, but...'

'Take your time,' she said. 'We'll go when you feel ready.'

He sat up in bed. 'So I probably didn't make it to the cabin?'

'What?'

'Last night, remember, you told me what Deeanna said, about losing me.'

'Did I? Oh yes, I did... sorry...'

Gil stretched and yawned. 'It's all right. Thought it was all a bit too surreal to be true.' He seemed disappointed, all the same.

'Let's go and see High Ridge like we planned,' Martina said. 'It's going to be another hot day, though, so be careful what you wear.'

'Nice dress,' he said.

She was about to leave when she turned back, 'Talking about clothes, you don't have a spare shirt I could borrow? I didn't really pack much besides this and I don't want to wear it if we're going to a farm. It gets dirty with dust so easily.'

Theo, Dolette's brother-in-law, had said to look out for the big fruit-stand. They were twenty minutes late finding the place. It seemed much more than five kilometres, all uphill away from the valley floor, and the drag up the canyon side took a while. The highway was busy with trucks and neither of them knew the way.

After a while they saw the fruit-stand. It certainly was big, made of plain unfinished timber, set back from the road and stretching a good fifty metres by the roadside. A rough handmade sign composed of large carved letters fixed to the apex of its roof announced: BEST FRUIT IN THE CANYON! HIGH RIDGE FARM. But all the shelves were empty and there was no sign of anyone tending it.

They parked, got out of the car and found a shady spot to wait. The house itself was about a hundred metres further up the hill, in a majestic setting on the edge of the ridge. They could see the farm faced due south as the sun was high and hot in front of them.

No one came.

'Maybe he was here on time and went away?'

'Could be.'

'Should we take a look up at the house?'

'Could do.'

'Tell you what, I'll go, in case he comes, you stay here. Come on, lad.'

She walked up the dirt track with the dog on the leash. About half-way, she turned to look back, but there was still no one there but Gil.

The view was absolutely stunning. The higher she climbed, the more she could see of the canyon. It seemed far greater in scope than she'd imagined. Driving up from Vancouver, reaching the crossing in that little flat valley she felt as if she'd seen its full compass, but now it was clear that this canyon went much much higher.

Into view came a small waterfall to the rear of the house and garden. Fresh running water – gravity would carry it down. The house was grander than she'd imagined. There was a big front deck with steps up on either side, and a fancy carved balustrade, supporting an ornate porch. The window casings too looked quite grand, in a European sort of way. The front door was padlocked, and behind the drawn shades was a hidden world.

She turned and took in the panorama, these great rocks and the life that clung to them. Thrived among them, some of it. In the fields below, she could see rows of fruit trees run in regiment downhill. She heard a far off buzzing, like a light aircraft or something, and it grew louder. She saw a flock of birds rise from among in the fields and over the crest of the slope a man riding a tiny motorbike appeared, kicking up dust as it went. She began to descend from the porch and was back at the foot of the hill by the time the rider arrived at the fruit-stand.

It was the guy from Dollette's, her brother-in-law. He switched off the engine, kicked the stand down, but continued to sit on the bike, sunglasses on.

'You guys found it?'

'Sure. Quite a place.'

'Big old farm. You only see a bit of it up here. There's fields and fields further down.'

'And your own water-supply, I see,' Martina said, nodding up towards the waterfall.

'Yup. That's why she's here. Old man Laurens, the guy who first broke the land, he was a clever old Dutchman. Brought the water down in flumes.'

'Like MacLeod down at the ferry?'

'Yup. Smaller falls here, closer to the house and barns so we aren't divertin it so far. Plus we got more elevation here so it works better. But same principle. I believe Macleod took the idea from old Laurens back in the day. Come on up, I'll show you round.'

He hit a button, the minibike roared to life, rocked it off its stand and he was off up the slope to the house in puff of fine dust and smoke.

By the time they'd walked up, he was on the porch with the front door unlocked, sunglasses still on.

'Here she is,' he said. 'You know if I'd had time to sort it out before, if I'd known you were coming, but hey, you got to look past the mess and see the potential. This is period everything. Cept my son's garbage. I let him stay up here while he's workin the fields.'

'So who was Laurens?' she asked.

'Old Laurens? He was just about the first settler up here. Maybe even was the first. Got lucky in the goldrush. So they say. Built this place with his stake.'

'You know, this explains something that puzzled me, Gil, when I read your writing. Why it was that Lyle's uncle John MacLeod suddenly set himself up here as a fruit-farmer. But if someone else was already doing it successfully, that would help explain it.'

'I don't know much about your MacCloud, but I know old Laurens knew what he was about all right. The evidence is still here. It all still works, just about.'

'So what's the connection with Lyle here?' she asked.

'He lived here about ten years. Married Laurens' daughter.'

'But he was married to Antko?'

The sunglasses were raised. 'Antko?'

'His wife,' Martina said.

Gil, who was subdued, said, 'She died and he remarried later.'

'The daughter of this settler?'

'Yup. Their kids were born here. There's graves up by the waterfall. I'll show you.'

'Later,' she said. 'Can we see round the house?'

So they went on in. It was like some old great grandma was living there with her untidy great-grandson. The widescreen tv and games console, the scattered clothes and the nude posters, hiding the old lady's painted walls and furniture. The corridors were runways between empty suitcases, mountain bikes and skis. But in the kitchen the old lady still held sway. In there was a perfect capsule of a life lived out long ago, the tins with their labels, the pots and the pans, the great black cooking range imported from Germany, the huge kitchen table which could seat all the farmworkers, the cupboards and the drawers. The framed embroidery on the wall.

'Wow,' she said. 'This is something.'

'Hardly been in here since we bought the farm, but yes, when you come to mention it, it's something alright.'

'You never lived here?'

'No, not us. We got a new house in town. It's a lonely place up here at High Ridge. We just work the farm.'

Gil called from another room. 'I see all the bookcases in the hall here are empty.'

'Ah, ya, Rick's wife Audrey from the inn, she bought them. They were just gettin spoiled here with damp.'

She crossed the threshold to where Gil was standing, looking out a window to the yard in the back. 'You seem a little down. Did you overdo it yesterday?'

'Aye. A bit,' he said. 'But empty bookshelves always make me sad, somehow.' His eyes travelled over the wood, shaped to fit the space perfectly, finished with a rough but true hand, to hold the family library. 'So I've been reading old man Laurens' books,' he said. 'I wondered where she got all those, if maybe they were MacLeod's or Lyle's.'

Theo the sun-glassed guide appeared in the doorway. 'Books,' she said to his puzzled expression, 'It's all Gil can think about.'

Theo laughed. 'Now who says a man can't multi-task? Like I always say, I can drink and smoke and watch hockey and eat chili all at the same.'

She was looking closely at the row of kitchen tools hanging above the range. 'What did they even use all these for? What do you think, Gil?' She looked around but he was still lingering in the hallway.

She found him looking up the canyon to the waterfall. 'You okay?'

'Yes,' he said. 'I mean sure. Just thinking about those graves up there. Wondering if he's among them.'

They headed out to see. The trail from the house through the alfalfa scrub wasn't far – they could see the small fenced-off area as they approached.

'You better watch your dog here – lotsa prickly pears,' their guide said.

'Maybe you'd better not come, lad,' she said and glanced at Gil.

'We're nearly there now. Look, I'll carry him.' Gil lifted the dog up so smoothly it didn't have time to complain. 'Lots a prickly pears and we don't want prickly paws,' he said. The dog seemed to understand and licked his face.

'Hero, I don't know what's come over you,' she said, but smiled, as if pleased by what he'd done. 'He's quite heavy, though.'

They advanced the last few strides along the narrowing path, the sun-glassed guy stepping on ahead, she thought looking from behind like Dennis Hopper in Easy Rider, she stepping carefully wondering about rattlesnakes and wearing Gil's plaid shirt loose, and the Scotsman behind carrying her collie named Hero, towards a fence the same as that around the Indian graveyard, the same criss-crossed pattern, the same iron posts. Even the bolt on the gate that the sun-glasses guy opened, and the sounds it seemed to make, were alike.

Inside was indeed a colony of prickly pear, with two small upright stones, side by side modestly in death. Walter and Floortje Laurens. Nothing beyond names and proximity was necessary, they were together. And then, almost hidden by the undergrowth, their guide revealed three smaller gravestones, laid flat.

'The grandkids. All scattered right here. Wanted to be back at High Ridge. Had their happiest times up here as kids.'

'Wow.' She looked at Gil as he stood holding her happy dog, his eyes running over the text, as if he was memorising it.

'So what about the middle generation?' he asked Theo.

Martina added, 'Yes, Lyle and Laurens' daughter? Are they buried here?'

Dennis Hopper stiffened. 'No, not here. Now I believe, but I haven't seen them, the graves are over in Merritt somewhere, cause when Jimmy Lyle got ill they moved over there. Right near the end of his life.'

They walked back to the house and Theo showed them the rest of the home spread, the yards and what was once the flower garden, ancient rose bushes now in the last battle of an old planting against nature.

Theo summarised it to them. 'You need a team to manage something like this. Back in the day there's a dozen folk living and working it all, and others when they needed them. Maybe didn't have a lot of money but they all ate and had somewhere to sleep.' He seemed quite proud of it all, yet saddened by the state of it and, worst of all perhaps, his inability to do anything about it. High Ridge was just frozen in time, a decaying edifice to the pioneers he saw as family, while the water ran from the falls, and the fields still produced fruit all around the old house.

As they walked back down the slope, their guide told them that if they wanted it, he could clear it up, for the movie. It wouldn't take long. All they had to do was let him know – and make the right offer, he grinned. They looked at each other, both wondering whether to bother trying to deny the rumour. Neither did, just thanked him for taking the time to show them round. He lifted his shades and gazed at her. 'Not at all, it was a great pleasure meeting you. I always liked you in that movie…'

Then she did interrupt. 'I don't know what you're talking about.'

He laughed. 'Sure, sure. I know. Hush my mouth.' And he winked.

'All roads lead to Merritt, it seems,' Gil said, as they watched the minibike blast off into the fields below once more. 'Country and Western capital of Canada.'

She popped the car-locks and got in. 'Hmm, looks like it.'

'You say that with little enthusiasm.'

'Maybe Country and Western capital doesn't have the same appeal to me as it obviously does for you? Is it far?'

'Not far, no. Couple of hours, maybe.'

On the drive back down the canyon, the road seemed much shorter. She hardly touched the accelerator, the VW just ran down the mountainside, cruising. Gil seemed quiet and Hero was glad to be back in the AC.

'Okay now?'

'Me or the dog?'

'You.'

He didn't respond right away, as if he was sorting out the words into the best order. 'Those kids – the graves – they could be Dad's half-brothers and sister.'

'Your father. He never spoke of them?'

'No. If they were, I don't think he knew.' The highway turned sharply towards the valley floor and the Falls. 'I'm sure he didn't know,' he added, as the old bridge came into view. 'Or maybe he did and just didn't want to…'

'What?'

'Deal with the sadness, maybe. The sense of separation. Loss.'

The VW was coasting then, The camber of the highway seemed to steer the wheels for her. As if it knew where to go.

'This movie stuff is getting a bit silly,' he said. 'Don't you think?'

'It is. But what can we do?'

'We could ride on outa here,' he said, in a cowboy drawl.

She laughed. 'Where to?'

'I'm a-headin north to see ma buddy Gordon,' he drawled on.

'Shut up,' she said. 'You sound ridiculous.' But after a moment she asked if he meant the man he'd told her about, the Scotsman who had never been to Scotland.

'Yup,' he said, and she punched his shoulder.

She was thinking about Vancouver, the mess she'd left behind, the texts that were probably waiting for her, whenever she found a signal for her cell phone. After a while, she said, 'You know, I was thinking, if you like, I could stick around for a while. I could drive you up to see your friend in the wilderness, what was his name, Gordon? Shall we make a road trip of it?'

He was surprised. 'Well, I'd like that, but it's a long way.'

'I've got time,' she mused. 'And maybe I can find a store somewhere to buy some clothes.'

'I think Merritt's got a bit of a centre, you'd probably find something.'

'You mean like cowgirl duds?'

'Have you ever been there?'

She shook her head. 'I didn't really know this part of BC existed before. Merritt. Kamloops. Just names on the weather forecast. It's like the wild west, desert and cactuses and cowboys and Indians. I mean, what's up with that? It should be forest and lumberjack.'

So the decision was made. That night they ate at the Apple Store, transformed back to the quiet restaurant from the country club of the night before, and Paulette was just herself, though slightly jaded. They told her they'd decided to drive on up to Merritt, to see if they could find the graves, like Theo suggested.

It was a quiet night, after the excitement of the previous. She slept well despite the heat. By next morning the news had spread, and George and his family came by to say goodbye. They were sorry he hadn't come for supper like they planned. Maybe when they came back?

They packed and loaded the car, spoke with Rick and Gil paid the bill, prepared to set off and, politely without actual commitment, said they would be back soon. It seemed to take forever, the shaking of hands and pleasantries, but finally, the car doors were shut and arms waved as they were pulling out, onto the highway to Merritt, intending to drive away from it all. But then she saw, behind the wiper of the car, a handwritten note: *I hear ur leavin but pls call in on the way out of town – I have smthin to show you. Call me. Deeanna.* So she went back into the inn to phone, and the whole farewell saga began again.

This time, they got away, left the inn going north and she drove past the old bridge, on up the bank of the river, parallel to the rail track like she'd been told to. A straight empty road stretched ahead. Hero lay down on the rear seat, as if sensing there was a way to go before the next stop. The AC was on and the car was the coolest place to be.

After a while, out of nowhere, she heard herself ask, 'So did you intend to die?'

'What?'

'When you came up here?'

'Did I?' He laughed. 'Maybe deep down, I didn't care all that much. But then I got caught up in the mystery. And I wanted to know more.'

They came to a crossing where the highway skipped the tracks, and zigzagged through it to the mountain foot, and the road that climbed over its shoulder. Slowly, from the rise, another valley came into view, heading away from the canyon. Another river, smaller and slower, a tributary, appeared from its upper slopes and flowed into the Thompson beneath a great steel rail bridge. Beyond that, the mountains. 'It's fantastic,' she said, stretching to see the highest peak. But her amazement quickly turned to the structure that appeared by the riverside. Huge cedar beams were shaped into mimetic life like feathers on a gigantic wing, and they shone vigour in the desert sun. It was an eagle's wing and it was ready for flight.

Deeanna was where they'd arranged to meet, at the corner of the trail down to the site. She was wearing a red poncho with a bold design – an animal of some kind, but it wasn't clear immediately.

'Hey, Veronika,' Deeanna said, as they got out of the car. 'It's good to see you.' She didn't acknowledge Gil till he spoke.

'That sounds weird,' Gil said, "Veronika."

'How come?'

'He calls me Martina. It's a long story.'

'O… kay,' Deeanna laughed, her upper lip curled as she did. Veronika hadn't seen her in daylight before, but the Elvis resemblance was strong from a certain angle. 'Anyway, like I said when you called, I thought after we talked the other night I really wanted you to see this. And when I heard you were leaving… anyways, most people just drive straight past cause it's right next to the reservation, but I think you guys'll like it.'

'This is a reservation?' he said. They looked around. The houses were well built and well maintained, better than many in the town.

'Sure.' Deeanna turned to Gil and said, deadpan, 'So anyway I guess I need to make things right for leaving you to the coyotes the other day.'

Gil stepped awkwardly from one foot to the other. 'Well, from what Mar… Veronika tells me, you actually saved my life,' he said.

'That makes three of us,' Veronika put in.

Deeanna smiled. 'Only three? Guy takes a lot of saving. Anyway, you're welcome… come on.'

She led them down the gravel slope, the three of them and Hero on a leash because of the nearby river, and as they approached the building, the scale of it was fully revealed. 'Beautiful,' Veronika breathed. 'Like a wing.'

It had five levels of stepped concrete, too big to be steps as such, more seats. Deeanna said, 'It's supposed to remind you of an open-air Greek theatre as well as an eagle's wing. Not a place for drama, but everything. A place of meeting and discussion for the elders. That was the architect's vision: a place where words would take flight.'

'So who is the architect?'

'She,' Deeanna said, 'is a young native woman over in Merritt.'

'So the elders stand around and discuss things, or do they lie down like senators in togas?' Gil asked, cheekily, and Veronika rebuked him with a look.

Deeanna laughed anyway. 'I dunno. I've never been.'

'Never?'

'I don't see them meet too often and, when I do, there's people here I like to avoid.'

'Meaning?'

She began to climb up the giant steps. 'Ah you don't know? Politics is dirty business everywhere.' At the top, she stood and gazed around her. 'Still and all, I love what they built here. Good things can some out of bad, I guess. Maybe they use a talking stick or something, keep them in their place. Me, I come when there's nobody around, which is most of the time. I love the wood, the cedar. The shapes its shadows make.' She stretched out her arms to stand like Samson between the pillars, but looked glad to find them strongly resistant.

'So this commemorates the signing of the document to the Premier that Lyle wrote?' Gil asked her.

'Helped word, is what I hear.'

He looked at her for a second, seeing the distinction, and bowed his head slightly. 'Aye,' he said. 'Of course.'

'It's really great,' Veronika said, as she reached the bottom step. She tried to climb up but Hero wouldn't attempt it. 'Come on, lad,' she urged. 'Jump!'

Gil was gazing around, as if looking for something. Then he said to her, 'But that, I believe, commemorates Jimmy Lyle,' pointing towards the river. A small stone stood alone, too far off for her to see. The scale of it seemed right, somehow. A tiny stone, next to this temple of sculpted trees threatening to take flight into the vast rocky wilderness around it. As much of a mark as any man could make on it.

'But there's no mention of Antko here?' Veronika called up to Deeanna.

'No. Not here,' she called back. 'This is a place for male heroes only.'

Hero, hearing his name, lifted his nose and barked, to remind them of the work done by all of his species too, and Veronika snuffled it affectionately with her palm.

They walked apart then, Deeanna along the great step-like seats, Veronika and Hero to watch the quiet river from the back of the temple. Gil had already strolled halfway to the stone. Each with their own understanding of the place, all affected deeply by it. For a long while there was no voice but the river's, and rustle of the trees in the ever-present breeze.

Veronika walked down to where Gil stood, in front of the memorial to James Lyle. The three written languages – N'laka'pamux, English and French – were a kind of triangulation point; two colonizing cultures and the local. Then they heard Deeanna call out, and when they looked for her they found she was standing at the highest level of the theatre banking, pointing skyward. They too looked up and saw, circling slowly high above them, a bald eagle.

'Wow!' Veronika shouted.

They stood a long time watching. It seemed as if it was circling the temple, watching them watch. The eagle above the eagle's wing.

'Maybe it'll drop you a feather like that raven did,' she said, winking dubiously. 'Or did you make that up?'

'That really happened,' he protested.

When they got back to the theatre, Deeanna had clambered down the seats to ground. 'That's auspicious,' she said, 'For your journey. But the eagle is telling us that this is the centre of it.'

'It?' he queried.

'Your travels. This is where you had to go to.' They walked up the gravel to where the VW was parked. Gil thanked her again and got in the car, while Veronika waited to say goodbye.

'I'd have invited you over,' Deeanna said, indicating the reservation houses behind them, 'but there's people there. Awkward maybe. Now if you had been just plain old Veronika and not Sigourney.'

'Haha. It's okay. I understand.'

She faced Veronika and put her arms around her. 'But listen, let's stay in touch. I like Veronika better anyway.'

'Sure. I'd like that. Come and see me, down in Van, why don't you?'

She drove off, climbing up the hill to the top of the ridge. He asked her to pull over and stop, so she did. He just wanted to look back at Cloud Falls for a while. So they got out of the car for a moment. They could see the theatre below, the CPR line running past it, the river and The Chief, and under his bulk, the little white houses of the town.

'It is beautiful, the temple, theatre thing, I mean,' he murmured.

'It's really like an eagle's wing.'

'It is…'

'Made of yellow cedar.'

'Yeah. And I like what it says about now as much as anything to do with the past.'

She looked around her at the canyon, as if it had become part of her world, her little town. 'So what do we do about all this?'

He was staring at it too, a slightly sad expression on his face. He put on his phoney American accent, 'I guess we just drive away, honey. Hit the highway. That's how you do it in the Americas, I believe. But we'll be back on the way south.'

After a while, her brown eyes turned to him, mischievously, 'But I like these characters, surely we can't just leave them here… what about the film?' she said.

He laughed. 'It does seem a pity, but where could it end? We'd be here forever. Think of it, no good coffee.'

'So you think there may be good coffee in Merritt?

'Let's hope.'

She drove on, the automatic gearbox changing up and down as the road curved along the ridge road, echoing the river's meanderings below.

'What's her background,' she asked, suddenly. 'This Martina of yours? What's her story? Or haven't you bothered giving her one?'

'Actually,' he said, 'I have three in mind. Do you want to choose one?'

'Sure.'

'Okay,' he began, 'So in the first Martina is the only daughter of two brilliant computer scientists who were given political asylum in Belgium while they were at a conference, before making their way to Canada, where they lived a quiet life and continued their research.'

'Hmmm,' she said. 'A little dull. What's two?'

A rig pulling a load of timber loomed up from a hidden hollow. Veronika hit the horsepower to accelerate away from its momentary menace.

'In two, Martina is the daughter of man who worked the black market in Communist times, not a gangster but a business man who supplied high party officials with western luxuries. It was all done under a blind eye.'

'Better. How did they get to Canada?'

'Hmm... well, he filled his car, a Skoda, with all his jewels and dollars, stuffing them into hidden compartments and simply drove through a checkpoint with official blessing. He had said he was taking his daughter on holiday whilst making a short trip to Munich for business.'

'So he arrived in the west with capital?'

'Yes, they lived in Paris at first, because the girl had been educated at a French school in Prague, so the transition was easy. And then moved from Paris to Montreal. He invested in property and became wealthy.'

'Hmm. Okay. What's three?'

'In three, Martina is the daughter of a two ballet dancers. Her father was famous in his youth as an actor too. He appeared in a few Czech films, state propaganda stuff. Martina was a brilliant pianist as a girl and they wanted her to go to the Juilliard in New York, but when they defected, they became trapped in the system and applied for asylum in Canada instead.'

'You're making this up as you go along, aren't you? She laughed and glanced at him sitting there in the passenger seat, still pink and ginger. He grinned back at her.

'Maybe...'

'And?'

'What?'

'What happened to them?'

'Ah... let's see now. The parents couldn't speak English well. They'd been dancers and let their bodies do the work, but they were getting older and had to seek new occupations. They tried to work as dance teachers, but without English, they found the teaching difficult. So Martina's father started in construction in Edmonton, and her mother did sewing repairs. Tutus and stuff.'

'Interesting. And the piano?'

'What piano?'

'Martina's gift. Her talent.'

'Ah... well, when they first emigrated they couldn't afford one, and when they could it was such a poor instrument compared with those at her conservatory, she couldn't play it without feeling very sad. It was many years before Martina played the piano again.'

'That's too sad. She's not that sad a woman.'

'She hides it well. She's bright and witty, but there is tragedy lurking.'

'No, it can't be three.'

'What then?'

'Two's a little less romantic, more real.'

'And one's the most boring and realistic of all?'

Another truck approached, and she slowed, pulled over as it thundered by. Hero got up and barked out the window loudly. She drove on, and slowly the road descended from the ridge, the valley opened out into a gentler terrain, grassy and fertile. After a while, she asked him, 'Does she have to be called Martina? And does she have to be Czech?'

'Well, kind of.'

'I think she should be allowed to choose her own identity.'

'So what do you think her name is, our Martina?'

'Okay... I'll accept Martina as her name, all right? But Czech... well, let's see if you can pull that off for the Czechs. So what about her story?'

'What do you mean? I just told you.'

'No, those were beginnings. How did she get to where she is now, in this car with you? This stranger who picked you up.'

He thought for a while, glanced at his driver. 'I think in all three stories she's someone who lost her way because of the cancer. The fundamentals of her life changed. And of course she's on sick leave. That's why she's free to be here.'

'And before the cancer?'

'I think she was happy. A translator of fine literature, with many famous clients, travelled a lot. And there was one famous writer who's more than a client.'

'So that first bit you stole from me?'

'Yes, I admit that.'

She had the feeling he was watching her closely as she drove, sensing his fiction overlap with their current reality. It was both disconcertingly intimate and somehow precious, this interest, but she wanted to put some distance between herself and this character he was dreaming up.

'So when's her birthday?' she asked, and he laughed.

'This is some interrogation!'

'I'm only helping you realise your fictional vision,' she said, her eyes on the road ahead, which was now getting busy with traffic.

'Em... Let's see, what was it she told me? Never ask a woman her age.'

Then she laughed. 'I like you, Gil,' she said. 'Like being with you. You kinda get me, don't you?'

He laughed too. 'Do I? I'm never sure.'

'I think so. But it's all a bit strange, this other identity you've drawn for me. Slightly creepy.'

'You weren't meant to read it. You weren't meant to turn up like that. You were just a....' His voice trailed off.

'A what?'

'A passing stranger.'

Another silent stretch. It looked as if they were getting somewhere, though, the roadside farms were large and well-tended, the houses set far back from the road with giant barns around. Herds of cattle filled the grassland. She rather liked this game of make-believe, she decided, especially the multiplicity, so she asked him, 'What were her three mothers like?'

He snorted, as if to say are you serious, but played along. 'Now the first was a scientist, remember, so very rational and self-disciplined. She never understood her daughter's ways. Art and literature. Though perhaps she admired it even more because she didn't understand it.'

'They sound quite a dull family. And the gangster's moll?'

'She died. Young. Martina was brought up by someone else.'

'Who?'

'I think the grandparents...'

'Did they emigrate too?'

'The plan was that they would retire with their son and grand-daughter in Canada, but when the time came they wouldn't leave the old country. They said it was too late.'

'Wait... that doesn't make sense. How could they bring her up then?'

'Ah,' he grinned again. 'You caught me out there.'

'No, I think leaving them behind was Martina's tragedy, not her parents dying.'

'Yes, maybe. She never saw them again.'

'Her love of Czech writing is down to them,' she suggested.

'Possibly.'

'They sent her a book when she was first in Canada, a big volume of Czech Literature. It was illustrated in such a bold and colourful style, she loved it immediately. It reminded her of her grandmother's kitchen, all her patterned crockery.'

He laughed. 'Hey, who's story is this?'

She came to an intersection and a line of cars, turned in her seat to check on Hero. He was half-asleep, enjoying the AC. 'What about the ballet dancer mother?'

'Maybe she gave up dancing when Martina came along and devoted herself to her daughter's education, especially the piano. When Martina stopped played, she broke her mother's heart. They still can't talk about it.'

'Does she ever play again?'

'I think so. When she came BC to meet her lover for the first time. In his flat, he had a baby grand he'd shipped out from his apartment in Prague. She found herself alone in the room, and the view over the sea and the forest through the balcony glass reminded her of the Czech mountains, and inspired her.'

'She played Ma Vlast.'

'That was when he first fell in love with her. The music floating through the cabin.'

'Haha, very romantic. Watch you don't overdo that.'

He laughed too. 'I have the feeling you're not taking this entirely seriously.'

'Of course I am... But I kinda think she should live all these lives. All these stories. These experiences.'

'And six parents?'

'Families are complex.' She shook her head slowly. 'Just sayin...'

She made it through the intersection finally. Gil said, 'So does this mean I have to call you Veronika from now on?

'It's my name. Still, I think Martina is quite sad to be leaving her fellow characters,' she said, to the windshield. He smiled, but didn't answer.

The land had now completely flattened out to become a rolling plain, dotted with farms. Cattle began to appear everywhere in fields. The land here was used, every acre. Fine tall horses paraded in corrals made of wooden poles.

'So this is different,' she said, peering out the windshield. 'No more canyon.'

'Reminds me of Shiloh,' he observed.

'Pardon me?'

'It's the name of a ranch in a Western series I used to watch on tv when I was young.'

Just then her cell phone, which had lain lifeless in her purse on the backseat of the VW, came to life with a succession of pings and pops. 'Looks like we're back on grid,' she said nervously.

He checked his phone. No messages, except one from the phone company to tell him he'd be spending a small fortune if he used it while in Canada.

'Yup. Movie's over,' he said, a little glumly.

'No way... this movie's not finished. You have the Country Capital and we have a road trip to your friend in Little Forks,' she said, reaching past the dog, to fetch her phone from her purse. 'Don't you, lad?'

The car veered towards the ditch. 'Look out!' he said loudly.

She turned to correct the steering just as the wheels ground into the grit at the roadside. 'I got it,' she said.

'Are you all right?'

'Ah, no, actually, let's stop for now. Unless you feel like driving?'

He didn't. She pulled in at the side of the highway where a patch of unfenced land and footpaths seemed to invite walkers. 'Would you take him out for a while, please? I want to check my cell properly.'

'Is everything all right?'

'Sure. Don't worry. I just need to reply to something.'

So Gil got out of the car and clipped Hero's leash on, and they walked away through the tall grass. She put on her pink-rimmed glasses, then flipped her cell. A missed call from her mother, even though she'd told her she wouldn't be able to answer. All the other calls and messages were from him, the last a day ago. It read: *Cant lose u. Wht shd I do?*

She sighed and counted ten messages, in reducing frequency from the day she left with her cell firmly off, in case he tried to change her mind. Reading them all now would feel as if she were falling into his web. She pressed reply on the last instead.

Do nothing. Stay where u r. Call u when I get back. Xox

The reply was almost immediate. *Darling! You got my msg? What d you say?*

Haven't read yr msgs. need time away

She waited a long time for the phone to ping again, but it didn't. It just lay there, plugged into the car, charging. Was that too cruel? Should she call and apologise? What was in the message he'd referred to? She couldn't move. She felt a pain in her breast, a sharp twinge where the scar was. What was he suggesting? That he leave his wife? That they should be married? She stared at the phone. It had the answer, but she wasn't sure if she could bear it.

Then Gil appeared with Hero padding alongside him, happy as a sandman. He gestured the question, was she done, with a tilt of his head and she nodded, picking up the charging phone and laying it on the top of her open purse. If it buzzed she'd hear it. Gil opened the rear door and Hero hopped in. His nose poked through between the front seats and he rubbed it against her cheek.

'Hey mister Hero,' she said. 'Nice walk?' Gil seemed not to notice the tears in her eyes as she glanced at him, and if he did, he didn't say anything. She pulled out onto the highway and off they went, as before.

'So if the movie isn't over, what do you think the woman on the plane from Calgary has in mind for us in Merritt?' he asked her, after a while.

'I don't know. She keeps on surprising me, that's for sure.'

Veronika grew silent then. Images of the past and other roads she'd driven merged with this, and the cars that passed. She kept a steady 90, holding the wheel lightly, and reached out to turn on the radio, but the channels were unfamiliar this far north. She pressed CD and KD Lang came through the speakers, her gloriously smooth voice instantly revealing.

'I know this. Almost Country, Veronika,' he said.

She only smiled and turned it up. The music filled the silence between them until they reached the limits of the town. At first it was just lot after lot of everyday houses, nothing in particular unusual about them, but as they reached the centre of town, the old colonial heart could still be seen, and what was more noticeable was a series of giant murals dedicated to country and western stars. Gil started to read the names out loud to her as they passed, but soon the density was too great. After Reba MacIntyre he gave up.

One brass cupola glinted above the other buildings, like a low-level minaret, and when they came to Main Street, they turned towards it. On the drive past, they both read out the name at the same time. Cold-water Hotel.

'Looks perfect,' he nodded.

'You aren't suggesting we stay at the Coldwater Hotel?' she said.

'I don't know. Look at it.' He drawled, 'Straight outta the Old West, Veronika.'

She grimaced. 'You're never going to stop that, are you?'

'Probably not.'

She parked in front of one of the murals, a huge painting of an old-time black vinyl 45 rpm record, completely covering the brick wall it adorned. Maybe it was even older than the wall, the royal blue central label looked it. 'Smiling Thru the Tears,' it was called.

'That's one for us,' Gil said, nodding towards it.

'Us? Why?'

'You know, being ill. You do remember that we're ill?'

'Ah!' she laughed, 'Yes.' But she was thinking of other things. He insisted posing her and Hero in front of the mural so he could take a photo. He said it was a landmark, and should be recorded. She didn't feel much like having her photo taken, but went along with it. Hero stood magnificently in front of the black and blue background, so she leaned back against the brick wall, relaxed, and knelt down a little to be closer to him. And then he insisted that she take one of him and Hero as well. When she felt the shutter click, she knew he was right, that it was a great image. And a threshold. Maybe she could smile through the tears.

'So, Veronika,' he said. 'Ready to take a look in the saloon?'

'You're joking?'

'I just want to ask if they have hot water too,' he smiled. 'But seriously, come on, why not?'

She stood and took in the full sight of the Coldwater Hotel –
'Est. 1909', it said, and not changed all that much, it would seem. It
did look like something out of a western, the kind of place where an
upper window might slide open and a gunman would stick a rifle out.
In fact, she could see the balcony the shootout would transfer too in
later scenes.

'Good location for the movie,' she said, finally. 'Okay. Let's go,
pardner.'

At the top of the steps to the wooden boardwalk, the entrance
split two ways, to the saloon and to a diner. Hero was on his leash and
seemed to smell dogs at the saloon door. When they asked if it was okay
to bring him in, the bartender came out and made a fuss of him. There
were a few drinkers at the bar, and one huge old bullnosed cowboy in
a Stetson asked where they were from, so they said they were passing
through on their way up north.

Gil ordered a beer and she a cup of tea. The bartender looked surprised, but unfazed. She chose a seat by a side window, away from the
bar, near an exit.

'It's great,' Gil said, sitting down. 'I love it.'

'If you say so,' she said. 'Feels a bit weird to me.' But Hero seemed
to like it, and settled down in the shade of the table while they waited
for her tea. She suddenly looked up, as if noticing something, then
pointed above his head. 'See!'

He turned round in his seat. On the wall was a framed picture. He
couldn't see it properly at first. When his eyes focused, he burst out
laughing. It was an old image, perhaps a nineteenth century engraving.
'A Good Day on the Moor,' the title ran. In it, an old Scotsman in a kilt
sat on the heather with a good kill of grouse strung on a pole.

'Well well,' he said. 'What did I say about New Caledonia?'

'I'm beginning to believe you.'

'You guys in town for the music?' the waitress asked, as she brought
the tea.

'Pardon me?'

'The music – y'know?'

The blank looks they gave were eloquent of ignorance. 'The festival. You should check it out. Some great stars.' She pointed to a poster
on a pillar nearby.

'You've brought me to a country music festival?' Veronika said,
incredulously.

Gil was grinning, straining to see the names and the dates. 'We're a couple of days early for the main acts,' he said. 'Unless you want to stay the weekend?'

She scoffed, but when the waitress came back with the check, he asked her if they had rooms here. She stood upright and took a double-take, caught Veronika's eye, then smiled.

'Yeah, we got rooms,' she said, 'But trust me, you guys wouldn't wanna stay in them.' Gil waited for more information, about outlaws or bedbugs or something, but the woman was gone as soon as she got the dollars.

Veronika smiled at Hero. 'No, we wouldn't want that, would we? You'd get fleas.'

'Ah well, just a foolish thought,' he sighed. She looked up from petting the dog.

'An airline ticket to romantic places…' she smiled, though for some reason the thought brought the tears to her eyes again.

The boy in the tourist place said they'd be lucky to find anywhere. The week of the festival was always the same, people booked ahead. Singers, musicians, crew, journalists. It was a big deal, he said. But he phoned around and found them a motel on the northern fringe of the town, one that didn't mind dogs. A cancellation. It wasn't too bad, he said. But when they got there it was a twin room, not two rooms.

'Ah well, I've already spent two nights with you. A third won't hurt, I guess,' she said.

'That's quite some testimonial,' he laughed.

'Anyways, we're only going to sleep here, it's not as if we'll be living in it. Just hope the sheets are clean.' She dropped her bag. 'I need to go find some shops. I need to buy a change of clothes.'

The three of them walked into town together, past a local diner that looked quite busy, and two rival truck dealers on opposite sides of the same road. The vast glitter of chrome and metal shone out as they passed, a loud beacon to drivers passing. They came upon a gang of workmen erecting a stage in the square, and another sorting out lighting. Still a third were putting together the scaffolding for some kind of theatre seating, and all the while a stream of country music came from the speakers they had already wired above the square.

'The jukebox is playin a honkytonk song…'

'Listen,' she said. 'Why don't I let you two have a look around, see the murals, sing along, whatever, and I'll go and buy what I need.'

'Meet back at the motel?'

'No, that diner we passed. At five?'

'You can text me now, whatever. I can pick up your messages. You'll be all right?

'Sure. I can shop, wherever I go. I have an instinct.'

'Shopstinct?'

'Yeah.'

'All right, lad. Let's go see the town,' he said.

She watched them walk away. 'No, hang on. Let me take him. He'll be okay outside a shop for a while.' But she looked around uncertainly, as if dog thieves may be lurking.

'Listen, why don't we come with you. Wait outside the shops. Keep guard.'

'Are you making fun? You better not be.'

He didn't answer, but they walked on anyway, the three of them, through the mean streets of town, passing a shop advertising 'cowboy supplies'. He stopped to gaze inside at the array of saddles and she pointed out a sign that advertised 'gold pans', joking that maybe he wasn't too late after all.

Another block, and she found a couple of promising clothes shops and, in the second, a pair of cotton trousers and a couple of new t-shirts. One was a reprint of an early CPR poster of a beaver, which she kept on, as Gil liked it so much. She went back to try on a blouse she saw in the window, and in the changing room, she pulled the cell from her purse. It was blinking, buzzing. It was him. For a second she resisted. And then it stopped. She picked it up and scrolled through his messages:

I miss u. ?? Where r u?

Then she found the message she'd been half-dreading, half-dying for. The one she needed to reply to. The one where he would say the right thing:

It read: *cd getaway fr the w/end, fly Kamloops, pick up car & meet u?*

So that was his great suggestion. A stolen weekend somewhere. A cabin by a hidden lake. Again.

It was all too brief, too stolen. Even the text message read like it had been written on the sly somewhere, while his wife was doing something else, and he pretended to be on his phone to someone else. She could picture it, the scene, the room, the music, the view out the window towards the mountains above Squamish, their affected Earl Grey tea at exactly four o'clock. Their funny shared habits were the glue that stuck them together and as long as he was there with her, sharing them even though he claimed they were hateful to him, he would never be with her in the way he'd said he would. Some day.

There didn't seem any need to reply. Her earlier message still covered it. There was no need to consider, as she had been doing all day with a part of her mind, the slim possibility that this suggestion of his was a radical redefinition of their relationship bringing about the thing that she had wanted for all these years… no, it wasn't like that. There was no need to cry, really. That was done with, had been for weeks. She had known it when she flew east, even. Long before meeting Gil on the plane. Long before this.

Hero was waiting outside the shop, with Gil leaning against the wall, whistling, when she emerged again from the shop.

'So?' he asked.

'No. Not me,' she said. 'It wasn't right for me.'

They walked back towards the centre of town where the stage was now in place, and picked up the road to the motel. A shop caught Gil's eye.

'Look. Stetsons,' he said, 'Just what you need to set that t-shirt off,'

'Yeah,' she said. 'Like that's going to happen.'

They sat on the deck of the diner so that Hero could be with them. He seemed to like the smells that seeped from the rear where the kitchen was. 'Ribs and salmon, steak,' she said, glancing over the menu. 'Burgers. Pancakes.'

'Good coffee?'

'Let's find out. I want a drink first. Wine.'

'White or red, that's what we got.' the waitress said.

'No wine list?'

'That's what we got,' she repeated, and smiled vacantly.

'Okay. White.'

Gil was petting Hero, who had stretched out on the decking under the table. She watched him for a while before he looked up and saw her, then the wine arrived.

'I kinda like being with you,' she said, after a half glass had been consumed.

'Good,' he said. 'Because you are. With me, I mean.'

'I don't know. Men are strange,' she said. 'But somehow you aren't.'

'We are twins, remember? Cancer twins brought together by fate in a movie being written by the woman on the plane from Calgary.'

'Ah, the woman on the plane from Calgary. I'd forgotten her for a moment. I thought it was just us.'

'The three of us.'

The wine went down well. Her sour mood soaked in the distilled sunshine in her glass and she tried to be happy. 'So this is nice,' she said, and winked, as she took another sip. He was playing with a coaster that read Ribs'n'Salmon and didn't look up.

'Anything wrong?'

'Well, don't tell me if you don't want to, but... that message,' he said, 'The one that upset you this morning. Was that from him? The man you went to see?'

'Ah! That.' She took another swig. The wine, poor as it was, was helping. 'Well, let me tell you, my Scotch friend, he doesn't know where I am, who I'm with, and what's more I am glad. It's good.' She poured more wine in her glass, spilled a little. 'Oops!' Hero stirred, but seeing no food, sighed and lay down again. She was a bit drunk.

'It's none of my business, I know.'

'You're right. It isn't. But since you asked, I've told you. And the matter endeth there. Anything else?' Her tone sounded light but false, she knew. But then their burgers appeared, a huge plate each with french-fries and salad. She ordered another glass of wine and a beer for him. He laughed, and nodded okay then.

She tried to stay in the moment over supper, but her mind kept drifting. At times she lost track of what Gil was saying. Something about Jimmy Lyle again. It was the wine, yes, and the long drive, but it was other things too. Her cell. Her purse. Him.

'Are you all right?' he asked.

'I think I'm a bit tipsy,' she said.

'Aye, I think you could be right,' he agreed, gazing at her.

'Can we go?'

It was a short walk home but she was staggering. 'I didn't drink much. Did I drink much?' she said.

'Most of a bottle.'

'Huh!'

'Anyway, it's very strategic of you to get blotto to avoid the discomfort of a third night with me.'

'Blotto?'

'Very drunk.'

'Oh... no... don't think that! It isn't like that.'

He laughed. 'Just teasing.'

She wagged a finger at him. 'Don't tease me. I don't like it.'

Once they'd reached the motel room, she threw her purse on the bedside cabinet, and quickly fell onto the faraway bed. She lay flat out, her feet sticking off the end of the bed, staring up at the ceiling.

'Wow,' she said. 'Country roads take me home.'

Gil sat down on the other bed and stretched out. 'Yeah,' he said, 'they do that.' He pulled off his boots. 'Think I'll take a shower.'

'Sure,' she said. 'Shower away.'

While he was gone, she changed into the nightdress she'd bought, switched the lights down and hopped into bed. She patted the cover and called Hero, who jumped up, budged around until he found a good way to lay out.

When Gil came out of the shower, she already had her eyes closed. He rounded the end of her bed and sat down on the far side of his, dried his hair off with a towel, and got between the sheets. Hero looked up at him, as if checking him out. They lay a long time like that, neither of them sleeping, but drifting into brief flights beyond waking. Only Hero's breath was even and restful. Finally his calm relaxed them too.

In the middle of the night, she woke from a dream that had drifted into nightmare. She'd been wearing a hat and when she looked in the mirror it was a living rattlesnake. Hero was barking at it and if she could have thrown the hat off, he would have chased it away, but she couldn't bring herself to put her hands near the snake to pull off the hat. And before that in the dream, the singer, the woman from the reservation.

She was sweating and had indigestion. She reached for her purse.

Gil was asleep in the other bed, she could hear him wheezing gently. Hero was still at her feet. She took the cell from under her pillow, but had no new messages. She lay down. The rattlesnake hat stayed in her mind's eye. She tried to get rid of it by thinking of other things, but that didn't work. At last the rectangle of window began to lighten behind the blinds and she found herself wide awake.

By the time Gil woke, she'd showered and straightened things, taken Hero for his morning walk to a football park where a carnival fair was set up, the rides all Western-themed. The sun wasn't yet above the hill and the dew on the grass was cool on her feet through her sandals. Hero ran after a stick until he was tired and then they sat together for a while on the bank of the Coldwater River, she watching the sun rise, he the ripples of water, doing his best to restrain his bark.

'Sounds good,' Gil said, when she'd told him what they'd done. 'I probably needed the extra sleep. You okay though? Not hungover?'

'Nah,' she answered. 'I'm fine. So what do you want to do?'

'Go to the graveyard? After coffee?'

The diner coffee wasn't as good as they'd hoped, but the pancakes and orange juice were better. Good enough to set them up for the trail to the old graveyard above the town Gil had found on googleearth, now that he had wifi again. They could have driven around there through the suburban lots, but Gil wanted to follow the pathway people would have used in Lyle's day, the route of procession along the river from the church to the place of burial. It was much shorter than the road, which ran around the foothills to get there, he said.

At first the walk was pleasant, the sun quite hot but not unbearable. They had hats and sunblock, water bottles, shorts and t-shirts. For the most part they walked in silence, occasionally observing something along the way. But as the trail left the riverbank and turned sharply uphill, out of the shade of the occasional tree, the sweat broke. Hero began to pant. They stopped halfway up for water and for breath, and to take in the view over the town.

The two rivers that met, here at the place they used to call 'the Forks', the Coldwater and the Nicola, were gentle flowing, compared with the canyon torrents. The bronze cupola of the Coldwater Hotel shone in the sun. They could see the expensive new houses around the golf course, the sprinklers dotted over its undulations trying to keep it an island of green in the midsummer sun. Big trucks cruised the streets. Somewhere in the middle was the little square with its stage and the C&W stream.

The old path emerged onto a tarmac road near to a fenced enclosure on the edge of the rise, an outcrop looking over the town to the valley beyond. 'I bet that's the place,' he said.

But it wasn't. It was a burial ground but far older and more exclusive, just a few settler families, laid together. Original ranchers, maybe, before the town grew, who'd brought their dead in from their spreads to The Forks and the chapel they shared. But then she spotted something in the distance, and when they walked a bit they saw it was a contemporary graveyard, laid out like the town below, whose dead it received, on a grid pattern, and covering a great acreage of the hillside.

By no means were all the plots taken. Those that were seemed to cluster like family groups.

'A lot of these names are Scottish,' he observed. 'And Welsh too.'

'Welsh?'

'They brought out miners from Wales and Scotland when they began digging coal here. And the railways came.'

It was only after they had visited all the taken sites and eliminated them one after another from the quest that they noticed the stones in the far corner that were laid flat, facing the sky. And there they found him, or least his remains, James Alexander Lyle. And Lotte Marie Lyle, his wife.

They stood a while, hats off, and gazed down at the twin stones. It struck them both as odd that the shared resting place was here above the town of Merritt when their lives were so closely linked with the Falls in the canyon, and that the children should have chosen to have their burial up at High Ridge, not here with their parents.

'And he lies here with her, and not with Antko,' Veronika said, as they walked downhill again, keen to get into the shade and have a drink.

'If he died first, it was Lotte's call, as you guys say here.'

The Coldwater River seemed a very good thing to her on the trail back. Cold clear water was exactly what this town needed, and indeed had, from these surrounding hills and their streams. That was its first commodity, before cattle or coal or Country music, he said.

They found a beer garden in the square by the stage, where a youthful band were warming up, presumably the first and least known of the day's fringe performers, and ordered two cold beers. Hero had a bowl of water in the shade. He looked a little happier there. The band came to life through the speaker above their head. The girl singer sang the first line of 'Coal Miner's Daughter' and a muted cheer went up from the few people listening.

Gil smiled. 'Girl's givin em what they want,' he said.

'Are you going to go on developing this fake Canadian hillbilly act?' she asked him, sipping her beer.

He considered a moment. 'No, ma'am, this is as good as it gets.'

She glanced up at the speaker. 'Come on, it's too loud.'

There was one place left he really wanted to go and they had decided after the beer to do that, and then head off north. A second night in the motel wasn't a good idea, so they went and settled up, packed the car and drove to where he thought the museum was. It turned out to be covered in large murals like much of the town, though these weren't of country singers but images of the valley's past. They circled its corrugated exterior walls, looking for narrative among the faces. Here, above the main entrance, the classic male 'Indian' pose from pre-contact times gazed down. Further round, hunters, cowboys and miners, schoolchildren and mothers. The first train. A vintage motor car.

Inside, they found the museum was actually part of the library and not the whole building. In fact, it was quite a small wing of the whole. They wandered in different directions through the exhibits. Then she heard him call her name, in a loud whisper. 'Veronika!' he repeated. She found him standing with a broad smile on his face, gazing at the glass cabinet in front of him.

'His things,' he said. 'Look. His buckskin suit from the photo I showed you.'

She looked closely at the collection of items while Gil took photos surreptitiously, with suppressed flash, so as not to attract the attendant's eye. The little typewritten card in the cabinet said they had been donated to the museum by Lyle's son, and that Lyle had been an early Canadian ethnographer and photographer who collected many songs and dances of the native peoples of the Nicola Valley.

The buckskin suit certainly was something. It struck her that she hadn't realised before how much it looked like something made by a First Nations hand. She wondered if it had been Antko who had cut and sewn it? Did the hand behind the hand that wrote also make him this suit of skin?

Then there were the scales and gold pan of his uncle 'John Mac-Cloud', spelled wrongly, who had claimed the falls for his own and who had also tried to imitate the old Dutchman's irrigation. They looked hardly used, perhaps coming north too late for the gold rush. There too was Lyle's camera. His rifle and its embroidered buckskin case. His hunting knife – used for skinning animals, the card said. She shivered. It suddenly sounded gruesome and bloody.

Then her eye was drawn to the far end of the cabinet where some of the children's things were gathered. A girl's buckskin embroidered dress. Their little beaded moccasins!

'Look at this. We saw their graves yesterday. These are their shoes.' She nearly cried, they were so very sweet.

'The incongruity of the juxtaposition of the old and the young,' he said. She looked at him. 'Wow. Write that one down.'

'Probably a quotation anyway,' he said. 'I've just forgotten where I heard it. But, yes, wow!' He seemed genuinely blown away by it all, stood for ages staring, until finally she wandered over to the lady at the front desk, and started chatting. She said Gil was related to Lyle and a second lady appeared, who said she knew the children when she was young. 'Especially the daughter.'

'You knew his daughter?' Gil asked, having been attracted from the glass cases.

'I knew her, yes. She was a bit older than me. She couldn't wait to get away from Merritt to the big city, but she always came back to visit in the summers. Now which of the children are you related through?'

'Ah,' he said. 'It's another branch of the family. From back in Scotland.'

'Scotland?'

'Aye…'

'Well, Marie, you see, she became a teacher in Vancouver, never married. She didn't have a good time growing up here. She was a target, you see, because of her father and the Indians back then. You know, times were different.'

'A target?'

'Oh you know. The clothes they wore when they first arrived in town. Name-calling, that sort of thing.' She said it innocently enough, but a sense of shame was vaguely evident in her eyes.

Suddenly Gil asked, 'I wonder if you ever heard of my father? He was here for a while between the two wars. He was a half-brother of Marie and her brothers.'

She listened blankly. 'No sorry, I have never heard of that story. And I wasn't around back then to remember him.'

Veronika was frowning, only half-listening. Those were the clothes the little girl wore that the others made fun of, she thought. And now they are here, in the museum tended by the kind of people who made fun of her. 'If their father was Scottish and their mother was Dutch, why do you think the kids wore native dress?' she asked.

Gil looked at the lady and the lady looked at him. 'Good question,' the lady responded, but she didn't attempt an answer at first. 'I guess Mr Lyle thought it was a good thing to do,' she said after a second or two.

Gil said, 'Maybe he saw it as a kind of mission. Something he had to do.' From the glance that passed between them, it seemed neither the woman nor Veronika quite understood what he meant.

They passed the reservation on their way out of town. It was big but looked weary, squeezed between the expanding town and the river. No room to go, or grow into. It had been strange, they agreed as she drove, to find this anomalous shrine to a man who loved Indians here in the very heart of this Cowboy festival world. But beautiful too, somehow, that these things had survived, from those days when frontiers between cultures were first crossed.

The reality of the current situation could be seen there in Merritt clearly, the First Nations presence still strong among the townsfolk on the street, a solid cornerstone to it. The road passed on under the banner proclaiming 'The Country and Western Capital of Canada' and then they were free of the gravity that had pulled them in.

'So remind me, why are you going to see this friend of yours you've never met?' she asked, the road dead straight ahead across the flat plain.

'He has a book to show me.'

'A book? You're travelling all this way to see a book?'

'Aye.'

Fourth Dance

'The Road to Happy Ever After'
(Quadrille)

THEY GOT ON to the old road north to Kamloops through the Nicola Valley outside of Merritt and, once they were clear of traffic, she tried again to persuade him to take the wheel for a bit. She pulled in. He protested that he'd never driven a left hand drive, nor on the right side of the road, nor an automatic, but she just said now was the time. The highway was quiet, straight and broad. So they switched seats and he got himself set. She explained the drive and park gears. He was feeling around for a clutch pedal and it was odd not to find one. Once she'd gone over things twice, he tentatively put them into action.

The VW pulled out onto the empty highway. 'It works!' he said. 'Now to remember to stay on the right side.' But they hadn't gone far before he decided to test the brakes, and nearly frightened the life from her, so sensitive was the pedal and so sudden the effect. Hero slid off the back seat and into the foot space. She gave him a questioning look, and he said he was sorry.

From then on, he proceeded carefully. He felt the automatic gear changes and thought at first that it would fail to catch if he didn't do something, but no, it went on like clockwork, which he supposed it was in a way, the clocking of miles.

'This is great,' he said after a few minutes. 'What fun.'

The road followed the valley's gentle undulations. It looked almost Scottish to his eye, a less grand sight than the canyon, but fertile and beautiful. When they came to the end of the lake, the valley floor widened out further.

As they passed a holiday ranch on the waterfront, she turned in her seat and read the name out loud. 'Hmm,' she said. 'We must be quite near Kamloops by now.'

'Why do you think that?'

'A friend of mine mentioned that place. Said it was near Kamloops.'

'Want me to stop?' Although he was now enjoying the drive, he would have welcomed a brief hesitation, a stop and start just to make sure it was really happening.

'Not here. I want to get down to the lake somewhere. Cool off a while. Can we?' He drove on a distance along the side of it, but nowhere seemed a good place to stop, until at last they came to track which went off to the waterside, a feeder road to some big new homes that were being built. One of the lots was empty so they walked down that gravel track to the lake, past thistles and thorns. Around the water's edge here, a bed of reeds grew, and it sheltered a small beach of yellow sand. The water sparkled.

'Look,' she said. 'No wind here.' And it was true. He could see where the lake bent in a dogleg, and where the wind that had blown in the south of its shores didn't reach. Up here it was glass-like, a perfect mirror to the clouds that hung in tiny clusters high over the valley. He stopped, took out his camera and tried to capture the panorama, as she and the dog walked on, until Veronika and Hero were in the right bottom corner of the frame by the water. Through the viewfinder, he saw her take her clothes off, down to her underwear, wade into the water, and then plunge under. He looked up, heard her whoop and then a great splash arose, and she was off, swimming freestyle like a marine-born creature.

'It's a thing we do, lake swimming,' she said, as she surfaced. 'Try it.'

'Hmm. Maybe I'll just wade,' he said. Hero was already in the water, cooling his paws. Because the water was still, he saw no reason to bark at it. 'Me and him are alike.'

The water was warm and tempting, so Gil did venture in a distance. And then he baptised himself in the N'laka waters, as it was called before 'Nicola'. It was gloriously fresh clean water and his skin, now healed after the worst of the sunburn, pricked and began to glow afterwards as the sun dried him off. He lay in the sun while she kept on swimming for a while longer. Hero waded further in too, far enough to cool his fur, so that when he came out he looked half himself, his lower body thin and his legs spindly.

When she came out she lay down next to him. 'It's nice to be cool again.' She pulled her bra up. 'Don't look at my scar,' she said.

'I wasn't,' he said.

'You were.'

He wandered off a bit. Then Veronika called him over, and revealed she had brought a picnic with her. She produced two sandwiches, peaches, nut bars and two small bottles of wine.

'When did you do that?'

'This morning, first thing.'

'Genius.'

'Picnic of the Year, I'd say.'

They stretched out on the sand in the sun. He noticed she seemed to be frowning at him, for some reason.

'What are you thinking?'

She studied him a while longer, sandwich in hand, chewing. Then she said, 'Who are you really, Gil?'

'Really?'

'Yes, it just occurred to me that I read your writing while you were ill and I formed an idea of who you were from that, but I don't really know if that was you or just something you wrote?'

'Now you're forgetting the Calgary woman who's writing us all.'

'Seriously?'

'Oh I'm the one thing I don't have to invent. That part's simple, as I am.'

She chewed a moment. 'I'm not so sure. My mother always says that everybody's got a twist to them, like on a candy paper. It's what keeps the sweet stuff in, she says.'

'Your mother's profound,' he said.

'But you seem all sweet stuff. Where's your twist?' She placed two fingertips in front of her eyes, and gave him the 'I'm watching you' gangster sign. 'I bet it's books, isn't it? That's what gets you twisted. Otherwise, why are you going to see this guy?'

He coughed. 'People are complicated. Isn't that what you said?'

'Families. I said families are complex.'

They drove on north through the valley, which just became more and more stunning as it narrowed again beyond the lake. It was relatively unspoiled too, the houses set back from the road. At last they came to a hill, beyond which lay Kamloops, and switched drivers so he wouldn't have to deal with busy intersections in the city. Later, he was glad of that when they got lost coming into Kamloops. The light was failing fast, slipping into a strangely luminous gloom that seemed to come on far too soon to be night, while the sun still shone through the murk. She pulled in at a gas bar to get directions and fill up. When she opened the car door the strong aroma of wood smoke snuck inside. Somewhere above the city, a wildfire burned.

At an intersection a white Volvo pulled up next to them. She glanced at it and for a second she thought the text message had come true and that he'd flown to Kamloops in pursuit of her. She quickly realised that, although the car was the same model, he wouldn't have been driving it if he'd flown. It made her nervous, though – maybe her phone had given away her location. Could GPS do that?

They found a liquor store and bought a malt for their hosts, then picked up a few snacks for the drive. She looked at the dashboard dials. They should make it before dark if they kept going.

However, once they were out of the city, visibility narrowed quickly, and they found it hard to see beyond the car in front for a while. A few miles further on, behind the line of pine trees on the high ridge's edge, they could see vapour rising like steam from a volcanic pool, twisting itself between black limbs and branches. But it was smoke - trees were burning, a halo of fire around them like St Elmo's Fire on a mast-head. A blue light flashed on a fire truck while, on an airstrip by the highway's edge, a helicopter sucked in water from a tanker through a hose.

The line was nine cars long. A pall of smoke rose high into the darkening sky, before swinging south toward the city. They both got out to watch the action. A few other drivers had done the same. The heat was pretty overwhelming, though, and before long they were back in the cool of the A/C. She put on a CD while they waited and he found he knew the song but not the version, and asked her who it was. She told him, KD Lang again, explained that this was an album of her favourite Canadian songs she'd made a while ago. They sang along, at least the lines they knew, and occasionally duetted, at least for the chorus 'Helpless, helpless ...'

Ages later, the helicopter took off, over the highway and up towards the burning hillside. Once it was gone, they were flagged through. The line was nineteen cars long by then, and it snaked slowly up the hill past the burning forest. At the road edge, the nearest tree was in flame. Not ablaze, but burning steadily. Alive. The smell was acrid and shocking, even though all the windows were up. Choking, indeed. Silently they rolled past, on up the hill, the image imprinted in both their minds as surely as if on film, of quietly flickering intensity strong enough to burn sappy wood.

Above the road, they saw dead trees not burning and wooden poles supporting a triangle of wires – once it was simple, he said, communication, the telegraph, now who knew what they transmitted?

'So tell me about this book?' she said, once they were back on the open highway.

'You've read all there is so far…'

'No, not what you're writing. I mean the book this friend of yours in Little Forks has got. The one you're traveling so far to see.'

'Ah, that book. Well, you've heard of Robert Burns?'

'Sure. Your national poet. The statue in Stanley Park.'

'Well, George Gordon Fergusson, to give him his full name, believes he has a copy of the Kilmarnock Edition.'

'Which is?'

'The very first printing of Burns' poems. 1786. 612 of them were made, and most are lost now. There's quite a few in libraries of course, and some in private collections.'

'But not so many on the market?'

'No. Precisely.'

KD had covered a Joni Mitchell they both knew. It seemed incredible that they should both have loved this so song much, so many thousands of miles apart, but at the same time. But then, thousands, maybe millions, did. And they would still be on their feet. Their voices sounded quite good together. Not that either were great singers, but both could hold a melodic line, if not a whole tune. Each remembered different lines, and sang loudest when these came along. Together they could almost sing the whole lyric, loudly and fairly badly. When it ended, they both laughed.

'So this Burns book is valuable?'

'In a way it is priceless. At least to a Scot.'

And so he told her the story of Robert Burns, his early struggles, his life as a rhymer and a carouser, Jean Armour and her father, the ill-fated Highland Mary, and the ride to Edinburgh on a borrowed pony to meet the literary elite when the book was first published. Nancy McLehose and 'Ae Fond Kiss'.

The darkness deepened. Now it was not just smoke blotting out the sun, but night, as it began to leech the light away. Soon they were in the night's void with only their twin headlamps to seek the way out. The road rising all the while, to the left or right, round the bend, out of sight. The names of places suddenly on the roadside – Henckey Creek, McClure's Ferry. Another Scot, no doubt. Then they were crossing the river in the dark and approaching Barriere.

'There was a big fire round here,' she said, 'a while back. I remember it being on the news. People were evacuated, houses burned.'

But there was nothing to see right then, just black night all around. The highway wound on ahead and they followed it hopefully. After a while she asked if he'd mind driving again. She didn't much like driving at night, so they switched again. He pulled out without mishap and, once they were back to speed, she stretched out and relaxed.

'So we're going to this place so you can look at this book of his? Or are you planning to buy it?'

'I've seen copies before,' he said, staring into the night, at the beams out in front and the stream of the river that occasionally glistened, briefly, as the road bent around it. 'The last one made £40,000 at auction in Edinburgh.'

She whistled through her teeth. He smiled. 'Not a fortune, compared, say, with a First Folio Shakespeare which would set you back a few million. But quite a lot. I'm not sure if he wants to sell it, though. More to be sure of what it is. There was a facsimile edition made in Toronto in the nineteenth century. It could be a Canadian copy.'

'But you would know?'

'I think so. He says his great-grandfather brought it out with him to Alberta from Scotland a century ago. I'll know if it's real. I have good bookstinct.'

She smiled. 'I bet you do.'

'Though of course it would have to be verified by the auctioneers before it could be sold.'

'And you could arrange all that for him?'

'I could. It's what I do. Or did, before I fell ill. Now I'm not so sure what it is I do. Or who I am.'

'You're writing now,' she said, and he grinned. That was true, he really was, at last.

Another long stretch without light or sign. Nothing passed, not even in the opposite direction. They were lonely travellers, companions in blindness bar all but the little beams that went in front of car. An age elapsed, just them, silent in the dark. The CD had ended and neither had moved to change it.

'I'm beginning to wonder if we've missed the intersection,' she said.

Then suddenly, as if summoned, the name they sought flashed up in front, passed before they had time to comment, as did the settlement. It was barely five streetlamps long. She realised they should have turned off, so he swung around, forgetting for a moment the direction of the loop on Canadian roads, travelling clockwise. But there was no traffic around, no people to confuse.

Little Forks was just a junction, a crossroads store, a diner and a gas bar. Everything was shut. They retraced tracks, took the turn off, and were back in utter darkness. The highway began to climb sharply once again. They had been going uphill since they left Cloud Falls, and yet they went up again, looking for the third turning on the right. A good few kilometres passed without even one, and only when Little Forks was far behind, did they see the first. Then another few kilometres, and a second, the darkness silent between them, as each sought the shape of an opening in the thick trees that lined the road, now hairpinning up the valleyside.

As they drove past what looked like a turn, they called out at exactly the same time. Another 180 turn and they were running down a dirt road. Darker and darker. She said, 'Are you sure this is alright? I mean, how do you know he isn't an axe murderer waiting for us?'

He laughed and said he didn't. Then, at the side of the track, they saw a tall standing stone, carved in an elaborate Celtic Revival style. That looks promising, he said. So she pulled up. The text ran top to bottom: F-E-R-G-U-S-S-O-N, it confirmed.

They turned off onto another still smaller rutted track, with green sward down the middle. He steered the car warily up the hill, afraid of hitting the bottom. Out of the darkness, dead ahead, a log cabin came into view in the headlamps. It appeared ancient, windowless, and above the gable end door hung a pair of gigantic antlers, and above them again, a skeleton moose head.

'Oh my giddy aunt!' he said, peering up at it, and she laughed at the expression. The road went on, until at last another rather more modern structure materialised in the clearing behind. It was straight out of the back of the backwoods, though, and stood lonely in the darkest forest night. Then the figure of a man appeared, with a great white dog at his side. It was impossible to see him properly, but at least she could tell he wasn't carrying an axe. Gil pulled up and they got out.

'Saw your lights,' the man said. 'I was beginning to wonder if you'd find us.'

Gil explained they'd stopped in Kamloops, then run into a forest fire and that they were sorry to come so late. The man, still shadowed, said that when he got their message from Merritt to say they were on their way, he'd wondered if they'd make it. Hero seemed a little reluctant to get out of the VW, with the great white beast there, but finally he hopped out and the two dogs began their ritual of rounding and sniffing. Veronika checked her phone – no service.

Aye, George Gordon Fergusson it was, and they embraced like blood brothers separated, met with again, generations later. He showed them inside the warm cabin where soon the whisky flowed.

Tales came fast in breathless conversation from the first large glass on, while supper bubbled on the elegant old stove. It was still somehow Scotch, their host's accent, well preserved across three Canadian generations first fathered by the tough young Scot who'd emigrated in 1886, who'd settled in Calgary before the First World War, fought in Flanders, a prize boxer, as hard as nails until the day he keeled over. This Canadian Scotch voice spoke of the world of cattle his ancestor knew as a lad in Aberdeenshire and in Calgary as a man, of his great buffalo coat worn on the long prairie rides, impervious to everything.

Gordon, as he was known, was talkative. He said he had chosen BC over Alberta, New Caledonia where the Scottish heritage he'd grown up revering seemed even more present; where he and his wife bought a piece of land first cleared around a century before, with an old cabin unchanged since the 1930s, from an old German settler. He told how they had set about building a home, one slow plank at a time, he and the wife who would join them soon – she couldn't for supper as she had an ageing mother nearby, and she shared care with her brother.

Later, over bowls of venison stew, wine made by one of Gordon's friends and vegetables from the garden, the two Scotsmen explained to Veronika how one book order had led to others, and letters led to emails, that led to a virtual friendship. They compared notes on the amazement of virtually being in the other person's world, 5000 miles away, and now being here together.

She listened as they talked so warmly, both new friends met and old reunited, and tried not to feel too left out of this global Scottish family. She knew how it was to meet someone from your childhood, from the world you had grown up in, to use the words and phrases known only to your most local tribe – to feel at home even if you meet abroad and the common place is far distant.

And then the lady of the house, Sara, arrived as they were talking, a blonde woman with a shy intelligence and an aura of strength. Veronika was glad to join her in the kitchen while she had supper, and Sara explained how they'd moved here as runaways from their respective families when they'd only just turned twenty. They had nothing when they started, just the land she'd bought with a small inheritance she got from her aunt. The original cabin had been home to an old Cariboo prospector who stayed on after the gold rush, panning about enough to keep him going, though it was a hard slog at times just to get a grubstake. To compensate for his unsuccessful mining, he cleared the land and improved it by keeping livestock – chicken, goats and a few cattle. So they'd inherited some well broken ground and the makings of a homestead. But with bears and wolves and other predators about, they were always wary – which accounted for Benji, the white bear dog, who lay outside the kitchen door jealously peering in through the glass to the warm stove where Hero lay curled up, as if wondering what other rare privileges might be afforded this visitor.

She and Sara washed up as they talked, then joined the men by the open fireplace in the large lounge, where logs crackled. George Gordon was explaining how the creek nearby was a blessing twice over. They'd been talking about the wildfires, and Gordon explained that only the previous year they'd had one that burned its way almost to their property. They'd had to seal everything valuable in plastic and put it in the creek just in case. And besides, it was pretty rudimentary up here back when they moved in, no power, but they'd built themselves a hydro plant successful enough to keep their various gadgets going, as well as tools. They'd get a tour tomorrow and he's show them all that. Veronika wanted to know more about the fire, but it seemed they didn't want to talk about it. Gordon changed the subject, saying he was eager to hear all about Gil's time in Cloud Falls.

So Gil told the tale, with Veronika's help, of the days they'd spent there, of Gil's 'adventure' in search of the hidden cabin, the Country and Western night and all the characters they'd met. They told them about the mistaken identity, the whole film farce, and they all laughed heartily at that.

'You do look a bit like her, though,' Sara said finally, after studying her.

Veronika told Gordon that Gil had said he knew about Lyle, and after a moment when she had to explain that she called Gilbert 'Gil' rather than 'Bert', Gordon replied he had made a study of Lyle's life for his own satisfaction, years ago, and knew quite a lot about Cloud Falls. It was one of the things that had cemented their friendship when he first began to buy books from Bookseller Bert, as he called him. He was about to explain his theories when Sara, teasingly, asked the book-seller who this woman was he'd brought with him. She'd thought him a confirmed bachelor.

Ah, now! Who was she? He said maybe she should answer that herself.

She laughed, said she had asked herself that very question just the night before, had found no answer. Gordon asked if she was Canadian and she said yes, she was a Canadian citizen, though she still identified with the culture of her parents' country. But she had grown up in Canada and identified with it more, particularly with the multicultural mix of Vancouver. A person has a lot of different levels of belonging, she said, and sure enough ethnicity is a part of that, but she felt a citizen of the world on one hand and a silent self that had no name on another. And in between, yes she was a Vancouverite, a Canadian, a citizen of the New World, yes, all of those. She couldn't just be one thing, her life had been too complicated, too dislocated by emigration, revolution, by the change in the political system that had entailed.

And Sara had a story too, which was similar in a way, although it had all taken place in Canada. She had been born into a Mennonite family in Manitoba and found herself rebelling against those values. Growing up was not a simple thing, not for her the unthinking adoption of a tradition. It was always complicated by the present moment, by the new ideas shared by different generations, the challenge those embodied to accepted beliefs. Everything was a revolution, in that sense.

True, George Gordon said. Even he, by moving across the Rockies and leaving behind the ranching, the Calgary stampede and all that, had rebelled. Though no one but he really saw it like that. By making their shared attempt at living like pioneers, self-sufficient and truly independent, both he and Sara had rebelled against their families.

Only Gil was without a story to tell. His life had always been one of taking the line of least resistance, doing the easy thing, staying safe – until the cancer had erupted, the danger within, the malfunction of the bodily self.

The whisky bottle slowly emptied, as their glasses remained permanently half-full. It was a tradition Sara didn't know, with her religious upbringing, but the drinking of spirits was one the others shared, whether whisky, vodka or plum brandy. When George Gordon turned the empty bottle on its head and carefully balanced it upside down, they all knew the ritual was over with. It was well after midnight, and they were all merrily drunk.

'Come on,' Sara said to Veronika, 'I'll show you your room.'

She explained how the log cabin they had begun to build as youngsters had grown, extension by extension, over their lifetime together. Doors led through one room to another. Each was full of craftwork and art, paintings and embroidery. They climbed a narrow handmade staircase, and when Sara opened the door which turned out to be the last, she opened it onto the vision of a fine hand-crafted quilt, in the classic Canadian style.

'This is really beautiful,' Veronika said, laying a hand on it. She put her bag down and sat on the bed. It was a high-mattressed double with a tubular brass frame. 'So comfy too.'

'I made it a few years back. Something I learned when I was a girl. The quilt that is, not the bed. Gordon made that.'

'Really? It looks shop-bought.'

'Sure. He can make almost anything. Show him a picture, tell him how it works, he'll figure it out.' Sara sat down next her. 'Gordon always had ideas about building his own place from scratch, you know a proper house with plans,' Sara said. 'So we have a half-built new house that's been half-built for ten years.'

'So where is the new house?'

'Down at the end of the property. You'll have passed it driving up here but wouldn't have noticed it in the dark. It's a beautiful spot above the creek. We built a summer house down there when the kids were little, a place they could go and play and, when they were older, sleep out. Course we made sure they took the dogs with them. We'll take you there tomorrow.' She stood up. 'Will you and Gil be all right in this room?

'Oh,' Veronika said, 'I thought this was just for me.'

'Ah, so you two aren't… I just assumed you were.'

'Well, not really. No.'

'Ok. Well, I guess I could make up a bed for him on the couch.'

Veronika laughed, thinking of the nights she'd shared a bed or a room with him already. She shrugged. 'No, don't go to any trouble, it's okay. Really. The bed's big.'

'But if you're…'

'Honestly, it's fine. As a matter of fact, we've shared a room the past three nights, for one reason or another.'

Sara didn't ask how come, but smiled. 'Sounds like fate,' she said, and turned to leave the room.

'Oh, one question,' Veronika said. 'Anywhere around here where I can get a signal for my cell?'

'Fraid not, but you can use our landline if you need to.'

Veronika was about to explain she was waiting for a text when Gil came struggling up the winding staircase with his luggage. Sara squeezed past and left.

He found her stretched out on the bed, with two large hand-embroidered cushions placed in the middle. Hero had been banished to the fireside – no dogs were allowed upstairs.

'You know, I can sleep on the couch,' he said, indicating the barrier.

'No, I actually think I want you nearby tonight.'

'Frightened of the bears?'

'No. Just… I don't know why, I just I want you near.'

'On the other side of that pillow wall?'

'Yes. That's to stop you rolling over on top of me.'

'I see…'

'Because of the operation.' She touched her left breast with her fingertips. 'It's still very painful.'

He sat down on the bed, sobered. 'Ah. Of course. I hadn't thought of that. Hasn't it healed?'

'It has, sort of. But it still hurts to the touch.'

'Is it very big?'

'What?'

'The scar.'

She didn't answer, but her look said none of your business. She got up, fished out the new toilet bag and nightdress she'd bought in Merritt from her case, and headed for the bathroom. At the door, she stopped and glanced back at him. He was already arranging his things on the stand by the bed, taking off his watch and bending to undo his shoelaces. He looked up at her. 'What?' he said.

'It feels huge,' she said, then left the room.

He was in bed behind the pillow divide when she came back, facing the wall. He'd switched the main light out and a blue-shaded lamp at her side on. She turned that off, slipped silently under the heavy quilt and lay facing away from him. Neither moved, listening instead for the sound of the other breathing, as their rhythms slowly synchronised, but neither slept. At length she turned onto her back and her hand fell on the pillow divide. He turned too and their arms touched. Her fingers closed around his, he stretched and below the pillow wall, his toes met her toes. They lay like that, connected yet apart, for what seemed hours of darkness. Then she asked softly if he was asleep. He said no, he couldn't, he was thinking.

'What?' she asked.

'Seems like they've spent their whole lives together here, slowly building a home piece by piece, making everything they need. And I was wondering, what have I built? Just a mountain of books by other people.'

She gave out a little sigh of amusement and squeezed his hand. 'There's worse things to have done.' After a moment, she added 'I was thinking what it must have felt like when the fires threatened, to have to put your things in the creek like that.'

'I know,' he said, and waited, but she didn't elaborate.

Slowly drunken sleep brought an end to a long long day.

Morning came in through the yellow curtains as a glow of light inching across the patterned quilt, square by square. By the time it reached the pillows, the kitchen downstairs was issuing aromas of a large breakfast.

He rose first, and went to the window to look out. Last night they'd arrived in the dark, and this first glimpse of where they'd got to amazed him.

'Good God!'

She opened her eyes and sat up. 'What's the matter?'

'The view,' he said. 'It's like the Canada I always pictured.'

She got out of bed in her new-bought nightie and peered out over his shoulder. In the far distance, a range of snow-caps shone almost pink in the morning light. In front of that lay ridge upon forested ridge of lower peaks, like ocean waves frozen in motion, until the nearest rose, louring above the valley where the cabin stood, and the creek ran dipping in and out of sight.

'Yep,' she said. 'That's my Canada.' But as soon as she'd said it, she knew that wasn't quite true. Her Canada was Vancouver, with its restaurants and bars, its high-rise downtown, its colonial suburban mansions, its beaches and parks - at best, the Gulf islands, with their easy wilderness, no more than a ferry journey away.

Here there was no human presence anywhere to be seen, no intervention in the wilderness, besides that of their hosts, but that, they could see, was fairly extensive. The clearing stretched away from the house quite a distance, and everywhere were signs of activity – a garden full of polytunnels, cultivated patches with healthy green growth visible, around that various greenhouses and sheds including the old timber structure with the moose head and antlers they had come upon in the darkness the night before. As they stood at the window, in that moment they felt the warmth of the other closer than ever before, and the vague yet clear scent of their true identities, regardless of what their names were.

He was the first to move away, to the clothes he'd pulled off drunkenly the night before, the jeans and the shirt he'd bundled. He found clean socks, and left her, expecting their hosts to be waiting. But there was no one bar Hero who was still moping at being left downstairs. He looked up, hopeful to see his love, but settled for Gil's petting anyway. On the stove lay eggs and bacon, hotcakes, beans and toast, a pot of coffee, all seemingly abandoned. Then he saw a note on the table: *Gone to do morning chores – will be back soon. Eat and make yourselves at home in the meantime, please!* It wasn't all that late, 8.30-ish, but of course they were busy people with lots to take care of.

She showered and dressed, and went down to find him sitting at the table, eating.

'All alone?' she asked, as she gave her dog a morning hug.

He pointed to the note and continued chewing.

'Hmm, okay,' she said, when she'd read it. 'Has he been out? Have you fed him?'

'Yes, he went out earlier and no, I thought you would want to.'

By the time Sara appeared at the back door with a bucket half-full of eggs, they had all eaten plenty, and she had washed their dishes at the sink. Hero jumped up, wagging his tail, and trotted over to Sara, greeting her like an old friend. She explained, while petting him, that

Gordon had some errands to run in Little Forks but would be back any minute, then they'd get a tour of the property.

'Not too hungover then,' Sara said, as she cleared away the leftovers. Then they heard the sound of an engine and Gordon's truck rolled into view. He brought a few grocery bags in, and once they'd unpacked them Sara suggested the tour. They set off, two dogs and four people, down the track through the garden with its teeming green life at high summer, wooden tipi frames of peas and beans, sunflowers, and the leafy heads of potatoes and carrots, down towards the old cabin with the moose skeleton. There, Gordon had something to show them — his great-grandfather's buffalo coat, worn on horseback while driving the herds. Gil was amazed.

'Don't you remember last night, you specifically asked to see it? Gordon asked.

Gil laughed. 'I don't recall too much of last night. The whole day was a blur.'

The coat was simply the hide of the beast, huge and heavy and smelly, shaped into something that would fit over a large man's shoulders. Gordon insisted that Gil try it on, then fished out from the cabin the buffalo rifle that went with it. The coat swamped him. Gordon handed the rifle to Gil, saying 'Sharps 1874. Highly accurate up to five hundred yards, maximum range a thousand. Fires eight to ten shots a minute.'

Gil took the gun from him and immediately felt the weight of the thing. 'It's pretty heavy,' he said, regaining his balance.

'Nearly ten pounds,' Gordon said, smiling.

'How could anybody move under all this weight?' Gil asked.

'Didn't have to move. Just had to be able to sit square on a horse and shoot. Would you like to feel its kick?"

'Ah no, I think this is enough,' Gil said, sheepishly. And so the Scotsman stood looking overwhelmed, draped in buffalo hide, holding the buffalo rifle across his chest like a greenhorn, next to his host, while Veronika took pictures and Hero sniffed at the coat, unsure what this new scent was. The fur on his neck and back bristled, while Benji the bear dog sat unmoved, watching him with faint canine disdain.

When the photo session was over and the laughter subsided, they carried on down the slope towards the creek. As soon as the water came into view, Hero set off towards it at full speed and disappeared over the bank.

'Where's he off to?' Sara asked.

They all looked at Veronika and she first shrugged, then smiled. 'It's just a thing he does,' she answered. 'Running water gets him all worked up.'

He began to bark and when they came to the bank he was up to his middle in the flowing stream, attempting to bite the breaking water where it tumbled over a rocky drop, and yapping at it when he couldn't.

Veronika said, 'I think he thinks he's herding it.'

Benji stood watching for a while, as if he couldn't figure what Hero was doing, then suddenly jumped into the pool beside him, splashing around, occasionally barking in a gruff beardog way.

'Would you look at him,' Sara laughed, 'the big puppy!'

Gordon grinned too, then carried on along the bank. At a point where the creek narrowed and the stream grew faster was another small shed, built astride the flow. 'This is our turbine,' he said, matter-of-factly, 'All our electricity comes from here.'

'Wow,' Veronika said. 'And you built this too?'

'Well, not the parts, but I put it all together. Essentially it's very simple. Creek drives a turbine, turbine drives a rotor which is a wheel with magnets inside. That spins around faced onto a stator, a static part with magnetic coils, and hey-ho, kinetic energy becomes electricity.'

'So how did you figure it out?' she asked.

'You recall a thing called the Whole Earth Catalogue?'

'Yes,' Gil said. 'I still see copies of that circulating. It was a kind of hippie guide to self-sufficiency, first produced in California, I think around 1970. Part of that back to the earth, post-Woodstock movement.'

'I believe so. Anyway, the rudiments were in there, plus places to order parts from. Took a while to get it up and running, but you know, there's no shortage of water up here. Of course, we've renewed it all since then, more efficient equipment, but the first plant was Whole Earth Catalogue.'

'So you guys were hippies?' Veronika asked Sara, who laughed.

'Lord no, not me,' she said. 'I was a good Mennonite daughter. Though Gordon had a lot of hair back then. But you know that was our generation and some of those ideas seemed like good ones. When we bought the land here one of the reasons we could afford it was because it had no amenities.'

The dogs caught up with them at the hydro plant, Hero wet from snout to tail, looking a fraction of the size he did when his fur was dry. He shook himself, sending a spray over everyone, and seemed intrigued by the sounds from the turbine, but had barked himself out. They walked on down the side of the creek until they came to a pool where the water ran slow.

'And this,' said Gordon, 'is where we had to put everything when the wildfires were threatening.' Gil stared at the pool of water, trying to picture the scene.

'Took us two days of wrapping everything in plastic and trying to seal it,' Sara added, ruefully. 'Still, when we put it all in the water, I did not expect to see any of it again.'

'So how close did the fires reach?' Gil asked.

'Came from southwest, behind the cabin,' Gordon said, pointing the direction. 'We could see the tops of the flames over there quite clearly when the smoke wasn't too bad. About 2k away at their closest.'

Veronika's horror at the thought was visible. 'What did you do?' she asked Sara, who shivered, remembering.

'There wasn't much we could do after we'd put all our things in the creek here. Gordon went off to see what he could do to help fight the fire. I sat and waited for the message to say we had to clear out. The truck was all packed up and we had friends we could stay with standing by. I was to drive up there as soon as I got the word. I suppose I wept some at the thought that everything we'd built here might be carried away in a day.'

They walked on down in silence, along the bank of the creek where it spread out onto a flat, a little meadow alive with summer green growth. They waded ankle-deep through clover, until, all of a sudden, Veronika gave out a yelp. Gil spun round, expecting to see her lying prostrate after some backwoods creature had bitten her, but instead she was standing beaming the broadest smile possible.

'I can't believe it!' she exclaimed, holding something up for them all to see. 'All my life I've searched for one.' They looked and saw that it was an actual four-leaved clover, and a very large one at that, each leaf almost the size of a loonie.

'Well, aren't you the lucky one,' Sara said, with a slightly envious tone. 'I've looked for one here for years myself and never found anything.'

Veronika's face at that moment was like a five-year-old girl's who had stumbled on the loveliest of jewels. She stood holding up the prize, saying, 'See!' to everyone, even Hero, who was gazing at his loved one as if he understood her joy precisely, with his tongue out and a faint doggy smile on his lips. 'Look, Gil,' she said. 'I can't believe it.'

So he went over to where she stood, closely examined the lucky find, then impulsively kissed her gently on the nose. 'It's perfect,' he said. 'And a very good omen, for what's behind you and what lies ahead.'

She was shocked by the little kiss, and slightly taken aback. She wondered what he could possibly know of her true situation, other than the cancer treatment. Probably that was what he meant. She hadn't thought about her cell all day, nor the messages there may be awaiting her when she got back on grid again, but now she did and it worried her – though the sight of the four-leaf clover lifted her mood again when she looked at it. She would keep staring at that, she decided. Focus on the good.

Sara and Gordon were already down the path a distance, with Benji close behind, but when they came to a bend in the creek, they stopped and waited. As Gil, Veronika and Hero caught them up, they saw the new house they'd spoken of gradually materialising from behind the rise.

It wasn't at all like anything else on the property, but a very modern design, not timber, blockwork, with big windows and a sloping pink pan-tiled roof that caught the sunlight. But as they approached they could see that only the section nearest the creek had a roof as yet, and that the remaining half or more of the structure was only partially built, and covered by a tarpaulin, under shelter of an enormous cedar.

'My dream kitchen,' Sara said, as she opened the door to the finished quarter. 'No smoky old stove in here, but the latest gas hob.'

'Well,' Veronika replied, looking around her. 'It's certainly different from the other house. And so spacious.'

'Different is good. I've been stoking that thing for thirty years and you get tired of trying to get a cranky old stove to the right temperature for baking. And keeping it there is another struggle.' She looked to Veronika for confirmation, but the glassy stare in the visitor's eyes suggested she wasn't much of a baker. Instead, she stood with her four-leaf clover in her hand, staring out through the windows to the forest over the water.

'Beautiful views, Sara,' she said.

'Yes, I suppose they are. To tell the truth, I tend to take it all for granted, how beautiful it is here, though that was why we first built the treehouse down here for the children.'

Gordon, who'd been rooting around, picking up some loose wiring cable and tucking it into a cupboard while Gil watched, suddenly connected with his wife's line of thought.

'Ah yes, the treehouse. You have to see that,' he said, grinning. So they followed him through a makeshift doorway into the rear of the house, an area still without a proper floor. 'Watch your step there,' he said, stopping to point to left and then right. 'The bedrooms will be two either side of the feature staircase. As you can see, it's not much of a feature so far.' And it wasn't, just a rudimentary ladder leading straight up to a hatch.

One by one they climbed the rungs, first Gordon, then Veronika, then Gil, and lastly Sara, entering a sawdusty realm filled with the scent of wood. This space above was stunning, wide and expansive, with open views across the creek, though the window frames were as yet without glass. And turning towards the shadowed side, they saw that the great cedar visible from outside was not simply behind the house, it was actually inside – at least, its trunk and some lower boughs were, all polished to a high finish. In fact, it was the centrepiece of everything. Gil and Veronika walked in slow circles around it, wowing, while staring up at the amazing structure, the organic puzzle of natural curves, odd shapes, and unfilled spaces where the tarp above still could be seen.

'This is incredible,' Veronika said at last.

'One day it will be, I hope,' Gordon said, grinning, 'The original treehouse is what you can see on that bough there.' And gazing up they could indeed see a small structure tucked into the trunk above, a little wooden boxhouse with a window, sat upon a platform on a strong bough. It was as if it was a kind of shrine, around which a great temple was being constructed, a temple to childhood.

'Where are your children now?' Veronika asked.

'All grown up,' Sara answered. 'One's in Vancouver, one's in Kamloops, and the youngest is travelling somewhere in the States right now.'

'They must have loved it here,' Gil said, meaning the treehouse, but Gordon responded with the place as a whole in mind.

'They did, but they outgrew it. Wanted to see what the rest of the world was like. Places where people didn't have to make everything themselves, where they could just buy stuff and order take-out. Gadgets and all that. Can't blame them, really, for being curious.' But something in his resigned tone suggested that he did, or at least had once done.

'Maybe they'll come back when they've seen enough,' Veronika said, more to Sara than to her husband. Sara gave a little smile in response, but there was a sadness underneath that surface.

'The world is full of wonders, that's true. But this, this is a work of art too,' Gil observed, running his hand over the fibrous lines on the smooth trunk of the cedar. 'It must have taken you forever to get this finish.'

'Sure has,' Gordon nodded.

'Hah! Finish! That's a fine word,' Sara said sharply. 'He's been spending all his time down here, just sanding that blasted tree.' Gil and Veronika exchanged knowing glances – the territory was clearly disputed – but Gordon didn't seem too troubled by her words. He just shrugged.

'Well, sanding costs nothing, honey. Trouble is, to get the house finished requires materials, and materials cost money. I can do the work myself, even source and cut the timber, but there's so much more needed. Like this wall here, where the picture windows will go. The right glass costs an arm and a leg.'

A brief silence fell on the four of them, as they stood in that strange cathedral to nature, the light glinting in through the place where the glass should be.

'That's where the Robbie Burns book comes in,' Sara prompted.

'Ah yes, the book,' Gil said eagerly, 'I was wondering when we'd get to that.'

'It's not *Robbie* Burns, Sara,' Gordon said, rather grimly. 'I've told you that.' Then as if realising he'd spoken harshly, he said more brightly, 'Come on, let's go back to the old house. Sara's made a picnic for lunch, and we're going to take you to one of our favourite spots.'

They went tentatively down the ladder and exited through another makeshift door to the rear, from where a grassy path led back up towards the road that Gil had driven in darkness the night before. The two women went ahead with Hero, while Gil waited with Gordon as he tried to make sure the door was properly closed against racoons, and Benji sniffed around.

'So the book is a touchy subject?' Veronika ventured, when she and Sara were a distance away.

Sara sighed. 'Yep, kinda. I'm not sure of its history, but I know it's been in his family forever, ever since they came over from Scotland.' They turned from the grassy trail onto the gravel road and Sara checked back to see where the men were. 'So you see it's hard for him to even think about parting with it, but if it is worth a lot, maybe this is the time. We could do with the money. We've been building the new house for the last ten years and Gordon can do all the work himself, but like he said we need materials. So I suggested we see if we can sell the book. We saw online that one similar had sold at auction for a lot of money a while back. At least we think it's similar. That's where Gil comes in. I guess he'll know, won't he?' She glanced at Veronika as if in hope of reassurance, who took her arm.

'I think he knows his business, yes. He was certainly interested enough to travel all the way up here.'

'Well, Gordon didn't want to send him the book. I mean, he seemed a good guy from the emails he sent, and the books we ordered from him came prompt and all, and now that we've met him I feel sure he is, but you know, just posting it off into the unknown didn't seem like a good idea.'

'No, I can see that. But I'm sure he's trustworthy.'

Sara glanced again at her, then laughed. 'You know, you do look very like her up close. I can see why the folks in Cloud Falls got the wrong idea.'

'So I'm told,' Veronika smiled, but she was tired of being someone else. 'I'm really looking forward to this surprise picnic,' she said. And they walked on, arm in arm, silently, but smiling at the ease of their new-found friendship.

Gil and Gordon came on behind, also silently at first. Gordon seemed a little put out as if the book was an off-limits topic at that moment, but Gil felt he should say something else, maybe something about the dreamhouse and the kids, yet he didn't quite know how to broach the subject without it seeming trivial. So he just followed Gordon up the narrow trail through the knee-high summer grass. Some of the plants that grew were familiar to him, but some were not, rather like this place and culture that he had landed himself in.

As they turned onto the road, Gordon waited for him to come alongside.

'It's hard for Sara,' he said, once they were walking together. 'I mean, the kids and all. Hard for me too. Everything we've built here is for them. The new house too, in a way. But now they've upped and gone and it's still not done. And now a lot of the time I don't really feel like doing it. Guess the motivation's lacking.'

'Maybe they'll come back – the kids and the motivation.'

'One might. The youngest. The one travelling.'

'That's something to look forward to, then.'

'I guess.' He quickened his pace a little. 'I'll show you the book tonight, okay?'

They caught up with the women who were walking slowly, arm in arm, and Benji gave Hero a friendly neck-bite which he then returned, both tails wagging.

'Happy trails,' Gordon said, and Sara chuckled at him as if it were a code, a phrase they shared, one that meant all's well.

Veronika had carefully placed the four-leaf clover into the pages of her journal, making sure that none of its delicate edges were folded, and had noted the date, time and place where she found it, when Gil tapped on the bedroom door.

'All right to come in?' he asked from outside.

'Sure,' she answered, putting the journal back into her purse. 'I was just getting ready for the picnic.'

'Sara says to bring a waterproof if you have one, and if you don't she'll loan you one,' he said, walking round to his side of the bed and opening his backpack, from which he fetched out a lightweight dark blue cagoule.

'Not something I brought,' she said. 'So where is this mysterious picnic spot?'

'Don't know. They're being very secretive about it. Like they want to surprise us.' He pulled the cagoule over his head and put the hood up. 'Somewhere wet, though, I suppose. There, how do I look?'

She grinned, thought for a moment. 'Well, with your burned red face and that blue top, a bit like a Facebook notification.'

'What's that?' he asked, crossing to the mirror and peering into it, rubbing his fingers over the worst of the peel. 'Think I need some maintenance.' He fetched some of the healing cream he'd got in Kamloops.

'You really are a creature from the dark ages, aren't you?' she teased, but he didn't respond and just carried on applying the salve to his cheekbones and nose, while she watched him.

'It's kinda sad,' she said, thoughtfully, 'Their kids not being here. Feels like such an empty nest.'

'And one they've not even finished building yet.' He dabbed one last blob onto the tip of his nose and rubbed it gently in.

'Speaking of, did Gordon mention the book to you yet?'

He sat down on the bed across from her, to put the cream back in his backpack. 'Said he'll show me it tonight.'

'I don't think he really wants to part with it, you know.'

'What makes you think that?'

'Oh, just what Sara said. How it's a family heirloom.'

'Hmm,' he said, standing up and swinging the backpack onto his shoulders. 'Well of course I can understand that. Anyway, it may not even be the real thing. Could be that Toronto facsimile I told you about. You ready?'

'Sure,' she said, getting up, 'Let's go picnic.'

Halfway down the staircase, she saw Hero waiting for them. He was still a bit wet from his creek-herding, and she gave a little snort of laughter. 'Hello lad! Wasn't that a good walk? Isn't it amazing that I found that four-leaf clover?'

Gil, who was a couple of steps ahead, didn't turn round to look at her, but said, kindly, 'I think you deserve it.'

The truck had its tailgate down, the hamper was already loaded and their hosts were waiting. All climbed aboard except for Benji who, as Sara noticed, was left looking forlorn as his new chum went off for a ride in his own truck. Worse still he was allowed to sit up front with the people, squeezed in between Veronika and Gil, his tongue out, smiling.

As they drove away from the homestead, Gil could see where he'd driven the night before and said to Veronika that they'd been lucky to find their way. Little Forks too revealed itself, more substantial than it had seemed when they turned off at the intersection the night before.

From there the highway north ran parallel to the North Thompson River and the views were so beautiful that conversation was minimal, other than when Gordon or Sara gave a name to some feature or landmark. The river was wide and running very slow, a labyrinth of channels, little islets and sandbars, reflecting the green trees that forested its banks, and the great mountains came in and out of view, some snow-capped, some not. They drove for about an hour before they came to any human habitation and then the highway took a sweep across a new bridge towards the town of Clearwater.

At that moment, a ping from Veronika's purse told her she was back on grid. Hero gave a woof when he heard it, as if it had awoken him from a dog daydream. She almost leapt in fright at first, and fished in her bag to try to silence it before the others heard, but she fumbled with the buttons and a succession of other pops and pings followed.

'Someone's popular,' Sara said. A little embarrassed, Veronika glanced at Gil who simply smiled benignly and turned his gaze to the town they'd arrived in.

'Work, probably,' she said, but she didn't sound convincing. She'd told them the night before that she was still on sick leave after her cancer treatment. 'I should probably see what the matter is.'

It was him again, more messages. She scrolled down her inbox. Five. She opened the earliest one. *R U trying to hold me to ransom?* it read, followed by a winking emoji. The second was just a row of questions marks. The third said; *I know we need to sort things out.* The fourth, *Where R U?* and the fifth: A*m going to tell her about u. Promise! xxx*

Amazing how text reduced an eloquent and literate man to such simplicity, she thought. But her heart began to pound, and silly tears welled up. She tried to pretend it was nothing, threw the phone back in her purse, but inside she was screaming. She took hold of Hero and squeezed him hard. She wanted to shout something. But what? For so long she'd wanted just that message, or those words, in one form or another. Through a fuzz of muddled emotion, she heard Gordon say something about this town, about it being on Sushwap land, and she nodded like she was paying attention but she couldn't concentrate. All that was in her mind was the thought of him confessing to his wife. Maybe it had already happened. Maybe it was all out in the open, had been for hours. Even days. She didn't even know what day it was any longer – Saturday? Sunday. It was still the weekend – wasn't it?

Gil was listening carefully to Gordon's account of the Sushwap people, the salmon fishing they did on the North Thompson, and their simple yet sophisticated method. But he was well aware of Veronika's turmoil when he looked briefly at her. She tried to smile at him, but the expression on her face barely hid her confusion behind a thin-lipped grimace, and the frown around her eyes gave her away.

In Clearwater, they turned off the highway onto a smaller one, two relatively narrow lanes by Canadian standards, divided by the ubiquitous yellow marking Gil was now familiar with – Clearwater Valley Road, which slowly climbed away from the Thompson, tracking a tributary, but at some distance above the valley floor. The landscape changed, became a degree more barren, less dramatic, more like the highlands of Scotland, Gil observed.

'I do hope to see that for myself one day, my friend,' Gordon said, and Gil agreed he must, one day.

Veronika couldn't resist another look at her cell. She was wondering about finding that four-leaf clover. Was this the good luck it would bring, this event she'd hoped for so long at last becoming a reality? But she wasn't even sure she wanted it, now that it was happening. Was it even happening? Inwardly she cursed the uncertainty, the poor mobile coverage, even herself for setting off on this impulsive journey at such a time. What had possessed her to leave Vancouver the way she did, in pursuit of this Scotsman she hardly knew? But then, if she hadn't, would he ever have told his wife?

The messages were there, five as she'd counted, but now the signal was gone again, and she felt a kind of relief at that. She sighed and stroked Hero's head. The fur she loved more than any man, those soft crimped locks under his ears.

'You're enjoying this road trip, aren't you, lad?' she said, looking around them. 'My my, it really is lovely up here,' she said, into the ear of Sara who sat in front of her, and Sara nodded, without turning.

'So what is the Scottish side of your family's story, Gordon?' she asked. 'You told us last night about the Canadian.'

'Well, I think I may have mentioned this in one of my emails to Gil, the two brothers who sailed out from the Clyde? But the family came from further north, near Stonehaven. I have some documents from my father.'

'That's similar to the journey the Burns family took – Robert's father came from the north-east, and ended up in Ayrshire, not so far from the Clyde,' Gil observed, after a minute's thought, and Gordon nodded, as if he knew.

She tried to listen, to tune out the texts, but couldn't. She needed to think through the relationship and tell its story to herself, so she could see how things had got to be as they are, so she could decide on a way forward. She remembered it began with a few sightings at events, across a room after a reading or at a conference. Then when they talked and he gave her his card, he said he might have some work for her. The emails gradually changed tone, to personal, and then, on his side, sexual. It was really an email affair at first, and email was new then, exciting. She'd never used it for anything other than business before, and hadn't really known how to respond – she knew that he was married by then, that he had a whole life in another place she had never seen.

'Must have been quite a thing for those boys to do,' Gordon was saying, 'They were not very old at that time.'

'Just how old were they?' Gil asked.

'Twenty-two and twenty. My great grandpop was the younger.'

Of course she had known that it was wrong, at least some part of her had, but it was fun too, as well as exciting. So new. Somewhere along the line the texts began – that was new tech too. They were in each other's lives, present in the sense of taking up time and giving companionship almost on a moment by moment level, as much as if they'd lived together, and the vibration of her phone had signalled that. She had never expected back then that it would last so long, had accepted they couldn't live together, though there was a time, once it was serious, she had desperately wanted to, when she'd created a kind of fantasy where they would make a world together, perfect partners. So why had she felt resentful of his presence in her real life, those times when he'd sleep over and stay a day, or even two, the way he seemed to colonise her space?

'Did you ever know him?' Gil asked Gordon, about his grandfather. The question cut into her mind, deeply personal, and resonated so that she lost the thread of thought, and gave out a sigh. Did she ever know him completely?

Gordon swung the steering wheel at a sharp bend, so that Hero almost overbalanced, and then nodded slowly, without taking his eyes from the camber.

'Look,' Sara said. The view was a conversation stopper.

'Wow,' Gil and Veronika said, almost simultaneously.

Sara laughed, from the front seat. 'Isn't it just wow?'

After a while, Gordon answered the question still hanging. 'Yes. I knew him some, Gilbert. I guess I was five when he passed on.'

'And he was the fellow with the buffalo coat and the rifle, the pioneer?' Veronika asked.

'That's him.'

'You know,' Gil said, 'There is a theory expounded by Alexander Carmichael, of the *Carmina Gaedelica*, that the Burns family came from the west coast, round Loch Etive or Loch Linnhe. Before they moved to the North-east.'

'Really? I'd like to read that sometime.'

'I'll send it to you, I have the text.'

Gordon smiled. 'That's what I love about you, Gilbert. You always have the text.' And Gil laughed in response, an actual hee-hee.

Sara twisted her neck around so she could make eye contact with Veronika. 'Just like brothers separated at birth,' she said.

'I see that now.'

'Who'd have thought you could hook up such a friendship on email, five thousand miles apart?'

'Yes,' Veronika answered slowly. 'Who'd have thought it?' she said to Hero. 'Eh lad?'

Hero, wise as ever, kept his own counsel, but Gil felt oddly cheered, uplifted by this acknowledgement of his expertise. Ever since Veronika's phone went off like a time bomb in the tight crawlspace between them on the back seat, his footing in this new world had felt tenuous, his knowledge limited. But here was a Canadian, a man he now respected, saying he was expert, even reliable. He knew he was, but it was good to hear it from someone else. He gave Hero's head an affectionate ruffle and looked over at Veronika, but she was staring out the window again.

'Yeah, just who?' he said.

She was thinking about the happiest times they'd had, the first long weekend in San Francisco, the nights in London, Prague, Chicago, and the times at his cabin on Bowen, when they'd been able to get away at the same time and she could bring Hero along. But none of them were truly domestic, no laundry, no dishes, no work to travel to. They'd been holidays, really, even if they'd met on the pretext of doing work. He'd been generous then, introducing her to people who'd since become friends and colleagues, and he knew so much about the old country, things she had no notion of, though some child-self inside her seemed to sense their importance in making her who she was.

They passed a sign which read Wells-Grey National Park. Gil spoke the name out loud and Gordon asked if he'd heard of it, but he said his research hadn't reached this far north. They drove on, along a road that narrowed, for another distance, then turned onto a track for a while, and finally Gordon brought the truck to a halt.

'It's a bit of a walk from here along the trail, but really worth it,' Sara said to her back-seat companions.

The two men carried the picnic hamper between them, Gordon leading the way. Sara came on behind, with Veronika and Hero on his leash following her. They walked for quite a way along a path through a young forest of Douglas Fir. The men were discussing David Douglas, the Scottish botanist whose name the trees now bore. They both knew quite a lot about him, though only Gil could say he'd been to where the botanist grew up in Perthshire. Gordon explained that the undergrowth was called falsebox, an evergreen that moose liked to graze. He said there would likely be some moose droppings somewhere along the path.

'What about bears?' Gil asked.

'Oh they'll be around here somewhere,' Gordon laughed.

Sara hung behind a bit, to let Veronika catch up. She'd been meandering, looking at the plants and trees, but lost in thought, letting Hero sniff at everything that caught his nose.

'Are you feeling okay?' Sara asked.

Veronika glanced up. 'Sure,' she said. 'I was wondering what Hero's so interested in.'

Sara looked at her intently. 'Could be bear or moose scent. Wolves even. But if you don't mind me saying, you do seem a little subdued since your cell went crazy back there.'

Veronika was a bit surprised at her forthrightness. 'Ah well, yes,' she admitted. 'There's stuff happening at home. In fact, I was just thinking that I really need to get back.'

'But you'll stay the weekend, won't you?'

'I don't know. I should really… this is Sunday, isn't it?'

'Yes, of course. Why?'

'It's just that I've lost track a little.'

Sara seemed to understand, though she appeared a little disappointed. 'Well,' she said, 'If it's something you feel you want to talk about, I am a good listener.'

Veronika looked into her kind face, her calm blue eyes, and believed her. She looked up to where the men were, some twenty or thirty metres ahead, each holding a leather handle on the hamper. Out of earshot.

'It's very complicated,' she said.

'Family?'

She thought of her mother, sitting at home on the porch, no doubt, after eating her tiny lunch, listening to CBC on the radio with her instant coffee as she always did. 'No,' she said. 'Not family as such. At least, not mine.'

'A friend's?'

'Kind of.'

'A man?'

Veronika felt an odd rush of relief. 'You're good at guessing games.'

'Well, I don't want to pry, but I feel you and I have connected. And if you do want to tell someone about it, maybe it can help make sense of things for you.'

'It's not that I don't want to, and yes, I feel we're friends too. But I wouldn't know where to begin.' And as they walked, she wondered then whether this woman she'd met, who'd spent her whole life with her teenage sweetheart, could hope to understand the mess she'd got herself into, any more than she herself could understand what it must be like to spend a life with just one person, away in the wilds, having a family, baking, making quilts, looking after animals and gardening, all those years of caring and tending to others. It was the kind of life she'd always been wary of, following her mother's example, the well-trodden path for women over centuries, and one she'd rejected out of hand when she was younger. Yet Sara seemed happy in a way her mother never had been, and her quiet calm suggested an inner repose, perhaps a kind of contentment that no quantity of yoga classes and therapy could provide. Or was that idealising the situation? Hadn't she suffered the loss of her children when they took off out into the world on their own?

The trail began to open out, and in the distance they could see a faint mist rising from a hidden valley. Veronika heard a roar.

'Where are you taking us?' she asked.

'That's the waterfall,' Sara replied, and at that instant, as if he'd heard the word and understood it, Hero lunged forward, pulling the leash out of Veronika's loose grip, and went haring down the trail.

'Hero!' she shouted, in a panic. Gordon and Gil turned at the sound of her call. 'Here boy!' But Hero wasn't stopping for anything, he was tearing along the trail at full speed towards the sound of water falling, and for a moment a terror gripped Veronika. She saw Gil drop his end of the hamper and step into the path of the dog, crouching down to try to tackle him. Hero kept on running, straight at the human obstacle and as he reached the two men he dodged between them. Gil spun round and grabbed him by the fur on his back as he went past, and then both disappeared out of sight, pulled along by Hero's velocity.

Veronika screamed. In her mind she saw them falling, down into whatever abyss was hidden, and she started to run towards the place they'd been, but felt her knees give way and she fell to the ground. The tears that had welled up earlier suddenly started to flow.

Then Gordon shouted back. 'It's okay, Gil's got him. He's okay. It's fine.' She looked up from where she'd fallen and saw Gil appear from below the rise with Hero in his arms, struggling a little but otherwise all right.

Sara helped her up. 'It's all right, he's fine,' she said.

'I wasn't paying attention,' Veronika sobbed. 'He just pulled the leash out of my hand.'

'It's okay, dear. Really, it's okay.'

And then Gil was there, Hero in his arms, perfectly fine, grinning in that mischievous doggie way of his.

'I thought you'd gone over the edge,' she said, to them both, sobbing a little.

Gil smiled. 'We did fall a bit, but there's a big wide shelf down there. I got him by the fur and just held on.'

'Hero,' she said, taking him in her arms. 'You are a one. And you, my Scotch friend, you're a hero too.'

'Yep, nice tackle, buddy,' Gordon said. 'You must have played football.'

'Rugby,' Gil said, smiling. 'Though I was never much good in the scrum.'

It took a little while before they were ready to carry on. Sara tried to clean the mud off Veronika's trousers, while Veronika smoothed out Hero's thick back fur and lectured him gently on the danger he'd so narrowly avoided. Gordon and Gil picked up the hamper, which was none the worse for the drop, though Gordon said the champagne would probably need to rest a while before they tried to open it.

'You brought champagne?' Veronika asked Sara.

'Yes. Well, prosecco. And I think you could do with a glass as soon as possible,' she said. 'I think you're suffering from shock a little. You're absolutely white.'

So they walked on, following the trail around the gorge above the hidden waterfall, fine mist settling gently on their clothes, their ears now engulfed by the constancy of the water's roar, and Hero's leash wound tightly around Gil's wrist. When it finally came into view, they stopped, Gil and Veronika completely overawed by the sight, Gordon and Sara standing proud, gauging their reaction. Cloud Falls was dwarfed in comparison. The waterfall emerged from a deep cleft in the cliff, falling in a perfect horsetail, arcing downwards. And it was big, the drop three times higher than Niagara Falls, Gordon said. In the winter, Sara told them the water froze into a cone that almost reached to its full height.

'Another wow?' she asked them, as they stood admiring.

Gil smiled. 'Beyond wow – triple wow. Sublime.'

'Multiple wows, I think,' Veronika said, and they all laughed, happy to hear her back amongst them, joking again. But she felt crushed inside, somehow, as if the day had robbed her of all strength. Her terror had lasted no more than ten seconds, but it was intimation of how swiftly things could be lost, and a reminder of the fear she'd endured when the diagnosis was confirmed. That was when she'd begun to think that his attention would never be fully on her. That time, when she needed someone more than ever before, he didn't step up. The flowers were nice, and the card poetic, but he wasn't there.

The picnic spot was a bench and table almost on the edge of the precipice, from where the majesty could be admired in comfort. Sara opened the hamper and began bringing out plates and glasses. Veronika sat on the bench next to her, and offered help, but none was required. The 'champagne' was still resting, but Sara had brought a bottle of white wine and passed a glass to her. Gil had tied Hero's leash firmly round a sapling, but Veronika took hold of him with her free arm and held on tightly all the same, while he stood gazing at the torrent below, as if trying to measure the sheer scale of it by some doggy calculation.

'Helmcken Falls,' Gordon said, 'named after an early settler, a medical man.'

'I think I've heard of him,' Gil added. 'Wasn't he Hudson's Bay?'

'I'm not sure it was The Bay, but he settled in Victoria over on the island and ran the first hospital, I believe. He was a well-loved man, did a lot for the early colonists.'

'There's a street named after him downtown in Vancouver,' Veronika said. 'At least I assume it's the same guy?'

'That's right. But the thing with these falls is, Helmcken never actually visited them. They were named in his honour.'

The picnic had emerged from the hamper – sandwiches neatly cut in triangles, salmon and cucumber salad, egg cress, chicken. Sara had brought plates and napkins for everyone, even salt and pepper shakers.

'I feel like we're Victorian pioneers ourselves,' Veronika said, as she ate and Hero sniffed the air in hope of landing a few scraps. It was a fine repast indeed, savoured and enjoyed by all, and when that was done, a homemade chocolate cake appeared from the basket too. After he'd eaten, Gil got up and wandered off along the cliff towards a wooden viewing platform that jutted out above the falls. He wanted a little time to himself, so didn't announce his intention, and he was glad when no one followed him. The incident with the dog had shaken him, and although he hadn't said anything, he'd banged his right elbow when he landed. Now it was aching. But what was worse was the space he felt had opened between him and Veronika. He'd detected it before, times when she'd withdraw without actually going anywhere, and he thought he knew the cause now – whoever it was who was sending those texts.

Standing above the torrent of water churning hundreds of feet below, he felt again the void that had troubled him so, the sense of the futility of existence that had hung around ever since his diagnosis. And his high-flown aim of writing the book that would justify his youthful ambition wasn't going anywhere. He'd barely written a word since he got lost in the Echte Valley, since she and he had begun their journey. And when they were attuned, joking and talking, he didn't wonder about that, or miss it. This dependency was a new and worrying thing – in a few days, he'd come to need her company in order to feel good. But their journey would end, she'd go back to her life and he'd have to leave.

When he got back to the picnic station, the others had packed the things away, and they began the return journey along the cliff path to the trail, and the parked truck.

The way home was quiet. Gordon put a CD of Bruce Cockburn on, and no one spoke for a long time, just let the acoustic guitar-picking ripple over them as they drove. As they approached Clearwater, Veronika waited apprehensively for her cell to find a signal again, as it had on the way north. It was in her purse, but she had positioned that so she could look at the phone inside. She'd turned it to 'vibrate', so no one else would know, but the screen would light and she would see that, if any new messages were received.

You thought it was over, but it's just like before, Bruce Cockburn sang. *Will there never be an end to the Indian wars?*

She waited, breathing lightly, but nothing happened and pretty soon they were south of the little town, heading down the highway at speed along the beautiful Thompson River. She smiled and leaned back, grabbed Hero's neck and rubbed her face in his fur.

'Well, I think that was one of the best picnics ever, lad, despite your bad behaviour,' she said, and looked at Gil, but he was gazing out the side window at the river and didn't acknowledge her.

'You know,' Gordon said, above the Cockburn soundtrack, 'Tomorrow we could go...'

'I think Veronika has to get back to Vancouver tomorrow,' Sara interrupted, and looked over her shoulder to check. 'Don't you?'

Gil turned to face Veronika, wondering what she'd say. 'I kinda have to,' she answered. 'I'd love to stay longer, but I really can't. But Gil could stay, take the Greyhound back, like he did going up to the canyon in the first place.'

He felt a terribly disproportionate sense of rejection at those words. But of course, he had anticipated something of this sort earlier. 'Of course I could,' he said, with no enthusiasm. 'It stops in Little Forks. That's how I was planning to get here in the first place, before you appeared, trying to save my life.'

He said this with a grin, but the tone had a little barb to it. In the front of the truck, Gordon and Sara looked at each other, but didn't speak. In the back seat, Veronika gave him another of her pained smiles, her forehead furrowed and her eyes worried.

When they got back to base, Veronika said she thought she'd take a nap. The wine had gone to her head, and she was still a little in shock after Hero's dash towards the precipice. Sara had work to do in the smallholding, and so Gil and Gordon were left by themselves.

Veronika put her glasses on and read his texts again upstairs, and lay on the bed wondering if he'd really gone and done it, or if he was just trying to reel her back in with promises. It wouldn't be the first time. In the years since they'd met, there had been a few occasions when she felt like it was pointless to continue on, that there would never be a good outcome. In her mind she heard Joni's 'Song for Sharon'. She'd always identified with that lyric, the white lace wedding dress haunting her.

But as she drifted off into sleep, all of that slipped away, and she heard instead Gil's voice, saying 'before you appeared, trying to save my life,' in that vaguely sarcastic tone of his. And then she saw him leaping after Hero, the two of them disappearing from her sight. She shivered at the thought of what could have happened. Sometimes I take a great notion, he'd sung at Jericho Beach, when they came to the bench with the little plaque that said *Goodnight Irene*. Which was one thing. But to fall when you didn't mean to jump, that was quite another.

She woke to footsteps on the stairs and someone talking – Gordon and Gil. Gordon said, 'The study's in here.' A nearby door opened. Then she heard Gil say, 'So this is where you keep the books.' And the door closed. Their voices were muffled then. She could catch the occasional word, but not the whole conversation.

In the study, Gil was scanning the bookshelves. He saw a few titles he himself had carefully wrapped and posted out, wondering then about the address, and this man with the Scottish name who seemed so keen to collect Scottish books. And not just any Scottish books, but good ones, volumes that not everyone knew, even if it was their field of interest. And there among them were four different editions of Burns' poems, well-thumbed, and one with its front cover hanging on by just a paper sliver.

'Guess you'll recognise some of these,' Gordon said.

'I was just thinking exactly that. Little did I realise that one day I'd be looking at them again, all the way over here.'

'Well, I'm very glad you are, buddy. Do you think we should get down to business?'

Gil laughed. 'You make it sound as if that's the only reason I'm here.'

'No, my friend, I know that's not how it is. But it is important to me and Sara.' Gordon bent down to a cupboard beneath the bookshelves and pulled out a plain dark wooden box. He set it on the desk and, from around his neck, he took a small brass key on a chain, and placed it into the lock.

'Mechanism's as good as new,' he said, turning the key.

The moment was upon them – the wooden box lay on the desk, lid still shut, but unlocked now. Gordon's hand put down the small brass key, opened the lid and lifted out a hand-sewn leather case, the size and shape of a book. He undid the button fastening, and inside lay a wrapping of thin yellowed paper. He lifted the contents out and laid it on the desk, then tentatively unwrapped the paper.

'Sit down,' Gordon said, 'Take a look.' He indicated the wooden captain's chair by the desk.

As soon as Gil caught sight of the blue covers, he knew it was the real thing. He took it gently from the careful hands that proffered it, and felt it was exactly what it was supposed to be. Gil smiled. 'So where was this when the wildfires came? Not in the river, I hope?'

Gordon laughed. 'No, this was in the truck ready for evacuation. But you know, that did make me stop and think, about what's really valuable in my life. When you have to sort out the essential from the rest. This, and a couple of other books I inherited, were the only ones that made the cut. Mind you, the truck was so full of animals, it was like Noah's ark. Don't think Noah took many books with him.'

'Papyrus, maybe, though probably it was too early even for that. Maybe the odd clay tablet.' He turned the book over in his hands, lifted it to his nose, sniffed at it.

Gordon laughed. 'So what do you think?'

'Well, when you first wrote to me about this, I thought it was probably just the facsimile printed in Toronto, just because you were in Canada. Then when you said your grandfather brought it out here with him, I thought it was probably one of the Edinburgh editions. That would be remarkable enough, but now that I see it, I think you may well have one of the lost firsts.'

He carefully opened the cover, feeling as if he should be wearing a pair of library gloves. The title page read as it should:

POEMS,
CHIEFLY IN THE
SCOTTISH DIALECT,
BY ROBERT BURNS.

followed by the anonymous epigraph:

THE Simple Bard, unbroken by rules of Art,
He pours the wild effuſions of his heart:
And if inſpir'd, 'tis Nature's pow'rs inſpire;
Her's all the melting thrill, and her's the kindling fire.

and below that again,

KILMARNOCK:
PRINTED BY JOHN WILSON.

and then the date: M,DCC,LXXXVI.

Gil could just make out a faint pencil insertion to the left of this, the word 'July'. He leaned back in the chair, looked up at Gordon and smiled. 'I think this looks very good, my friend. Very fine indeed.'

Gordon gave out a huge sigh, blowing his cheeks out as it escaped his lungs. 'Wow,' he said. 'So you think it's real?'

'I do. As if it's hardly been read,' he said, then laughed, remembering Veronika's comment at the waterfall: multiple wows.

'They say my grandfather never took it out of the case. My father wasn't so interested in books, so he never did either.'

'You know, when they printed these, they stitched them and then it was up to the subscribers to decide how they wanted them bound. This never has been. It's like it's hardly been touched. There's some spotting but that's to be expected.' He turned the pages slowly, examining the type closely, looking for marks. 'Although, now, I can see it has been read. Here, some thumbmarks where the pages are turned.'

Gordon looked. 'Yeah, I know. Must have been great-great-grandfather. It was him who supplied the leather case, I believe. He gave it to my great-grandfather when he was leaving Scotland, like I said, the cattleman I told you about. It travelled out in the bottom of his trunk. And he never took it out again. Well, hardly ever. Maybe on Burns Night. Or St Andrews.'

Gil sighed, then let out a little laugh. 'Well, it's remarkable that it's survived. Who'd have thought it? Five thousand miles and, what, two hundred and twenty-five years?'

Gordon nodded, then frowned. 'So it not being bound, does that add to the value or otherwise?'

'I'd think it would add.'

'That one that sold at auction for £40,000, that was bound, wasn't it?'

'Yes.'

'So how would this compare, value-wise?'

'Something like this, almost pristine, still with its blue covers, well… if a couple of libraries or collectors went head to head after it… you may well double it. Maybe more.'

'You're kidding, buddy? That's getting on for a lot of dollars.'

'I really have no idea. But there would be a lot of bidders, all round the world. Big libraries and private collectors.' Gil leaned back in the wooden captain's chair. 'You know, I'm wondering if your great-great-grandfather might have been one of the subscribers, if he was around at the time. He may even have known Burns. If his name is on the list, that would prove the provenance conclusively.'

'I think we should have a wee dram to celebrate,' Gordon said, and went over to the small cupboard under the bookshelves, from where he'd brought the wooden box. He fetched out a crystal decanter with a silver thistle adorning it, and two small nip glasses. 'This is the good one,' he said. 'For very special occasions.'

'What do you think your grandfather would say if he was here with us now?' Gil asked.

Through the wall, Veronika heard a sudden 'Whoopee!' She'd been lying half-awake, listening to the low mumbles of their voices, gently massaging the scar on her left breast and musing on the last few days. The lump was gone, but the scar was itself a knot in her skin. She thought she would never have been here, would never have followed Gil north, had it not been for it, the cancer, their shared bond. She would never have acted so impulsively before it. Some deep change had taken place, or was still taking place, in her psyche, in her attitude to life. Things that in the past she would hardly have noticed or, if she did, would have ignored, the tangents and side roads, the back alleys she drove past without a glance, the little marvels of nature she'd begun to discover while walking in Pacific Spirit – since she'd been forced to stop her onward course, she'd had time to look around her, to notice things, and to reassess what was important. She looked down at the scar, something she had hardly ever done since the operation, because it seemed too awful, too dreadful a reminder of her vulnerability. She saw the little blue indelible mark that the radiographers had made, the target guide for the lasers they had shot her with. It was tiny, but it was forever.

She heard laughter from the next room, and wanted to share in it, so she rose from under the quilt Sara had made, as the sound of their voices rose in volume.

'Whoopee,' she said to herself quietly, stretching. 'Whoopee indeed.'

She went downstairs and found Sara sitting, almost napping herself, with Hero on her knee. Sara asked how she was feeling and she said fine, it was just the shock, she'd like to take a walk before dinner. At the word 'walk', Hero leapt to the ground.

'That's another word he knows,' Sara said. 'He's a very clever boy. Would you like some company, or do you want some time alone?'

'I think alone,' she said. 'Or just with him.'

'Sure,' Sara said. 'I understand. But don't go too far, supper's almost ready. Oh, and just to warn you, Hero seems a bit too interested in the chickens, so best not to go that way.'

'I heard a cheer upstairs,' she said, as she was fixing his leash.

'Did you?' Sara was suddenly alert. 'Think I'll go up and see what's going on.'

Outside they were joined by Benji, who went a distance with them, as if shepherding Hero away from the livestock. Then she walked down the dirt-road away from the house, and cut across the grassy path to the new place they were building. She guessed that 'whoopee' meant money, that the work here could perhaps be finished because of it. Hero was sniffing around the backdoor, as if he'd got the scent of a racoon or some other creature, but she pulled him away and carried on down to the creek. Ahead of her was the little bit of meadowland where she'd found the four-leaf clover. Funny that happening, now, at her age. As a girl it had been one of the treasures she sought after and never found. Once she'd even spilt a leaf to make a four, but her mother wasn't fooled.

Hero was straining at the leash, drawn to the sound of the water, but she gave a yank on it, and turned away. 'Enough of that for today,' she said to him. 'You naughty boy, I thought I'd lost you for a second. It's a very good thing Gil was there.'

When they got back to the old house, they found the three gathered around the table in the dining area. Gil and Gordon were clearly a little drunk already – their faces flushed, their beaming smiles and gleaming eyes rather gave it away. In the middle of the table was a leather case, lying opening, with a package wrapped in yellowed paper.

'Veronika!' Gordon called out when he saw her, 'Come in, join the celebration!'

She caught Sara's eye, where she sat at the far end of the table. There was no glass in front of her and her expression said she was tolerating, not participating.

'So this is because?'

'The book!' Gil cried out.

'To the bonnie bonnie book!' Gordon said, and they raised their glasses, to clink in toast. 'To Rab!'

'Rhymer Rab!'

She leaned forward so she could what was behind the wrapping, where it peeked out. She read the title to herself. 'So it's what you thought it was, Gordon?'

'According to our visiting expert from Auld Reekie, it is the real McCoy,' Gordon replied, emphasising the word 'real'.

'What's Auld Reekie?' she asked, frowning, but with a faint smile on her lips.

'Edinburgh!' Gordon called out.

'Scotia's darling seat!' Gil clarified.

'Okay…' she said dubiously, and looked over at Sara, who seemed quietly pleased, but not quite on page with them.

'Scotchmen,' Sara shrugged, with a smirk. 'What can you do with them when they get together?'

Veronika sat down on a vacant chair and took the leash from Hero's collar. 'I really don't know,' she answered. 'It's not a problem I've ever encountered before.'

'Come on now, lassie, will you no hae a dram, to celebrate our good fortune?' Gordon said loudly, and set the bottle in front of her. 'I'll get you a glass, so I will.' He seemed to be becoming more Scotch in his speech the more whisky he drank.

'No, really, thanks, after last night…'

'He's getting more Scottish by the minute,' Gil confirmed, and slapped him on the back. 'You must come over, my trusty frere. As soon as you like.' And they guffawed and nodded, as if nothing could be more certain.

'So this is because of the book?' Veronika said, across the table to Sara. 'That's great.'

'Yes, yes it is,' Sara said. 'As long as we can do something with it.'

'Ah…'

'Gordon,' Sara said, leaning over to put her hand gently on his forearm, the one that led to the hand holding his glass. 'We should eat. And maybe put the book somewhere safe. You wouldn't want to spill whisky on it, now of all times?'

Her calm words had immediate effect. It was if she had a secret power, to make things as they should be, to control man and beast alike.

'Oh! Sure, sure, sorry.' And the mood in the little dining room changed as if by magic. Gordon got up with one last guffaw at Gil, and carried his precious heirloom out. Sara followed him as far as the stairs, and watched as he went up, slightly unsteadily. Then, she turned and seemed to glide across the floor to the kitchen, with a little wink to the others as she passed the open doorway.

Gil and Veronika were left by themselves, with Hero stretched out on the floor between them. If the atmosphere should have been a little awkward after what happened earlier in the truck, neither noticed.

'Really good news,' Gil said, and he drained his glass. 'Sorry if we were a bit rowdy.'

'It's fine,' she said. 'I've seen much worse. Anyway, after what you did at the waterfall, you deserve to do whatever you like.'

He gazed into her deep brown eyes for an instant. There was gentleness, kindness, companionship. She was back from wherever it was she went to.

'I'm sorry I have to go tomorrow.'

'Do you have to?'

'I think so, yes. I'll miss you taking a shift on the road. Even if you drive on the wrong side of the highway.'

He thought for a moment. 'I suppose I could come with you. If you wanted me to.'

'Would you? Just to take a turn at the wheel?'

'Of course. It's a long drive. And well, now I've checked out the book…' He shrugged, and smiled at her, that slightly sheepish look on his face.

'Your sunburn's healing,' she said, and reached out to run her fingers over his cheek.

Hero looked up at them, sitting face to face, staring into the other's eyes. He gave a little dog groan and stretched out on the floor between them.

'He'll be happy if you do. Won't you, lad?' she said, and stroked the fur on his belly. Hero didn't reply, one way or the other, but as he stretched, his front paws touched her feet, and his rear paws, his.

'You're Hero's hero now, Gil.'

Supper was a chicken pie Sara had made, with beautiful golden-brown pastry, sweet potato from the garden and salad too. The mood was more subdued, both men slightly drunk, but trying to pretend they weren't. Conversation drifted to the book, and what should happen next. Should Gil take it away and look to auction it in Edinburgh, like the one they'd read about, Sara wondered? Gordon visibly

stiffened in his seat at that idea. Gil, sensing that, said 'There's no reason why it has to be sold in Edinburgh. Could be anywhere. This is a
global market.' Gordon's mien didn't alter. It wasn't Edinburgh that
was the problem, Gil realised, but the taking away.

'I don't know,' Gordon said, after a while. 'It's great that's its real
and worth so much, and we could truly do with the money as you
know, but it's not easy for me to consider parting with it.'

An awkward silence fell around the table. 'This pie is delicious,'
Veronika said. 'Such great pastry! I wish I could bake like this.' Sara
thanked her, but she was watching Gordon carefully. His face was so
easily read, his emotions so near the surface.

The wine flowed and they talked about the trip they'd made to the
falls, how much fun the picnic had been, and how Gil's lunge had saved
the day from potential disaster. But Robert Burns was a proverbial ele-
phant among the company now, unacknowledged and unspoken, but
very present. The talk further retraced the steps of the day and arrived
at the creek where Veronika had found her good luck symbol, and
again they said what an amazing day they'd shared, quite unforgetta-
ble. She was going to get it framed, she said, when she got home. From
there it wasn't far to the new house, the half-built dream, and Burns
was there again, in all their minds. Veronika so hoped that the children would come back home again soon, to visit if not to stay, so they
could see them all, and she said that if they were ever coming down to
Vancouver to visit the one who lived there, they must, absolutely must,
come and see her.

'Build it and they will come,' Gil said, not knowing why the phrase
had popped into his mind at that moment.

Veronika stared at him. 'I thought you never watched movies?'

'Why?'

'What you just said. It's from 'Field of Dreams'.'

'Is it? Huh,' he said. 'I had no idea. I thought it was from a book.
What's 'Field of Dreams'?'

Gordon and Sara knew the movie and they began to tell him the
plot in outline.

'Hang on,' Gil said. 'That *is* a book. 'Shoeless Joe'. Kinsella.' None
of the others had heard of it, but there was a hopefulness to their tone
now, as if the phrase he'd spouted had tapped into their essential opti-
mism unwittingly, the shared energy that had helped build what they
had already built, over the many years of their marriage.

'I suppose we'll manage it somehow,' Sara observed. 'It's not as if we're broke. And we do own the property. Maybe we can raise some money against it. I don't want you to sell the book if it makes you unhappy, honey.'

At that moment, a thought popped into Veronika's mind, one of those inspired ideas she sometimes had. 'Couldn't you raise money against the book? Like with a great artwork. Not actually sell it. If it's worth what you say it is. And it's not as if it's going to lose value, is it?'

'Huh,' Gordon said. 'That's a thought, indeed it is.'

'If you had a letter from a respected antiquarian bookseller in Edinburgh, and proof of provenance, I reckon you probably could,' Sara said.

'Happy to help,' Gil ventured. 'It may take a little time, but I feel sure we can get the papers required. It's as close to pure gold as a Scot can get. As far as verification goes, I know of a professor at Simon Fraser University who's an expert in Scottish Literature in the eighteenth century. I'm sure Leith could check it out and corroborate.'

A broad smile burst across Gordon's face and he began to chuckle. 'What?' Sara asked, as if recognising the signs of some funny thought bubbling up in his mind. He chuckled again, as she leaned in close, waiting for his words.

'I was just thinking, honey, our bank manager in Kamloops is a MacDonald. Nothing he'd like better than something like that, safe in a bank vault.'

'And it would be safe, and it would still be yours.'

'Huh,' he said again. 'Veronika, I think you may well be a genius.'

'I think she is,' Gil agreed. 'That's an inspired solution. And you know, if you wanted to sell the story to the newspapers, it's a great outcome all round.'

Gordon went on. 'The thing with it is, what has always troubled me, is that it has never really felt as if it was mine. I always thought of it as my great-grandfather's, see? Like I was just the custodian for a generation, that one of our kids would have it sooner or later.'

'But if this works out, one of them will,' Sara said. 'And there will be a new house here too. Right,' she said. 'Time for pudding.'

'But won't it belong to the bank?' he thought out loud.

'Not if we pay the loan off.'

Gordon helped her clear the table and followed her through to the kitchen. Moments later he was back. He raised his eyebrows and winked, then closed the doors.

Gil looked at Veronika. 'What do you think's going on?'

'A little quiet whoopee, maybe?'

He laughed. 'It's nice to see them so happy, whatever. You're a very smart woman, whatever your name is,' he said. He added, 'Sigourney', and grinned.

She punched his shoulder, but laughed. 'Yup. So they tell me.'

'And good at making other people happy.'

'Sometimes,' she said. 'Sometimes I am. I just hope it works out for them.'

The aroma of dessert began to creep into the dining room, and when the doors opened again, it was to the sound of Gordon with a toy trumpet, playing Auld Lang Syne, though it sounded more like a kazoo.

'In honour of our dear departing guests,' Gordon said, and then in came Sara with a tray, as he root-toot-tooted his trumpet.

'This is one of my grandmother's recipes. Old-fashioned Mennonite Blueberry Cobbler,' she said.

'And this,' said Gordon, putting the trumpet down, 'Is the champagne that was sacrificed in the dramatic rescue of our other departing guest, the king of Rough Collies, our Hero.'

'Gordon's drunk,' Sara said. 'Please excuse him.'

'Not drunk, my love, just very happy. Merry, you might say. Because the book is the real McCoy, and our genius new friend here has pointed out a way to both keep it and profit by it.'

'Anyway, enough about that book of yours,' Sara said, as she sat back down and began spooning out the cobbler. 'I want to hear about your book, Gil. The one you're writing.'

'Ah, the book,' he said. 'Yes, my great labour.'

'This looks wonderful, Sara,' Veronika said, as her eyes saw the blueberry appear from under the golden brown topping. Sara passed the first plate to Veronika, who took a taste. It was delicious.

'Wow... if you were to open a restaurant in Vancouver, you'd do really well.'

Sara laughed and poured a little cream onto her bowl. 'I can't think of anything worse than having to cook for lots of people all the time in exchange for money. To me, food is about love. This cobbler is full of Grandma's love to me. The secret ingredient. But Gil, do go on.'

'Are you sure?' he asked her. 'If I start I may not finish. And this wonderful pudding will go cold.'

'Gil knows so much about that place,' Veronika put in. 'I was amazed.'

'Well, as Gordon knows, I've been researching for a while now. There's quite a lot of material – Lyle's diaries, though they tend to be just a list of where he went and what he did, so no great revelations as to what he thought or felt. There's letters between him and Franz Boas, but they're none too revealing on a personal level either. Mostly it's just business, very often requests for certain artefacts by Boas, for the museum. Lyle would sometimes send newly made copies of the things Boas wanted, because he'd come to understand that taking the originals from people wasn't right, that they were family heirlooms. A bit like your book. Boas of course has been written about many times, and he had an unsavoury side to him, I think. And there's the historical context, John MacLeod and the falls, and the canyon. So quite a lot.'

He took another spoon from his bowl. 'Mmm, this is so good.'

Sara smiled. 'I'm glad you like it. So this will be a biography, then?'

'That's what I firstly thought. But since I came over here I've started to wonder if I can do that, or even if it's the kind of book I want to write. It seems to me that all the things on record are just a small part of the whole story.'

'And the rest is... where?' Gordon asked.

'Lost forever. Or at best, somewhere in the oral traditions of the people there, in fragmentary form.'

'You mean the First Nations?'

'The N'laka'pamux, yes. One of the things I learned while I was there is that to them the key person in recording their stories wasn't Lyle but his wife. It's her they revere, more than him. He was just the scribe to them. Important in a way, but not the source. That was Antko. And she left no archive.'

'Huh,' Gordon said. 'She died young, didn't she?'

'She did. In 1899. I found her grave there.'

'So couldn't you just put together your research, into book form, anyway?'

'Well, maybe I could. I've written a few pieces. Or tried to. But it seems a bit forced, false even, too historical. What I wanted was to bring the man and the time alive. But I realised something when I was in Cloud Falls. This isn't simply a historical situation, so-called Indian

Rights of a hundred years ago, it's still going on right now. And I don't think I can write that kind of book, no matter how much research I do. It isn't my story to tell. It's matter of perspective. What's valid.'

'You mean, it's a question of appropriation?' Veronika said.

'Well, I suppose so. To what extent can anybody tell another person's story, if they're far distant from the source, in terms of time, or culture. Even gender.'

For a minute, they ate quietly, enjoying the flavours, as if chewing over the idea. Then Gordon said, 'But what about Burns? He wrote from different perspectives, didn't he? Women included.'

'He did, that's true. It's possible, maybe for a short lyric, like 'The Slave's Lament', to get inside the head of the other person. But I think to sustain it for a whole book would be hard.'

'What about 'Sunset Song'?' Gordon asked.

'What's that?' Veronika queried, as she finished her helping and placed her spoon inside the bowl. Sara gestured, offering a little more, and Veronika nodded, please.

'It's the great Scottish novel of the last century. Written by a man, but the main character is a woman,' Gordon explained.

'Hmm,' she said. 'I haven't heard of that. And it's good?'

'Great,' Gil said. 'And from the women I know who've read it, he gets it right. The female perspective, that is.'

'Well gender isn't clear cut, is it? Not really, despite all the stereotypes we live with, and boy do we have them round here,' Sara said. 'One of the Native American tribes, I can't recall offhand which, reckoned there were five genders. And with writing, surely it's about empathy? Maybe it's impossible to really understand the other person, their view of what you've shared. And impossible to tell anybody's else's story truthfully. Maybe. But it's worth trying. Of course men and woman are different. You may as well say Mennonites are different. But we're all human, first and foremost, aren't we? If we don't try to see the other person's perspective, what hope is there?'

'And people would only be able to write about themselves,' Gordon added.

'Which is kind of where you're at, Gil, aren't you?' Veronika smiled across the table. Gordon looked at him, awaiting further enlightenment.

'Oh well, I've been keeping a journal since I got here. At least I was. Haven't kept up with it these last few days.'

'I think it's a little more than that, Gil,' she said. 'You are writing a book. Maybe not the one you thought you'd write, but another kind. The one you have to. About what's happening to you.'

Gil looked a little perplexed at her comment, but didn't deny it. In fact, it sounded true, coming from her. Maybe he needed to hear someone say it, to make it real? 'The muse has spoken,' he said finally.

'Well, I think today has been worthy of being in a book,' Gordon said. 'The things that have happened. Just remember to tell the reader how handsome I am.' He refused the offer of a second helping from the Mennonite cobbler dish, saying 'That was, as ever, delicious, honey,' and stood up from the table. 'It's been a long day, indeed it has, but I think a small nightcap to round it off, by the fireside. What say you?'

'That was fabulous,' Veronika said to Sara. 'But I think I'll pass on the nightcap, Gordon, if I'm going to drive in the morning.'

'Gil?'

'Well, actually, we've decided I'm going to go with her. It's a long drive and we can share the duties.' He'd been reluctant to tell them he was leaving, anticipating some protest, but to his surprise Sara gave Gordon a look, and none emerged.

Gordon smiled. 'That's a very good idea, my friend, though I'm truly sorry you're not staying longer. I would have liked to show you the interior plateau tomorrow.'

Sara, who was placing the dishes on a tray, said 'Maybe they could drive back that way? It's not that much farther, and such a beautiful time of year to see it. It's what they call alpine meadow.'

'Yeah, that could work. Come on, I'll show you the map,' he said.

'You go,' Veronika nodded to Gil. 'I'm going to help Sara.'

They carried the dishes to the kitchen, while the men went into the sitting room, and Gordon unfolded a map of BC. Sara and Veronika worked together, doing the washing up, Veronika drying. They spoke about the day, the friendship they'd discovered, how deep it seemed in so short a time. It was a day like no other they'd known, so full of things to wonder at, so significant the moments they'd lived through. And of course it was a shame it was over so soon, but it was good that Gil would go with her to share the drive.

As Sara poured the water from the basin down the sink, and washed it under the faucet, she suddenly stopped, turned to Veronika and said, 'I don't know anything about this situation you have to go back to, but I do know one thing. I've seen you and Gil together and you are very good for each other. What you've been through, both of you, with the cancer, it's a very deep bond. That I can see.'

And she took Veronika in her bosom, and hugged her for what seemed a very long time indeed. Her body pressed against the scar and it hurt a little but she didn't wince. Tears formed in Veronika's eyes and when Sara finally released her, she too was crying gently.

With Hero on the leash, she walked out into the northern summer night. The sky was still vaguely bright, an odd luminosity hanging over the forest ridge. They could hear the creek below, but she didn't go there. At this time of night, who knew what creatures were roaming in the dark? She listened, expecting perhaps a howl or the hooting of an owl. But there was nothing to hear but water. The water that kept on flowing, whatever. It went wherever it was pulled, falling down, always down, wearing away at the rock till something gave way beneath it, and its route subtly changed, forever.

Gil was in bed, asleep, when she went upstairs. He had switched out the main light and turned her lamp on, had placed the cushion wall as she had done the night before, in the middle of the mattress. She switched the lamp out, undressed and put on her new nightdress, and went in between the sheets, under the heavy quilt, then sat up and took the cushions away. Her hand slipped towards him, found his and her fingers closed around it. Her foot sought his too. He didn't stir. Probably the whisky had caught up with him, as it must surely do finally. Even if he was a Scotchman.

When Gil awoke, the first thing he saw was her face right next to his on the pillow. She was still fast asleep, her hands tucked under her cheek, like a child's. He didn't move, but lay there looking at her face, studying it. With her eyes closed, she seemed so different. When they were open and he looked at her, they dazzled him so he hardly noticed her other features. But now he could study at her nose, her lips, her ears, her beautiful hair where it cascaded over the pillow. He felt like reaching out to trace the lines, to memorise them, but didn't dare in case he woke her. And then she stirred, turned and the quilt slipped from her shoulders, so he could see how her neck curved perfectly, to meet the skin across her clavicle, the curve of her shoulder to her upper arm and the lines that led to her waist beneath her white cotton nightdress. He wanted her, wanted to kiss that beautiful neck, but instead he got up from the bed as gently as possible and went to take a shower, the image of her impressed on his mind's eye. And then it struck him that the wall of cushions he'd placed between them had been missing.

As he was dressing, quiet though he was, she woke. 'Hmmph,' she said. 'Morning already?'

'It's still early. Just after seven.'

'Okay,' she said sleepily, and rolled over onto her side.

He finished drying his hair with a towel and went downstairs, leaving her to her rest. Sara was already at work, preparing breakfast in the kitchen, and there was the smell of something baking. She smiled up at him when he appeared in the doorway.

'Good morning!' she said. 'Sleep okay?' He said yes, and she poured him a cup of coffee from the pot on the stove.

'I thought you might be feeling the effects of that whisky. Gordon sure is,' she said. He laughed and said no, he was fine. Surprisingly.

'Well, I'm glad you and I have a moment to ourselves. We've hardly had a chance to speak, just the two of us. Sit down, won't you?' So he sat, and so did she, at the table in the kitchen. 'I'm so glad you're going to go with Veronika,' she said. 'Not that we wouldn't love to have you stay, but it's a long road south and I'd worry if she was setting off on her own.'

He said he'd do his best to take care of her – and you too, Hero, he added to the dog under the table. 'It's been an amazing trip,' he added. 'And you, you've been so kind.'

'Well,' she said, 'It's certainly meant a lot to us, the fact that you came. Gordon... well, he's not lonely, he has plenty of friends round about, but no one who shares his deeper passions, really – apart from me. He's a very creative man, a very learned man though he never went to college or anything.'

He said he could see that, from all the things he'd made, the paintings on the walls, and all the books he'd read.

'Yes, so you see your friendship over the last year or two has meant a lot to him. Especially with you being Scottish. He's forever reading out bits from your emails to me. And every parcel that arrives, whatever the new book is, he's like a kid at Christmas. It's been a kind of lifeline for him, all that.'

'Maybe you'll come over to visit soon,' Gil said. 'Don't spend all the money on the new house, keep some for that.'

'I'd like that,' she said. 'But getting away isn't so easy, what with all the livestock. Maybe when our youngest comes back from his travels, though.'

At that moment, Gordon appeared in the doorway, stretching his arms out and yawning.

'Honey, you look like a bear in spring,' Sara said. 'Come over here and I'll fix you some breakfast.' He staggered to the table, and winked at Gil as he sat down heavily.

'Some night,' he said. 'And some day.'

Veronika joined them, and they ate breakfast while Gordon and Sara explained the alternative route to Vancouver they had in mind. He fetched his map again. Two hours to reach the Cariboo Highway, he reckoned, another two or three to Hope when they'd see the full extent of the canyon they'd been in at Cloud Falls, which they would pass through, and then the road down to Vancouver through the Fraser Valley – another two maybe. It was a full day's drive, but they'd easily be back by nightfall if they started early.

Sara said they should really go by Green Lake, it was one of her favourite places, and Veronika asked, wasn't that near Whistler, but no, it was another Green Lake she meant, and very beautiful, especially at this time of year. That would mean making for 70 Mile House then, Gordon said. He asked how they were fixed for gas, because that would be their first station.

Veronika said she was sure they'd have enough, they'd filled up in Kamloops. So pretty soon their bags were in the VW, and they were setting off. Gordon, Sara and Benji came out to say goodbye, and various hugs and entreaties to take care and come visit followed. Then Sara handed Veronika something wrapped in a dish cloth, something warm.

'It's what we call a friendship bread,' Sara said. 'For the road.'

'Hey, I've got something for you too,' Gordon said, to Gil, and he pulled out a baseball cap from his pocket. 'Little Forks B.C.', the stitching read, around a picture of a moose, standing proud as the monarch of the glen. Inside it was a small book.

'Now I'm thinking that since you've been researching BC, you won't maybe have seen this, as it's about the life on the other side of the Rockies over in Alberta where I came from. It was one of my favourites, growing up. You've sent me so many books, I feel I ought to give you at least one. You haven't seen it before, have you?'

'Ballad of a Stonepicker,' the cover read. George Ryga. 'No,' Gil said, I haven't.'

With the book safe in Gil's bag, the time had come to go. Before long, Veronika was turning the car, and they were heading down the dirt-road past all the sheds and polytunnels, down towards the gate.

'Amazing place,' Gil said, looking around back up the track.

'Amazing people,' Veronika added. 'I'm so glad I came with you and got to meet them. And you, Hero,' she said to the dog, who was standing with his head in between the two front seats, panting, 'You've had quite an adventure too.'

He turned the book Gordon had given him over, and read the blurb aloud. "Ballad of a Stonepicker' is George Ryga's novel about the Prairie Dirt farmers in the 1940's and early 1950's – about two brothers, one who forsakes the farm for the world of the educated elite, the other who stays behind to work the soil, bound to a land that takes more than it gives in return.'

'Sounds good,' she said. 'A bit of a message there too.'

'I wonder if that is how he sees me? As some kind of great scholar? Because he's pretty far off the mark, if he does.'

'I don't know, Gil, but I think you need to give yourself a little credit. Seems to me you've read a lot and learned a lot, even if you're not a big professor. Cut yourself a little slack. If not now, when?'

He smiled. 'Is that another movie quote?'

'Probably.'

She drove on, climbing up through the canyon, away from the Thompson valley, wilderness on every side. Then into view came a vista where there was nothing green at all, and only the black bristles of burned out tree trunks, stretching away into the distance. It went on for miles and miles.

'I wonder if that was the fire they told us about, the one they were ready to run away from?'

'Could be,' he said. 'Must have been terrifying.'

'I know. Hard to imagine.'

Whether it was imagination or not, they thought they could smell the charcoal remains, somewhere off in the distance, still smouldering. Then the road began to flatten out, and forest returned to green, while the landscape transformed into a sequence of lakes and hills that looked to Gil like Perthshire. For a long time, neither spoke, just gazed around them at the beauty as it unfolded, a new vista around each bend.

'This really is more like Scotland than any part of Canada I've seen so far,' Gil said at last. 'The scale's the same.' She pulled over at a rest area, so they could appreciate it properly. *Lac Du Roches*, the sign said. *South Cariboo*. They took pictures of each other with the blue lake behind, with Hero, of course, in all of them. A large map on an information board had all the lakes and trails marked.

'See here,' Gil said, pointing. 'Scot Lake, and here, Little Scot Lake. We could hike there.' But she was looking at another part of the board.

'And here's Loch Lomond,' she grinned. 'You Scots get everywhere.'

'I'd really like to see that,' he said, but there was no time for meandering, a long road lay ahead of them. So she drove on, as the bonnie bonnie banks sounded in his head and he sang a few lines, but she didn't know it, only laughed at his exaggerated accent.

A small corner of his mind was waiting for her phone to go off again, as and when they reached some place where a signal existed, but up here among the hills and lakes that seemed unlikely.

'I suppose you'll be glad to get back to Vancouver again,' he wondered out loud, inviting her to elaborate on her feelings. She took a while to answer, but not for the reasons he suspected. She had switched her cell phone off that morning, a decision that instantly made her feel better. The last thing she wanted was another shock, especially whilst driving these twisting mountain roads.

'I'm looking forward to seeing the sea again – and a proper coffee,' she said, finally. And they hadn't gone very much further before one of her wishes was granted, when out of nowhere a billboard appeared, a large sign which said, simply, ESPRESSO 2km.

'Incredible,' he laughed. 'You really do have magic powers.'

'I never did before,' she replied. 'Must be that four-leaf clover.'

Further billboards followed, each more tempting than the last, so they had their morning coffee on the western shores of Lac Du Roche at an Italian restaurant run by a family which had emigrated from Bergamo.

'O Canada, you never fail to amaze,' he said, as they set off again. The landscape changed subtly once more, becoming flatter than before, and every kilometre or so, there were numbered mailboxes by the roadside, suggesting homes or farms hidden from the motorist. The area seemed quite populous, though the highway itself was almost empty and had no houses on its fringe and they recalled Gordon had told them that the Cariboo plateau was the first part of the interior to be settled, from around the time of the gold rush. The habitations grew in frequency and pretty soon they saw signs for Lone Butte. He had his BC map out and was following the route that Gordon had indicated.

'I think we've gone too far,' he said, 'If we want to see Green Lake, we don't want to go to Lone Butte.'

'Who does?' she smiled. So they found their way onto a side road that would take them back towards the place Sara had said was one of her favourites. And it was very lovely when they reached it, green as promised. The land around its shores made sense of the term 'alpine meadow'. Fattening cattle grazed among the bushes, or lay lazily in the sunshine, chewing their cud. Everything seemed to be in bloom.

'I feel like Julie Andrews could come running across the fields towards us at any time,' he said. Veronika asked if he meant Maria, and he said, yes, Maria von Trapp, that was it.

'So you have at least seen one film?'

'That was one of my mother's favourites.'

'Mine too!'

'She took me to see it four times.'

'We had the recording.'

'So did we!'

'I used to play it all the time when I was a girl.' And so, as they drove through the beautiful flowering alpine meadows around Green Lake, they also ran through the 'Sound of Music' songbook, one by one. Veronika knew almost every lyric, and Gil knew plenty, but their best effort was 'The Lonely Goatherd,' where Hero joined in on the chorus. They sang it again, then again, and every time they came to the yodelling part, he did the same thing, a doggy howl that was surprisingly tuneful. They were sore with laughing by the time the road reached 70 Mile House, where she pulled in at the gas bar to refuel.

She took Hero in search of a patch of grass for him to do his business, while Gil pumped gas. 70 Mile House was a sudden and stark reminder of the modern world, where huge trucks lumbered by on the Cariboo Highway to and from the north, making the little intersection world shake with noise and vibration. There wasn't much to it besides the store and one tired-looking roadhouse motel.

She walked a way back up the quieter road they'd come down, with Hero on the leash while he snooted around, and as she did, she felt a surge of sadness at the thought that their trip was nearly over, that soon she'd be back in Kitsilano and he'd be on a plane, heading for Scotland again. They had laughed so much on that last stretch, singing and listening to Hero's howls. And then it struck her, that she could probably pick up a cell phone signal here. It seemed likely. Her hand went into her purse, found it there among the other things she carried, between her make-up bag and her hairbrush.

It was cold. Off.

He had filled the tank and gone inside to pay. It was quite a store, stocking just about everything imaginable, and had a great deli where you could have just about anything you liked on any kind of bread or roll. But as he queued to pay, he felt suddenly saddened after all their laughter. The road was almost done. Tonight he'd find a room somewhere in Vancouver, and she'd go home to her apartment with Hero and who knew who else? He didn't feel ready to say goodbye.

He saw a stand full of CDs by the till and searched through the titles with his eyes, as the cashier took her time in selling the guy in front something that involved paperwork – a hunting permit, he thought. His gaze came to rest on one CD that interested him and he took it from the rack, to pay for it with the gas – *The Man Comes Around*.

She was waiting in the car when he came out, with Hero on her lap in the passenger seat. 'So I'm driving?' he said, as he got in.

'Yeah. Your turn,' she said. 'Let's get out of here.'

'On the busy highway?'

'I trust you,' she said, shoving Hero towards the back seat, where he scrambled unwillingly.

'Well okay,' he said, and pulled out onto the highway heading south, as trucks rumbled past. He settled back into the automatic drive position and followed the yellow lines south through a flat and fairly featureless territory.

'So did the book come first?' she asked him, after they'd gone a distance in silence.

'What book?'

'Your book. Did you start working on that idea before you got to know Gordon? Was it that that brought you over here, or him and that Burns' book?'

'I suppose it was around the same time. But it was a while before I did anything about coming over.' He laughed. 'You know what really triggered it?'

'What?'

'I bought a Stetson.'

She looked at him and laughed. 'What?'

'It was my last day of radiotherapy. The nurses and me were talking, and they asked what I was planning to do next. I said I just wanted to sit in the sun for a while, and they said I should take care not to let the sun get at my neck, you know, where I'd had the laser treatment. So I walked out of the hospital for the last time, went down to the nearest shops and into a charity shop – what you call a thrift store – to look at the books and there was this Stetson. A leather one. So I tried it on and it fitted perfectly. I thought I'd be able to wear it the garden in the sun, use it for shade.'

'Huh,' she said. 'So where is it now, this Stetson?'

'I left it out in the garden in the rain and it shrank. But by then I'd booked my flight. Talking of Stetsons, I bought you a present back there at the petrol station.' He felt in his pocket and found the CD, then handed it to her.

'Johnny Cash?' she said, without much enthusiasm. 'You still trying to convert me to Country music?'

'Look at the tracklist,' he said.

She ran her eyes over it. 'Okay, interesting,' she said.

'It's one of the last he did. With Rick Rubin producing. Very stripped back. A year after it came out, he died.'

'That sounds cheery,' she said, but took the CD from its case and put it into the player. 'So when do you fly back?' she asked, as the first chords emerged from the speakers.

'Don't know yet.'

'What, you haven't booked?'

'No.'

'And they let you through at passport control?'

'I just said I was here to research a book and didn't know how long it would take. I showed the man my card. You know, the one that says I'm a proper antiquarian bookseller. It looks quite smart.'

'Huh,' she said again, and leaned back in the passenger seat to listen.

'He asked me what the book was about, and I told him. He seemed impressed.'

'Must have been,' she said, smiling to herself. So he wasn't flying off right away. He'd be around a while. In Vancouver.

'So what about tonight?' she asked. 'Where are you staying?'

'Don't know,' he replied, without taking his eyes of the road. 'I suppose I'll find something.'

'You really are flying by the seat of your pants, aren't you?' she teased. 'But you know, I do have a couch. You could sleep there. If you're very good. You'd have to share with Hero, though, but I don't think he'll mind, not after you saved his life.'

'You saved my life, I saved his. Now all that's left to complete the triangle is for him to save yours.'

'Oh he already has, a thousand times over, haven't you, lad?' she said, turning to him and ruffling his head again. Hero smiled his doggy smile at her, scrambled his way into the space between their seats until all of their heads were lined up in a row of three, and he stood there gazing out the windshield, panting.

'And if you don't behave yourself, it's not too far to the YMCA, is it, Hero?'

'Hah, don't think I'd qualify, being neither young nor Christian.'

She smiled. 'And just how old are you, Mr. Johnson?

He snorted gently, in amusement. 'I'm AC+1.'

With cold air blasting from the vents of the VW, all she could think of was 'air-conditioning'. But when she said it, he laughed.

'AC - After Cancer. I've been reborn.'

And she laughed too. 'Then we're the same age.'

But both of them knew that 'after' was too strong a word. The living ghost of recurrence was with them both, always.

The highway bent left and a sign flashed by – CHASM, it read.

'Now is that a place name or a warning?' he asked.

'I've heard of this,' she answered. 'It's a national park.'

The road began to slope downwards steeply. To their left, an abyss began to open. He took his foot from the accelerator. Gravity alone was enough, even too much, and his foot went to the brake pedal, to control their progress.

'It's like we're entering the underworld,' she said.

And then the CD he'd bought at the gas station began a new track. At first she didn't recognise it yet, once the lyrics started, she knew it well. But it wasn't Art Garfunkel's high reedy tenor singing about a bridge over troubled water, it was the gruff shot-to-pieces choking voice of a man close to death, who was savouring every single note, measuring it out like it could be the last his throat would issue.

The chasm opened, as if to swallow them. And then a female voice appeared, out of nowhere, coming in on the chorus, and there was someone, someone there with the dying man, hearing his vow, returning it, a companion, a harmony – someone holding his hand as he faced the inevitable.

'His daughter,' he said.

They listened, silently, as they descended. When at last the road began to flatten out, and the gaping chasm was behind them, the last note sounded and she looked at him, her eyes full of tears, and when he glanced back at her, sensing her gaze, she saw that he was crying too. But he couldn't know the real cause of her crying, and she couldn't guess at the true reason for his. What the song stirred in each of them was unspeakably deep, many strata of experience, as layered and complex as the geology of the chasm itself. Both were old enough to have known intimate loss first-hand, of family and friends, of lives left behind – or those which had left them. They had lived long enough to know how quickly the wilderness reclaimed the little clearings people made, how tenuous a human's hold on life really was.

Another sign appeared, advertising the 'Clinton Rodeo and Ball'. It was welcome distraction, and she said she'd heard that Clinton was nice from a friend, but the dates were already a week past, and the sign rather tattered and bleached out. Still, Clinton was indeed a pretty little town and he drove slowly through. She suggested they stop and find something to eat, as it was already after one o'clock, so he found a place next to a small park and she said she'd walk back into town to a shop she'd seen, if he took Hero for a walk.

The sun was high in the blue sky and it was hot, outside the AC of the VW. Around the perimeter of the park, a small stream ran slow, and Hero was happy to play there, though the flow was so slight there was little to bark at. Still, it was cooling, and he lapped the water, glad to be in the open air again.

It was a while before she reappeared, carrying a bag with sandwiches, bottles of water and a couple of ripe peaches. They sat on the grass to eat, and she produced a package from the bag which she handed to him.

'It's a gift,' she said. 'In return for the CD.'

It was about a foot long, and thin, wrapped in tissue paper, taped securely. He began to ease it open and pulled out a dark-stained piece of wood, carved with faces and heads like a tiny totem pole, but with a handle at the bottom. He looked puzzled at first.

'It's a talking stick,' she informed him.

'It talks?'

'No, stupid. It's...' She was about to explain to him how it was used at pow-wows, but then realised he was teasing her. 'You do know, don't you?'

He waved the thing in the air in front of her face. 'Ah ah...,' he said in commanding tone, 'I have the talking stick, so I do the talking.' Then he began to study it closely. The carving was really very good. The head had canine ears, above a bird's beak and body, and below that was something more like a bear, then another bird-like creature.

'Like it?'

'It's great. Where'd you find this?'

'There was an antique shop back there. I saw it in the window. Don't think it's actually an antique, but it's First Nations. The carver's name is on the tag.'

He looked, and saw it said 'Bob Davidson'. 'Sounds like another Scot,' he smiled.

'Or another residential school renaming,' she said, more seriously. 'So what I thought was, it can be like your writing stick. So whenever you're in doubt about whether you can write, you have to take hold of this and remember that you can.'

'I will do exactly that. It's a real treasure, thank you.'

South of Clinton, the canyon proper began. The highway sloped down, down, down, and he barely used the accelerator at all. Trucks coming in the opposite direction strained and groaned, as if pulling the weight of the world below behind them. After a while, she put the passenger seat back and said she was going to take a nap as she hadn't slept enough the night before.

The canyon went on, deeper down and deeper, the river at its bottom a long distance below the highway, railway tracks on the far side. The landscape changed into the dry desert he knew and, as the miles went by, he began to see place-names appear on road signs that he recognised from his time in Cloud Falls. They had almost completed the loop, arriving back where they'd started out from just a few days before. But it felt like weeks had passed. Here he was, steering a left-hand drive automatic on the wrong side of the road, with a beautiful sleeping woman next to him, and a sleeping dog on the back seat behind. He'd met the internet friend he'd made, at his home in the place that had been almost mythical to him beforehand, and had seen their pioneer existence for himself. He'd held a lost Kilmarnock Edition in his hands. He'd really been in New Caledonia. It barely seemed credible.

Down and further down he drove. When he'd pitched up in Cloud Falls on the Greyhound, it had seemed like he'd been travelling up the canyon forever, and that flat stretch of land alongside the Thompson river felt like the extremity, but now he understood that it was just a brief flat hardly midway, that there was even more to the north. And thinking about the interior plateau at the top, he wondered just what altitude that alpine meadow was at. Higher probably than any part of Scotland, even Ben Nevis.

She woke when they were about fifteen kilometres north of Cloud Falls, feeling groggy and confused. She drank almost half a bottle of water. Gil was still at the wheel, and they were still going down.

'Where are we?'

'Coming down to High Ridge. Remember, the fruit farm where Lyle's children are buried?'

She nodded, groaned a little, then put her seat back in the upright position. 'So almost back where we started?'

'Yup.'

She saw the desert around them, the steep canyon sides with their sparse twisted trees, the sage growing everywhere, the river and the railway below. All the memories of those strange days they'd spent in the little settlement by the great river began to seep back into her consciousness. Gil being lost. The people mistaking her for a film star. The country and western night. The woman she'd talked with that evening on the bridge. The graves. The new wooden temple. It had all been so intense, so dream-like.

'Do you want stop?' she asked him.

'Now?'

'No, at Cloud Falls.'

'I don't know,' he said. 'I could do with a break soon, but we don't have to.'

'What time is it?'

'Half past three.'

'Already? It's about another five hours to Vancouver from here.'

'Not according to Gordon, he said more like three and a half.'

'He must drive a lot faster than you or me, then. Took me ages getting up here.'

The old colonial house above the fruit-stand at the side of the highway, where the guy on the mini-motorbike had met them, came into view on a ridge below. It was a splendid, commanding situation, above the valley where the two rivers met.

'I'm not sure I want to see anyone here,' she said. 'I don't want to start in with all that film stuff again.'

'Well Ms Weaver, if you say so. I'm only your driver.'

'Stop it. You better know who I am by now. No more 'Martina' or 'Ms Weaver' or any of that nonsense, okay?'

'Do I know you? I'm not so sure. You're just a strange woman I met on a plane. I haven't any evidence.'

'Stop it,' she said again, grumpily. 'I've just woken up and I'm really not in the mood.'

'Whatever you say, madam,' he answered, flatly, and tipped the brim of the Little Forks cap he had on his head, the one Gordon had given him.

And she began to laugh.

He pulled over at the abandoned Rumours restaurant, which was still advertising the best food in the canyon. No one had bought the cars that were for sale either. From there, they could see the whole of the settlement below, so they got out and stood in the warm canyon wind, which was blowing strong, following the river's race to the south. The old bridge was still there, so too the inn on the far bank. The row of acacias that had once led to John MacLeod's ranch house. The settler houses crowded around the bridge end, the tipi at Lyle's house. The Apple Store. And in the distance, the little Indian church and the old reservation. But no one was to be seen, not a soul was moving, and the traffic on the highway just kept on going to wherever it was going, like the interminable flow of water and wind, the sun above moving through the blue summer sky.

It seemed so small, so tiny to them then, but only a few days before it had been alive with characters, complicated histories, tales to tell.

'We could just drive through,' he said.

So they did, slowly. She took the wheel so he could look around, taking in the details one last time, drove across the old bridge and down along the CPR rail tracks where a line of trucks waited for Ken to make sure the two ends talked to each other. Past the inn where the tree-planters trucks were absent, the community hall with its silhouettes of times gone by, and on by the graveyard where Antko's stone marked the very edge of the settlement.

On the far side of the river, behind the new highway bridge that bypassed the town, the waterfall that had once been 'MacLeod Falls' and was now just 'Cloud Falls' emerged from the rock face, and he asked her to stop for a while. It was nothing like as tall as Helmcken, not nearly so impressive. The name seemed too grand, inappropriate – just wrong, somehow. And behind that again was the track that he had followed in the hope of finding the mysterious cabin, where he'd been so close to being lost.

She was walking Hero, a clouded expression on her face, and he asked what the matter was. She glanced up at him. 'Wish I'd gone to see that healer.'

'Ah well, maybe next time?'

'You think there will be one?'

'Who knows?' he answered, a little sadly. 'Anyway, let's go.' He got back into the car. So she pulled out onto the highway south, and they left it behind them, this strange oasis where fruit once famed throughout the Empire had grown. The canyon, though, went on as steep and wild as at any point, more so still when they reached the gorge known as Hell's Gate.

'I couldn't live up here,' she said, as she piloted the VW through the narrows. 'This place really freaks me out.'

The drive to Hope would take another hour and a half – down, always down and further down. She seemed to withdraw as she drove, her gaze fixed on the yellow line ahead, and she put on the KD Lang CD she'd played on the way north. Neither of them sang this time so the miles passed in silence, while he studied the talking-stick and looked out at the passing towns, checking them off one by one on the map. When the CD ended, there was no sound at all except that of the engine as it ground out the miles.

After a while, he turned to Hero, who was sleeping on the back seat and said, 'It's all so quiet, isn't it?'

'Hero says you're the one with the talking stick,' she answered. 'Why don't you tell us a story or something?'

He thought for a moment, then held up the talking stick, just as the signpost for Spuzzum flashed by. 'Once upon a time,' he began, 'not far from Spuzzum, the wind ran wild through the canyon, blowing down people's houses and creating havoc. Finally one brave young fellow announced to his family that he was fed up with the wind and he was going to go out and catch it. They told him he was crazy, that the wind was invisible, but he said he had an idea of what to do. So he went to the narrowest part of the whole canyon and there he set a great snare, because he knew the wind must pass through that place. That night the wind howled and when he went out in morning the snare was empty. He thought that maybe he'd made it too big and that the wind had just run through it. So the next night he made it smaller, and waited while the wind howled and when he went out in the morning the snare was empty. So that night he made it smaller again, and waited, and around the middle of the night the wind stopped howling and in the morning, when he went to the narrow place, there it was in the snare...'

'What was it like?' she asked, enchanted. But he held the stick up and said he was the one who was telling the story.

'The wind was very small and invisible but he knew it was there because the snare was moving, so he took his blanket and wrapped it around the snare, then tied it up. The wind must have been frightened because it stopped struggling and lay very still while he carried it home. When he went into the house he laid the blanket on the ground and announced to everybody that he had caught the wind. They laughed at him, of course, so to prove he was telling the truth he undid a corner of the blanket and suddenly a breeze blew through the house and almost put the fire out.'

'And...?'

'That's it I think.'

She laughed quietly. 'Nice. Did you just make that up?'

'No,' he said, 'That's a N'laka'pamux story, sort of. Classic appropriation. I'm not sure I told it properly. Lyle wrote it down in his book, and you know, when I read it, I thought if you just changed 'canyon' to 'glen' and 'blanket' to 'plaid', it could easily be a Scottish folktale.'

'I wonder if Antko told him that one? Anyway, I think you told it well,' she said. 'That stick must have magic powers. Tell me another.'

He thought for a bit. That was the only story from Lyle that had really stuck in his mind. But then he did remember another, and held up the talking stick again. 'There was once a wolf that was causing the people great trouble, taking their animals and even their children, so they asked the best hunter they knew to go and kill it. So the hunter took his two sons and off they went, tracking the wolf, until they came to a cave where it had its lair. The mouth of the cave was narrow, but the hunter could hear the sound of cubs inside, so he looked in and in the darkness he could just make out the eyes of five youngsters. There was no sign of the mother anywhere, and he knew he should kill her young while he had a chance. But the mouth of the cave was too small for him to get inside, so he told his two sons to climb in with their knives and make sure the cubs were all dead. The boys did as they were ordered and so from inside the cave came the terrible howling of the young as they died. The mother wolf was some distance away, but when she heard the noise she came bounding back to her lair as quickly as she could. She leapt straight past the hunter, trying to get inside to protect her young, but as she passed him, the hunter grabbed a hold of her tail and held on tight. So the wolf was stuck in the mouth of that cave, and the hunter heard one of his boys shout out to him, asking what it was that was blocking the light, and he shouted back that if the tail came off, they would soon find out. But the tail held, and the hunter was able to get his knife from his belt and kill the she-wolf.'

For a while, she didn't say anything, as if waiting for some coda. When none came, and he laid the talking stick on his knee, she said 'That's horrid. Hero was rooting for the wolf, weren't you, lad?' But Hero didn't confirm. He was stretched out on the back seat, with one ear bent over, considering the question.

'That one's Scottish,' he said. 'I forget the hunter's name, but it's a true story about the last wolf to live there. Or one of them. A couple of hundred years ago now, if I remember rightly.'

'Huh,' she said. 'I wouldn't have guessed. I thought it was another local one.'

'No, I know. Could just as easily be First Nations.'

'Don't you know any with happy endings?'

'Let me think about that,' he replied. But he didn't come up with anything, except for the Margaret Atwood story of that name.

He asked if she knew it, and she laughed. 'John and Mary died. John and Mary died. John and Mary died?' she said.

'That's the one.'

When they finally reached Hope, she felt tired and worn out, so they stopped and changed places again. He asked if she'd like to take a break before he started up the engine, but she said no, she wanted to get back, to get home. When the big green signpost announced Vancouver, her mind was already there. The resolve that she'd felt when she switched her cell phone off that morning in Little Forks had gradually weakened. She knew there would be a signal now and the temptation to check for messages grew, but while she was sitting next to Gil in the car she felt she couldn't. What kind of world was she returning to, what had happened since she drove this same highway in the other direction, filled with a sense of dread? It felt as if everything had changed. But had it, truly?

The flatland of the Fraser Valley began to open up as they sped along, though the steeps on either side continued. He felt a true sense of the scale of this territory, understood just what energy it was that had poured southwards from the highlands over the millennia, just why the alluvial soils were so rich and why the great farms were there – why, in fact, the whole conurbation around Vancouver was there, on the estuary plains that the great river had created.

The road was busy then. Traffic flowed constantly in both directions. Hero, who'd been asleep on the back seat ever since they left the Falls, stirred and scrambled into the space between them. She looked at him and smiled, ruffled his head and gave him a hug.

'I think he needs a stop,' she said. 'See if you can get off the highway somewhere.'

He spotted a signpost leading them off to a place called Bridal Falls.

'Here we are,' she said, 'Somewhere between Hope and Bridal Falls.'

'That must be a train trip,' he said, but she didn't get it, or if she did she wasn't amused. He drove along the side road looking for a place to stop, until he saw a hand-painted sign pointing up a track leading into the forest.

'THE ROAD TO HAPPY EVER AFTER', it announced, boldly.

'Well well. Sounds just the place for us,' he said, and she laughed a little. Once he'd found a place to pull off, she got out of the car and Hero jumped after her. She looked back in through the open door. 'I'm just going to take him a walk.' Her tone implied solitude. She was telling the driver to wait, so he got out and stretched his legs, while she disappeared off up the track. He noticed she'd taken her hand-bag with her and was reaching inside for something, as she moved out of sight. He guessed what it was.

The cell took a minute to power up as she waited impatiently. It sang its little start-up tune, before the home screen appeared. Hero found a good tree to pee on, and pulled on the leash until he had enough latitude. The phone pinged three times and the little envelope icon materialised three times. Clumsily, she tried to click on the app, but missed and instead it loaded something else. She closed that and tried again. The inbox opened. Three unread messages popped up as promised, but she saw immediately that none of them were from him. Another missed call from her mother. Some spam message, one from her network provider and one from her friend John asking if she wanted to watch the hockey.

'Huh,' she said, and put the phone back in her purse. When Hero was ready, she walked further on up the track, wondering what the lack of a message meant, and getting annoyed with herself for thinking there would be something. But step by step, she felt a growing sense of relief, somehow, a lightening of her mood, and then she saw another smaller sign, written on a blackboard that stood in an old wheelbarrow. The Road to Happy Ever After, it said in the same hand as the first, and it pointed further on. Intrigued, she followed it and came into a clearing with half a dozen small log cabins, identically built and perfectly finished, and she saw, up the slope a little further, a wooden chapel. She carried on up, peering about her. The grass was manicured, and bunting hung between the trees. There were flowers in standing pots, and everywhere little humorous touches. It was like some fairyland wedding place. She thought she'd just walk up and look at the chapel.

Gil waited a while, like a chauffeur attending, then got back in the car and did what he always did when things were quiet. He picked up 'Ballad of a Stonepicker' and began to read. It was a strange opening, a one-sided conversation, but the voice was strong, colloquial, and as he read he thought he could learn from it when it came to writing Canadian characters. It would be useful. Then he wondered where she'd gone. Had she got lost? Should he go after her? But he pictured her talking on her phone to the man, whoever he was, and thought better of it.

He leaned back in the driver's seat and thought he would just find a room when they got back to Vancouver. It was a big city, shouldn't be a problem, even if it was late. Yes, she'd offered a couch, but he didn't want to wake up there, in the way, when she had her life to get on with. As did he. He thought he'd just get a room somewhere for a night, and in the morning he'd see about a flight home. Maybe he'd stay a couple of days, visit the library again, see if he could get back on track with his research. He'd hardly done a thing since she turned up. But then everything he'd seen and done had its uses, he'd learned so much about BC, and when he got home, he'd have stories to tell. He could be Bookshop Bert again, but he'd have new things to share – funny thinking of himself as Bert again, he'd got acquainted with Gil, somehow. Maybe he wouldn't even go back to the shop. He could sell up, cherry-pick the best editions, and just work online. He had his mother's place to live in now. And he pictured himself in her garden, watching the planes come and go from Edinburgh airport as he'd done before he left, remembering this journey and working on his book, focused and free of manning the shop. But somehow it didn't fill him with any great sense of enthusiasm. Had he fallen in love? So long had passed since he'd even considered love to be an actual thing, as opposed to some kind of illusion. Desire, yes, that existed, and when it was frustrated, it was unhealthy, dangerous even. He looked again at the talking-stick where it lay on the passenger seat. It was a beautiful gift, and he would remember her words whenever he picked it up, back home in Edinburgh. But no, not love – she had helped him, and he had helped her. They weren't about to drift off into some romantic mist. They had shared something special, a brief yet essential period of transition, like a pivot or a hinge, between one life and another. But love – no.

He looked up the road she'd taken, the road to happy ever after. She'd gone up there without him, though he had taken her to its beginning. He wished her well. She was a remarkable woman, a special person, and he was glad they'd met. But it was time to go home, to get real as they say over here, once more. He leaned back in the driver's seat and closed his eyes, tried to picture his new life at home. But all he could see were her brown eyes with those flecks of gold shining in the Interior sun, her flashing smile.

'Gil!' He woke with a start as the door opened. 'Bring the car up,' she said, getting back inside. 'We're staying the night here.' She explained, as he drove tentatively up the track, that it was a wedding venue but it wasn't properly open yet. She'd met the woman who owned it, who had said they'd just held their first wedding ceremony two days ago for a couple of friends of hers, they'd only put those signs up to guide the guests in, that there was one couple who couldn't make it at the last minute so she happened to have one cabin all made up and ready if they wanted it. And it was such a darling place, she'd just said they did.

'You'll see,' she added. Gil was surprised at her sudden change of mood, all smiles and chatty, but it made him happy too. So he said nothing, until the VW crept into the clearing and he saw it for himself.

'Multiple wows,' he breathed, looking around at flowers and bunting. 'And traditional nuptial emus, I see.' For there were emus, at least three of them, in an enclosure off to the side and Hero was lying in the grass staring up at them, as if completely flummoxed by these crazy creatures with their long legs, huge bodies and snake-like necks, as they stared back at him.

'I know!' she said. 'Isn't it weird? She has donkeys too.'

He parked the car and they got out.

'I was just so tired of the drive,' she said. 'And it's not as if we have to get back to Vancouver tonight.'

'No,' he said, surprised. 'I certainly don't.'

The owner came over and introduced herself as Kathy. She shook Gil's hand and showed them to their cabin, all the while explaining how she and her partner had moved up from Vancouver the previous year, how she had always loved weddings and how this was a sort of dream for her, though her partner was the architect and builder, of course. And how well the wedding had gone, she'd been so nervous because it was their first, but everything went off wonderfully well, and everyone was so happy.

It was as if they had stumbled into the afterglow of the most fabulous party, which the hostess did not want to come to an end, which she wanted to tell the world about, and Gil realised then that Veronika's mood shift had been wrought by exposure to this bubbling joy.

'You know, you really remind me of somebody,' she said at last to Veronika, who smiled at Gil.

'Maybe we met in Vancouver. Where did you live?'

'Kitsilano.'

'So do I!'

'Well, that must explain it. Where exactly are you?' And they went on to compare notes on streets and shops, while Gil headed back to the car to pick up their bags, thinking to himself that this journey was endlessly surprising. It even had emus in it. When he got back, Veronika told him that they had gone to the same hairdresser, wasn't that a coincidence?

The cabin had a little hand-carved sign on it which said 'Bliss' – each one had a name, Kathy said, all synonyms for 'Paradise'. Though she would probably run out of ideas when they built the second phase the following year. Inside, everything was brand new and first class, and little wedding favours adorned the room – chocolates and flowers, still fresh, and in the fridge a bottle of champagne.

'Just you help yourselves,' Kathy said, handing them their keys. 'And if you need anything, our house is just over the rise there. I'm so glad you turned up. This empty cabin was the one thing that didn't go to plan, and now you're like the guests who came late, to make it perfect.'

Gil picked up a card that was sitting on the table. 'Welcome to Bliss, Jack and Marianne!' it read.

There were two bedrooms, one double downstairs, and one small single up above in the rafters. 'Well, at least we don't have to share a bed tonight,' he said, 'No need for pillow walls.' She didn't answer, but gave him another of her slightly pained smiles. 'It's all so well done,' he went on. 'This woodwork is real craftsmanship.'

'Her husband did it all. She said he was an architect before he retired, but that he loved carpentry more than anything.' She too picked up the welcome card. 'So you're Jack and I'm Marianne tonight, are we?'

'Looks like it,' he smiled. 'And she doesn't mind Hero?'

'She loves animals. Though she said not to let him on the beds.'

'Well, I think it's a very lucky find.'

'Another one. That four leaf-clover is really doing good work.' She opened the fridge and saw it was stocked with food, and the kitchen area was equipped with everything they could ever need, all unused. 'We can have supper here,' she said enthusiastically. 'Maybe barbeque and eat out on the deck?'

'Sounds great.'

After they'd unpacked, they went for a stroll around the wedding complex with Hero, who reluctantly abandoned his emu-watch. At first neither spoke, but they fell into step with each other naturally. They found a little stream that ran through the heart of the clearing, with a perfect wooden bridge arched over it. Hero was immediately interested, but the water ran smooth and there were no waves to herd.

'You know, I really didn't mind sharing a bed with you in Little Forks,' she said. 'That wasn't why I made the pillow wall.'

'I know, Marianne.'

'Stop it, Jack,' she said, feigning annoyance. 'Seriously, these last few days with you I've probably been happier than at any time for ages.'

'Same here,' he said. 'But?'

'But what?'

'I sense a but…'

'Ah… well, I guess I'm not much good at relationships.'

'My track record isn't so great either.'

'But I do love being with you. It's so free of friction, somehow.'

'That's a 'but' I like. I feel that too.'

'It's almost like being alone.'

He laughed. 'That's the nicest thing anybody ever said to me.'

As they walked on up the hill towards the chapel, Gil found the moment to ask the question he'd had on his mind for a while. 'But there is another man, isn't there?'

'There is… was… half of a man. One I share… shared.'

'Interesting. And these messages your phone keeps jumping into life with. They're from him?'

'Some. I'm sort of on the run from him right now.'

'Ah! One of the pursued. He's not using GPS to track us or anything? He's not suddenly going to appear?'

'God, I hope not,' she gasped.

'Well, it sounds like a fine mess you're in. But as sure as my name's Jack, you are a very remarkable person, and you deserve to be happy.'

She laughed, and took his arm as they walked. 'You're very witty, but sometimes I wish you'd be a bit more direct.'

'Jack may be my first name, but my middle name is Irony,' he said, and she pulled her arm away to punch him gently on the shoulder.

'You know, if you could write like you talk,' she said, 'You wouldn't need that stick.' And she took his arm again.

They came to a signpost, which indicated one way to Chapel and the other to Dining and Dancing. He said he thought that dining sounded good, but she replied that chapel must be first, so they carried on up the path till they came to a low building, covered in shingles, that reminded him of the little Indian church in Cloud Falls. Outside an arrow pointed towards the doors: 'I DO', it said, and further off, behind that, leading out from the exit at the other end, another similar arrow read 'WE DID'.

'I guess you go in one end single and come out the other married,' she said. 'And inside you jump the broomstick, or whatever.' She tried the handles and they turned. 'The doors are open,' she said. 'Shall we have a look?'

'Hang on, though, shouldn't I be waiting for you at the altar and then you make your entrance?'

She laughed. 'You're taking this all a bit seriously, suddenly. Anyway, I haven't got anyone to give me away.'

'You have Hero,' he said. 'Who could be better?'

'He would never give me away,' she said. 'Not even on my wedding day, would you, lad?' She pulled open the double doors and went inside. The little chapel smelled of new wood, and some fragrance or incense that had been burning there during the ceremony. It had proper pews, old ones that must have come from some disused church, but the rest of it was newly v-lined pine, both floor and walls. In the far end was a piece of stained glass, in the window of the exit door.

'It's charming,' she said.

Gil followed her in, looking around. It reminded him of one of the plain wooden kirk interiors in Scotland, bereft of decoration since the Reformation, where the little congregation would gather to sing unaccompanied psalms, led by their minister. But there was no altar, no crosses, nothing Christian about the building, and nothing particularly new age or wacky either. Aside from the pews, the only furnishing was a kind of cast-iron trolley, which bore an abstract metal candelabra and a large book with the single word WEDDINGS embossed in gold. He opened it and saw that there was only one entry, Mr John and Mrs Chris Chang-Powick, two days prior, with their address and their signatures, as if it were a guest house's visitors' book.

She was peering out the window beside the exit. 'Wow,' she said. 'What a view to step out on in your new life together!' He came over to where she stood and looked. It was indeed spectacular, forested into the far distance, but with a small lake, almost hidden by the contours, shining bright blue.

'Fabulous,' he said, and tried to open the exit door, but it was locked. 'Oh well, I suppose we can't because we didn't.'

'Look,' she said. 'The confetti is still here.'

He stepped back to where she was standing. 'Where?' he asked.

'See, there,' she said, 'Among the grass.'

He leaned close, to look at it from her angle, and saw the pastel-coloured paper shapes of tiny hearts and stars. Their breath met the window glass at the same time, and clouded together. For one moment, each felt the warmth of the other. Then she put her head on his shoulder and said, quietly, 'So do you remember that woman from Calgary on the plane who's writing our story?'

'I do.'

'She thought you should have kissed me then.'

'Should I have?'

'It was in the script.'

'And it isn't any longer?'

'Not such a good shot. You'd have to twist your neck around and it would be awkward.'

'Ah,' he said. 'That's true, I could do myself an injury. Or show my red neck to the camera.'

She laughed, pulled his collar down, and examined the laser mark closely. 'It's not so bad, Gil. It's hard to see with all your sunburn. It's not like you have a scar.' And she kissed the burn mark gently. 'There,' she said. 'It's all better now.'

No one had touched his neck since the hospital, and it made him flinch. He felt a cold shiver pass through him, right down to his toes, and he stepped away from her. 'We'll have to go back the way we came in,' he said. 'This door's locked.'

A little troubled by his reaction, she followed him back through the pews. 'If we go out this door, does 'I do' become 'Do I?' she wondered out loud.

He didn't respond, but said, instead, 'I think it's time for the dining and dancing now.'

Hero was waiting by the entrance, and together the three of them walked in silence across the clearing in the direction indicated, till they saw a covered deck with balloons still hanging from its beams, the guest tables all set out, some with the odd empty glass and wilting flowers in vases. Against the back wall, on a raised dais, was a long table for the bride and groom and their attendants and, further over, a small bandstand with a piano under a rain cover. Behind the bridal table, a banner read 'JOHN & CHRIS'.

'It's so pretty here,' she said. 'Must have been a lovely wedding.'

They stopped at the steps to the dais. He held out his hand for her, and she took it, then climbed up, crossed behind the chairs and sat in the middle, where the bride would have been. And he took the chair beside her. They looked out over the empty tables and seats to where Hero was staring back at them, as if wondering what they were doing.

'It's so wonderful that all our friends and family are here with us to share this special day,' Gil said to the curious dog, who tilted his head to one side, aware that he was being addressed, but not understanding the irony.

'And especially you, lad,' she added. Hero wagged his tail a little, but didn't move.

They sat a while looking out at the scene, the beautiful setting beyond the deck, where the sun was shining and everything was summery green.

'Do you remember, back in Vancouver, how I told you that if I was dying, I'd get married?'

'You said it was on your bucket list, I believe.'

'Yes. Well, this is the place.'

He put a cupped hand to his ear. 'What's that you say, Hero? I may kiss the bride? Really?'

'Stop it,' she said, laughing. 'Remember, we didn't do it?'

'No. That's true,' he said. 'So what about some dancing, anyway?'

Without a word, she got up and went over to the upright piano, pulled the cover off, then lifted the lid. 'I hope they don't keep this out here all the time,' she said, 'It'll ruin it.' And she tinkled the keys, then played a few scales. 'Not too out of tune,' she said.

'Do you play then?' he asked, from his bridegroom seat.

'I used to,' she answered, and sat down on the stool. 'Remember you told me that story about Martina the pianist? That was closer to the truth than you knew.'

She gazed at the black and white keys, from which a million colours could arise. The last time she'd played had been on his beautiful piano at his cabin on Bowen, looking out through the glass facade across the sea. He liked her to play while he was working in the other room.

Hero trotted over and lay at her feet, looking up expectantly. Her fingers found their place, were poised, ready, for a piece she knew by heart, had known by heart since she was a girl.

Gil waited, wondering what she'd do. What emerged from the piano was not what he expected, though, not some familiar song but a gentle repeated melody he thought he'd heard before, but not one he knew. She played with such assurance, her hands flowing over the keys while she gazed straight ahead, as if in a trance. Then the mood changed, became minor key and melancholic, and another melody drifted across to where he sat, played on the bass notes but with the same insistent repetition. Her eyes closed, and then he heard another change, from minor to major, and as she played he saw that pained smile of hers spread slowly over her face, while her hands picked out the melody and kept the same punctuating repetition. As the last notes sounded, a single handclap that became a sequence sounded from behind them. They both turned to look and saw a tall thin man with thick jet-black hair was standing just outside the awning, listening. For a moment Gil thought it was him, her lover, having tracked them down.

'I heard the music. Chopin, wasn't it?' the interloper said.

'His Raindrop Prelude,' she answered, slightly surprised by the audience, but pleased he'd recognised it.

'Yes,' the man said. 'Written in Majorca while he and Georges Sand were living there. She overheard him composing it and thought it sounded like rain on the tiles of the roof.'

'That's right.'

He stepped forward. 'I'm Kirk, by the way. Kirk Douglas, Kathy's husband.' Veronika and Gil looked at each other. 'I know, I know, I get that all the time. Guess my mother thought it would be a good name.'

'I hope you don't mind me playing your piano.'

'No, it was wonderful. I swear that old thing never sounded near as good before.'

'So you're the architect?' Gil said.

'I am.'

'It's wonderful what you're building here,' she said.

The man laughed, a deep musical chuckle. 'It's Kathy's dream, really. She's always been a romantic. I don't have too much to do with it. She just tells me what she wants and I build it. The idea and all the little touches are hers, though. She tells me you guys have been on a road trip up in the interior? Where'd you go?'

Gil got up from the bride's table and stepped down on to the deck, as Veronika came over from the piano, until the three stood in the sunlight outside.

'We started out from Cloud Falls,' he said, 'Then went on through Merritt and up the Nicola Valley to Kamloops. From there, we drove north to visit friends in Little Forks.'

'They took us up to Helmcken Falls,' Veronika added. 'And wow, was that a sight!'

'And then driving back we came through the Southern Cariboo and down to Clinton, then followed the canyon back to Cloud Falls, and south from there.'

'Yeah?' he said. 'So you've seen a fair bit of the interior. And what's so special about Cloud Falls?

Veronika spoke first. 'Gil's been researching a relative who used to live there,' she said. 'He's from Scotland.'

'You know the place? Cloud Falls, I mean,' Gil asked.

'I do. You know the new outdoor theatre there? That was designed by a local woman who trained with us,' the architect said.

'Huh! That's amazing you should know her,' Veronika observed.

The architect smiled at her. 'Well, not really. It's not amazing that a place like that would have an architect, and although there's not all that many aboriginal architects in BC, there are quite a few these days. And we're all very well aware of that project.' He spoke with the authority of a man who'd been responding to surprise over what he was doing all his life, and had worked out all arguments. He didn't bristle with defensiveness, on the contrary he seemed genial and friendly, even as he undermined the implicit assumption. 'What's really amazing is that you found your way up here when we're not even open,' he added.

Gil explained. 'We just pulled off the highway and saw the sign. I mean, who wouldn't be intrigued by the road to happy ever after.'

'And you were looking for a happy ending? Must be fate,' he said with a grin.

Veronika remembered Sara using the same phrase just the day before.

'Listen, why don't you come over and eat with us tonight? I was just going to spark the barbie, as they say in Australia. Unless you'd prefer to be alone?'

'Oh I don't know,' Veronika said, a little taken aback by his gentle put-down. 'Thanks all the same. We've been on the road since early and I'm dead beat.' She looked at Gil, who seemed a little disappointed. 'But you go. Sounds as if you two have things to talk about.'

'Well, come on over if you like. The house is just there and there'll be plenty of food.'

He left them then, walking down the slope together, towards their cabin. Towards 'Bliss'.

'I didn't know you could play piano like that,' Gil said. 'It was so beautiful.'

'There's a whole lot you don't know about me.'

'I'll bet there is. Are you sure you don't mind if I go over there for a while? I won't stay late. It's just I'd like to know more about that new building up in Cloud Falls.'

'No of course not. It's not like we're some married couple who have to check everything we do with the other, now is it? You go. I could do with some down-time, to be honest.'

'But you'll be hungry.'

'No I won't. There's plenty to snack on back at the cabin.'

She watched as he went after the architect, speeding his stride to catch him. At the top of the rise he did, and the two of them walked on, already deep in conversation. Talk about lucky, she thought.

Did lucky things always happen around him? He seemed to think it was her magic touch. Or was it the combination, the two of them together? Maybe this was just one of those lucky sequences that come along once or twice in a lifetime – if you're lucky. She laughed to herself. Twin lucky. Doubly lucky. Dublucky, Gil would say.

When she got back to the cabin called Bliss, she took her journal out and opened it carefully to where the four-leaf clover lay pressed. It was drying out, fading a little, but it was real. She wrote for a while, a few notes on what she'd seen that day. Then she checked her cell. There was no reception, though she was picking up a wifi signal, HEA123, probably the business, but it was passworded.

Hero came over and tried to jump up on the bed, but she shooed him down, and he went to lie in the shadow, sulking. So she went to the bathroom, to the sunken bath she'd had her eye on ever since Kathy first showed her the cabin. After a day on the road, the chance to test it out, and see what nice free toiletries there were, seemed very appealing. She found a robe and slippers still wrapped, set the taps to run, then undressed. Her feet felt sore, though she really hadn't walked all that far. They were more swollen from the heat and the nail polish was chipped and worn. She blamed those shoes, they'd never quite fitted, though they looked good on. Deciding to have a pedicure when she got back to Vancouver, she put the robe on and went to check the water.

As she waved her hand through the foaming water, the thought occurred that he might be there. What if he was waiting outside her apartment with his bag, if he'd told his wife like he'd said he was going to in his text, and had left her? And then his mistress turned up, laughing and joking with another man? She pictured the scene, him sitting in his white Volvo across the road, then her car pulling up, driven by Gil. It made her smile for moment, but only because she knew it would never ever happen. Would it?

When the temperature was right and depth nearly perfect, she slipped into the water. Wow. It felt good. And she lay back, thinking of how she'd played piano again, for Gil. How different it had been, that slightly out of tune upright, from the day she first played on Bowen, that perfect baby grand overlooking the straights and all the little islands in the sun. She closed her eyes and hummed the Chopin quietly to herself.

Gil was sitting on the deck out the back of the architect's house, with Kirk Douglas and his wife. They'd been talking as they drank, and ate the barbequed food, about Cloud Falls, and the outdoor theatre. Kirk explained how the construction drew on aboriginal methods, in the detail of how the great timber was jointed. And he asked Gil about this relative of his who had lived there, and when Jimmy Lyle's name was mentioned, Kirk said yes, of course, he knew something about him, the work he'd done for Boas and his part in the Indian Rights movement of the time. And he asked what the family connection was.

So Gil had told the tale again of how Lyle had left a pregnant woman behind when he came out to BC, and how he had suspected that this child was his father. How he'd wanted to find some evidence and hadn't. How he'd planned to write a book about Lyle, but found he wasn't up to it. That there was so much more to the story than he could have imagined, for all his research. How he had met Veronika on the plane, and what connected them. About the couple in Little Forks, their Burns book, the fire and the creek.

The wine had loosened his tongue. In fact, he'd been talking so much that his hosts seemed a little overwhelmed, and he stopped, realising he'd most likely been boring them with all sorts of details he found fascinating, but probably didn't mean all that much to them, however polite they'd been.

So he asked the architect about his name, pointing out that it was as Scottish as any, and Kirk explained that, yes, his great-grandfather had indeed been Scottish, one of the Hudson's Bay men, that he'd married a Musqueam woman. But his own background was thoroughly aboriginal, despite the surname, and he'd grown up on a reservation near Squamish. He said he'd been one of the first aboriginal students at Simon Fraser University.

'Guess I've always been what the old folks would have called a lucky Indian,' he added, with a wry smile, which seemed to Gil to have hidden within it the same testing directness he'd gently admonished Veronika with, earlier.

'I don't think luck could account for it,' Kathy said. 'You've worked so hard. And you're so clever.'

Kirk shrugged. 'Well, sure, I was a bright kid, but there has to be somebody around to notice that and help. I was lucky. I had a teacher who saw something in me. I got scholarships, all that stuff.'

'But you deserved it.'

'Sure, but so do lots of other kids and they don't get lucky. That's why it's so important we give something back.' And he went on to explain about some of the work he did, besides his work as an architect, committees he sat on, trusts and social concerns. 'There's a long road to go here in Canada,' he said. 'So many problems that are hidden away. But we are working to correct them.'

And they talked more about the issues around First Nations, the need for them to own their own discourse, eventually returning to Lyle's role as the man who wrote down the BC chiefs' wishes a hundred years before, and how important that had been, though Kirk pointed out if it hadn't been him, then it would have been someone else.

The sun began to slip behind the trees. Gil finally got up to go, and thanked them both. The architect walked a distance up the path towards the cabin with him. As they parted, he said to Gil, 'You must write whatever you feel you have to. Even if you can't tell the story in a complete form, and you haven't found the answers you were looking for, you have the right to write your partial truth, as much as anybody does. It's all a contribution.'

Gil walked on up the last stretch himself. He'd stayed longer than he meant to, it was almost ten o'clock, and 'Bliss' was lying in silence in the faint gloom of a late summer evening, the VW parked outside. He didn't see any lights on in the windows, so he took his boots off outside and opened the door as silently as he could, shushing Hero gently as he passed by where he lay sprawled, then padded across the new floor to the bathroom in semi-darkness. He was more than a little tipsy, and a wet towel she'd left on the floor tripped him up. He almost went headlong into the sunken bath, but managed to grab the towel rail and right himself.

As he came out, he noticed the main bedroom door was ajar and he heard her breathing, slow and regular. He went to the little staircase and began to climb up quietly, but when he reached the top, the step squeaked. The sound roused the sleeper below.

'Gil?' she called out. 'Is that you?'

'Who else?' he said.

'I waited for you.'

'Sorry,' he said. 'We got talking.' For a moment neither spoke, and he was about to carry on into the little bedroom when her voice came echoing up to him again.

'I missed you,' she said.

'Sorry,' he said again.

'Come down here, will you?'

So he retraced his steps in the half-dark, and pushed open the main bedroom door. He could just make out her shape in the bed, as she shifted over and flicked the duvet back.

'Sleep with me,' she said. It was a whisper, but a command.

'Are you sure the woman in Calgary has scripted this?' he said, quietly.

'Just shut up and get in,' she whispered again, 'But be careful, remember I'm one of the wounded. And no more words. It's time we let our bodies talk.'

'All right,' he said, laying his head on the pillow. 'But one last thing… what's with the emus?' He felt her body gently convulse with suppressed laughter, then her hand covered his mouth, and her thumb and index finger pinched his nostrils.

'I should never have saved your life,' she whispered.

Through the darkness, the sound of claws clipping over the bare floor approached, and before she could say no, a large furry creature landed heavily on the duvet on top of them. It wasn't a bear.

Fifth Dance
'The Best of Seven'
(Finale)

HE WALKED AGAIN along the shore that had become his retreat on his last day, the little stretch of wilderness coast on the south of English Bay. Mist enshrouded the twin peaks of Cypress and Grouse, like a steam cloud rising from the land in the heat of summer. Downtown Vancouver shimmered in the sun, as he stood on the sand watching a skein of geese fly towards the ocean. His mother used to say that was a sign of rain to come.

Tomorrow he too would fly above the city, on the first leg of the journey back to Scotland - across the Rockies where he'd first met her, then on across the vast wastes of Northern Canada, Greenland, Ice-land and the Atlantic, back to the North Sea, far from this strange Pacific shore. The day of departure would carry him through the night towards home, but also towards the end of this companionship. This love he now felt. He could call it that, on his side at least.

But she had withdrawn again, since they got back to Vancouver. Though they'd met and talked, joked and laughed as they did before, she wasn't physically present in the same way as during those few short crazy days in the Interior when they'd had to share a bed. And now he was about to leave.

But he had written – feverishly - something, not the story he'd imagined with an invented historical reality, the heroic adventures of a Scottish pioneer, but the story of what had happened to him, and how it had changed him. Meeting her. Their story. It was far from finished and he could never bring it to a conclusion here. The hours were running short. It occurred to him that time accelerates as the end of something approaches, or at least a person's perception of it. The closer to the conclusion, the harder it seems to fit in everything that remains to be done or said, and still more things occur as the mind races in dread of ending – always, the tyranny of the undone. Once there was time for everything but now the finish looms, the bucket list is too full, it's spilling over. Finally you give up, accept stillness, accept silence. This place of quiet by the shore. Acceptance, as with death, with the cancer and the sense he'd felt of hurtling towards non-existence, of being sucked into some invisible black hole. An unseen nothing. That river in the canyon and his urge to jump. Of course there were options, but they were all final acts, deeds to be done once, not a life plan to slowly unfold, to evolve and grow into shapes and places unimagined.

He turned and left the panorama behind, a last over-shoulder glimpse imprinted on his mind's eye. As he headed up MacDonald Street away from the shore, a bus passed going downtown. The usual destination display read 'GO CANUCKS GO!', as did all such signs he'd seen in the last few days. The hockey fever had reached a peak. It was the day of the final match, Game Seven of seven, the decider with the score tied at 3-3. The Canucks were hosting the Boston Bruins and the city was full of fans, all dressed for the occasion. It was a day to make history, for the city to claim its first Stanley Cup. The citizens had all disappeared indoors to watch the showdown, and the streets were silent.

SHE was vacuuming her apartment, moving furniture, doing some serious tidying up, seeking out every little dust bunny or ancient crumb of dog biscuit. Hero was locked in her bedroom, barking periodically at his enemy, the dreaded Hoover. Since she got back from the interior, she'd felt so exhausted, so in need of downtime that the days had drifted past with the minimum of maintenance. Now that she'd restored her energy a little, the importance of restoring order in her domestic life seemed paramount.

The noise of the vacuum rang through the rooms, the growl of the roller brush beating hard floor, followed by the gentler rumbling as it passed over carpet, all punctuated by Hero's stifled bark. She swung the electric beast around her like a reluctant dance partner - or a cowgirl roping a calf, the cord looped over her right shoulder like a lasso.

This was how she had prepared for death. Everything in place, all arrangements made, awaiting the inevitable, so that when the hour came, she would leave behind a perfect little nest, containing a record of her life laid out for anyone to find. All ends knotted, all her tangled yarn neatly sorted. She thought about what people would find after-wards. Her mother, mostly.

Yes, she had created order. She had finished her last translation, had seen all her friends, had even succeeded in ordering her mother's phone calls and constant need for reassurance by saying the doctor told her she must rest, and so she would unplug her phone when doing so, something her mother had finally accepted.

Then Gil's appearance in her life had brought with it a kind of chaos she was unprepared for. He had burst through the detachment she had so carefully cultivated in those final months, had caused her to feel panic and anxiety for someone's fate other than her own. She had gone to places she had never been before; into a Canada she barely knew except for the odd news bulletin.

But that week of madness was behind her and she required tran-quillity. She had said no to going out to watch the hockey with her friends. She didn't have the energy for it, and besides it was Gil's last night and she wanted to make it special for him. Though she hardly knew him, the time they'd had together had been so intense she felt bonded to him in a deep way, as if they had passed through some fire or forge, and had melded one to the other.

When she switched off the vacuum, she heard the sound of the buzzer and realised it was already quite late. It was almost time for the puck to drop.

THEY found it very different watching the game at her place, rather than in the crammed pub. Just the three of them, the sound turned quite low, and the screen rather small. Hero didn't seem to care at all, and the humans seemed more preoccupied by the behaviour of the other than the sporting history waiting to be made. They sat on opposite chairs, the game between them. An awkwardness pervaded, their glances and smiles brief, their words light, barely circumstantial. Hero gave a sigh and lay down in front of the tv, his head by her feet, his tail by Gil's.

Right from the first face-off, it seemed Boston were up for the fight. Three straight losses at the Canucks' home in the series so far hadn't blunted their self-belief. They seemed keener, skating hard and chas-ing their opponents down. The Canucks, the best team over the whole season's record, looked as if their composure was busted. They looked second-best out on that ice.

When the first Boston goal went in, she stood up and left the room, shaking her head saying she knew it would end badly. That she'd had a feeling, and neither of them questioned that, after what had happened in Cloud Falls.

Gil called after her, that maybe losing the first goal would spur Vancouver on, but she ignored him, and nothing changed. They had shots aplenty from distance, but nothing to trouble the Boston goal-tender, who was playing at the top of his game. At the end of the first period, the Canucks still trailed. She left the room again, came back with another beer and some chips and salsa.

The second period went the same way. Vancouver huffed and puffed, blowing hard but Boston had the whip-hand, and a second goal for the visitors went in. Still time, he told her, but she scoffed at that, only half watching the match now. Then a collision between two play-ers took out the Canucks' goaltender too, and the puck slid slowly into the unguarded net. They waited as the referees reviewed it, to see if a foul had been committed, but the goal stood. 3-0 Boston, and the Canucks still hadn't really threatened. It was beginning to look like the cause was lost.

She said she couldn't stand it any longer, so they decided they should go out, but without Hero who would chase the waves madly, down to the shore he had come from, to watch the sunset. They walked to the little park at Tatlow together, side by side, step by step, in silence. Sunlight filtered through full-leafed boughs. Two small kids still clam-bered over the play area although it was late, while a mother waited to one side with a double stroller, studying her cell phone.

They walked on, across the little bridge and down to the steps that led to the beach. The vista opened out before them, the glittering sea hardly moving, the freighters reflecting, mountains opposite dwarf-ing downtown to the right, and then, emerging to their left as they approached, the sun as a disc of molten gold falling deathly slow to the ocean in the narrows between Point Grey and Bowen Island, through a sky of fire. They turned to face each other, smiling. It was truly awe-some. Beyond words.

From the top of the steps, they could see the tide was right in, cutting off the path where it met the beach, so that a small gathering of people had assembled to watch the spectacle, standing in a huddle where the metal railings ended, some swinging from the rails. A posse of giant logs churning in the waves kept thumping up against the concrete of the steps, pushing against one another, twisting slowly. Escapees from some logging boom looking for a place to land.

The gathering was mainly a group of local kids who'd given up on the hockey like them. Or maybe they weren't all that interested in the first place. They were passing round a bottle of whiskey, and a joint too, from the pungent smell. They didn't seem to mind being joined by the two old people who stepped gingerly down the stair to where they stood.

It was all so peaceful, and hard to believe that over in the city centre, thousands of people crammed into an arena, hearts racing, blood pumping, anger mounting, as the hockey match played out.

She took hold of his hand. 'So… tomorrow,' she said.

He nodded. 'Aye. I'll miss all this. And you.'

'Maybe you should stay.' He glanced at her to gauge her seriousness, but her eyes were gazing out at the setting sun, at that moment merging into the horizon.

'What would I do?'

'You could open a bookshop,' she smiled. But he knew that his life was back in Scotland, what remained of it, and said nothing. He had things to do there, he wasn't ready to die, not quite yet.

Yet they both knew well that they would both die. How long it took, and where they met their end, and from what cause, all that remained unknown. But they had been to each other a kind of promise that there could be some kind of life with cancer, an existence on the other side of radiation. Of surgery. An intimation of a possible afterwards. And although they would die, probably sooner rather than later, they would not die together, unless some cataclysmic event happened to envelop them, like those lovers at Pompeii, in the next few hours.

No, they would part. But they would see each other again, as often as they could, and when the time came, one of them would be there to help the other die, the one who would mourn. They knew this somehow, though which one it would be, they did not know.

And yes, it was sad to contemplate that end, the physical and emotional pain of dying. The former at least could be soothed by drugs. But the latter could only be ameliorated by the presence of another person, the gentleness of one who understands, who is prepared to suffer loss and grief close at hand, to nurse. That was real love.

It was sad, yes, but they both knew that all stories must end.

Some other books published by **LUATH PRESS**

Nort Atlantik Drift

Robert Alan Jamieson
ISBN: 9781906307134 HBK £15

North Atlantic Drift – the warm ocean current that runs past Shetland, keeping the climate mellower than equivalent latitudes anywhere else in the world. For centuries Shetland's artistic tradition has been nurtured by the rhythms of the sea and the lyrical cadences of a unique dialect. Set halfway between Scotland and Norway, these North Atlantic isles have produced a distinct and vibrant culture. Robert Alan Jamieson mixes mythology, autobiography and history with photographs in a beautiful book not only for Shetlanders, but everyone who has visited, or dreams of visiting.

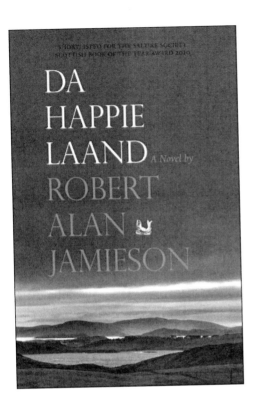

Da Happie Laand

Robert Alan Jamieson
ISBN: 9781906817862 PBK £9.99
ISBN: 9781906817336 HBK £12.99

In the summer of the year of the Millennium, a barefoot stranger comes to the door of the manse for help. But three days later he disappears without trace, leaving a bundle of papers behind.

Da Happie Laand weaves the old minister's attempt to make sense of the mysteries left behind by his 'lost sheep' with an older story relating the fate of a Zetlandic community across the centuries – the tales of those people who emigrated to New Zealand in the South Pacific to build a new life in the promised land, and those who stayed behind.

Scots in Canada

Jenni Calder

ISBN: 9781908373038 PBK £8.99

In Canada there are nearly as many descendants of Scots as there are people living in Scotland; almost 5 million Canadians ticked the 'Scottish origin' box in the most recent Canadian Census. Many Scottish families have friends or relatives in Canada. Who left Scotland? Why did they leave? What did they do when they got there? What was their impact on the developing nation?

Thousands of Scots were forced from their homeland, while others chose to leave, seeking a better life. As individuals, families and communities, they braved the wild Atlantic Ocean, many crossing in cramped under-rationed ships, unprepared for the fierce Canadian winter. And yet Scots went on to lay railroads, found banks and exploit the fur trade, and helped form the political infrastructure of modern-day Canada.

This book follows the pioneers west from Nova Scotia to the prairie frontier and on to the Pacific coast. It examines the reasons why so many Scots left their land and families. The legacy of centuries of trade and communication still binds the two countries, and Scottish Canadians keep alive the traditions that crossed the Atlantic with their ancestors.

Scots in the USA

Jenni Calder

ISBN: 9781908373380 PBK £9.99

The map of the United States is peppered with Scottish place-names and America's telephone directories are filled with surnames illustrating Scottish ancestry. Increasingly, Americans of Scottish extraction are visiting Scotland in search of their family history. All over Scotland and the United States there are clues to the Scottish-American relationship, the legacy of centuries of trade and communication as well as that of departure and heritage.

The experiences of Scottish settlers in the United States varied enormously, as did their attitudes to the lifestyles that they left behind and those that they began anew once they arrived in North America.

Scots in the USA discusses why they left Scotland, where they went once they reached the United States, and what they did when they got there.

Luath Press Limited

committed to publishing well written books worth reading

LUATH PRESS takes its name from Robert Burns, whose little collie Luath (*Gael.*, swift or nimble) tripped up Jean Armour at a wedding and gave him the chance to speak to the woman who was to be his wife and the abiding love of his life. Burns called one of the 'Twa Dogs' Luath after Cuchullin's hunting dog in Ossian's *Fingal*. Luath Press was established in 1981 in the heart of Burns country, and is now based a few steps up the road from Burns' first lodgings on Edinburgh's Royal Mile. Luath offers you distinctive writing with a hint of unexpected pleasures.

Most bookshops in the UK, the US, Canada, Australia, New Zealand and parts of Europe, either carry our books in stock or can order them for you. To order direct from us, please send a £sterling cheque, postal order, international money order or your credit card details (number, address of cardholder and expiry date) to us at the address below. Please add post and packing as follows: UK – £1.00 per delivery address; overseas surface mail – £2.50 per delivery address; overseas airmail – £3.50 for the first book to each delivery address, plus £1.00 for each additional book by airmail to the same address. If your order is a gift, we will happily enclose your card or message at no extra charge.

Luath Press Limited
543/2 Castlehill
The Royal Mile
Edinburgh EH1 2ND
Scotland
Telephone: +44 (0)131 225 4326 (24 hours)
email: sales@luath. co.uk
Website: www. luath.co.uk